## PRAISE FOR THE SEVENTH AGE: DAWN

"Visceral, funny, relentless, and clever, *The Seventh Age: Dawn* is the rollicking tour of supernatural Chicago you never knew you needed. A mix of Jim Butcher and Terry Pratchett—with just a little Mike Royko thrown in for good measure—an urban fantasy tale with real bite."
—Scott Kenemore, national bestselling author of *Zombie, Ohio* and *The Grand Hotel*

"Unrelenting, unfiltered urban fantasy with a two-pack-a-day habit. Heinz has crammed more supernatural spectacle per square inch than is probably legal."
—G. Derek Adams, author of *Asteroid Made of Dragons*

"A riveting read that showcases a supernatural side of Chicago that even Jim Butcher hasn't seen. *Dawn* is a suspenseful, page-turning urban fantasy that leaves you waiting for more."
—April Carvelli, PopCultHQ.com

"A delightfully macabre roller coaster right from the first page. The more you learn about Mike and the world he inhabits, the more you'll want to know—this book will grab you by the throat until the very end."
—Dailen Ogden, author and illustrator of *The Liminal*

"Heinz crafts a dark conspiracy of secret organizations so unique and believable that you"ll want your own bottle of demon's blood before looking into the shadows again."
—Zachary Tyler Linville, author of *Welcome to Deadland*

THE SEVENTH AGE: DAWN

# RICK HEINZ

# THE 7 SEVENTH AGE: DAWN

INKSHARES

Published by Inkshares, Inc., San Francisco, California
www.inkshares.com

Edited and designed by Girl Friday Productions
www.girlfridayproductions.com

Cover design by Scott Barrie
Cover illustration by Ashley Witter
Cover images © Katja Gerasimova/Shutterstock; © Roberto Castillo/
Shutterstock

ISBN: 9781941758892
e-ISBN: 9781941758908

Library of Congress Control Number: 2015959898

First edition

Printed in the United States of America

*To Michelle Heinz, for inspiring me to actually do it; Cheryl Nabors for working with me till the end; and all the friends I've made over the years while building* The Seventh Age. *A story woven together orally is now tangible.*

# CHAPTER 1

The adrenaline caused his heart to race faster as sweat formed on his face, only to be whisked away by the cold winds of the creeping winter in Chicago. Twenty-one floors up, Mike Auburn stood on a six-inch I beam, looking at the city below him. The blood-red sun on the horizon added a grim look to the city when shining on the swaths of people leaving their daily jobs. *Go back home to your reality TV and frozen pizza,* Mike thought. *I'm out here for a reason. I can't turn back now.*

He reached down and decoupled his safety harness, inching farther on the beam. His worn, duct-taped boots gripped the cold steel as he leaned over to look down before performing a slow balancing act, moving out a bit more. His arms were stretched to each side, and his fingerless gloves offered little protection against the biting wind. With each gust, Mike's heart jumped as he adjusted his balance. He dared himself to not look down and to keep pushing farther out than he had the last time. *One step. And then another. And another . . . Ah, fuck it. Just get out there, man. Quit screwing around. What's the worst that can happen, fourteen seconds of free fall?* He broke into a sprint. One boot after another, pushing him forward, closer to the concrete void below.

Fear of the fall, that tumbling sensation when you're turned upside down with no sense of control, spiked instantly in him as he came to the end of the beam. His red dragon bandanna, already soaked with sweat, flew off in a gust of frozen wind. Instinctively, Mike shot his arm out like a cannon and grabbed it.

For a single beat of his heart, his destination of oblivion forgotten, claws of gravity latched onto him as the city below attempted to claim one more soul for her bloody belly. The world turned gray as Mike began his descent. Chicago was ready to embrace her soon-to-be-shattered lover's body when his training as an ironworker kicked in. He hooked his knee around the beam at the last second. Gasping for breath, he grabbed for safety with every bone, muscle, and, he was pretty sure, organ. Mike steeled himself to embrace the feeling rushing through him and kept his eyes wide open. *There!* Right there at the edge of death, Mike saw it, the decayed city of Chicago, covered in ash from a fire that raged nearly a century ago. The buildings around him exposed their flaws in construction, their secrets laid bare like an old whore.

He took them in, along with the ghosts of the past, his son down below standing in the middle of the street with a look of surprise on his face before the yellow cab would speed through the red light. Looking into the office building across the street, he saw his first girlfriend being strangled with a necktie by an executive she was cheating with. His wife in a cherry-print dress, paralyzed with terror before the crane would fall. Everywhere he looked in that fleeting instant showed the dead in his life, frozen in their moments of time. Countless lives lost over his twenty-eight years. Here, on the precipice of death, Mike could see them. If only for an instant.

The sharp pain in his knee jerked him back to the situation at hand. He was dangling twenty-one floors up in a new skyscraper being built for some obscenely rich bank. People the size of his thumb walked below him, too interested in their cell phones to look around at the wonder of this city. Mike pulled his other leg around the I beam and dangled there, taking in the sights of the city and his past. The wind whisked away a few tears. He used his bandanna to clean his face. *I had it for a second. I can feel it. I can see the afterlife. Death can't be the end. Why not just let go?*

It was the sight of a cigar being lit in the building across the street that paused the thought. The warm orange glow didn't provide enough light for him to make out the figure, as the red hue of the setting sun obscured the view inside. By squinting, he could see the silhouette, someone in a long coat with a cabby hat, the cherry of the cigar playing a trick with the light, casting a shadow on his face. No phone in hand, no rushing to call emergency services, he was just standing there . . . watching him.

An upside-down Mike chuckled for a second and flipped his strange death admirer the bird. With the same hand, he grabbed the beam and let his legs go, showing off a bit. Mike's hands had a grip like a vice. He'd never lost a thumb war in his life. *Meh, got a doctor's appointment anyway. Daneka will just show up at the Billy Goat if I miss the appointment, and the last thing I need is my doc showing up around my crew. Better get going.*

Mike pulled himself up and took one last look at the sun's vanishing rays, the soft glow glinting off Chicago's skin of brick and steel. The cold no longer bothered him, his adrenaline already subsiding. He glanced across the street toward his voyeur but only saw an empty room. Shrugging, he trotted back across the beam to the construction site. He would slide down like a spider monkey before he would reach the freight elevator, a nightly ritual that stayed the same regardless of what building was under construction.

Stepping out onto the street, Mike lit a cigarette and began bumping shoulders with people during the pedestrian rush hour. One of the best things about Chicago was that any guy in dirty construction clothes was completely invisible to everyone else. Only women and power suits got attention from the masses. The homeless were a different story. They always saw everyone. Mike flipped a bill and a spare lighter into the case of someone setting up his homemade string instrument. He reached out to shake the musician's gnarled hand and paused when he saw his face, leaving his hand awkwardly hanging in midair. The guy had one shoe, camouflage pants, and a brown coat, but no eyes. Blood still ran down his cheeks like tears as the empty sockets looked back at him.

"He sees you," No Eyes said in a raspy voice. "Watches you every day. We watch you . . . always."

Mike shut his eyes and backed up quickly, bumping into the train of people. "Fuck. Longer visions this time."

Opening his eyes, Mike realized his foray had pissed off a suit who was clearly on important business. A completely mundane street musician setting up his gear looked at Mike like he was out of his mind. *Doc is going to put me on so many meds, I'm going to start calling myself the second Son of Sam.* Adjusting his Carhartt coat, he went back to shouldering people out of his way with more haste than before. He had an unfair advantage walking in crowded streets, as he was a hand taller than most, with a scrappy frame forged in mosh pits and by hanging off buildings. Pushing his way through, he made it to the street corner, where he could hail a cab.

In any major city, hailing a cab was always fun for Mike Auburn. Today it was a bidding war versus three other hands waving in the air. A grin crept across his face as he eyed this evening's competition. In one corner was a lady in those furry ski boots and a hat fashioned from a dead animal. In the other, a set of Japanese businessmen carrying poster boards of some pitch. *Almost unfair today.* The yellow cabs waiting at the red light saw their marks and inched closer, waiting for the second they could hit the gas. Putting his fingers to his mouth, he let out an ear-piercing whistle, summoning a chariot to his side. He hopped in. With the door almost closed, he saw the other cabs speed by, ignoring his challengers.

"One sec," he told the driver. Then, leaning out, he said, "Hey, you three want in?"

They exchanged apprehensive looks before shaking their heads and going back to gazing down the street for the next set of cabs.

"Fullerton and State, please," Mike said.

As the cab pulled away, Mike looked out the window at the people before turning to the driver to start chatting him up. The cabbie's skinless hands gripped the wheel. Bones, tendons, and muscles left a trail of fluid on the wheel as it spun under his palms. The driver looked backward casually.

"Rough day at work?" he asked.

"Meh, you know how it is," Mike said. "Don't even know why we do the grind. Build stuff, get paid, drink, smoke, watch a movie"—he took a drag—"and hang upside down from a beam trying to prove to yourself there's an afterlife. 'Nough about me. How's yours, Frank?"

"Awww, ya know. Bears*hh* lost again. Got some cash riding on the next game, though. You know, he wants to see*hh* you, right, Mikey?" Frank said, his skinless face and torn lips slurring his speech.

"Yeah, you've said that every day for the past . . . hundred and forty-seven days now, is it? So who the hell is *he* anyway? I keep asking, and you keep beating around the bush. You suck at the pitch line." Mike laid his head on the cold window and looked out at the pedestrians, unsurprised he had ended up in this particular cab again. *Good for them. They get to live normal lives.* He couldn't help the feeling of longing clenching his chest and did his best to push the feeling away. "Ha! He's probably some very dead guy like you," Mike said.

"No more dead than you'll be if you keep about the way ya are, Mikey. Ya know who, boy. O'Neil, the guy who runs this town. He's a patient man, but nice invitations do wear out."

Mike ran his finger along the picture on the cab info card that showed Frank as a larger man of Indian descent with a warm smile. "Frank . . . you are O'Neil. Frank O'Neil, it says so on your card back here, annnnd you've been dead since the sixties. So, how could I meet you? Besides, you're all imaginary anyway." Mike changed his voice to a higher pitch like his doctor's. "Just my messed-up projections of guilt made manifest." He chuckled. Smoke started to fill up the cab, so he cracked a window. "Whatever. Hey, drop me off here. Tell your boss if he sees"—he counted on his hands quickly—"my three girlfriends, kid, mom, dad, aunts, uncles, my barista, and my last few crews, and my 7-Eleven porn dealer in hell with the rest of you, tell them I said they all still owe me money." Mike made eye contact with the skinless driver in the mirror. "Except Gabe. I still have his stuffed turtle." Tapping the glass with his knuckles, he signaled it was time to pull over.

"Ya don't have much time left. S*h*even days*h* left. Twenty-one days*h* *aftah dat*." Frank looked back again. Mike could never tell if he was smiling or just staring at him. So Mike threw some cash into the front seat, flicked his cigarette out the window, and stepped into the bitter November night. He watched as he imagined a very confused, mundane cab driver pulling away. *Well, what did you expect, buddy? You are dropping me off near my shrink's office.*

# CHAPTER 2

Doctor Joseph Daneka had a small office above a Chinese noodle joint on the north side of the city. Mike walked up the narrow staircase, reminding himself to never eat at that place again. The restaurant's owners left their food in large plastic bins to marinate and used them to prop open the door to the hallway, saturating the entire stairwell with the sickening smell of meat mixed with sweet-and-sour sauce. *Every time Doc brings it, I end up eating it. Not this time, Doc. Not this time.*

Walking into the vacant reception area of the eccentric doctor's office, Mike inhaled the welcome smell of polished leather and old books. *For a self-proclaimed minimalist, Joseph Daneka fails spectacularly at it.* Mike looked around the room as he sank deep into a cool leather chair. A prized swordfish took up most of the space on the wall across from the door. Doc recounted the story of it every time he had a new patient. He had battled the scaly beast in the seas off the coast of Brazil for six hours on a rickety fishing boat. But Mike knew the truth: he bought it from a disgruntled taxidermist in a back alleyway, like a junkie buying drugs with a briefcase full of cash.

Books piled up on every table in the room ensured people like Mike wouldn't put their feet on them. Most of the books related in some fashion to Senator McCarthy and famous media figures of the 1950s. Still, if he peered carefully, Mike could find some obscure 1970s science fiction and the obligatory copy of *Highlights* over five years old. He had never seen a medical office without one. Lastly, about fourteen chess and go sets stolen from coffee shops in the area were stacked in the corner. He had known Doc for years. They were roommates once in another lifetime. While Mike joined the Ironworkers Union, Doc spent the next decade racking up enough student-loan debt to buy a small third-world country. Considering that he was the doc's only repeat client, Mike was not exactly sure how he remained in business.

He laid his head back and began to finally relax when the door flung open, ushering in the awful odor from the stairwell. A malnourished, balding man with a tweed coat came stumbling in, carrying bags of Chinese food and another stolen chess set. Despite his relatively young age, Doc could have easily passed for a forty-nine-year-old. He looked at Mike, gave a curt nod, and dropped the takeout bags on top of a stack of books.

"Food," he said. Then, stepping over the table with his lanky legs, he slid into the therapy room with haste, closing the side-office door behind him.

"Great session, Doc. Real insightful. I think I'm cured now. You've done it by destroying what is left of my intestines," Mike said. A growl in his stomach forced him to instinctively grab the bag. Realizing he still had his fingerless gloves on and his fingers were still blackened from work, he paused for a second before shrugging and tearing the bag open. *Damn it, Mike, stop going on impulse. Ah, screw it. Rotten stairwell mystery meat hasn't killed me yet.* Doc's closed door was an attempt to avoid hearing the sounds of slurping noodles, Mike's preferred method of revenge for the most vile food on the planet. He smiled mischievously as he locked the doctor's office and plopped himself down on the therapist couch while tossing Doc the beef fried rice container.

"So, the visions are lasting longer. The walking, talking dead ones. I feel like I'm living in a horror movie. If it was real, it would be much cooler. I think zombies would make great cashiers and retail employees," Mike said as he slurped his slimy noodles.

"Well, Mike, you have survivor's guilt. It's natural you would start projecting this. Not many have had as many people around them die, like you. You're a good person, Mike. There is no rhyme or reason to your destiny. No divine plan. It's just a matter of life. People live, life happens, then they die. It's what you do during that life that matters." He paused to stare at Mike's noodle-eating habits and began to eat his food with precise care. "Are you still trying to overdose on adrenaline?"

"Yeah. I'm tellin' you, what I see is real. When I push myself, right when I'm hanging there on the edge, I can see them. The world changes for me. Becomes this sort of . . . shadow world? It's even clearer if I do it near a haunted place. Speaking of that, I'm going to the theater where Dillinger died this weekend. Wanna go?" Mike asked. He realized he was talking with his hands again. This presented a problem with the food delivery system of chopsticks, and he paid more attention to devouring his foul meal.

"Nah. If the dead were real, Mike, the entire world would know. There are nearly seven and a half billion humans, living people who do things like go fishing. Everyone accepts tragedy in their own way, and that the dead stay dead. As your therapist, I can give you a clinical diagnosis. As your friend, I'm just going to tell you that you are insane. You already know this of course. However—"

"You know this is why you don't have any clients, right?" Mike cut in.

"Why would I need other clients when I have you? I could write a book about you." He got up and moved to a white-board and started writing names down. "As I was saying, every time you find a place where tragedy happened and pull off a death-defying stunt, you get these visions. Let me take an educated guess about today. You have been working on accident-prone job sites. It's why your company gets the high-risk work. This job site is no different, correct?"

"Yup. Three-man accident. One survived, two didn't. Every one of them family men. I worked with one of them on a few different jobs. He had a temper and rode everyone pretty hard, but was a saint at heart if you could avoid talking politics with him." Mike paused and stared at the names appearing on the board. "Why?"

"I want to focus on something here, so follow me, if you will. You've mentioned the names of the ghosts you talk to. There is a pattern. All of them are people who nobody would notice. Janitors, cab drivers, the lady at the security desk, and so forth. Yet all of them have the same last name. O'Neil." Doc kept writing names on the board from memory; it showed in his handwriting. Twenty-one of them, Mike guessed. Doc ran his fingers through his hair and started picking at loose neck skin while staring at the board. "I think you see them in these roles because you respect them. You value the common man, the working class. To you, the world ignores them and sees their lives as tools to be used. Dead things. But this isn't just coincidence, and has not been for a while. Tell me again what they ask you."

"Well, they're always asking me to meet *him*. They're always vague, just that he runs this city and he is being polite by waiting. This time, one of 'em reminded me I have seven days left?" Mike counted on his fingers. "November thirtieth, right? Anyway, I don't talk to all of them. Sometimes I just see them in the distance. Always disfigured or dead in some way. The worst is when they're kids or the pizza delivery guy. Creepy as shit, really, even though I've become jaded." A tingling sensation started creeping through his hands as he remembered flashes of his encounters. *Jaded my ass. I wish I could help them.*

Mike slid a small end table in front of himself and put his dusty boots on it while Doc's back was turned. "Here's the thing, though. It's never during the daytime. Always at night, like I said, horror movie. They keep giving me a deadline, and I'm running out of time. It started after—" Mike could not stop his hand from shaking. "It started after the drunk cabbie ran the red light." He wasn't sure if fear or nervousness made it difficult to talk about it so honestly with someone who was not dead.

Doc lowered his voice. "Are you still positive that you want to hold on? You are not taking any truly suicidal actions, are you? I do have some obligations to uphold about your mental health."

"I'm still afraid to die, so not there yet, Doc. No reason for Linden Oaks—currently." Mike elected to leave out that this day had a closer call than usual due to some unfortunate wind.

Doc continued staring at the board while writing down numbers. Then he put dates on the calendar in illegible doctor scribble. "December twenty-first. They say the world is going to end on that day. Maybe you want it to happen. It could be that you are getting wrapped up in all the hubbub about it." He circled November 30. "This day, however, seven days from now, is completely insignificant. Did you know anybody who died on that day?"

Mike closed his eyes, trying to jog his memory, counting with his fingers. Doc watched him reset the count more than a few times. "Nope." Mike said. "Nobody, which is a relief. Maybe I should make that day a holiday."

"I think you should. Make a special day for you and take some personal time. Call it Mike's Fiesta of the Not Dead. I also think you should do something else, though. Something unusual for me to suggest." Doc sat down and leaned forward, putting his elbow patches on his bony knees with an excited look on his face. "I've been doing research into the ghosts you only see versus the dead ones that actually talk to you. You, my friend, might have stumbled onto a conspiracy."

"Uh, Doc, I'm talking to . . . dead . . . people. The last time we had this session, you went on about how I do what I do in trying to prove I'm still alive. Which, hey, actually makes some kind of sense. Took over a year to get to that point. Now you are shifting gears into conspiracy?"

"Perhaps it's all in your head, yes, and Senator McCarthy saw communists everywhere as well. My father was his therapist in confidence during the worst of it. I'm continuing the family practice, and after reading his notes, Dad concluded that allowing McCarthy to radically play out his fantasy was the best method of therapy for him." Doc's feet began to twitch with anticipation. "The private session notes are missing, unfortunately. Wish they weren't confiscated . . ."

"This isn't one of your fish stories, is it? Besides, McCarthy ended up trashing the entire country. Hell, man, he even added *under God*, to the Pledge of Allegiance."

"Actually, that had more to do with Eisenhower and potentially a conspiracy with the Catholic fraternities for a few decades." Doc waved his hand in the air frantically to prevent himself going off on a tangent. "Unlike McCarthy, you see the dead instead of communists. You imagine that one man runs this city, and the working-class dead end up in his employ, that they want you to join them." Doc reached behind him and pulled out a folder. "The O'Neils. It's a common enough name, particularly here in Chicago." He started holding up pictures of strangers to Mike. "Now I know you're not the type of person to put in late nights going through newspaper reels. So I did. The thing is, the more I started digging into dead people you've specifically named and encountered, I keep finding real people who went missing or who died of unknown causes. In a few cases, they died of outright murders."

Doc produced an old 1920s picture of a curly-haired policeman with round cheeks and spots of freckles. "Patrick O'Neil. Every single person you have named is somewhere on this man's family tree, despite their ethnicity. The dead you see are all maimed or disfigured. I think he is faking deaths or burying secrets. I think you should go see him. I think this is your *him*." Doc smiled ear to ear, his glasses nearly falling off his nose.

"Patrick O'Neil? Really? The imaginary leader of the dead that runs Chicago from the shadows . . . You want me to see him?" Mike smirked in doubt and began looking away from the photos.

"Somewhere in your subconscious is a buried connection. Maybe hypnosis is something we could look into. The mind works in curious ways, and humanity has barely begun to understand how it works. I not only think he's real, but he's connected, and you're seeing ghosts and projections because your subconscious can't rationalize what you've seen. Maybe he's behind all the accidents?"

They looked at each other in silence. The only sounds were sirens outside rushing through the city. Mike let the information on the whiteboard flow into him. Despite his best efforts every day to forget the names, he always found them wandering into his thoughts like tiny maggots. He would try to forget after each encounter happened. Like an addict, though, he kept coming back and placing himself in death-defying situations, and afterward, the encounters would happen. His fists began to unclench from the stress of uncertainty as he slowly nodded in acceptance. The Chinese food's pungent odor reminded him of his surroundings and that he was no longer ravenously hungry. *Hunger is the best spice.*

"Okay. Why not? There aren't many things left that can hurt, right?" Mike said at last.

"Excellent!" Doc raised his hands above his head in triumph. He reached over and patted Mike on the legs. "By the way, if you put these ratty boots on my table again, I'll stab you with my swordfish. Then you'll have your final answers about the afterlife." The doctor extended his hand, helping his friend off the couch and patting him on the back, causing concrete dust to fly off as they walked into the waiting room. "I'll keep researching to find a location for this Patrick fellow before then. Meet back here on the thirtieth. You said at night, right? Let's do dinner first. Chinese?"

"Nice incentive. Real nice. You know that place will kill you faster than my smokes, right? See ya then."

Mike took the stairs two at a time and stepped out into the cold, already fumbling in his pockets for a lighter. Across the street, he saw a man in a long coat with a cabby hat dodging around the corner. *Nah, can't be the same guy. Everyone wears that style of clothes now. Fucking hipsters.* Mike looked back at the building, the neon glow of a noodles sign providing the only light on its facade. *Doc did good research, though, and if it's real and he's causing accidents . . . Well, I don't have anything else going on tonight.* Mike began a slow jog across the street after the man.

# CHAPTER 3

The pace picked up after Mike rounded the corner about two blocks away. Mike saw the man flick a cigar and start running into the street after Mike began catching up. *That's gotta be him. Oh, shit. Doc was right! He was waiting for me to fall today! Motherfucker.* His boots pounded on the pavement as he worked to close the distance. It was the only sound he focused on. Running through a red light, a beat-up car came to a screeching halt, its duct-taped bumper just two inches away from Mike's shins. *It's all or nothing.* Jumping onto the hood of the car, leaving another dent in the car's body, Mike committed to the chase. Ignoring the inevitable stream of vulgarities, he kept running. Gasping for air as his lungs burned, Mike threw one foot in front of the other as he broke into a full sprint. *Gotta quit smoking. I can't keep this up.*

His pace started to falter as his legs began to burn too. *For an old man, this guy can keep a hell of a pace. I guess that says something about me.* Mike could see him a half block up, his brown duster coat flapping in the wind like a superhero's cape.

He held his hat from the wind, and his checkered scarf was pulled up around his face.

The man bolted into an alley at a frantic sprint. Mike, running like a freight train, tried to round the corner and slammed into the wall with his shoulder, the impact forcing his breath out in a loud grunt. His momentum shattered, Mike turned down the alley to refocus.

"Hey!" Mike shouted. "Dude! I . . . just . . . wanna . . ." By now his lungs had given up, and Mike put his hands on his knees to catch his breath. He looked down the alley, but there was nobody in sight. Metal-halide floodlights gave the space an orange glow. Garage doors along the lane were closed. Garbage Dumpsters were filled to the brim with trash bags. Empty beer cases were stacked near their sides. *He couldn't have made it to the other end in that time. He's gotta be hiding.*

Mike straightened himself, popped his knuckles, and stretched his arms to crack his back. Satisfied with the noise and the release of tension, he readied himself for a back-alley brawl. He took cautious steps, wary of anyone coming out of hiding. At each Dumpster, Mike leaned back and kicked it before walking along its side. Hoping that the noise would give tell to a hiding coward. *Hey, it works for the raccoons that hide in mine. What if he's got a gun?*

His breath was visible in the air, and his lungs were still sore, but the cold no longer bothered Mike. In the middle of the alley, Mike smiled to himself and picked up an empty beer bottle. He smashed it open as he continued. Inch by inch, he eliminated places to hide. His fingers tingled with anticipation, blood coursed through his limbs as his muscles braced themselves for any surprise movements. With a running start, Mike kicked the last Dumpster as hard as he could. Rusty wheels creaked in protest, and a black garbage bag hung like a limp wrist for a second before dropping to the ground with a thud. No signs of movement. No creepy old cigar-smoking man flushed out from the other side. Disappointed, Mike looked around the alley, finding nothing, and took a deep breath. He threw the broken bottle back into the Dumpster and began walking back the way he entered just in case he missed something.

A red-and-blue flash of light caused Mike to stop in his tracks. The quick pierce of a siren echoed off the walls, warning him that it was time for an unpleasant conversation with a cop. He turned around with a dejected look on his face. He knew he fit all the profiles, with a bandanna, ripped-up jeans, and hands that smelled of spilled beer. *My arrest record for obtrusive protests isn't going to do me any favors either.* He placed his hands up.

A barrel-chested officer stepped out of the car. *Does this guy spend every waking moment at the gym?* Mike watched his partner, a shorter woman with her hair pulled back in a knot and a warm smile on her face, hold out her hand for him to stand down as she stepped out.

"Easy there, sir. Everything okay here?" she asked.

Mike looked at both of them and relaxed his arms. "Yeah, peachy. What can I do for you?"

"Noise and vandal complaints. You mind stepping over here for some questions? Have you been drinking? Hands on the car, please," she said.

As Mike walked up to their car and put his hands on the hood, he caught a glimpse of the checkered-scarf man across the street, putting his cell phone back into his pocket. The cops slammed Mike down face-first into the patrol car before a sound could slip out of his mouth. The metallic embrace of handcuffs and their ominous clicking as they tightened brought back memories. After a little rough handling, they thrust him into the back of the car. *Great way to start a night. I fucking swear that cops put these damn handcuffs in a freezer before throwing them on people.* While the door slammed shut, he twisted his neck to try to get a better view of the man across the street. He stood between streetlights and had the audacity to tip his hat to Mike before walking away. *That son of a bitch . . . I know where you work, at least.*

"Hey, why the hell are you guys arresting me?" Mike asked as the pair of cops got into the car. They didn't say anything and just started driving. "I mean, come on, guys, at least give me a clue. Aren't you supposed to read me my rights? I think I saw a guy recording everything on his cell. You'll be on YouTube soon enough. Chicago's famous police brutality."

"Just relax, sir." The man's voice displayed a small hint of nervousness. Mike caught a glimpse of his eyes in the mirror, full of sadness and sorrow.

"Everything will be okay, Mike. Just enjoy the free ride. A concerned friend said you haven't been taking your medicine," the woman said before picking up the radio to inform dispatch that everything was okay and there was no one at the scene.

"Ooookaaaay . . . yeah, this doesn't jibe with me. Obviously you know more about me than I do you. What's this? A shakedown or something? Guys, this really perpetuates the stereotype of corrupt cops. Did I interrupt your coffee break?" Mike looked through the metal grate at the laptop. Next to his arrest record, a mug shot of him grinning from ear to ear with a black eye and a broken nose stared back from the small coffee-stained screen. *Yup. I'm fucked.* "Okay, listen, the arrests were all for minor incidents and protests." He tried his best to sound appeasing.

"Like we said, Mr. Auburn, we're taking you home," the male said. "Enjoy the silence for now. You've caused a lot of noise today." He flashed his partner a look, and she shook her head. That silent language two people have after working together for a long time was all the communication they needed.

Mike sat back and resigned himself to the car ride. He put his head on the window, fogging it up as they drove. *This is the longest and slowest way home possible.* They came to a full stop at every red light, even when making a right turn, which caused Mike's eyes to roll in frustration. He resisted the urge to be a backseat driver. *Last time I had a tour of this type, it was for "gerrymandering" the homes of a few congressmen in protest over voter suppression. Heh, that was a good time. Allison was stunning that night, all covered in red paint as we divided their houses to match their districts.*

After a full tour of Chicago, they finally rolled their cruiser in front of his apartment. A three-level flat in a neighborhood where finding parking was impossible any time of the year. The female officer let Mike out, removing his restraints. By now every bone and muscle ached in his body and his wrists had nice red marks from the day's activities.

"So that's it?" Mike asked.

"You tell us. Is it? Go inside," she said as she leaned on the back of the car.

# CHAPTER 4

Mike reached into his pockets for his pack of smokes as he climbed the steps to his apartment. The door dangled, bouncing off a wall with the breeze, its handle broken. He stopped the rattling and held it open. Cigarette hanging from his lips, he stood in the doorframe and stared at his violated home. *Great. Just great. No matter where I move, this happens every year. Why do I even bother?*

The streetlight cast a small bluish beam inside. Mike flicked his lighter on, revealing everything he already came to expect. A trashed apartment. Cheap lamps lay shattered in the middle of the floor. His old, ratty couch had been upturned, and homemade shelves were thrown to the floor, their contents strewn about like the splattered brains of a murder victim. Mike took careful steps, trying to avoid crushing things that might be important. Picking up a lamp and turning it on caused a small shower of sparks. *Lighter it is. They better not have broken my pool cue.*

Entering his kitchen, he saw the light from his fridge that lay sideways on the floor. Its feeble glow was enough for him to take in the scene that matched his living room. He pulled a broken chair from the floor and wedged the fridge under the missing leg for a place to sit down. He took a deep drag and let the taste of tobacco hang in his mouth as he looked around. Nothing was stolen from what he could tell. *Just a message.* He pulled off his bandanna and put his head in his hands, letting the smoke and silence settle in. *This day sure as shit could've been better, but at least nobody died. I don't care what else happens. I want nothing more out of this night than the sweet warm embrace of sleep.*

Getting up and lumbering through his kitchen, Mike no longer cared about the noise or where he stepped. A knife lay buried in the wall, pinning a coat to it right in his line of sight. Pulling it free, he ran his fingers over the coat, feeling its texture. He brought it up to his face and inhaled deeply, pulling in the smell of polished leather and rotten Chinese food. Doc's tweed jacket.

Mike threw his fist through a wall and stumbled into his bedroom as the world became fuzzy. *November 30 is too far away. I'm coming. I can't lose another friend.* Loneliness and panic wrenched in his chest as he fought back tears. He collapsed on his bed and curled up as the world spun with an array of dizzying thoughts.

Mike snapped back to his reality after what seemed like an eternity. His knuckles were almost as white as the sheets he clutched, his whole body covered in a cold sweat. Falling. He'd reached out for the handkerchief, his foot had slipped, and this time, his training hadn't helped him—he'd plummeted straight toward the concrete. He could swear he'd felt the beginning of the impact just before his thoughts aligned. His gut felt twisted and gnarled.

The chopper-motorcycle-shaped alarm clock flashed three thirty, and the morning air was cold enough to form puffs with his breath. *Only five minutes have passed.* Events of the day were becoming clearer to Mike as he sat there in the dark. Something happened to Doc, he had a stalker, and the police were in on it. *They are right outside.* He tried to swallow but a lump in his throat prevented it. *I gotta do something, but what can I do?* He got out of bed and lumbered back and forth around his room, stepping on the clothes and tools strewn about. *Should I call the cops? There's no way all of them could be in on this, right?* He remembered how one of the officers, the big one, had seemed nervous about the scenario. Doc was right about a conspiracy. Maybe Doc's research into the topic had been what set things in motion. *Or me chasing that guy pushed the envelope too far.*

Thinking about Doc, Mike searched the tweed coat. He pulled out a folded piece of paper, and after trying to get the right amount of light on it by holding it up at odd angles, he determined it was the calendar from the office, with November 30 circled. *They could have at least left a phone number. All right. Let's be real. There is no way they could all be involved.* He patted himself down, pulled out his cell phone, and dialed 911.

"Nine one one," the voice said.

"Yeah, I need to report a break-in and kidnapping," Mike said.

"Are you in any danger?"

"Not immediately. The address is fifty-three forty-three Paulina."

There was a pause on the phone as information was probably being entered. Mike took the moment to grab a glass of water.

"Mr. Auburn, we are currently handling the situation there. Your landlord, Frank O'Neil, already called the officers, and they are on location," the voice said in a low, more matter-of-fact tone. Mike got the hint and hung up the phone. He had enough experience with dispatchers before, and this wasn't legit.

*Shit. Okay, maybe they* can *have all the cops in on this. Rerouting perhaps? Bugged phone?* There were not many options. He could perhaps hire a private detective, or maybe even make enough of a noise to bring attention to internal corruption in the Chicago Police Department. The mere thought of this caused Mike to crack himself up. He pounded the countertop while holding his stomach, still aching from all the running and climbing earlier. *Internal . . . corruption . . . Chicago. Well, there's only one option I can think of. Might as well go for it.* He gave a quick kick to his fridge door, making sure it was open all the way so more light could help him find a flashlight. It didn't take him long to find it, and he was off to his room.

Mike started going through all the clothes on the floor. He would need gear, and he might as well dress the part. He pulled out a green World War I army trench coat covered in patches, union buttons, and many burn marks. His protest coat. He held it up in triumph and threw it on. He started throwing more items on his bed that he would need. A gun case, his pool cue kit, spray paint, a carton of smokes, and some motorcycle body armor. He looked at it and nodded, shining the light on them. The gun and body armor were obvious choices. The pool cue kit, however—Mike had won more than a few bar fights throwing a nine ball at someone's face. Everyone always underestimated how much those things hurt, so he decided to grab it. A few more random objects went into his worn backpack.

He flung the drapes aside in his room and waved at the two officers outside before dropping trow and pressing ham against the window. The juvenile nature of the gesture was totally worth the initial shock of a frozen window pressed against parts where the sun didn't shine. *You want me so bad, come arrest me. I'm going in protest!*

He didn't have to wait long. Mike heard the front door open and watched the two officers from earlier enter with their guns drawn. When they noticed him still pressed against the window, Mike gave a two-fingered wave.

"Welcome to my humble abode. You two ready for our second date?" Mike asked. "So, since you two are my new drivers around Chicago, I figure we could get to know each other a little better. I myself am a huge fan of *Project Runway*, I hate ma po tofu with a passion, and when I grow up, I want to be the chief of staff." He put his arms out wide and gave his best performance grin.

The warm smile from earlier was gone from the female officer. She rolled her eyes as she gestured for her partner to flank Mike while the handcuffs once again came out. "Cuff him," she said. Then she turned to Mike as she holstered her weapon and took his bag. "Let's just play this out. You stay quiet, let us do our job, and you'll be back to binge watching *Project Runway* in no time."

The cuffs squeezed tighter on Mike's wrists and felt even colder than the first time. He was pretty sure the big guy could bench-press him with one hand. "So how about some names? I mean, I can start guessing, but you really don't want that. I'll just start making up drag queen names for you."

"I'm Officer Paul Winters, and that's Officer Janine Matsen," Winters said as he put his massive paw on the back of Mike's head, pushing him off to the side into a corner like a child in time-out. "Matsen, what's in the bag?"

Officer Matsen was going through the bag with her flashlight, pulling out its contents. "Nothing threatening, a set of pool table balls, a gun, duct tape, socks . . ." She paused as she held up a set of ThunderCats boxers and stared at them, eyes back to Mike, and then to her hands. "A set of clean underwear."

"Mom always said to be prepared. Janine, eh? Nice name, I dated a Janine once—" Jerked into the wall by Winters, Mike let out a loud grunt and spat on Winters's shoe in protest.

"Stuff the sock in his mouth and duct-tape him. I can't handle a car ride with a chatty anarchist," Winters said.

Mike gave his best puppy-dog eyes as he accepted their makeshift gag. His plan was to go with them after all, not fight and make a run for it. His shoulders let tension release as he watched Officer Matsen pack all his bag contents and bring it with them.

# CHAPTER 5

Throughout the drive, the taste of sweaty socks in his mouth was only a fraction better than the Chinese food Doc "forced" him to eat earlier at his office. *Next time you pull this, pack clean socks.* As the squad car approached the Drake Hotel, the man with the checkered scarf approached with three security guards behind him. Mike glared out the window to get a clearer picture of his adversary. Mike's earlier assumption about his age seemed right. He was clearly in his late forties. The wrinkles around the eyes and the five-o'clock shadow speckled with gray hairs gave it away.

"He's all yours. If I were you, I'd leave the gag in," Winters said.

"I think our guest can use some proper hospitality. We are gentlemen after all. Mr. Auburn is not going to violate any rules of etiquette, is he now?" he said while holding two fingers under Mike's chin and looking into his eyes. Mike gave him a nod.

"It is a pleasure to finally make your acquaintance, Mr. Auburn. You may call me Edward. Edward Morris." The cuffs came off.

Mike clinched his eyes shut to brace himself as the duct tape was ripped off. It didn't work. "Son of a . . . man that stings," Mike said as he grasped his jaw, half wondering if he just got a fresh shave. "Edward Morris, eh?" Mike thrust out his hand, giving his best business handshake. "So, what's the deal? You realize a phone call and a fruit basket would have worked."

"It is not my place to explain such things. I am merely the head of . . . security. This operation and my employer requested your presence. We will escort you to him and his associates, who have been waiting for you at the pub." Morris started to straighten Mike's collar and cleaned off the ratty coat a bit, but his eyes never left Mike's. "Under no circumstances are you to speak louder than casual conversation or make any sudden movements. Are we clear?"

Somehow, Mike heard the statement reverberate through him. *I am to speak no louder than casual conversation nor make any sudden movements.* It was a fact to him. He wasn't sure if it was the gravity of the situation that made it sink in, but the goose bumps rising along his arms added to the weight of it. "Yeah, crystal. Bar, then? Let's get this over with."

Mike's eyes glanced sideways to Officer Matsen, and a coy smile crept along his face. "What are you doing next Thursday night?" Mike got his response when she dropped the bag at his feet.

Victorian opulence inside Chicago's older hotels never impressed Mike. Everything was gold and red with twisting patterns carved into every surface. Massive crystal chandeliers tried to hide cracked plaster and nicotine stains from the good ol' days when smoking indoors was allowed. At four thirty in the morning, the only people to be seen were a pair of new carpet cleaners in the main lobby, trying to wrestle their machines. The bar matched his expectations, dimly backlit bottles lined the wall, and it was empty except for employees and Morris. *Not many associates after all. Looks like the boss has a hard time making friends. This is meant to be a one-on-one meeting anyway.*

The goons accompanying Morris stood at attention in the entryway, reinforcing Mike's thought. Morris pulled up a chair at the end of the bar and reached over to grab a half-full bottle of red wine. Unsure of what to do, Mike thought he deserved a drink after the crazy night and sat down at the bar. The bartender, sleeves rolled up with an open vest, had polished the bar so much Mike could see his reflection.

"Whiskey," Mike said.

"You're a hard kid to push," the bartender said while pouring his drink in a swift, fluid motion. "Had a rough day, I heard." He slid the drink over to Mike.

He concluded that the bartender looked like an old man you would see playing Vegas slot machines all night and day. "It's been a peach. So where is everyone?"

"Here," he said, gesturing to the empty bar. "You see what you want when it suits you. It's much easier to ignore the crumbling world hidden just out of sight."

"Yeah, clearly, you don't know me very well." Mike craned his head to spy into the back room behind the bar, expecting to see mobsters smoking cigars and playing cards. He turned back to his whiskey when he only saw an empty room.

"Did you know that Senator McCarthy led another campaign concurrent with the Red Scare? They call it the Lavender

Scare. His quest was to eradicate homosexuality," the bartender said.

"Yeah, he was a freak. You should've heard what he told his
therapist."

"It's never brought up that the Vatican and the Catholics
were the driving force behind that. Even forced a friendship
between McCarthy and the Kennedy family."

"Another one of the dynasty families that really pull the
strings." Mike gave a nod. *Where you going with this, buddy?*

"The Lavender Scare was an experiment to see if the
Vatican could control a nation by sacrificing its minorities
for a sense of greater good. McCarthy became the villain in
history. Kennedy later won as the first Catholic president and
sparked the imagination of a nation to put a man on the moon."
He gave a salute to a nicotine-stained American flag dangling
in the corner before continuing. "One nation, *under God*. Yet
putting a man on the moon is an act of science. The concept
would have been heresy by the same god hundreds of years
before. What changed upstairs that could spark such a policy
shift? Or was that change done below?"

"Okay, now you're just jumping the shark. I got shit to do."
Mike pushed his stool away from the bar and stood up, planning his assault. *Guy is a crackpot.*

"Kid, I'm going to level with you. The night is almost over,
so I'm going to cut the bullshit for the sake of time. My patrons
and I have an aversion to the sunlight, and as their caretaker, I
need to make this quick. You have the deathsight. It happens
every now and then. Someone brushes with death enough
times, they start to see into purgatory and it looks back at you.
You're one of them. I want you to come work for me. Do some
real good in the world rather than waste away and rot with the
rest." He put his hands on the counter and leaned in. "It's going
to be undergoing some . . . changes soon."

"What? The bar? It's old, sure, but perfectly reusable. Maybe hang some new drapes?"

The man smiled. "The world."

Mike nodded, not to what the man was saying, but to his own internal conclusion. *Yup, I've officially gone insane.* "Who are *you*? What happened to Doc? Are you this O'Neil guy? What changes? Deathsight? Aversion to sunlight? Do you offer dental?" Mike pointed and raised his glass in a toast and slammed it back, feeling the burn down his throat. It was the most refreshing thing of the day, and it cleaned out the taste of sock.

"Your friend Joseph Daneka uncovered secrets sooner than the timetable allowed. I take kindly to researchers who start piecing the puzzle together like him. A potential future prospect. The Unification, my employer, takes a more violent approach. I made the call to scoop up Joseph. His father was a member of the Unification, so I can call off the hounds without ruffling feathers. You, however, needed a stronger hand to force you out of your slump." He smiled and started polishing his bar again. "Technically it's the Unification Proclamation, but that's the legal name of the treaty all the vampires signed years ago. Monsters are real, kid, and we do indeed offer dental coverage."

He let Mike reflect before he continued. "We've been watching you since you were born. You refuse to be passive, you notice people who others don't, and you've had a rough life. These are some of the beginning signs of a prospect for me. What really got our attention, however, is when you started seeing our organization for what it really was. Frank isn't a figment of your imagination. He had his skin ripped off in the seventies as he went through the change. Everyone in this room has their own unique story that caused them to shed their innocence. Normally, everyone is so blissfully ignorant of the creatures in their midst. The Unification likes to keep it that way. People live happier lives if they are kept in the dark. Can you imagine the mass panic? We barely made it out of the Dark Ages. Reason and silence had to become our tools. Otherwise, the human race would have died off long ago. The Nazis were our last big threat to unraveling everything by thrusting the occult world out in the open. Until now . . ."

Mike nodded and pointed to below the bar. "Hey, buddy, I'm going to need the whole bottle right next to me if you want to continue the full history lesson."

O'Neil reached down and pulled out a bottle filled with black ichor from a cabinet and set it down. Mike's eyes went wide as he looked at the countertop. He felt hairs on his neck rise when he saw no reflection of O'Neil. Deep down inside, he wanted to scream, get up, and run away, to dive back. He felt Morris place his hand on his shoulder. *Hold still* . . . He heard Morris in his head again.

Mike's hands shook while he reached for the bottle, but Morris placed his hand on it first.

"I'll handle this," Morris said. "Boss, you sure you wanna do this? This kid's a rabble-rouser, defiant, not to mention a socialist bordering on the kind of progressive who . . ." He let the thought trail off as Mike felt an unnatural degree of strength pinning him to the bar stool. "He's got a built-in resistance to control. It's taking all of my concentration just to get him to sit still. I think we would be better off throwing his soul in as fuel for the society in the Twin Cities." Morris wrinkled his brow as he tightened his grip on Mike's shoulder. Mike could not shake the feeling that Morris was afraid of the old man.

Mike looked at the stare-down the two of them were having and butted in. "So why me? Why Doc? I'm just a construction worker. Because I saw you? That's why you want me?" he asked.

The barkeep added, "Most people who develop the death-sight end their lives, kid. You keep running into danger to trigger it. That means you have guts deep down inside. It means we can train you." He looked at Morris and continued. "It means you are worth bringing into the fold. If we didn't reach out to you and bring you in, someone else would eventually find you. I assure you, that's not a scenario you want. Since you haven't shed your innocence yet, you can only see us for what we are right after you've had a close encounter with death. It's why you think this room is empty."

"Like the nineties movie *Flatliners*?" Mike asked.

"I suppose." O'Neil looked behind Mike.

In the dimly lit mirror behind the bar, Mike noticed that Morris began to bleed drops of black blood by his right eye.

O'Neil placed his hand on Mike's shoulder to keep his attention. "Listen, I want you to come join us before the month is out. Work for me. Put that fight you have inside to some proper use. World-changing events are going to happen shortly. The kind I'll fill you in on once you decide which side of the fence you're on. Our side, or those good folk out there." O'Neil gestured out the window to the city.

"That's a pretty easy choice if you're asking now. When did I strike you as the kidnapping, accident-causing, horror-movie stand-in like yourself?" Mike laughed.

"Lady Fate is a fickle bitch, kid. And I've wagered my *name* on protecting this city. The Second City has been chosen as a safe haven for what's to come and the damned who survive. You can be a leader, or just another face in the horde. Make your choice. But time's running out. You might not have a mouth left to voice your decision after it's burned off by demon fire."

O'Neil snatched the bottle out of Morris's hand and uncorked it. A rich aroma of sweetness filled the room. Mike thought he heard chairs slide out of place, and suddenly he felt a bit crowded in a bar with only the three of them. "Morris, would you be so kind as to keep an eye on our guest. Make sure he doesn't get into any trouble or a demon doesn't sniff him out in the next three days. Keep our cops on him during the day," O'Neil said. "I already have eyes on the society. We've given them more than enough fuel. We need men like him here in case that goes wrong."

Morris placed his hands over the glass, defying O'Neil, while Mike's hand was still trembling. "We are the rejects of the Unification for our perceived loyalty issues. They've sent more of our family diving down than any other group that joined them. Now we hide in the shadows like starved hyenas for the coming global change. Are you sure you want to bring this kid into the Unification, the noisy rioter? By making him Nosferatu with one of your last vials? What makes you think he'll change our fortune?" As Morris spoke, Mike had the feeling that he was in a crowded room. He could almost hear the whispers from behind him, yet Morris was keeping him pinned.

O'Neil placed a towel over his arm and rocked back and forth on his feet, letting the silence sit while he contemplated. His gaze wandered across the entire bar before finally resting on Mike, who he regarded with a wry grin. "People like you are born once a decade. You'd never even know it, but Lady Fate spins you into action one way or another." O'Neil grabbed the bottle from Morris without further protest and slowly poured the thick black ichor into Mike's glass. "So drink up."

Mike raised the glass and took a sip. It tasted like an incredibly sweet peach, with a fiery burn as it went down. He licked his lips and held up the glass for closer inspection. "What the hell is this?" *Poison, probably. Now he's going to say if I don't accept his offer, I don't get the cure. I am way too tired to be doing this.* He didn't feel tired, however. He felt as alive as ever, the pain in his wrists and legs washing right out of him. A sense of renewed vigor filled him.

"Demon blood," the bartender said. "Has a different effect on everyone. Kills some people and gives others strength. I'm sure you'll love it. You're gonna take that bottle home and finish it off. I've already taken the liberty of getting you a replacement for your job. Daneka is going to stay with us for a while and study his father's missing notes. You figure out if you like where your life is going and make your own choice."

"Morris will get you a cab home. When you're ready for more, we'll be here, kid. Remember, though, it's okay to gamble with your life, but Lady Fate will make you pay thrice if you gamble with other lives." He reached over and rubbed Mike's head like a father tussling his kid's hair. "Hey, you'll be fine. Your life is going to come into focus. Now get outta here before my associates decide to make a meal of you."

Mike began to feel more than a bit drunk and was grateful for Morris helping him outside into a cab. He didn't notice skinless Frank driving him home and tucking him into bed. Mike only noticed that he felt like a paradox. Half wanting to scream and shout at the world, and half wanting to cuddle up with his pillow and sleep. *At least I brought clean underwear . . .* was his last thought of the night.

# CHAPTER 6

Talking heads bobbed up and down on an array of monitors. Sounds of the drivel echoed off the glass windows in the vast penthouse of Walsh Tower. Thirteen figures in tattered gray Masonic robes stood in silent judgment of the chattering screens as the moon cast a peaceful light on the Twin Cities. Only the porcelain-skinned creature daintily sipping on a goblet of blood seemed amused by the events unfolding before them.

"... and that, Janice, wraps up our highlight on Macgregor Brewery's newest addition of local brewers to their line. On to you, Michael."

"Pause!" All monitors except one went dark. Charles Walsh stepped out from the corner of the room, jamming buttons on a remote. His bright-blue vest, lavender tie, and sandy-blond hair stood in contrast to the rest of the room's inhabitants. "Okay, my lords and ladies, watch this!" Charles had a face perfect for the front page of magazines, accented now by sideways light from the screens.

"... in other news, international pop star Molly LeMuse is starting her tour right here in . . ."

"Did you see that?" Walsh asked. "Alexandria, you of all vampires had to appreciate that." Flicking a pocket watch open and closed out of habit, he let the quiet linger to that moment where everyone was standing in awkward silence. "Okay, let me rewind it."

"I saw you cut away from news of my favorite singer, Walsh," Alexandria said at last.

"Right, right. Let me play it again."

"Please. Heavens no. Even immortals have busy nightlives. Enlighten us."

Slamming the pocket watch shut, he straightened his position. "Very well. What you did not see is a video made a few days ago in which a crane fell in Chicago, killing two people and injuring fourteen."

One of the robed figures spoke. "Your point, please."

"That we can control the narrative fully now. Everything is on schedule. We've fully perfected our technique that the Unification started with McCarthy in controlling public discourse. Uh . . . here, let me highlight." Walsh snapped his fingers and pointed to one of the smaller figures. "Lord of Murder, over forty shootings happened in Detroit this weekend alone. Here's the news."

". . . caught in a sexting scandal . . ."

"Lady of Age, warlords in Africa continue to press children into their ranks for their wars, even going so far as to sacrifice them, drinking their blood, and having them charge naked into battle. Because we want to prove the point, here is the coverage." Charles turned off all the monitors. "Absolutely nothing." He took a flourishing bow in front of the middle figure. "Lord of Heaven's Wrath, a tiny fraction of the world's total population is killed by supernaturals each year. That's still thousands of people. Yet the news of strange accidents is replaced with this."

". . . this winter's must-see blockbuster . . ."

"The Treaty of Unification is working. With the majority of the world's occult groups on board controlling the flow of blood—"

"The rockin' sockin' business hour is up next with Tim . . ."

Walsh turned on more monitors, each showing people of influence in developed nations. "After McCarthy, we've been giving demon blood to those with power and influence to shape the direction of the masses, relying on the trickle-down effect, and it's worked."

Lord of Heaven's Wrath took a step forward and placed his hand on Charles's shoulder. "We are grateful for your efforts, my child, yet until our work is complete, souls of the dying are still sorted by demons and angels of all the world's religions. Often with a great deal of inconsistency. One goes to a heaven for slaughter in his god's name while another goes to a hell for killing."

Charles tapped the remote on the creature's shoulder. "We can finally save the souls trapped in purgatory. We've slowly recruited descendants of Lazarus for centuries and trained them in helldiving and how to navigate purgatory." Charles winked at Alexandria. "We've made the warlocks, located and readied all the prime ritual sites into the underworld, and now, thanks to the beta run by the Unification with McCarthy, we can control collective will for what comes after."

Alexandria applauded. "So the sheep can be herded because we gave the sheepdogs demon blood. It doesn't matter, when we bring Lazarus back for the third time, we can just slap all the angels and demons in line like the good little servants they were created to be."

Robed figures next to her shuffled away quietly. "Or we could do it peacefully, as intended by the accord of the Unification," Walsh replied. *I really wish we could muzzle a three-thousand-year-old vampire.* "It's proven that by focusing man's will, anything can be done. We put a man on the moon because they longed for it." He turned back to the monitors. "All the regional directors are on board. The great ritual to bring back Lazarus can be done, with miniscule casualties by our projections. When he returns, the entire world will be ready to receive his message. One world thought, one world nation, one world humanity. All heavens and all hells will be forced to follow a united world. Our suffering in purgatory will end, and all will be saved." He smiled at the thought, but knew deep down he acted out of fear. *Tow the party line.*

Lord of Heaven's Wrath let out a warm chuckle. "A true believer if I ever saw one. I understand that our last hurdle is here? An emergency *certamen* is under way for replacements?"

"Uh . . . oh, yes, but an emergency it is not. There are plenty of occult groups looking for glory and blood from you lords. They've sent their finest sorcerers in contest here. Delilah has already picked her favorite, however. And . . . and . . . the Second City has enough death for the walls to power the ritual for a week, easily, longer than most. Delilah Dumont is holding the contest now." *How did they find out about this?*

"Ooooh, trouble in paradise," Alexandria chimed in before she took a swig.

"What happened to the original first seed we sent to Primus Vryce?"

"The fireman? He—"

"It doesn't really matter. Delilah has, as always, found the best way to settle things. We only need the portal open for three nights at best. All other regions are ready." He gestured to the others in the room. "Come, let us enjoy a final *certamen*."

Charles waited for the death lords to shuffle out of the room. He stared at the pale bare skin on Alexandria's back while she looked out the window at Chicago. *Eater of a demon lord's heart, a noble vampire. Without creatures like her, this wouldn't be possible.* She slowly drank the remaining blood out of her glass while looking back at Walsh in the reflection.

# CHAPTER 7

The body twitched on the ground, its jaw opening and shutting as it tried to scream and hold on for life. Smoke rose from its blackened skin like a bonfire that had just been doused with water. Ceremonial robes fused with flesh gave off a nice fragrance, Gabriel thought. It would serve this failing apprentice well to learn a lesson he should never forget before stepping into a certamen circle. Gabriel reached down and tried to brush soot off his jeans, letting out a tsk sound in frustration, as he knew the stains would not yield easily. *At least my Chucks are still clean*, he thought as he retied his shoelaces and looked up at the scoreboard. Gabriel D'Angelo stood firmly in first place. Out of the forty-nine applicants for the position, Gabriel had bested over half of them in the arena.

The certamen arena was carved into the basement of a Masonic Temple in the heart of Minneapolis. Large, overlapping circles were etched into the concrete, with Latin markings and formulas from every Hermetic introductory manual. Inside one of them lay the twitching body of the second-best applicant. Gabriel had already forgotten his name. He did not just think he was the best; he knew it. Gabriel looked at the judges' table. Thirteen of them sat in full old Freemason robes with deep hoods. Before them, a diminutive blonde girl with stick-straight hair and golden spectacles wore a modern, immaculately clean pine-green suit. *She has no business being here. The Council of Death Lords rules over the Unification and all its occult groups. They alone should determine the victor.* Gabriel straightened his back and stared straight ahead while awaiting acknowledgment. Robed men dragged the body of the second best free from his circle and got to work pouring demon blood back into the etchings. Ever since magic had gotten scarce centuries ago, such trappings were now required for the most basic of spells.

"Satisfactory work, Gabriel. Tell us, you believe you are performing well in this tribunal, correct?" came a voice from behind a hood.

"My success is the only measure of performance, sir," Gabriel said. *This is my chance to prove my lineage, even if I have to endure these rituals.* He kept his face calm by clenching his jaw and focusing on the circles in the floor.

"Tell us, what do you believe is the purpose of this barbarism?" asked another.

"Primus Vryce, the warlock for the third circle of ten, requires apprentices to complete his coven for your worldwide ritual. A mandate to bring the divine presence of Lazarus back into this world offering humanity guidance into the next age," Gabriel said. The first of his family to be born with his talents in generations, he spoke with confidence. This was his chance to break the cycle of addiction the Unification had trapped his family in. "Of the forty-nine applicants selected by the Society of Deus's ambassador, Delilah Dumont, the victor of the tribunal will be granted the glory of becoming the first seed. The right hand of the primus. The following nine shall serve as proxy for the other nine rituals happening worldwide. The remaining thirty-nine will lend their power as if they were the base of a pyramid." *In other words, I get to prove that sorcerous lineage will always be better than these blooded hacks who have cut deals with demons and become junkies.* He liked his version better.

"Have you read Primus Vryce's *Arcannum Arcannimusim,* his thesis on Gnostic Hermeticism in the modern age?" another voice said.

"No, sir."

"Have you read Warlock Lucian Montegue's manual on the Vodun Loa and the risks of tampering with Bondye?"

"No, sir."

"Perhaps, have you studied the radical theory of techno-logically inspired magic by Warlock Peter Culmen?"

"No, ma'am."

"Then tell us, Gabriel, how is it that an uneducated member of the Unification, such as yourself, believes he is fit for such a position?" yet another said, placing his hands on his robust belly while a servant poured him another glass of black ichor.

"Because I am better than them, sir," Gabriel said. He failed at containing a small smirk. "My mother, Maria D'Angelo, served the Italian branch of the Unification within the Order of the Eastern Star. She saw fit to train her seventh son in the arts of controlling his will. Unlike the rest of the apprentices in this room, I do not imbibe the demon blood to fuel my magic. I control it by birthright granted to me, an art form far faster and simpler, yet deemed useless by the *educated* Unification. I am proving everyone wrong." Gabriel pressed his hands to the sides of his jeans. His palms were starting to sweat. *That was probably the wrong thing to say.* He returned his focus to clenching his jaw.

The judge who sat on the highest chair stood up. He had long brown hair that frayed at its edges and a beard, but candlelight played tricks with the shadows to obscure the rest. "Centuries ago when magic flowed freely, that method was vital. Now it is only practical as a counter to magic. Demon blood is in such rare quantities that outside a certamen circle, or facing a Unification sorcerer, you will never cast more than a single spell. Your style of magic burns the divine blood around you, rather than from within. Perhaps in the past when demons were more prevalent . . ." He let the words hang in the air. "Now, unless you consume the blood yourself, you are as useful as a wolf to a sheepherder." He placed his hand gently on the shoulder of the woman. "Delilah, we shall accept your recommendation of Visago as the first seed," he said.

She entered a sequence of numbers into her tablet and made a few notes with her stylus, then nodded curtly. "Yes, Lord of Heaven's Wrath. What shall be done with the remaining recruits?" Her accent was remarkably British.

"We will leave them in the capable hands of Vryce to rank as he sees fit. See to it Visago's wounds are attended to immediately. He must grasp glory from the heavens soon enough. We verified your initial assessment, Delilah. Gabriel is unfit to be a first seed. You may use him for your ritual as you see fit. We must return to Rome. As always, it is a pleasure to see your work, my dear." Lord of Heaven's Wrath stepped off his podium and proceeded to leave the room. In ranking, displayed as golden rings along the back of the robes, each of the other judges left the room in procession after wishing Delilah farewell.

Gabriel's face was quickly turning shades of red and purple. The Masonic ring dug into his fingers with its sharp edges, leaving a punctured indent. The pain provided only a sense of focus and calm in the room. *What useless old wretches. I dropped their best on the floor like a sack of bricks. What am I supposed to do now?* Gabriel stayed motionless in the circle as the rest of the applicants filed out of the basement, most of them limping or holding bandaged arms from wounds Gabriel had given them. None of them displayed the courage to look Gabriel in the eye. He bit his tongue to remain silent while staring at the circles until the last of them was gone. Thoughts raced through his head at a frantic pace. *Dismissed so quickly? What a farce.* His entire life of practicing his family's craft was utterly insulted by the aging order of the Unification.

If he returned home to Italy a failure, his mother and older sisters would be expelled from the Unification and disgraced. While he could survive and forge his own path, his family would perish without the rationed quantities of blood the council shipped them. He wanted to free them. His mother, Maria, had sacrificed everything to bring the seven of them into this world. Yet only he, the youngest, was the first to ignite the flames of sorcery hidden in his lineage. Without his success, his fate-bending witch sisters would have no choice but to continue down their path of blooded addicts or die. *No. I need to break this cycle.*

Servants whispered among themselves, debating whether they should start cleaning while there was still someone in the room. The boldest of them began sweeping at the farthest end of the chambers from Gabriel, leaving a wide circle around him, and then left the room.

The sound of metal against concrete echoed throughout the chamber, followed by a muffled scream. Two sharp pings, one . . . two. Gabriel spun around to look at the stairs. The torches in the room began to wisp out and flare up suddenly as if they were trying to fight for life. It was the servant who was in the room earlier, only now adorned with two cold-iron nails in its bare feet. One . . . two. Gabriel took a step back and readied himself. *I'm useless to them, so they are going to have me killed? Not today.*

"Indeed. Not today." The voice was raspy and seemed to come from the shadow tied to the servant by the nails. Without much light in the chamber, however, that shadow seemed all-encompassing. "What a piece of work is a man, how noble in reason, how infinite in faculties, in form and moving, how express and admirable in action, how like an angel in apprehension. How like a *god!*"

Sparks flew from the candles, and electric arcs danced from each to the next. With every movement, the shadow danced around the room. "The beauty of the world, the paragon of animals—and yet to me, what is this quintessence of dust?" As if to make a point, demon blood still etched in the circles gave off an amber glow of warm coals before turning to ash and flowing upward. "Man delights not me—no, nor woman neither—though by your smiling, you seem to say so." The servant took a low bow, craning its head to look up at Gabriel. Its eyes were a mix of green and gold that illuminated themselves from within. With a twirl of its hand, it conjured a letter, sealed with the symbol of the Society of Deus. The personal occult group of Warlock Vryce that either joined or was created by the Unification for this ritual. Gabriel wasn't sure of its origins entirely.

"There are few visionaries left in the world. True architects worthy of mentorship. You will join the others at Walsh Tower, Gabriel. Failure is a matter of perspective. I will give you the chance to succeed, or die." The eyes quickly faded back to a dull brown. The servant, clutching his feet with panic, struggled with the choice to pull out the nails or not. He looked at Gabriel as if he were the source of his current torment.

"Wrap those up and take some aspirin. You'll be fine. Better off than everyone else who was in here," Gabriel said. He broke into a trot up the spiral stairs leading out. *Finally, recognition. This is not over yet.*

# CHAPTER 8

Sunrise over the Twin Cities brought hues of purple with red streaks that cascaded onto the reflective glass of downtown, creating a rather scenic mural. Delilah Dumont took in the quiet moment outside her favorite coffee shop as the morning's first customer. The heat from her obsidian macchiato along her thin hands served its purpose to fight back the cold air. Her head nodded and jerked back up as she fought off fatigue. She had just come to accept the bags under her eyes as part of the job. Trying her best to shake it off, she made sure that the nails and hammer were out of sight in her bag. Unfortunately for the servant, Primus Vryce required arcane rituals for possession. *That reminds me, I need to give that servant a raise. I may be ruthless, but that doesn't mean I don't pay my people well.*

Delilah pulled out her tablet and set to work while she waited. Her notification list informed her of her tasks for the day:

- Meet with JJ Bollard—deliver containment protocols.
- Blackmail the mayor's wife.
- Test Stockholm procedures on society soldiers.

- Lunch.
- Prep media cover stories.
- Acquire weapons-grade nerve gas agents.
- Set plan in motion to destroy human life as we know it.
- ~~Sleep.~~
- Attend to Boss's dry cleaning.

*Well, at least it's a slow day.* Delilah smiled as she reflected upon the upcoming day. The Unification Proclamation was filled with ancient people. Her talents navigating modern-day bureaucracy made her an invaluable employee. After all, juggling a worldwide conspiracy was not something best suited to those who had a hard time understanding the concept of e-mail. Later tonight she would have to meet with dignitaries from a variety of organizations that had signed the Treaty of Unification. The list seemed endless.

Scores of centuries-old occult organizations collectively made up the Unification. The Freemasons, the Illuminati, the Brotherhood of Skulls, and the Order of the Eastern Star were some of the most prominent. A wry grin crept onto Delilah's face as she fondly recalled outmaneuvering many immortal creatures to bolster the Unification's ranks before her master recruited her to make their own society. Each one fell in line in order to use the Unification as their own individual means to instrumentality. *And they will soon all be dancing to my master.* Delicately managing inflated egos was one of her specialties. She pondered what the world would be like today if everyone did exactly as she instructed.

Delilah slammed back the rest of her drink and decided to stand while waiting for JJ. He was always a prompt fellow. Unlike the rest of the creatures she would meet with later, JJ was at least one other human, like her, who embraced the wonder of the hidden world. *A healthy résumé of multiple secret societies and the prestige of an artifact hunter. His résumé is perfect. Too perfect* . . . She began fingering a crimson coin with the law of thermodynamics on it, her own symbol of the Society of Deus. *Right now we are just one cog in the machine of the Unification. Not for long.*

It was one of her many jobs to vet applicants sent by the council to the Society of Deus. She chuckled at the thought that she was the closest thing the creature had to a friend. After exhaling and watching her breath, she closed her eyes and thought back to how much she owed Vryce for her second life.

A white Lexus pulled up in front of Delilah exactly on schedule. She looked inside to see JJ, gave a curt signal to her security team down the street, and stepped into the backseat. As the sun's rays cast a wonderful canvas of paint on building glass, gazing at JJ Bollard's polished head would be like looking into a mirror. His stocky shoulders and frame marked him for a soldier. Delilah reminded herself to track down the exact composition of his ethnicity at some point. She took in his islander skin tone and eye shape with admiration. JJ did not fit the demographic of the area.

"Morning, Mr. Bollard. Are we ready to begin?" Delilah asked. "Driver, head around the city counterclockwise at five miles above the speed limit. Stay on Hennepin and shadow I-94." She reached into her bag, moving aside the cold-iron nails, and pulled out a sealed envelope. "You will be allowed to read the contents of this letter containing your offer. Afterward, it must be burned in my presence." She handed it to Mr. Bollard in the passenger seat. *His car is impeccably clean, a man of taste after all. Or with much to hide.* "As you have been informed, Primus Vryce would like to officially thank you for your past five years of service. Without you and your associates' funding for the construction of the new Twin Cities, it would have never happened. As the prime investor in his vision and the Unification, Primus Vryce is willing to offer you title and membership within this city once the new world order has been established. Your reward is that of a *ridari*, a ranking officer in the military, and command of your own legion." Delilah looked back to ensure her security team was in their proper position. Satisfied with the results, her shoulders dropped, and she relaxed slightly.

"You have nothing to fear from the likes of me, my dear. But I am disappointed. I had hoped to speak with the warlock himself. I'm just going to assume such pleasantries are not going to be granted to me just yet? Guess money really can't buy everything." Bollard straightened his cuff link and smiled at Delilah. "Most of these buildings I'm seeing now do not exist on any map. You've managed to insert alternate Google Earth images in their database. I can see the signs of your impressive skills, Lady Dumont."

"This city has become something of a libertarian paradise. Everything you see is built and controlled by private enterprise, using shell companies that are controlled by one of the *pillars* of the Unification," Delilah said. To JJ, "pillars" would mean one of the secret societies that signed the treaty. *It also means I have many societies that owe me favors.* "For over a decade, the populace of the Twin Cities was groomed to accept energy independence, local gun rights, and an absence of government control. Unlike Texas, we've managed to keep it subtle here. Thanks to the *honorable* donations and influence to our society, every officer is now a full member in our ranks. Those who caused difficulty were transferred to other cities." She rapped the glass on the left side of the car with her knuckles and pointed outward. "You may be disappointed that the warlock is not meeting you in person, but look outside to see your money in action. Every building code has been upgraded to support the most robust construction practices in the country, certifiable bomb shelters hidden beneath their facade. Thanks to your funding, we were able to keep the cost to private enterprise low. Everybody answers to the call of money, Bollard. Even centuries-old warlocks," she said.

"Everyone except *your* warlock," said JJ. "It has been over nine decades since he last made an appearance in person to the Council of Death Lords who are organizing all of this. You do know he can't go jamming iron nails in everyone's feet, right? My partners are understandably worried. It's why I was flown in with them last night. So much rests on the warlock's shoulders. Without absolute success in the coming ritual, the idea of one world, one nation, one unification will spiral out of control. Globalization of mankind has been in the making for a while now, but only with the resurrection will our plan come to fruition." JJ kept eyeing his driver, enough that Delilah inferred that the gentleman in front was recording any reactions in her demeanor for later study.

"Let the Council of Death Lords be nervous. That apprehension does not fall on Vryce's shoulders. There are no less than ten concurrent rituals around the world. Each led by its own warlock, converts who have done more than drink demon blood. Soul stealers of the highest regard, sacrificing everything it meant to be human for the resurrection. Their divinity, their holiness, and their sanctity, to practice the paths of left-handed sorcery." She paused to push up her thin spectacles, subtly forcing JJ to maintain eye contact. "There is no room for you here if you even think to question our master."

"I assumed you felt quite strongly about this. If you want another mind-washed soldier who just says yes, I'm indeed afraid I have no place here either," he said, tossing the envelope on the seat between them.

"In order to rip open the gates, rescue Lazarus, and then cover it up, the tools of the demons must be utilized, an unfortunate hypocrisy for those who would do the lord's work. Should not the death lords of the council be more concerned with the recent events in Japan? Rumor has it, the emperor's family pulled their support and assassinated the Unification's puppet there?" *Vryce has given everything he's loved for his vision and this world. Our loyalty to ascension will not be questioned.* Delilah pushed back her sleeve and put her bare arm next to Bollard's face. "If you doubt us, take my blood as sacrifice."

JJ looked at her arm and gave a deep laugh. "You can take that back, Ambassador. I'm on your side. The coming days are not going to go smoothly. Do we honestly believe with all the world's religions and fanaticism, that rivers of blood will not be flowing? Besides, just like you, I'm not blooded." He pulled back his coat and revealed a holstered custom-made gun. "That doesn't mean I haven't killed countless Faustian junkies in my years. The rogue ones always think they can summon a demon and get away with it." He paused as he signaled the driver to pull over. He grabbed the envelope and got out of the car.

"We have not even made it halfway around the city," Delilah said, while following him.

"Neither of us have time to waste. I am here to stay."

The sunrise was in its full morning glory, shining through a mirrored city that was designed to be a fortress. *And even more secrets underneath.* "You'll find the security protocols inside, and further instructions," Delilah said. "Time will be on my side today it seems."

JJ broke the seal on the envelope and reread every line multiple times. More than a few times his eyes widened. "Vryce is very . . . thorough," he said.

"Actually, I wrote those. As long as the Unification does its job in Chicago, I'm confident our location will be victorious." She held her rustic brown bag in front of her with both hands and admired the city while leaning on the car, waiting for JJ to finish.

"I stand corrected, then. It is you who should run this city when it is over. I for one would gladly stand by your side. In all our time working together, I have always enjoyed your professionalism and discretion in all matters," he said, stepping close to her.

"That is in the cards for neither of us. We are both lacking in power and age." She reached out, accepted the letter, and proceeded to burn it from the bottom. The flames danced along the edges, taking on a multitude of colors, before consuming their prey. "One last order of business, for old times' sake. Do you have any connections that might assist me in obtaining several canisters of nerve gas?" She smiled and curtsied, looking more cute than professional in her green dress and brown scarf. Bollard's slight blush let her know she managed to cut through his demeanor.

"I might. I just might. But I want a tour of your prison—the real one, below the city. The council wants access to your technique. I can trade that and a meeting for me. In person," he said.

"Tour and technique. A meeting is not mine to grant. You'll have to prove your usefulness to Vryce, personally, for the meeting." She offered her hand to seal the deal.

"Done." Bollard refused the shake and took a deep bow instead. "My lady."

Delilah's security detail pulled up and both parties left their meeting place. She pulled out her tablet and updated her daily list. *Perfect, I get to cross off two items. I might be able to get an extra hour of sleep today.*

*Check. Aaaannnd check.*

- ~~Meet with JJ Bollard—deliver containment protocols.~~
- Blackmail the mayor's wife.

- Test Stockholm procedures on society soldiers.
- Lunch.
- Prep media cover stories.
- ~~Acquire weapons-grade nerve gas agents.~~
- Set plan in motion to destroy human life as we know it.
- ~~Sleep.~~
- Attend to Boss's dry cleaning.

# CHAPTER 9

Walsh Tower, a fresh building finished only recently, stood between Minneapolis and St. Paul. Like most modern-day construction, it could be viewed as an eyesore compared to its surroundings. It was still impressive on its own. White marble columns stretched up four stories tall. Floodlights shone upward, adding a regal element to the building. Manicured landscaping, cultivated rock gardens, and an impressive array of fountains dominated the surrounding grounds. In any other city, the impressive headquarters of Walsh Construction Company would seem more fitting. Here, the Gothic architecture of St. Paul mixed with the fresh steel construction of Minneapolis and its skyways made the tower seem overly lavish. Gabriel judged the building as an outcast. *They should fire the architect.*

Gabriel had received his instructions a few days ago. Three days had passed since his combat in the certamen circle, and the few wounds he'd received had nearly healed. He opened his envelope and pulled out his security RFID key pass. *I would not have expected the great ritual to feel like I was working at an IT firm.* Gabriel kneeled down to tie his shoes while he prepared his best cocky demeanor, and then he read the timeline in the envelope.

*December 1, 9:33 p.m. Meet with Roger Queneco*
*at Walsh Tower.*

*December 1, 10:17 p.m. Take elevator down.*

He adopted a swagger as he walked into the marble palace. It came surprisingly easy to him.

Security was impressive to say the least. Filling the cavernous lobby was an entire SWAT team of the local finest, each bearing a Masonic Fraternal Order of Police patch. People maintained a fast power-walking pace as they rushed to elevators. Everyone in this building today would be a person in the employ of the Unification one way or another.

"Aha! There you are!" The shout came from a little man, lanky with oily hair and an ugly handlebar mustache that seemed out of place on his face. He took steps over to Gabriel and extended his hand. "Roger Queneco at your service. Do you prefer Gabriel? Or Mr. D'Angelo?" Roger spoke at a clip, causing Gabriel to replay the words in his head in order to keep up.

"Gabriel is fine."

"Good, good, D'Angelo it is. Primus Vryce has chosen me to relay instructions for your operations here within the society. Only a handful work directly with him, so you should count yourself fortunate." Roger gave a wicked grin, revealing his vampire fangs, and shook Gabriel's hand longer than normal.

Gabriel pried his hand away and looked down at him. "Charmed, I'm sure. You're telling me that you work directly for Vryce, then?"

"I'm both his apprentice and his herald. Your rejection must have really burned. How did it feel to fail so badly? Did . . . it make you cry?" Roger rose up on his toes with a curious look and studied Gabriel closely.

Taking a step back, Gabriel held up his hands. "I have a thing against vampires getting near my neck. What is it you want?"

"To make sure that you are worthy. Delilah brought you to the society's attention, and I'm going to make sure that you have a chance at success." Roger moved in faster than Gabriel could react, a blur of unnatural speed and grace, and put his arm around Gabriel's shoulders. "Do you see those fine gentlemen over there?" Roger pointed to the other side of the foyer.

Gabriel spied nine of the apprentices waiting off to the side in the lobby near a massive pine tree brought in for the season's festivities. He recognized Visago, a large man whose neck swallowed his chin, gesturing to the tree as if he was explaining its history, trying to sound important. He still wore bandages on his arms but tried to hide them under a winter coat. Gabriel was surprised to see that of the nine victors, many had been replaced by lower-ranking candidates. *The certamen was just a showcase of talent. Nice.*

Roger grabbed Gabriel's chin to refocus his attention back on him. "Your task is simple. I want you to piss them off. I want you to be an absolute, unrepentant jerk of the highest caliber to everyone."

"How is that going to help? Is this what Vryce wants?"

Roger hesitated a bit. "I'm his herald, aren't I? I'll be monitoring your performance in our courts and reporting back to him on your success . . . or failure. When you fail, I'm going to watch you cry." He paused and held up his finger. "Don't take this the wrong way. This has a purpose. I was passed up for the job because I'm so likable. We need you to keep your distance from them. You're already an outcast and a failure in the Unification. We need to increase that. This helps us determine who's *really* loyal, and who is just . . . loyal." Roger slapped Gabriel on the ass with a slight pinch added in and pointed to Visago. "Get to work."

Gabriel's face was already reddening with anger and embarrassment as he watched Roger give a fancy bow and begin to skip away. *Make enemies with the most powerful, clandestine organization in the history of mankind? Well, this is my leap of faith.*

"Why are you hiding your suntan there, Visago?" Gabriel smirked as he walked right up to them and patted him on the back in alpha-male fashion. "Don't like the new skin tone my flames gave you?"

Visago frowned and leaned forward with a scowl. "Quiet, you fool, there are still humans around. They could hear you."

"Fuck 'em. They're going to learn soon enough. What's it to you if the world knows you're a crap sorcerer? Who brought a set of knee pads in order to get Vryce to sign off on you being his *yesod* in the ritual?" Gabriel leaned down, his nose almost touching Visago's. Gabriel realized he looked down on everyone here. "Did you kick Cael McManus and Mitch Slade off your team? Is that why they aren't here? Didn't want them showing you up?" Gabriel put a single finger on Visago's forehead and pushed him back, claiming Visago's spot by the tree. *If Visago is still this afraid of me, I am going to exploit that.*

"He . . . he . . . he w-w-won't stand for this," Visago stuttered. "I am his *yesod* in this ritual. I am the understanding of concepts and actions, which places us above animals on the tree of life, something an ignorant swine like you failed to study. That is why you are not invited," he said.

"Do you even know what you just said? You sound like a mental patient. You are nothing so glorious. You might as well be his altar boy." Gabriel turned to the rest of the apprentices, their eyes fixed to the floor. Most of them were old, almost geriatric by Gabriel's system of measurement. "A bunch of old men with scraps of power they stole from a vial of blood in their youth, holding on to what glory they can in their final days. Just like the old warlock. Come on, tell me you wouldn't want to take his spot in the ritual."

Gabriel leaned in so close that he could smell Visago's rotting teeth. "You know, at Vryce's post on the sphere of *da'at*. The sphere of progress." *I've studied plenty divine magic that actually worked. It was all the useless fluff I ignored.* "None of you can tell me you would not shoot Vryce in the back if you could take his spot for the prestige you would earn in the Unification. You are all one bullet away from treason."

"*Enough.* Not today."

The voice cut through the gathering, stopping even occupied workers. One of them almost tripped into a fountain as she looked to the sound. Delilah Dumont marched through the lobby, watching Gabriel. Filing in with her were Roger Queneco and Charles Walsh, the Unification's regional director. Gabriel was pretty sure he recognized most of the faces in the crowd behind them. He leaned from side to side to see around and glimpse Roger giving him a nod of approval.

"Museum tour of the area's foremost occultists? Where is the hotline psychic?" Gabriel asked with a smile. *Am I pushing this too far? With that scowl on her face . . .* He saw a few nods come his way from the crowd and even a snicker. *They are supposed to be staunchly loyal to the Unification. Guess not.*

Roger Queneco nudged a few of them with his elbow and leaned in to start whispering in their ears. While some in the crowd looked like they hated Gabriel, the ones who snickered looked like they wanted to recruit him. *They are fools if they fall for this. Centuries reading books and not a day of life experience. Sheep, I suppose, with no real quality among them. They are going to fall right into Roger's trap. This cannot be that easy.*

Delilah continued, "You do realize that I can revoke your invitation here? Furthermore, you stand in a room full of not just blooded apprentices, but in the presence of those who have fully shed their innocence and eaten a heart." Delilah seemed to be talking to the lot of them, despite dressing down Gabriel.

Some in the crowd behind her looked at each other as if she were talking to them.

"Let us move to the correct floor and begin preparations. Ladies and gentlemen, Charles Walsh will escort dignitaries to the top-floor ballroom. While the opening events must be conducted in private below ground, you will be able to see the results from the ballroom over the next month at your leisure." She gestured to the main elevators.

Delilah entered a password into her tablet and pressed her hand on a marble column. The white marble gave way and a concealed elevator opened. Every inch of the elevator was bathed in a warm yet dull white light, designed in such a way to keep out shadows. "Apprentices," she gestured.

Gabriel waited for the rest of the apprentices to file into the elevator. He winked at Visago as he got on last and turned around to face the crowd. Gabriel gave the crowd a face of boredom and an eye roll. *I could probably get very good at this job.* The elevator lurched before picking up a very smooth pace. His ear seemed to pop, and Gabriel worked his jaw to relieve some of the pressure from the descent. He did not know what he should be doing next. The instructions only went this far. *A chance to prove myself. Success instead of failure. Keeping my record clean would be ideal.*

Lights in the elevator started to go dark, causing a quick shout from one of the old men. The glass panels of the elevator, which were providing light, began dimming to reveal a landscape behind them. Deep underground, a massive cavern, a geofront, was hollowed out well beneath the city. Gabriel placed his hand on the glass and took in the view even more, his brow scrunching up like two caterpillars moving along a tree. *Impressive. Well done, Master.*

He slowly began to nod to himself. "You scum suckers ready for this?" he asked. Looking down below them, Gabriel saw a forest full of vines and overgrowth. Geothermal wells served as a power plant up to the north. The top of the cavern had its own source of lights. They mimicked stars in the sky with only a fraction of them lit in the pattern of constellations.

A solid stone pyramid sat in the middle of the geofront. *And that's where we are going to change the world.* A temple to Hermes Trismegistus the Thrice Great. The other apprentices started to marvel as well.

"Equal parts of alchemy, astrology, and theurgy," one said.

"The holy trinity," another added.

"As written in the Emerald Tablet, 'That which is above is the same as that which is below,'" Visago concluded. "But for that to work here, there would need to be a floating structure above Walsh Tower."

"I think you're missing the point," Gabriel said. "This is just one structure of many in a series of points connected in the world. That's where you will set about ensuring that Lazarus has a safe return and all of you get your reward for loyal service." He paused. "That or you ambassadors of Dumbfuckistan will toss it all away, happier than a pig rolling in shit." *Which better happen if I want to free us from the cycle. Not that my job prospects look very good if this goes south. What's Vryce's real plan here?*

The elevator touched the bottom, letting the apprentices out into the garden full of vines as thick as jungle snakes with thorns to match. They began walking down a path, admiring the various blood-drenched roses and the array of plants. The entire cavern felt infused with magic. Never had Gabriel's fingers felt so alive before. *For a man of my pedigree, I could light this place ablaze. Could I be useful here?* The cobbled path led into the side of the pyramid.

An imposing stone door stood as a barrier preventing all who would enter without admittance. *A proper hermetic seal, bound by magic.* In front of it stood a man equally imposing. He wore an ivory-and-crimson porcelain mask cracked with a deep scar across one eye. On his shirtless chest rested a golden ouroboros pendant, one snake with green eyes, the other with gold. The fingertips of his hands were blackened with soot and blood.

Visago took the lead and gave a deep bow. "Primus Vryce."

The other apprentices and Gabriel followed and bowed as well. Gabriel noticed that under the wide black hakama pants, the man was barefoot with two nails in his feet. *It's not really him, technically speaking.*

"Welcome to the ritual chamber and libraries for the Society of Deus. The microcosm we will utilize to affect the macrocosm. Inside this door you will find a keystone. To gain entry past this chamber you must speak your true name while letting your blood flow on the stone. Any magic, demonic possession, shape-shifting, or form of arcane deception will be detected. You will be incinerated on the spot should you be found guilty or fail to perform this task." As Vryce spoke, the sound of his voice came from all angles, mixed with the voice of his host body.

"Surrender your true name and your life to the temple inside. You will enter one at a time so that your true name is revealed to none other. You will be . . . transported to your personal ritual components. Then you shall take your place on a symbol for the tree of life." His voice was not as raspy as the first time Gabriel heard it. It sounded more vibrant instead.

"As Delilah Dumont promised, for your services in this ritual you will be granted first access to *my* library of magic. Inside these walls are the assembled collections and works of every warlock, demon, angel, prophet, and other such occultists, including my prized possession, the Emerald Tablet of Hermes Trismegistus himself, which contains the base formula for all spells. Ask yourselves, what spell could you invent with private access to such a tablet? Twenty-one days of learning magic without having to cut a deal with demons because the remaining occultists who assisted with the construction of this city will be invited after that for a final night."

Primus Vryce's puppet turned around. The massive stone door shook and grated against the building as it opened for him as if on command. The keystone chamber was just beyond the threshold. The last sight of Vryce was of him slicing open his hand as the stone door shut with a thud behind him.

*Offering knowledge such as the keys to immortality, shape-shifting, and spells from the dark ages is a rather impressive payment.* "So that's the bribe to force you blood junkies into working together," Gabriel said while they were waiting.

"It is what Delilah went to great lengths to recruit us for, and why we chose to come to this site rather than go elsewhere in the world. We are sorcerers; let the vampires and shape changers flock to a place more suited for them," one of the old men said.

"We each have our own agenda, no doubt. We do this one favor and lend our strength to Lazarus. You should be thankful, child, that you stand among us. Your purpose here is no doubt our sacrifice for fuel. A death that may yet resurrect your lineage from fallen glory, just like Lazarus," another said as he spat at Gabriel's feet.

"All the knowledge in that library isn't going to save your souls. A demon king will always come to collect the blood and knowledge he gifted you. In one way or another," Gabriel said. *Sacrifice? I'm just one person. My blood alone could not fuel a ritual of this size.*

He was excited to study the Emerald Tablet. Perhaps he could find spells that would work without divine blood as fuel. Or something, anything he could use to get the power he needed to show the old ways could work again. *Even normal people are awed by tales of magic, right? Even if the almighty dollar is the new magic.* It saddened his heart to realize that not only would he be last inside, but he would probably never get much alone time in the library.

Gabriel had to wait, of course, for each of the other men to walk through. They were all part of the ritual. *Why am I here? Am I really a sacrifice?* The fact that nobody questioned him made the doubt rise within him even more. *No. No way. I'm here to showcase glory.* My *turn now.*

# CHAPTER 10

Gabriel entered the keystone chamber and waited until he was alone, his only companions silence and the absence of light. He did not even feel the pain of the cut from placing his hand on the sharp stone, warm to the touch. Smooth yet covered with a flowing blood as it ran over his fingers, defying gravity. He recited his true name aloud to the room, his voice coming back to him in the echoed chamber with a slight delay. It was uneasy being deprived of sight and hearing the delay of his own voice.

A true name was more than your birth name. To any occultist or creature, no matter the type, it was a recount of your deeds and the name of your soul spoken in the language of the divine. A secret anyone would guard with his life. Yet without knowledge of one's true name, working magic was completely impossible, with or without the crutch of demon blood. You were . . . *innocent.* Or as Gabriel liked to put it, more ignorant. Still, for all the secrecy, there was always one person who knew your true name. Usually it was the demon you sold it to for his blood. People such as Vryce hid it with their own sorcery after killing anyone who once knew it. For Gabriel, a sorcerer of birthright, it was his parents. Because of this, he said his name proudly and with conviction.

He felt the magic of the keystone chamber send a chill through his legs. The walls oozed charcoal gray liquid as a doorway opened up into the instrument room. It was less dark due to a red amber glow from the ceiling and etched circles that reminded him of the certamen chamber. A single sword leaned against the wall. *A sword is my ritual component? At least I will have a weapon.* Its blade absorbed the dim light around it, making it difficult to focus, but Gabriel could tell it was shaped like a cavalry sabre. A clear crystal about the size of an eye was centered in the hilt, appropriate since Gabriel noticed that it was one of the fabled eyes of Mammon, a demon of greed. *That means this is a soul blade.*

Forged by an apprentice and master together in ritual, the blade would steal the souls of its victims, granting the bearer of the blade all knowledge and powers of those killed in sacrifice to its forging. *I may not read like the rest, but no one will ever say my study of artifacts in museums is lacking. I just hate long manuscripts. But why a soul blade? It is useless to anyone but the two who forged it.* Gabriel inspected the blade, hands trembling as they came close to the blade, but he dared not lay a finger on it. He knew well enough that it would be hazardous to his health to wield it. *I thought the eye was supposed to be green and glowing. Wait. Is this an invitation? It is still not forged completely. Only the master's work has been completed on it. It still needs an apprentice to satiate it with souls.* In the red light, crouched down in front of the soul blade, Gabriel weighed his options. *This is hardly a tough choice.* He reached out. The hilt felt cold as ice in his hands. He stood and readied himself as the final chamber door opened, the ritual already beginning. *I accept.*

The ritual room was immense, the size of an airplane hangar. Gabriel paused on a mezzanine with spiral staircases on both sides. *Wonderful. The very stones themselves emanate magic.* The obsidian floor sprawled the entire length, the ten circles of the Sephirot etched into it with streams of blood, bile, and water flowing between them. Each Sephirot circle laid in the tree-of-life pattern was large enough to contain all the instruments of ritual and the apprentice within. Gabriel felt his stomach knot up in anxiety. *This chamber has been built with the purest of substances and etched with divine magic that has only been used at the turning of each age.*

The ceiling was constructed of a blue stone that reminded Gabriel of sapphire. It had markings mirroring the floor with the exception of language. The etchings above were not in Latin, nor in Hebrew, nor any language Gabriel had seen before. The sapphire ceiling had dark spots where each of the ten Sephirot rested below them. Gabriel could see faces through the blue crystal behind each circle. The smell of bile permeated the room as Gabriel traced the lines from the ceiling. *Eleven of the apprentices I beat earlier, now dead, to fuel the ritual, no doubt.* The rank smell of bile from above and boiling blood from below started to make Gabriel gag a bit. He quickly made the choice to take a spiral staircase down to where the other apprentices were already stationed.

On the ground level, the smell was worse. Now it smelled of hot, sticky sulfur, and he could taste the blood on the air. His eyes began to water. It was almost too much for him, and he took a moment to pull off his T-shirt and tie it around his face. *I doubt that's why Vryce wears a mask, but I've never wanted one of those deep hooded robes so badly before.* He could only see some of the apprentices. The rest were surrounded in a storm of magical energy, the ritual already beginning. Four of them were visible in the circles of the bottom Sephirot; kingdom, victory, glory, and yesod, the elements of all things.

The old men and the bandaged, plump Visago looked nowhere near as feeble as before. Infused with the strength of demon blood in the circle of magic, their robes almost floated off as wind whipped around each of them. All contained within their own circle, as if they were in their own magical prison. They chanted and gestured centuries-old arcane glyphs with haste. Gabriel watched the ritual unfold. Each of the Unification ritual sites connected together in a worldwide practice that would pry open the barriers between worlds. The Unification had twenty-one days to free Lazarus and then shut the doors. *For a third time. Some people should just stay down for the count. Can't we find someone better to bring back?*

Sweat dripped from the sorcerer nearest to Gabriel. Droplets fizzled into steam instantly after touching the ground. Even the eyes behind the mask on Vryce's puppet were focused with intent. Leaning against the wall, Gabriel made incidental eye contact with Vryce. *I could swear he is smiling under that mask.* A cool breeze provided relief from the heat and gagging smell of sulfur. The sorcerers in the circles widened their eyes in surprise and began to reverse the pattern of their gestures. The breeze became a torrent of wind that spiraled quickly around half the chamber, obscuring vision as the cool mist spread throughout the room. The seventh sorcerer stopped gesturing.

The sorcerer in the Sephirot of victory let out a shout and slammed the ground with his fist. A pillar of black-and-green hellfire erupted from the far end of the chamber, returning the oppressive heat.

Visago shouted, "Hurry, we must undo what he's opened! He is betraying Lazarus! I can save this ritual. Kill him while he is distracted with summoning!" Visago himself summoned up from the floor a creature made of obsidian that charged through the chamber.

Each of the four sorcerers he saw were attacking Primus Vryce at the far end of the chamber, where he stood at the da'at. *So this is your offer. Join you in betrayal?* He didn't care about the Unification as much as he cared about proving himself. *I could just sit back and watch this play out. Or use this blade on you . . . you're leaving this choice to me, aren't you?* He shook his head as he stepped into the tenth Sephirot. He knew deep down he had already made his choice to side with the warlock the moment he came here.

The sorcerer occupying it was focused on finishing a spell and had no time to react before Gabriel thrust the blade into his back. He felt the ribs snap as the blade sunk deep into the man. Gabriel pulled on the tassels hanging off the ceremonial robes and gave a second push, causing the blade to erupt out of his chest. Black tendrils from the blade spread like mold in the sorcerer's veins, and he could only choke up ichor and fall to his knees with a scowl of hatred on his face.

The blade worked its magic. The eye of Mammon pulsed with emerald light. The sorcerer, demonic blood giving him strength, attempted to stand. Gabriel gave him a quick kick in the back of his head, then sealed the deal by grabbing a clump of hair and smashing his skull on the floor until the body stopped twitching. *Just die already.* As the last gasp of air left the body, it crumpled and folded as if gravity collapsed on itself. The process of ripping a soul out of a half-human demonic sorcerer is not a process that Gabriel would describe as clean.

Free of distractions in the tenth Sephirot, he could see more of what was going on. The floor faded away, as if all sorcerers stood on air itself, revealing a hellscape below. A shadow world, bodies heaped up in skyscraper-sized piles and rivers of lime-green ghostly souls floating through them. *Purgatory? Hell? It's very green and gray. Not what I was expecting.*

Looking above, Gabriel saw a scene with a massive tree, littered with sparrows, winged angels martialing swords of fire to protect the tree on another plane of existence. *Okay . . . each of the worldwide rituals is supposed to open portals to the Kingdom of Hades so helldivers can locate Lazarus's cave. What is this? Questions later.*

Pulsing colors of light—greens, oranges, pinks, blues, even black, and reds of all spectrums—were emanating from the Sephirot circles. Gabriel could see each with clarity inside his own circle. Rivers and pathways connected them, but only if his eyes followed the correct stream. Fully empowered, the sorcerers were launching everything they had at Primus Vryce, who had some shield or magical defense active. Most of the fireballs snuffed out before crossing the barrier, but some of their spells were starting to get through as if they shattered glass.

Vryce seemed more focused on pulling something from above with his right hand. Sparrows would fly from the tree while angels would try to cut them down, but the little birds that made it flew around the chamber. While below with his left hand, Vryce poured out a bag of gold coins to a hooded reaper on a reed boat. Souls, *which I guess are the color green,* floated up into the chamber from below.

"Kill them, my child. Claim your birthright," Vryce said, his voice echoing off all the walls in the room.

The sorcerers turned their attention away from Vryce and briefly looked back to Gabriel.

Gabriel tilted his head to the side, cracked his neck, and smirked. Here in the middle of this chamber, in the circle, this would be easy. He could control demon blood by strength of will alone. Each of these men relied on a crutch to fuel their magic, one he could bend to his own edge.

The eighth circle sorcerer sent an arc of lightning along the path to Gabriel. With a simple gesture, Gabriel caused the sorcerer's bloody hands to ignite in white fire, canceling the spell. Gabriel ran down the pathway, impaling him with the blade before another spell could be cast. With both hands on the sword's hilt, he lifted the man off the ground and let gravity do the work as the blade creaked past bone and flesh. The blade finished the job, absorbing the strength of the sorcerer. *Speed and efficiency. Don't lose momentum. Initiative is your friend.*

The fifth circle sorcerer attempted to turn Gabriel into some sort of harmless creature. Gabriel countered the spell in the same fashion as the first. Sprinting along the pathway, his gym shoes splattered in the ankle-high rivers of blood. The momentum was enough to bury the blade deep into the sorcerer's neck.

Looking at the pathways in the floor, he saw that he could not reach Visago yet. There was a path leading to him now, but that would leave him open to more attacks. The other sorcerers were buying Visago time to undo whatever had been done. *I guess I'll kill you in order, then. Efficiently.*

With each circle, the killing became easier and faster. Gabriel danced between them, letting the blade do the work while he countered their magic, each death more satisfying than the last as he meted out vengeance for years of laughter as an outcast sorcerer.

The warlock Vryce floated with magic inches off the ground. The cracks in his mask grew while streams of energy flew into the mask from above and below, into the ouroboros pendant. His body was bleeding profusely from spells that made it through his defenses. Angels from above whipped him with lashes made of fire to stop him. From below, souls clawed at his bare feet, trying to drag him into the rivers. Wounds simply appeared upon him like stigmata.

In both Visago's and Vryce's circles, Gabriel saw reflections of other sorcerers or vampires that he knew were from elsewhere in the world. *Each of the worldwide circles is con-nected. There is not just fighting here, but also at the other nine.* Drenched in blood and flecks of bone, the last sorcerer fell to Gabriel's blade. He took a moment to catch his breath, to ana-lyze the elementals Visago had summoned and surrounded himself with. The simple act of running along the path and stabbing him was not an option. In the tribunal, Gabriel had bested him before Visago even created his first elemental.

"It's over, Visago," Gabriel said. "Give up."

"Are you blind, you ignorant sap! He's opened too many gates. Too many paths! Nobody will find Lazarus and close the gate. It will only spread! Do you realize the cost alone to keep this many portals open!" Visago shouted. He was crying, a bro-ken man trying to give his last breath to a cause he believed in. "We were supposed to save everyone, to correct the heavens!" A creature made of fire charged forth and tackled Vryce, his leg breaking from the fall, twisting in a way it was not meant to.

Gabriel could not wait. He had already committed to this act. He threw the soul blade like a javelin at Visago, praying it would find its mark. Fate was on his side, as it was a water ele-mental that tried to offer protection. The blade pierced through the water without resistance and found purchase in the robust gut of Visago. Black veins spread up his neck, and soon his eyes turned black, tears no longer flowing. He mouthed out his last words. Without breath to give them weight, they went unheard. Gabriel read what he could from his lips. *Something about Lazarus and his return.* The elementals crumpled and simmered out as Visago's soul entered the blade, which clat-tered to the ground. No longer in the hand of the apprentice, the blade's edges were defined and static, easier to look upon, the eye of Mammon in its hilt a deep green. The blade had been satiated and the ritual completed.

# CHAPTER 11

For his part, now undistracted by enemy attacks, Vryce propped himself up and gestured with his remaining hand, completing what he had intended. All the lights from the circles merged, blindingly white. Gabriel could hear the sounds of a symphony, which felt infinite and distant, yet played wonderfully for him just out of reach.

The light faded, only to reveal the grim reality of the dark, hot, pungent ritual chamber. Gabriel was not happy to have this return. He picked up the sword, feeling a rush of power and knowledge that invigorated him. *I know all their spells and skills. Perfect.* He smiled and crouched next to Vryce, his leg twisted and mangled, with wounds, cuts, and scrapes everywhere. He was not long for this world. Gabriel reached down to pull the mask off when a shadow grabbed his arm.

"I'm not dead yet," a voice echoed from the shadows in the room and behind the mask. "This body is just another vessel. Surely you know that. A criminal from the prison system who will not be missed."

"I've obviously taken your offer," Gabriel said as he studied the variety of magic rings and the ouroboros pendant on his master.

The voice rang out again. "The Unification believes that God is dead. They are power hungry, greedy, and very wrong. Oh, so, so wrong." The body sat up, pulled as if it were a marionette dangling from strings of shadows. "They have engineered a pathway to ascension over the heavens." Strings of shadow lifted the body further as the voice continued. "They make mankind forget its true nature. Humans are willfully ignorant of the wondrous world, so creatures of myth and legend have been banished and snuffed out by collective disbelief.

"In the past century, faith has even become a matter of prestige, a trite and token membership club to keep up appearances. Magic is all but dead. Reduced to cutting deals with the last active demons. I seek to change all of that. To awaken God from *its* slumber and save *it* from *their* own ignorance. I will defile *its* grave if I have to."

Gabriel fell to his knees in front of the floating marionette. "How? What the hell did you do here? Ancient creatures that have walked this earth for millennia lead the Unification. What hope do the two of us have against them? I did not sign on to be your ritual sacrifice so you could battle full-blooded demons and other warlocks on their payroll," Gabriel said as he studied the room. Two massive black statues near the far end stood blocking an exit. *Gargoyles, protectors of a sanctum.*

"On the seventh day, he rested," the voice said. "To the angels and demons, God died on the seventh day, *she* stopped talking to them. They have been waiting for countless millennia to hear *her* voice again. God made humanity in his image, both him and her, equally. Humanity is God and God is humanity. All the creatures, myths, and pantheons are created by humanity and given form, power, and truth. From a child's dream to a scientist's greatest invention, the act of creation is a distinctly divine act. One which only a human soul can perform." A bone snapped back into place as the vessel worked to repair itself while it contorted in agony. A reflex quickly brought to heel by Vryce's magic.

"I led six others around the world to betray the Council of Death Lords. We created tears in the Innocence. Only warlocks could shatter the barrier between earth, heavens, and hells. I was not there to witness the barrier erected after the eradication of the Roman pantheon. So born into this ignorant world, I long for what comes next," Vryce said as the vessel reached out with a mangled hand to help Gabriel off the floor.

Gabriel refused and rose on his own, his eyes tracking the shadows as they danced around the room.

Vryce's fragmented voice continued from another shadow in the corner. "Over the next twenty-one days, the battle begins. Finally connected once again, demons, angels, ancient gods, those who wait beyond, and others will find their way back to humanity. Then punish her for willful ignorance. We have set in motion the plans to usher in a thousand years of darkness. On the dawn of the twenty-first, the sun will die and rise as a blackened shadow of itself. Finally allowing those banished to walk in the light once again. Returning all magic to the world freely. Or the death lords will succeed."

"How can that still happen?"

"Their path to success has not changed. All they required from us was to open the gates. The bold within the Unification will seek fame and fortune by diving into purgatory to hunt for Lazarus's prison. Should this pass, and they close the gates before the twenty-first, they will succeed. They have already prepared mankind to forget what transpired. As you said, they have planned for millennia. We must fight and distract them for each night that passes. While not ideal, we must hide, deflect, and distract until we have complete success."

"Are we alone?" Gabriel asked, following the floating marionette to the exit by the gargoyles.

"Correct, my child, we are alone, and yet not. As the Unification dives past the Innocence, demons and others will bleed out, slowly at first. Divinity sleeps within mankind, but it can only awaken after the masses are culled and the weak removed. I seek to awaken the god in all who have the will to grasp at divinity. What aids us, who aids us, and when can just as easily destroy us."

Gabriel flipped the soul blade up in the air and caught it by the hilt. "Bold plan. If it works. Just don't get too cocky thinking you can take on everyone. That's my role." He grinned and flicked the blade, making a sharp ping echo in the chamber.

Vryce's raspy voice laughed as he gestured for the gargoyles to move. "It is indeed, Apprentice." The marionette glided through the door, and the creatures followed inside. Before Gabriel could step within, a stone door slammed shut inches away from his nose.

"Wait . . . that's really it?" Gabriel asked to no avail.

"Hello?" He looked around the room, noting the way out was back to the library. Gabriel caught a wind of the odor left over from the night's battle. As if on cue, a mop near a bucket in a far corner fell over.

"Apprentice," he said as the true meaning sank in.

# CHAPTER 12

Mike vaulted over the gap between two buildings, landing with a solid thud. Without hesitation he rolled with his momentum, putting his shoulder into it and coming out into a sprint. His duct-taped boot found purchase on the parapet, and he launched himself another fourteen feet between rooftops, laughing the entire time. Days after drinking the ichor, Mike felt stronger than ever. Dashing, ducking, rolling, weaving, and vaulting, Mike was having the time of his life as he tore through the city. The winter air didn't bother him or his lungs for once. He felt a furnace raging inside him, hot coals in his belly powering him like an old unstoppable train.

He stumbled and tripped over a DirecTV satellite dish, sending it tumbling while recovering from his last leap. *Crap! At least twenty feet that time. Probably ruined some dude's night. Sorry, bro.* Picking up the mangled dish and setting it back on its post with gentle care was almost futile. It took a few tries. Crouching and backing away like a person facing an angry raccoon, Mike eased himself off that particular rooftop before breaking into a sprint.

He hadn't experienced nightmares the past few nights. Gone were the cold shakes and vomiting, replaced now with the strength to lift a car and move very fast. Electrical wires and transformers overhead whizzed by in the December night as he continued his run. Mike didn't worry about the skinless taxicab driver burning rubber like a bat out of hell to catch him.

Mike grinned. *Come on, Frankie. You can do better. I'm three blocks ahead of you, and I'm not even tryin.'* Mike grabbed a fire escape rail and slid down a few stories, hopping with loud clangs at each landing before getting impatient and vaulting over the rail. It just seemed like a good time to walk in the street and give out some high fives.

A little yippy dog barked at him from the purse of a Lincoln Park Trixie, her North Face vest buttoned up and giant Versace sunglasses resting on her head. Mike waved and smiled. When she pulled back, Mike gave a deep bow, his green coat fanning out behind him as she hurried on her way. *I did just land in front of her after jumping from two stories up.* "Have a nice night!" he shouted after her.

It reminded him of his three ex-girlfriends who were visiting him over the past few days. Yelling and belittling him for forgetting birthdays, anniversaries, and flowers. To the dead, it was as if they were trapped, waiting for someone to notice them. To Mike, it meant that they were not gone forever. It meant they had a second chance. It also meant that he was alive. More alive than ever.

The only thing that Mike didn't like about his newfound power was that he could see how the living were doing. The world appeared duller, more ashen and gray to him all the time now. He could tell the girl he just walked past was a smoker and, if he focused hard enough, that she would die hooked up to a set of oxygen tanks with a hole in her neck. He couldn't quite remember if it was Frankie or Morris who told him there was a drawback to drinking the blood. *If I could pass the tests, I'd make a hell of a doctor now. Ha! Who am I kidding? I'll take the super strength.*

Mike saw a landing of buildings across the street that looked very interesting to run across. Before he could reach them, Frankie's cab screeched around the corner in a nice burnout. Mike raised his fist and cheered him on as he slammed to a stop in front of Mike. The obligatory Bears bobblehead almost decapitating itself on the dashboard.

"Nice, Frank. You caught up faster this time," Mike said.

"Get in. Just how much of a death wish do you have? Boss will kill us if you get caught," Frank said. Ever since the change in Mike, he could understand Frank clearer than before. While his lipless mouth still moved, the words seemed to come from his throat. Another perk of being attuned to the land of the dead was that hidden things were now revealed to him.

"No way. It's a fantastic night out. Come on. I'm starving. I'll buy you some street tacos if you walk with me. No running. Promise." Mike extended his pinky finger. Frank just let out a sigh of frustration and parked his cab in a no-parking zone.

"Nobody can refuse street tacos. Enjoy them while you can. Remind me to introduce you to an ol' friend of mine who is a fantastic cook. If you take off, though, I'm telling each of your dead girlfriends the secrets of ghostly possession," Frank said.

"Charming. What would I do without you?"

"End up a bloody mess on the ground when you fall from a skyscraper in sixty-three days?"

"Well, isn't that just peachy." Mike pulled out his phone and opened the Taco Tracker app. "The taco guy should be at the bar up on the corner real soon. Let's go."

"A few hundred years of evolution, science, and technology, and you humans use all your gifts to track tacos."

"Look, Frank, hunting for good Mexican food is a fine art. It takes skill and patience. Unlike Chinese food, which throws itself at you like a lemur, fine Mexican cuisine is like a seven-horned, white-tailed buck. This taco guy is the prize stallion. His mom spends all day making the tacos and tamales." Mike could almost taste the food. He was ravenous.

"Do you even listen to yourself speak? I mean, is there a pause from your brain to your mouth? Wait, don't answer. I already know." Frank put his bony hands in his brown aviator jacket, and the two of them crossed the street at a red light.

"So how long is this going to last? I'm immortal now, right? Bulletproof? What's the catch? Why not just give vials of the stuff to every hospital in the world?"

"If only those with power were that caring. Besides, it will only last a little bit. You'll have to keep drinking demon blood if you wanna keep the perks, or avoid withdrawal the likes of which you've never seen yet, boy. You are not bulletproof and can be killed. For Lady of Fate, who we work for, your rite of passage is when you die while you have the blood in you. You'll come back as a ghost, with whatever scars you earned in death."

"So why didn't you just stick your head in an oven and gas yourself instead of getting your skin ripped off?" Mike asked as they walked through a crowd of people. To them, Frank was just an Irishman not worthy of any notice. They were still innocent.

"For starters, I'm not a ghost. We'll cover that spicy pepper when you're ready." Frank replied. "Suicides, however, send ya screamin' straight to a different death lord. Politics of the Unification can make the electoral college look like kindergarten. The stupid version is that all humans go to an afterlife. Where you go is sorted by the ruling belief of humans. The death lords all wedged their way into the process somewhere along the line. They siphon off souls for their own ranks and make purgatory less full, stealing them away from being demon food or waiting for judgment. Sure, this shit don't make angels or demons happy. They didn't have much of a choice, though, when we got our hands on magic a long time ago." Frank paused as a train rattled by on the elevated platform above them, drowning out any conversation.

"So, shit. I don't know, man. I just work here. All I know is that magic is fueled by divine blood." Frank tossed his arms up. "Lazarus coming back is gonna give the Unification the strength it needs to sort all human souls. Cutting the divine out of the picture. The boss gambled away his fate for us with his demons for a special source of blood to help the cause. That little act makes some question our loyalty to Lazarus. O'Neil's agents only hafta die on their own, each in their own way, to join our death lord, Lady of Fate." He patted Mike on the back. "Of course, there are tons of ways to mess that up as well. You ain't anything special, boy. You're just another one of my fares this decade. If ya are special, I'll be cartin' you around the lands of the dead for a few more centuries."

"So O'Neil serves some demon, then? What's her name?"

"His, in this case. Also no, he doesn't. The rakshasa vanished, actually, in the nineteen twenties. Boss was pretty torn up when it went down. I guess it had to do with some infighting on the council. Either way, it meant Boss doesn't need the council. Sort of put us on the Unification shit list at the same time. Makes me wonder how he landed the current gig."

"Yeah, shit list. Right. How the fuck could a group of superpowered badasses get on a shit list? Much less ever get fired. You guys gotta be some sort of special pacifists if you can get your hands on this juice and decide to sit idly by while the world goes to shit." Punching Frank in the shoulder, Mike chuckled.

Frank reached out and latched his bony hand on Mike's shoulder. "Listen. For most people, you drink the blood, ya end up being able to cast spells. Still gotta know 'em first. Demons are like coke dealers, keeping ya comin' back for more. The more ya use it, the more you crave it." His grip felt like an iron vice as he kept on. "Boss broke that cycle for his men. Cost him his name. It also meant the Unification didn't have a lock-down on divine blood. We're wild cards to them. You think immortals care about money? You think people with this kind of power give two fucks about mortal trappings? Blood is all they have to offer us. The Unification keeps their various groups in check by controllin' the flow. Succeed, the council sends you a crate. Fail . . ." Frank shut up as a stumbling man wandered by.

Mike's smile faded as he realized the man was going to die of liver cancer. He tapped Frank's hand while his eyes followed the man. "Easy there with the claw of death. So why work for 'em if you don't need to?"

Frank pulled his hand away and tucked it back into his bomber jacket. "What else we gonna do, sit in a castle and rot for eternity?" Frank shrugged. "Besides, Boss has a plan or somethin'. Our job is to make sure that people survive. Do some damn good for once. Feels better than runnin' an extortion racket if ya ask me." He tilted his head up the street. "Let's keep going."

They walked up to the street corner where their prize stallion would soon be found, a drunken line already starting to form in search of late-night snacks to sober up on. "Good? A demon is a demon. Not that it matters much to me, I suppose, if you guys have your own source," Mike said taking a spot in line.

"Nothing is black-and-white. We also don't hand out that ichor to every Tom on the street or sick person, because it's the rarest substance on earth. It's not like demons are falling out of the sky. Most of it dried up after the witch hunts, they say. It was the last time the blood was easily accessible," Frank said. "The Unification was formed for our survival as much as yours.

Had to shift to rationing what's left. You humans fucked shit up. Now drastic crap has gotta go down to restore the balance."

A drunk couple wobbling in front of them slurred a cheer. "Woooo, witches! Yeaaaah."

Frank and Mike eyed each other and mutually shrugged. Frank looked normal to the living, but words were still words. Mike started bouncing as he smelled tamales and tacos and did his best to ignore the realization that the taco guy would die from being stabbed. The man was a saint to Mike. Sixteen dollars later, Mike tipped extra, and they were back to walking and enjoying some amazing flour soft tacos. Except Frank. Frank was dead.

"I'll eat that if you won't," Mike said.

"I hate you."

"Not my fault you crossed Joe the Alderman," Mike said as they ducked into an alleyway to keep talking without passersby listening in.

"I'm tellin' you, he cheated—" Frank said as Mike cut him off.

"What's that?"

"What?"

"That." Mike gestured with taco in hand to a corner by a garage. Something that looked like a small hairless squirrel crawled out of the shadow. It seemed afraid of the floodlight, like it was cornered by it. When it moved, the motion sensor would kick on, and it would scurry back to the shadow and hiss at the light.

Mike and Frank moved to flank the creature on each side of the alley. Mike crouched down to not startle it, trying to get a closer look. From here, he could see that it was much larger than he'd initially thought, about the size of a cat, ugly without any fur. Its eyes glowed like small laser pointers, and it had green skin with three-fingered hands. *Smells like shit over here.* The light clicked off again.

The ugly thing hopped back out, appearing to raise its tiny fist in defiance. It tried a new path, inching itself along the fence. It had yet to notice either of them. Mike slipped his coat off and secured his gloves, getting ready to make a dive and catch it.

"Now!" Mike shouted, jumping forward. Frank followed from his side and rushed to it. The floodlight kicked back on, freezing the small creature in its tracks. Mike quickly wrapped his coat around it. It let out a series of kicks and noises as if it were an angry cat held over a bathtub. "Got it!"

He held up his makeshift sack, and both of them stared at it and listened. "That's a demon," Frank said at last. He was pressing his hands against his coat, maintaining a distance.

"Oh, please tell me this is not a succubus," Mike said. "That would just be way too funny."

"No, no, I'm not sure, but I think that's a *nefrit*. Uh, a librarian of hell? Homunculus, imp, goblin kind of thingy," Frank replied.

"Kind of thingy? Do you even hear yourself speak? What kind of zombie tour guide are you?" Mike grinned.

"It shouldn't be here, Mikey."

"Sure. But it is. Hey, can we use its blood? You said they are rare, right? This is like winning the lottery?" When Mike said that, the creature picked up the pace of its frenzy.

"Mikey, this isn't a joke. It *should not* be here."

Farther down the alleyway, another motion light clicked on, and a similar screech was heard. It was another one of the little buggers. Only this one was looking right at them.

"Mike, we need to go. If there are more of them, they stop being afraid. Unless you have a cat, or some salt, more will keep coming," Frank said as he backed away. Another one appeared on top of the garage. "Let him go. The sunrise will send him back to hell, Mikey."

Mike looked over at Frank with a grin. "Man, for a dead guy, you're really scared of a lot of things."

"You see a lot of shit as one of us. If you wanna keep existing, run when you see something ya aren't prepared for. Sunlight, hunters, magic, angels, demons, the YouTube . . . children . . ." He shuddered. Mike heard Frank's bones rattle and a tendon pop.

One of the imps scuttled along the shadows under the floodlights at Mike, jumping and screeching at the same time. With a swift kick, Mike punted the imp like a football back down the alleyway. The remaining ones scampered away. Mike would have laughed if it weren't for the scream from the crowd of people walking past where they ran.

"Okay, I'm new here, but I know *that* shouldn't happen," Mike said. "Why can they see them? I thought you had to be initiated to see this stuff."

Frank's face held all the expression it possibly could. Mike was sure he somehow managed to make his eye sockets wider. "They ain't kids. They shouldn't be able to see."

"Come on, Frank. Let's go home. I'll bite. One of them is bound to have 'the YouTube.' If you are this freaked out . . ." Mike said, grabbing Frank's arm and pulling him out of the alley. *Luckily most people are drunk at 3:00 a.m. on Friday.*

# CHAPTER 13

Peace and quiet were things that Mike had learned to let go of in recent nights. His new permanent residents floated around the place, displacing his belongings only to pick them up again later and put them back. *More than just a little bit haunted is an understatement now that I can see ghosts all the time. But do they have to trash the place?* Almost everyone he knew who died was still lingering around, lost in a perpetual cycle of awareness that they were dead and then forgetting that very fact.

Drones or poltergeists, either term was fitting. Mike thought he was never going to have a clean house again in his life. *I'm probably going to have to handcuff my car keys to my wrist at this rate. Ugly cat things appear and my ghosts turn into ferrets.* Great. At this particular moment, however, the location of household knickknacks was not the focus of the five people standing in the kitchen.

Officers Winters and Matsen brought an old cat carrier to hold the ugly critter. It took Mike, Morris, and Frank an epic battle full of tiny claw marks and bites to jam the imp into the carrier. The five of them now relaxed a bit and inspected the tiny hell beast.

"So it just appeared in an alley?" asked Morris for the third time.

"Yeah, with a few others. Which kind are these again? I'm not exactly a demonologist," Frank replied.

Morris leaned in close, and the imp tried to claw his nose. "The kind that steal souls from children. Legend says they sneak in and steal the breath of kids. Cats are their natural enemy." Morris waved Matsen over. "You guys need to arm up. This is most likely additional feedback from the Twin Cities ritual. We need to keep it quiet if people can see these things. That part is an added twist. Hear any reports?"

"There hasn't been any chatter on the radio tonight. Nobody has called anything like this in yet. But it's late, and from what you've said, these things are afraid of bright lights and cats. If anyone did see one, it's nothing that can't be thought of as a deformed bird." Matsen chuckled. "You guys really thought this looked like a cat? Look, it's got tiny wings. I'm telling you it's a featherless bird."

"Any rules we should know about it? Don't feed it after midnight? Keep it away from water?" Mike asked the room. "I take it that this is the kind of stuff your boss was talking about with the world changing? Are cats *really* going to become man's new best friend? The imp might be a better companion. So, million-dollar question: How did it get here?"

"It was summoned," Officer Winters said as he stood by the back door. "We got a rogue sorcerer in town."

Morris gave a dirty look to Frank. "No, I don't think that's it. Summoned ones can usually speak the language of whoever summoned it. This thing just chitters and clacks. Also, Boss has been on a recruiting spree," Morris said, pointing at Mike. "It's here because when people mess with this stuff, it never goes according to plan. All you can hope is that this is as bad as it gets. I'm not going to bet on that, though. This is just the start. Boss needs to know about this." He folded his arms in front of him and leaned back on the kitchen counter. "We've been at this too long, and I need to get out of here before sunrise. I want good news by sunset. Make a plan."

Mike threw his feet up on his kitchen table and leaned back. Matsen's lips pressed together and gave a disapproving look. "Hey. My house. My table. My pet cat-bird-demon thing," Mike said, holding up a finger. "Look, chief, you guys kidnapped my friend, ransacked my house, and had me drink the blood of demons. Frank is pleasurable company and all, but now I have the ghost of everyone I ever knew walking around in circles. You really fucking think I'm actually going to work for you?" he asked.

Everyone in the room looked at each other, mouths open and then closing, but nobody talked. In the awkward silence, their eyes eventually turned to the floor or away from Mike. Frank threw his hands up in the air. "None of ya guys are going to tell him, are you? Fine. I will. Mikey, the Unification already put its plans in motion while you were asleep." Frank avoided looking at Morris.

Mike dropped his feet and stood up, leaning into Frank and raising one eyebrow. "What plans?" Mike poked Frank on the shoulder.

"At least the boss was right about recruiting Doc," Morris cut in. "The dead don't exactly keep hours conducive with most businesses. His father was a member. Doc figured it out. Now he's our therapist. Let's just say that *some* of us carry a lot of issues. I mean, look at Frank. He had his skin ripped off him. Matsen? Well, she struggles with the things she has to do. And Win—"

"Do not finish that sentence, Morris," Winters said.

"Right. Look, friend. We're the good guys, but we can't fill you in until you decide you want in. Your pal Doc? He's doing real good now. Has actual clients. For some reason the boss wants you. I can't figure out what the Unification would want with you. What good are you at keeping people alive?" Morris spat at the room full of ghosts.

Mike laughed. "Therapist of the dead. Fitting for Doc. You mean to tell me that the skeptic signed on to your little merry troupe? Hope you realize that he probably thinks you're all clinically insane and that this is all one giant conspiracy to control the world."

"We're leaving. You already know what to do if you want answers. Keep the imp locked up. Might give you some perspective. If you are right in the head, you'll run in the other direction from us. Matsen, Winters, he's back on your watch now," Morris said. He grabbed Frank and headed out of Mike's place.

Matsen stepped forward and put her hand on Mike's shoulder. "It's for the best, you know. You can help all of them." She nodded to a ghost learning to throw a spoon across the room. "We'll be outside in the car." They followed the others out and closed the door, leaving Mike alone with a demon and an apartment full of ghosts.

Even Mike was starting to get tired. He let out a long yawn. He could still stand the sun, but even drinking the blood made you want to sleep all day. He looked at the imp inside the cage, cowering near the back, trying to hide as much as it could. "I suppose you aren't a fan of the sun if a flashlight scares the crap out of you. You need a name." *Also some food, I imagine.*

Mike rummaged through his fridge and pulled out a slice of pizza from an old box. It was the only choice he had. He picked up the cat carrier and set it in his closet and slipped the piece of pizza in between the bars. "Full of bad manners, you bite, you come from the pits of hell, and you smell like shit. You need some cheer in your life. A good foot forward makes all the difference. I'm going to call you Sparkles from now on." Mike closed the closet door and plopped on his bed. Four ghosts curled up next to him, one of them smaller than the rest.

# CHAPTER 14

"Wake up!"

Mike felt someone shaking him. His eyes opened in panic, and he braced himself against the bed as if the world were ending.

"Wake up, Mike. We gotta go. Shit hit the fan," Officer Matsen said.

"It's morning . . . coffee . . . gotta feed . . . Sparkles. Crap, there's a fucking demon in my closet!" Mike said running his hand over his face as he stifled a yawn. *What the hell? Last night. The past few days. I'm spinning. Get it together. You're alive, right?*

"Sparkles? Tell me you didn't name it. No, wait, I know the answer. You named it. You idiot. Grab it," Matsen said as she was thrusting clothes and stuff in one of Mike's backpacks. "We gotta go. Now!" Mike had not seen her so pale before. She wasn't kidding around, and her voice trembled as she spoke. Something was wrong.

Mike got his act together as fast as he could manage. It was dusk. He slept through an entire day, an occurrence becoming all the more common. *I take it I'm fired by now. Lifetime gas station attendant, here I come. Hmm, screw that. Taco salesman.* He opened the closet to grab Sparkles, both disappointed and relieved that the imp was still in its carrier. It had also eaten the pizza. "If you like pizza, you and I are going to get along just fine. You can't be evil if you like pizza. That's the new rule." Mike turned around to Matsen. "What's going on?"

"It's all over the police scanner. Once the sun set, rabid dog attacks started pouring in. Instead of German shepherds, they're three-headed hellhounds. Your time for a choice is over. We gotta meet with the boss. This can boil over quickly out of our control. There are a few million people in Chicago, and trust me—YouTube is not our friend. We don't have much time," she said.

Mike followed her outside, remembering to grab his earlier kit of mayhem. Winters was already in the black police cruiser. "I take it calling shotgun is out of the question?" Mike held his smile back as he looked down the street.

The moon sat fat and large on the horizon, its color a shade of deep lilac purple, so large Mike felt he could hug it. From the moon's direction, clouds reached out like six fingers across the sky to the other side. The dying rays of sun, a quickly fading crimson. Mike saw winged creatures, flying in the sky.

Matsen caught him looking up. "Relax. Not everyone can see the way we can," she said.

"Tonight's not going to be a good night, is it?" Mike asked.

She shook her head and got in the car. Mike took one last look at the moon and followed. Winters hit the gas pedal almost immediately. "We need to take a detour. While you were inside, a call came over the radio. Hellhounds have been sighted around the United Center, and there is a game going on. Boss has already mobilized everyone else," Winters said. He turned up the police radio.

Nobody in the car, not even Mike, felt like talking as the radio reports streamed in: An attack by a mutant dog on the north side that killed four. A home invasion where people locked themselves in the bathroom with crazy ugly cats clawing at the door. A neighbor calling in that the next-door neighbors were on their knees praying in the yard, covered in blood. Calls about people being attacked and eaten by rabid dogs kept coming in. One after another.

Mike unpacked his smokes in the backseat and put one in his mouth. *Chill, man. Just get ready.* Straightening his bandanna and putting his gloves on helped him focus. Another report blasted on the tiny radio. Officer down. Medical requested. Sinkholes were forming, causing accidents. Mike couldn't take the silence anymore.

"You know we've seen this movie before, right?" Mike asked. "Some douchebag flips the switch and releases all the ghosts into the world. So it's important to remember that as we go through this, if someone asks you, 'Are you a god?' you say yes." Looking out the window, he saw a figure dash into shadow. "Hey, over there!"

They were near the United Center, in a neighborhood that had run-down houses placed so close to each other Winters could touch both at once without stretching his arms out. Fate was on their side at least; there did not seem to be anyone outside. The police cruiser came to a roll, gliding through the night like a mountain cat stalking its prey. All of them looked out the windows for a sign. *There.* Matsen flashed a spotlight at the same spot. She saw it as well.

A red-and-black dog with a beak for a nose and bony whips protruding from the base of its skull. It growled at them and narrowed its eyes while it backed away from the light into the narrow gap between houses. Just like the little ones last night, it was afraid of the light.

Matsen didn't hesitate as she got out of the car and started shooting. Her aim was exceptional. Three shots fired, one in each eye and one in the forehead. The hellhound crumpled to the ground. Mike started to run closer to it before Winters grabbed him and pointed over to Matsen. She took a few more measured steps closer, firing three more shots with bull's-eye accuracy.

"Okay," she said. "It's down." Mike noticed that her eyes seemed to emit a soft glow when she turned back.

"I kinda figured demon hounds would be a little stronger," Mike said.

"That makes two of us," she said.

They walked single file in between the houses, Mike bringing up the rear. Winters was a giant man, near impossible to see around. Mike had to climb up a bit by putting his feet on one wall and back on another to see over. The hellhound was falling apart, into ash, rather, crumpling in on itself like it was burned from the inside out. Matsen kneeled down in front and was working some of the ash between her fingers.

"At least this makes cleanup a cinch," Mike said. From where he was perched, he could see out over the fence behind the houses. The United Center was in the distance, the stadium illuminated with symbols of sports teams. Mike felt a wave of relief wash over him. *That place is so well lit these things would never get near it.* It was not a feeling that lasted long. Between them and the United Center stood an abandoned parking lot without any lighting. It had contained a row of houses that were torn down. Mike could see an entire pack of the hellhounds in a circle growling and snapping at each other, their bony spines digging at the ground and scratching.

"How many more bullets do you guys have?" Mike asked.

Winters looked up at him and smiled. "Enough."

"Let me guess, behind that fence there is a bunch of them," Matsen said.

"Yup! They are doing something, like clawing at the dirt. Maybe trying to find a place to hide during the day?" Mike said.

"Hey, Winters, go get the shotguns. We can take care of this," Matsen said.

Mike shimmied up higher to allow Winters to walk underneath him. A sharp squeal and whimpering came from the back of the car. Mike realized the door was still open. Mike could see the cage he had Sparkles in, now rolled over onto the floor. It was shaking, and tiny hands from the imp rattled the bars, trying to undo the latch. Winters and Matsen crouched and braced themselves.

The ground started to shake first, hard enough to knock Mike off his high post. The heat built up in a second. To Mike it felt like a furnace blast door had just been opened. A giant pillar of flame shot up from behind the fence, green and black, twisting and winding in upon itself, the third warning sign.

Mike pushed Matsen out of the way and ran to the fence, easily vaulting over it and landing on the other side. *I can lift a damn car. Fuck this shit. I'm not letting anyone get hurt by these things. Why have powers if you don't use them?* Mike began bracing himself for a fight as a red light from a rift in the middle of the circle pierced into the sky.

The hounds were backing away from the pit, unaware of the new visitor behind them. If they cared, they didn't show it when they turned away and ran right past Mike with their tails between their legs, leaping over the fence. Mike heard Matsen swear and fire her handgun. The deep, satisfying sounds of shotgun blasts followed. *They got that. I'll take this.*

A giant claw, roughly the size of a large SUV, grabbed the earth from within the rift. A giant hook grafted onto a second arm, easily the size of a crane, followed the first out of the rift.

They worked together to lift out a demon, easily three or four stories tall, its horned head adorned with rings and piercings. It had the same bony whips coming out from under its neck.

*This thing looks more like a gorilla than a dog or feather-less bird.* The spines on the beast fanned out, and green fire filled the gaps between them, creating massive wings of flame. It leaned back and bellowed, causing Mike to put his hands on his ears and drop to a knee. *"I am Golgoroth."* Unlike the rest, Golgoroth started running directly at the United Center, unafraid of any lights. It reached down with its claw and snuffed out a streetlight like a candle.

Mike could see it now, thousands of people inside the sta-dium enjoying a game and this thing crashing in. It would be over. Everyone would know about demons. He had to do some-thing. At the very least, he could distract it and lead it away. Mike got into a sprinter's position, digging his boots into the dirt. *We can do this, guys.* He imagined all his haunted friends at his back.

Mike took off, demon blood surging in his veins. He was faster than Golgoroth, and as he came near, Mike jumped and put all his momentum into his shoulder, aiming for the back of Golgoroth's knee. The impact took the wind out of Mike, and he continued tumbling on the ground a good twenty feet away. Golgoroth toppled forward, and a tremor shot through the ground. Mike gasped for breath. *That should get its attention.* Adrenaline, his drug of choice, returned to him. Mike dug his knuckles into the ground, sprang up, and dusted himself off.

"Hey, big guy!" Mike called as he did a little boxer dance.

Golgoroth was also standing back up. His flaming eyes pulsed with hatred. *So if it's a demon, is it a he . . . she? Nah, it's an it.* It leaned back and slammed its foot down, causing concrete and debris to fly up. The shock wave moved in a direct line toward Mike, who could not move in time. Mike was sent flying farther, crashing into a parked car, shattering the glass of the rear window and leaving an imprint. Golgoroth sniffed the air. *"Demon slayer. Your stolen blood will be reclaimed."* It charged at Mike, each step rattling the earth and setting off car alarms.

Mike panicked. His heart was racing. His body ached. *I'm an idiot! What was I thinking? Run!* He scrambled to get off the car. In the backseat, he saw a crowbar. Grabbing it through the glass without a second thought, he sprinted as Golgoroth stepped down. Metal crunching where he had just been, he felt the demon continue chasing as the ground shook with each step. Mike ran. His pace faltering with doubt and his balance shaken, it was not a fast run. He wanted to lead Golgoroth away, but instead he was running toward the United Center.

A crowd of Chicagoans in sports jerseys was already streaming out the doors. They had only two reactions to a three-story-tall demon with flaming wings chasing a scrappy little guy with a crowbar. They either froze, cheeks red from the cold, and grabbed the hand of the person nearest them, or they ran in a full-on sprint of sheer terror.

The game was over. If Mike kept running straight, he would lead Golgoroth right into an exit door, with people flooding out. Behind him was inevitable death. He could see how these people would die. Crushed, burned, and sliced in half. All Mike saw when he looked at the crowd was the dead. It would be his fault.

"Fuck it," Mike said. "Time I join my friends in death."

Mike turned around and faced his reaper. Golgoroth itself came to a halt before sweeping its giant hook out. Mike tried to jump over it but couldn't get high enough as the claw shattered into his knees and sent him spinning. With its other hand, Golgoroth grabbed Mike in midair, hoisting him up higher. Mike felt his stomach drop as he winced in pain. Golgoroth slammed Mike into the concrete with rib-shattering force.

*What options do I have?* Mike's hand clenched onto the crowbar for life. He coughed up a thick pool of black blood. The heat from Golgoroth's grasp burned his skin as he was thrown. Wind whisked past his face as he spun, the crushing pain from being slammed into a pole made flecks of white stars appear in his vision. He dropped to the ground like a rag doll, gasping for breath.

*How . . .* He was standing over his broken body suddenly. The world an ashen color of its former self, yet Golgoroth towered over him with its flaming crown. He watched his body vomit more black ichor out and pull itself back to the demon, who seemed content to watch a life be snuffed out slowly. Even though his body was broken, it tried to lick the blood off the pavement. Mike realized that the body was already dead, kept animated only by the blood inside it. *I've had only a small amount of demon blood, and I think I can take that? The thing is full of it. Its strength is insane. Wait . . . blood. That's it!*

Clawing at his body and pounding it with his hands, Mike screamed with desperation as he tried to get back inside. Ghostly hands with fingerless gloves reached through the animated body's chest as Mike focused every ounce of his willpower. Searing pain like serrated daggers thrust into his lower body brought him back to his senses. He didn't know how, but he forced his way back into his body. A gasp of air filled his lungs, bringing him back from the brink of death with a scream that followed. Every bit of strength he had went into licking the blood off the concrete. Even mixed with the taste of granite, it was still as delicious as the first time he tasted it. The sharp pains he was feeling were from his body stitching itself back together. *I'll only have one chance at this.*

Mike flipped the crowbar in his hand. He smiled knowing that on the precipice of death, he was at his finest. Fight returning to his limbs, he was there on the edge of death again, adrenaline surging through him. The ashen world stayed visible. He could see his family and friends in the crowd. He wiped the sweat and blood off his forehead.

Mike vaulted himself up and charged. Golgoroth raised its giant hook and brought it down, shattering the ground where Mike had been. Dashing to the side, grabbing the top of the hook, and jumping to avoid the earth shock, he held on. The hook felt like a hot fire poker through Mike's gloves. He pulled himself up and ran along Golgoroth's arm. It was no different than moving along steel beams at a construction site. Golgoroth was so large it felt like Mike was walking along an I beam that was being hoisted by a crane. He was at home.

Focusing on balance, Mike made it to the shoulder. The heat from the wings scorched him. He could already feel his skin blackening and red sores erupting on his exposed flesh. Golgoroth brought its claw around to pull Mike off, but he was committed. He ran forward to its massive head. *I'm either gonna be incinerated by green fire or impaled by that claw. Neither sounds like a great way to be taken out.*

All his strength went into plunging the crowbar into the demon's temple. It felt like trying to move through a concrete wall, but it worked. Blood streamed out like a geyser from Golgoroth's head. Its screams shattered glass as it shook its head. Mike did what he could to drink as much of the blood as possible while holding on to the embedded crowbar. He grabbed some of the rings pierced into Golgoroth's flesh for extra purchase. The blood tasted sweet, like plums and peaches simmered and spiced. It was so much more fulfilling than the bit he drank nights ago, and its effect was even greater. Mike's hands started to glow with their own heat. A rage took hold deep within him, the simmering coals in his stomach now a full raging fire.

Mike stabbed and punched. His kicks and elbow strikes caused their own impacts as he hammered into Golgoroth's face. The demon was backing away from the crowd, trying to stop Mike's onslaught. Everything was red to Mike, a crimson rage as he hacked and punched.

Mike began ripping out giant hooks from Golgoroth in his fury, causing more streams of blood as Golgoroth fell to its knees. No longer conscious of what he was doing, Mike let the fury consume him. Riding the wave of death, he punched through the demon's flesh with his hands. With each drop of blood Mike stole, he became stronger.

Golgoroth was on its back now, chest heaving as Mike ripped it open. *There!* Mike saw the heart. *If blood is life, if blood is strength, what can the heart do?* He grabbed the pumpkin-sized heart with both hands and pulled with all his strength to wrest it free. Without a second thought, Mike bit into it, searing the flesh around his mouth. He didn't care. With each bite, he felt stronger, better, faster. His teeth started to grow into fangs, to help him devour the heart faster. It was all-consuming. The ashen world faded. The friends and family faded. The crowd was gone. All that mattered was devouring the heart.

Until it was gone.

The world came back into focus. Ash was already floating up into the air from the dead Golgoroth. Mike tried to breathe, only to find that his lungs didn't work. Fangs that protruded from his mouth snapped back into his jaw, hiding themselves. His hands were no longer shaking or glowing, and the rage that consumed him now rested at the back of his mind. He knew, deep down, he was no longer human. He did feel full, however. He *felt* alive. He also *felt* dirty somehow.

The crowd cheered, snapping Mike out of it. He heard words like *awesome* and *amazing* and cries of *"What the hell was that?"* Mike looked at the assembled crowd. *We can beat* them. *This is our chance to change the world. For all of us.* Mike knew he wasn't thinking only of demons. Images flashed in his head of privatized prison systems and debutants laughing while people burned alive in factories to make their clothes. Mike grabbed the crowbar, hopped onto a car tipped on its side, and turned to the crowd.

"Everyone! Listen up!" He waved his hand and the crowd fell silent. "They *will* try to cover this up! They will keep the truth from you! Ignore the news! Ignore the government! Demons are real. So are angels, ghosts, vampires, monsters, and everything else you can imagine. Even I don't know the half of it. But I know this. I've shown you! You can beat them." He pulled off his protest coat and held it up. "I am one of you. One of the many caught in the cog of the machine. We toil. We crawl. We sweat so we can try and feed our families. For what! So systemic wealth distribution flows from your pockets? So you can be thrown into prison if you don't pay your debts? We deserve more than thrown-away scraps! You may believe that you have a good life. It's a lie crafted to fool you!" He waved his coat like a flag as he was speaking.

Mike pointed behind him to the decaying body of Golgoroth. "Their blood gives you strength. It heals wounds. It can fucking cure cancer, and they have kept it from us! This is your chance to rise up. They are trying to summon more of these in secret to force us into another lie. They messed it up worse than every oil spill that's ever happened. You have this one chance. One chance in your life to change your lot." Mike gestured to the crowbar. "Our founders knew the right to bear arms was important. They knew that weapons would hurt these creatures. Imagine what modern guns could do."

He watched them nod in understanding. They hung on his every word. Mike could feel his soul bristling with energy given to him from the crowd. "Demons are afraid of light! The daylight is your friend. When you see them, do not run. Do not be afraid. Face them. Kill them. Eat them." Mike raised his fist in the air with each word. "We are the living! We are the future! Spread the word. Don't become cattle herded into sacrifice for the needs of the few," Mike shouted. The crowd cheered with him. Every word Mike spoke carried the weight of his emotions to the crowd. He watched their reactions as his spark and drive took hold of them. They were his.

*"Mike!"* One voice rang over the rest.

Mike looked down and saw Matsen flailing her arms while loading the chamber in her shotgun. Winters flanked the other side of the car yet was still facing the pit by the fence.

"Put down the crowbar, Mike. We gotta get them out of here," Matsen said, pointing at the crowd. "You're gonna get them killed, you moron! It's why we fucking keep them in the dark! More could come at any minute!" Matsen almost drew her gun on Mike but looked at the crowd instead. She kept it ready instead at the pit and spat at him. "You wanna lead them all down that hole? Means less cover-up to be done. Because that's what's gonna fucking happen. Or they are going to get crushed, burned, and sliced in half by more. I'll stop you myself if I have to."

Mike took in the scene and dropped the crowbar. "Remember me! Mike Auburn! A son to a father, and a father to a son, just like all of you. We are the Sons and Daughters of the world! Go now. Protect your own!" he shouted, and waved for them to disperse. Looking at Matsen, Mike said, "I'm not going to fight you two. You are good working people just trying to get by. Take me to O'Neil. I have my answer." He hopped down. The righteousness burning through him shone in his eyes. *I am alive, even in death.* He tried his best to ignore his lack of heartbeat as he went back with Matsen and Winters to their cruiser. They never lowered their guns.

# CHAPTER 15

- Initiate demon harvest protocols.
- Rewrite channel 12 news reports.
- Locate security leak.
- Lunch.
- Verify satellite monitoring of Walsh.
- Sleep for ten minutes.
- Feed the dog, Alexandria.
- ~~Exercise.~~
- Pull off double double cross and live.

Delilah took a moment to update her schedule before entering a complex sequence of codes into her pad to activate the gateway before her. After a retina scan, voice authorization, and a small pinprick of blood from her finger for verification, the chrome-plated doors began to unlock with a series of clanks. She was down in the bowels of the city, deep underground. *The Unification will learn of our treachery soon enough. Let's strike now while we have the upper hand.*

Her heels echoed in the chambers as she made her way to the middle. Sterile and gleaming rooms filled with a soft white glow surrounded her on all sides. Shadowed figures locked behind cells paced with anticipation when they saw her. *Oh . . . death lords . . . what did you think would be the result of your lock-down on blood?* Monsters and rogues that were deemed a waste by the council were sentenced to death. Delilah plied her influence to acquire them instead under the pretense of cannon fodder for the second phase of their plan. The Society of Deus, as the Unification knew, was built to store and utilize the souls harvested by the Second City. Fuel for the walls surrounding the city to power and create a beachhead into other worlds, where their divers would scour the underworld, retrieving lost things, like Lazarus. She and Vryce had been collecting this menagerie on the side for years. Their army of damned soldiers would assist in this. "Better useful alive than dead, he always says," she said. "I couldn't agree more."

Delilah had been working half a decade on the mental programming of these soldiers. The master himself took care of the supernatural enforcement, ripping out portions of their soul and binding them to his will. Delilah had long ago suggested that they not rely entirely on anything that could be undone by another sorcerer. She had personally overseen their mind control using the que neuro-stim technique she perfected to control sorcerers.

After McCarthy took his initial program too far, the Unification blackballed any further research into the subject for decades out of fear. Delilah had recruited many of the forgotten researchers before they were executed and advanced the cold-war technique to work on blooded sorcerers and vampires. One security leak from a treacherous apprentice and now the Unification was always asking her for the technique to keep world leaders in check. *Old, wretched bygones.*

*Who wants another thousand years of insipid control?* The process wasn't simple and required hiding vast amounts of divine blood from Regional Director Walsh. Fortunately for Delilah, the Second City seemed to cook their books about divine blood as well, which helped keep the cover. *Even if they are probably the source of my security leak.*

Her cell phone vibrated in protest as she moved deeper into the reinforced concrete facility, informing her that she was now cut off from the world above. *So much can go wrong in even an hour's time.* She felt her love-hate relationship of being down here more than necessary flush her cheeks.

She came to the central chamber, her heels echoing with each step. Every wall contained prison cells that were stacked upon each other so high it made her seem tiny in comparison. Inside, her monsters paced, awaiting their chance. Only those who drank of demon blood were housed within. Most of them were soldiers for hire, but a few were tried-and-true killers sentenced to death. Here they would be given a second chance at life.

The middle of the chamber housed what Delilah was here for today. Seven special prisons were buried in the floor. Each of them was a solid frozen cylinder of ice lowered into the floor. The prisons served as a means to hide the society's strongest soldiers from the Unification's seers and sorcerers that knew magic to scry upon them. Water was a fantastic foil to a scrying spell, and being placed in stasis reduced the need for blood. Within each cylinder was a full-fledged vampire, violent slayers and eaters of a powerful demon's heart.

Her master had stolen them from the clutches of the Nazis' Thule Society after they were betrayed by the Third Reich. *A perfect example of what happens when the world unites against you.* They helped Vryce until just after the moon landing verified the Unification's theory of a unified consciousness. For the past forty-five years, they were kept off the radar while tubes of fresh blood had been giving them strength. Each prison would have to be opened manually.

Alexander Lex DuPris was the leader. Trained to kill other supernaturals, he was a master of shape-shifting. With a long rap sheet of successful battles versus multiple enemies in solo combat, he was perhaps the master's favorite. As the prison rose out of the ground, Lex's eyes were already open, and he wore a monstrous grin on his face. His flesh seemed to shift around inside the ice as he appraised the face of Delilah. His unique way of saying hello. She began the sequence to release him.

Symon Vasyl was next. A fellow soldier like Lex, they fought in the same unit in World War II. Unlike Lex, however, he wasn't thrilled with his friend's choice to sign up for this fifty-year imprisonment. Symon preferred to wander from battle to battle, feasting on the blood of soldiers instead of being fed like a cow. He was a master tracker and saboteur. Delilah was particularly fond of Symon due to his unique skill sets. Nobody else could turn a building into a fortress with booby traps made from piano wire and duct tape and have it be lethal enough to disable an entire Special Forces unit.

The last soldier Delilah was going to release today was her ace in the hole. The ice cylinder rose from the ground. A man with a suit and thin black tie waited with patience inside. His face had no features, no markings, no nose, mouth, or even eyes. Just empty eye sockets. The Whisper, he was called, a master infiltrator and espionage genius with no knowledge of his past lives. Each life he lived, each name he stole, he became in full: mind, body, and soul. This single vampire would be Delilah's spy. *I finally found the correct target for you to replace, Whisper.*

She waited for the heaters to melt the ice and release her soldiers. She was only releasing three of them today. The rest would have their time. It would be rude for her to release everyone. There was some etiquette as to how her master wished events to unfold that she vehemently disagreed with. *Still, he has six hundred years of practice. He is just keeping his cards close to his chest. I much rather prefer a crushing victory.* She reassured herself. The three of them began to move closer to her, all three not making a sound. Even with the puddles of water at their feet, no ripples were cast. *The merits of the true undead, kings of the night, I suppose.*

"Your time to usher in a new age for the world is at hand. All of your training is about to be put to the test. You will be my agents for the salvation of the Society of Deus. Our army will be marching forth in the coming nights to defend this kingdom from all enemies, both above and below," Delilah said.

"Yesss. That we shall, my princess. Is *his* ascension complete yet?" Lex asked.

"Vryce has only begun. It's why only three of you are activated at this time. You will be assisting his new apprentice, Gabriel D'Angelo. These are the orders I have been given," she replied. The look of dejection on Lex's face didn't belong on a creature such as him. *Pretending to have emotions is below him.*

"Vryce found another vampire more competent than us, you say?" Lex replied. "We follow him on the promises to further our own ascension," he snarled. "Amo-a-Deus, the name of his army, *like a god*, it means. We have trained it. Forged them to a weapon. He will replace us so quickly with a child vampire? History knows *not* of this Gabriel. Therefore, he is young and insignificant."

"Silence!" she snapped. "You presume much. This is why you are an assassin and not a visionary. Gabriel has his place in *his* plans as much as you do. Where blades are needed, you will be found. Your task for now is simple." She waited as the three of them recoiled and stood at attention.

Delilah stepped inches away from Lex. She could smell the sweet scent of blood as she looked up at him with determination. "There are sixty-three dignitaries within the city. Vampires, shape-shifters, and sorcerers waiting for centuries to dive into Hades and hunt for glory."

Lex lowered his gaze in submission and spoke in a softer voice. "Yes, my princess." A toothy grin began to creep along his face. "You want us to quietly assassinate any of those who get too close."

Delilah paused and let that thought sit for a moment. *Good. You already understand the real objective.* She gave a curt nod of approval. "This city will soon be overrun by demons who find themselves on the edge of hell ready to crawl up. Let us liberate ourselves from the council's shackles while the blood roams freely. Kill them all. Kill them and claim their hearts. You were promised strength and a new world if you fought for it. These are your first orders in *his* plan. Now go forth and do his work until you hear from me again." She gestured to the exit chamber.

"As you wish, my lady," Symon said in a thick French accent. "How you say? You look divine today. Perhaps a dance you will grant me under the moon?"

The three of them walked off to wage war. Delilah looked at the remaining four chambers, wishing she could just unleash them and end this in a single night. *Not yet. Not yet.* Delilah updated her list with a smile as she left the chamber.

- ~~Initiate demon harvest protocols.~~
- Rewrite channel 12 news reports.
- Locate security leak.
- Lunch.
- Verify satellite monitoring of Walsh.
- Sleep for ten minutes.

- Feed the dog, Alexandria.
- ~~Exercise.~~
- Pull off double double cross and live.

# CHAPTER 16

It almost seemed to look at him. Tiny and small, it protruded from behind his glove, spiraling up in defiance. A mistake. One that was soon to be plucked away with utmost precision. Bollard felt a twinge of pain as he plucked the defiant hair out of his wrist with his right hand. He placed the rebel weed with delicate care into his vest. Mr. Bollard had no room in his life for deviants. Not a single hair of his body could fall within the walls of the Twin Cities. A single mistake, a single hair, a single drop of blood was all Vryce would need in order to utilize his sorcery and learn the truth. Every single act Bollard committed within these walls was one of careful precision.

He stood outside Walsh Tower with his driver and waited for Ms. Dumont to return. He struggled with his host body, a mortal descendant of Lazarus. Mr. Bollard was tasked with embedding himself deep within the organization and as close to Vryce as possible in a limited time window. Per the wishes of Lord of Heaven's Wrath, Mr. Bollard would locate the best path to free Lazarus before anyone else, including the society. Countless layers of espionage over the nine decades had paved the way for Mr. Bollard. *Don't fool yourself, demon. You were one of Lazarus's jailers. You bartered your escape from hell on the promise of his location. You've been paying lip service by helping O'Neil. It's time to pay up.* Mr. Bollard tried to silence JJ's voice in his head while biting his lip.

"O'Neil is a cunning monster to keep me wrapped in his affairs," Mr. Bollard spoke under his breath.

*Cunning? Dare I say it was you that wanted freedom from the pits of hell and entrapments of heaven? In your desperation, you bargained with Lord of Heaven's Wrath. I never brought you to me, so try and tell me you do not enjoy your time here. Hidden from all sides by borrowing half my name and body.*

"You are, of course, correct," Mr. Bollard said while inspecting the rest of his clothing.

*The society is a tool for us to use,* JJ's voice came bubbling up from within. *One which needs to be handled carefully.*

JJ and Bollard were brought together by the Unification in Chicago, deep below the city, over the protest of all but two death lords. Many saw the alliance with a demon king as a sin. None believed it was possible to navigate the eternal landscape of purgatory, as they had tried for a millennium, much less return even a tiny fragmented soul across the barrier. So a challenge was put forth by all other death lords. O'Neil's teams of helldivers would jump in and locate specified lost artifacts and soul fragments, a daunting and nearly impossible task for even the world's strongest vampires, sorcerers, or most experienced helldivers.

The expedition was launched beneath the city, a city that had been burned to ash once, forging its close connection with death. The more death and sacrifice in an area, the farther one could dive into purgatory, or hell. Cities, with their concentrated populations, allowed for missions unattainable in past centuries. Twenty-four from O'Neil's team went in. Only three returned: Morris, Frank, and O'Neil. A small wooden cross, a set of grave clothes, and a single soul fragment were brought back. Upon realizing that Mr. Bollard's information was true, Lady of Fate quickly bound Mr. Bollard to JJ with the fragment before it evaporated. And it worked.

It only took small whispers into the ears of the death lords to convince them a worldwide ritual was required to return an entire soul, or person. A massive undertaking had begun. The Unification bound demons for information, exploring the depths of purgatory in earnest. Lost objects and forgotten secrets were recovered as the art of helldiving was perfected. Yet souls, entire souls, required the current undertaking, and Mr. Bollard knew exactly where to go.

Currently, the goals of many groups were aligned: Bollard and JJ, bound demons and the Unification, Deus and the Unification. "Step one, open up the barrier between the worlds, the one part that requires everyone working together," Mr. Bollard mused. Every organization intended to use the great alignment of December 21 to its own ends. Perhaps, he thought, a similar battle is waging at each ritual around the world. It was not the first time this decade he had such thoughts. For his part, he only wished for true freedom, no longer in debt or bound in service, a goal achieved by freeing Lazarus before any other. All the death lords wished success to be theirs first, so Mr. Bollard played his cards close to his chest.

*Don't forget, you will need me if you wish to remain anchored and hidden in this world.*

"The first part is done. Now we need access to the perfect threshold to dive in, a location which we still need. According to O'Neil's information, the Society of Deus will have the best beachhead."

*And the stiffest competition. "Joining" the society itself will put us closer.*

"If they kill you, JJ, any blood-hungry sorcerer will see me instantly, potentially sending me screaming back into Vitala."

*Ah, one of your dreaded seven Hindu hells. Fear not. If I kill you—well, that is my step three, actually. I can't kill competitors without your power. So let's just focus on step two.*

"Silence." Mr. Bollard ran his hand over his bald head, feeling the crisp cold air and taking a deep breath. He refocused his efforts to keep his thoughts on the task at hand.

"Are you ready?" Delilah asked.

Startled by the diminutive woman who walked up behind him, and without hesitation, Mr. Bollard was forced to the back of his mind as JJ stole control of the body.

"Yes, of course. To dinner, then?" JJ replied. He successfully masked his counterpart's surprise.

"Dinner is pushed back three hours and twenty minutes," she replied. "The ritual is having some residual effects, bleeding out of these walls. The dignitaries must be hastened to explore so the gates can be sealed again upon the return of Lazarus." Delilah pointed inside the building, and JJ followed her gaze, letting his awareness of his surroundings falter briefly.

"Why shatter the gates open so far? I have been meaning to ask but was unable to find the perfect opportunity to pick your ear until we were alone," JJ said as they began their walk.

"I love the color purple," she said, looking up at the moon.

"That is out of character for you. You never let yourself relax on business."

"The world is changing. Can you fault a lady for taking in the sights?" She smiled. "Was your tour of the prison satisfactory earlier?"

"Quite. I don't think the United Nations will feel as kindly, though, when your technique is applied. You know, I've always enjoyed a harvest moon myself. Fall is my favorite time of year."

*You are becoming too fond of her. She could still be an enemy.*

JJ chided Mr. Bollard internally before looking at Delilah with a warm smile. "Did you find the chemical agents to your liking?"

"They say the secret to a real woman's heart is weapons-grade chemical warfare." She smiled. "How is this going to play out, JJ? Soon you'll be leading forces of the Unification against demons pouring out of rifts. All to protect this." She gestured out to the city. "Don't die. The world would be less without men of integrity and taste. I feel Primus Vryce views this as a game. He's holding back and took a risk holding his end of the ritual open longer." She placed her arm around his. "All to compensate for some of the gates not opening as planned. As punishment, this region is going to be hit harder with the feed-back of shredding the Innocence." She reached down to hold his hand. It was cold, as if he had dipped it into ice. Mr. Bollard accepted and JJ embraced it.

"I know your loyalty to him is unwavering. Just remember that it is you who orchestrated all of this. Without your ser-vice, our survival and our future would not exist. If the bleed is going to hit harder here, I'd like to know what I am going to face in the coming nights."

"Already prepared," she said. "You will find all relevant information in your room tonight."

"I wish all my co-conspirators were as thorough as you. You truly have a gift, Delilah. I meant what I said a few days ago." JJ paused and looked into her eyes. In another life per-haps, JJ thought, there would be something there.

*Not this one, however. I will force you to destroy her.*

"Do you truly need my assistance above with the dignitar-ies, or might I prepare our forces for the coming nights?" JJ held both her hands now. Mr. Bollard was unprepared when she leaned up and gave him a kiss on the cheek. JJ desired more. Mr. Bollard howled with fury just beneath the demeanor and resumed control. For a second, Delilah was the only thing in the world. Nobody saw the feet of JJ's driver being dragged away in the distance.

"Go. Do what you do best," she said.

JJ bowed, holding the position until Delilah had walked off. His next move was clear to him. He must warn Patrick O'Neil to prepare for even greater challenges from what would soon break into this world from the pits of hell. The driver opened the door to the car for JJ. Closing the door, the Whisper gave a slight nod to Delilah, letting her know that she had provided him with enough distraction to embed himself.

Delilah waved before making a quick swipe on her tablet with a look of happiness.

# CHAPTER 17

*For something called the Emerald Tablet, it sure doesn't look emerald. Or like a tablet,* Gabriel thought as he opened more grimoires and arranged them on display within the Library of Deus. In the middle of the room sat the famous Emerald Tablet, displayed next to Vryce's own works of the *Arcannum Arcannimusim.* The tablet, if that's what it could be called, was more of a giant gray slab with circular grooves and arcane sigils carved into it. *Of course, any markings on it are written in some godforsaken secret language that nobody probably knows anymore.*

It was a cruel irony, Gabriel mused as he continued dusting and cleaning. His first task as an apprentice was wholesale slaughter. His second, housekeeping. The library sat above the ritual chamber and was far more grandiose. Stained-glass windows lined the ceiling among carved marble columns. It was a cathedral for the arcane. Locked in a room filled with hundreds of magical spells, thanks to the oversight of his new best friend, Queneco, he had yet to open a single book for actual study. *Just show me how to do it. I'll pick it up with practice.*

"Ahem, missed a spot up here on the nineteenth shelf," Roger said. "Did your mother not teach you how to work a dust mop?"

Gabriel craned his neck, following the massive ladder up to Roger's position. Where he held up one finger of his white gloves, faintly soiled by a slight smudge of dust. "My mother has six daughters," said Gabriel. "If you think battling the Unification will be hard, just try and keep up with laundry."

"Tsk, tsk. Go grab the other ladder, Apprentice. I see a bloodstain down the way on sixteen." Roger paused as something fetched his eye outside the window. "Hey, Gabriel."

"Yes?"

"It's just your mother, right, and a bunch of daughters, right? No men around, right?"

"Yeah, what of it?"

"That's why you're so angry, right? Can't find a man to sweep you off your feet?"

Delivering a swift kick to the base of Roger's ladder, Gabriel gave an Italian flip-off. "They are all fate witches. Just wait until they are free."

Roger looked down at him. "We'll let you bring them here, you know. Once this ritual is over. We have medical clinics that are designed to help people through blood withdrawal. Soon enough, hearts as well, to get them bending all the fate they want as well." His lips quivered as he suppressed a laugh.

"Kindness doesn't suit you."

"I'm actually not kidding. You were handpicked by the big shots. Vryce only takes on apprentices once a century, and you're this century's pick. Even more, he made you a blade, so you better claim your sacrificial role. And fast," Roger said, grabbing both ends of the ladder and sliding down like a fireman.

"Fast?" Gabriel asked as the glass above the library shattered into a thousand pieces, falling down like stain-glassed rain. The severed torso of a society member thudded on the Emerald Tablet. "Sacrifice?" Gabriel fell backward as silver-winged creatures shattered through library windows.

"Yes, shield me with your body!" Roger said as he ran past Gabriel out the exit. "I'm a lover, not a fighter!" His voice trailed off.

"Coward," Gabriel said, as he stared down one of the several long-armed luminescent creatures. Their bodies were disproportionate and frail-looking. They moved with a slight flicker, as if they skipped seconds in time. Gabriel smirked and snapped his fingers to command the blood within the nearest demon to ignite.

His smirk quickly faded as nothing happened. *That's . . . not a . . . demon.* Fear welled up within Gabriel as he ran for the exit. In a flicker, it was blocked by three more creatures. *The sword! Where did I leave it?* He sprinted to the other side of the library, sliding underneath the Emerald Tablet as silver blades stabbed the ground around him. He planted his shoe to recover momentum and swung at a creature in front of him. As his fist passed through the surprisingly ethereal creature, an overwhelming urge for survival flooded into Gabriel, followed by the raw emotion of judgmental disdain.

He lost his balance and fell to the ground, winded on impact. He was only meters away from the sword when the futility set in. The room was swarming with the creatures.

"Your role is not sacrifice, but to build our own piece of the kingdom," Vryce's voice echoed from the shadows on the library walls. The creatures wretched in agony from the sound alone and glowed brighter with hatred. Vryce continued. "I was born just as you were, who auspiciously knew his true name by birthright, allowing command of demon blood."

Gabriel was frozen with a soul-gripping terror. The creatures were only concerned with locating the source of the voice. They cared little for the useless human at their feet.

"To become a warlock, a soul stealer, I had to shatter my own soul in ritual and consume the hearts of an angel and demon. My body is animated by my will alone. What happens to your body if you die, Gabriel?" A bolt of electricity slammed into a creature near Gabriel, causing an explosion of light. "This has allowed me to be a vessel for six hundred years, collecting the souls of others to survive. We warlocks have nearly infinite temporal magic as long as souls exist to feed us."

*Get it together. I refuse to be useless.* Pushing back the fear in his mind, Gabriel heaved himself off the ground, making a mad dash for the blade. A silver dagger was thrust through his right hand in a skip through time, pinning it to a bookshelf. With his left hand, he stretched to the blade, only inches away from his fingertips. From behind him came the dull thud of several blades stabbing wood.

The ill-formed assailants stalked the room. Gabriel felt their warmth on the back of his neck as they hovered by the blade and him. "Oh, just do it already!" he shouted.

"The divinity of man is lost to us forever. Like Lilith, exiled from the gardens. Without our human souls, we can never be *more*." A pulse of frozen air filled the room before all light was extinguished, covered in complete shadow. Inhuman screeches were muffled as Gabriel felt Vryce do . . . something. "Or so they say." Gabriel heard clearly over the wailing in the shadows. "I have a once-in-a-thousand-years opportunity to piece my shattered soul back together. I have mere days to steal it back and bind it. You have but a second in time to decide your fate."

A small whimper came out from behind the Emerald Tablet. Gabriel saw a hint of a feathered wing as the shadows retreated back to the corners. Wincing, he pulled the dagger out of his hand and crept around the side. Crouched up, arms around her knees, was a lady with golden hair, longer than she was tall, and angel wings with feathers covered in ash and blood. "We have a visitor," Gabriel said to the room.

"Meet your first angel, or in this specific case, a virtue of growth. I cannot fend off the Unification demons that cross over here or the multitude of enemies we make while I hunt for what's mine. So you will do that. You will be the weapon that ensures the Society of Deus succeeds. By your hand, you shall judge which souls lend us fuel. To do that, you are going to need power, power which I hand to you on a silver platter. This rare angel has *agreed* so kindly for you to kill her and consume her heart." The voice dripped with disdain.

"She may not agree with my means"—a spell of telekinesis lifted the angel—"but she understands the ends. We have given them a beacon leading them home. To restore the kingdom of magic, the divine must be shackled under our rule, uniting them with that divine spark latent in all human souls once again. Some will come with swords drawn, seeking vengeance for their banishment. Others, I've learned over the past century, believe in my vision." A moment of sadness filled the room before the internal fire of Vryce's conviction continued. "So she will serve in ushering in the dawn of the Seventh Age. Give her a quick death."

Gabriel was amazed at her small, frail frame and fingered the cold blade in his hand. "You want me to toss aside my soul, everything I am, and become like those losers outside we sacrifice by eating her heart?" Gabriel took a step closer to the angel. The desire for power of this magnitude being offered to him caused his hands to clench the sword, yet his pride was strong enough to stay the blade.

"No. Do not mistake yourself for a demon-blooded junkie, a mere blooded sorcerer. Angel hearts do not offer strength on demand. They grow within you over time as you push limits. The cost is banishment from the sun's rays. Your soul will not be shredded unless you are made into a warlock. Even then, there are *ways* to reclaim your birthright. You face vampires of immeasurable strength or demon hordes. Look beyond your myopic viewpoint of pride. If you want magic to return to the world in force, along with all the freedom it brings, then you must do this," Vryce said, his presence fading from the room.

Gabriel ran his injured, trembling hand along the blade and looked out the shattered windows, witnessing another battle begin in the distance. Minutes crawled by in silence. *This is a terrible thing. Does the end justify the means?*

For the first time that week Gabriel did not enjoy killing.

# CHAPTER 18

"But the cowardly, the unbelieving, the vile, the murderers, the sexually immoral, those who practice magic arts, the idolaters, and all liars. They will be consigned to the fiery lake of burning sulfur. This is the second death!" Reverend Matthews shouted to his congregation. He stood with an assault rifle pointed at the head of a visibly shaking teenage girl who could only manage a quiet whimper.

A hellhound was flayed open on the altar, its legs still twitching. "The seven seals are being broken! Soon shall come forth the blackening of the sun, the sixth seal before the seventh, where heaven itself is silent." The reverend raised his free hand over the girl's head. "We shall be martyrs and die here today in the name of the alpha and omega. We shall be reborn in glory to fight the forces of darkness at the side of our savior when the sixth bowl is poured from the heavens unto earth!" His finger began to squeeze the trigger. A millimeter away from oblivion, the reverend and his ninety-eight congregation members froze. All within the church was silent.

Charles Walsh fidgeted with his pocket watch, opening and closing it, the ticking was the only sound that echoed through the church in St. Paul. He took his time as he slid open the tall doors to the church and walked into the sermon. "I don't mean to interrupt, but you do know that book was written by men in Rome, right?" Charles said to himself. Nobody in the congregation could hear him. *I often wonder what is in their thoughts during these precious moments. A great gift this is, the ability to freeze time itself. Even if the cost means I die sooner.* Charles took a stroll and admired the vaulted ceilings and stained-glass artwork. The odd colors of the night sky only added to their wonder.

Walsh had a love of architecture, and in these moments where his life was ticking away by the minute, he made sure to enjoy every flaw and imperfection that was to be found. For every person in the room that was forced to stand frozen in time, Charles lost three minutes at the end of his life per minute purchased. Of course, no deal for blood was ever without its cost. Charles had to set the amount of time he wished up front. He had purchased seven minutes for this endeavor.

A reverend getting his hands on a hellhound and killing his entire congregation would be difficult for him to cover up. Regardless of the celebrity weddings, divorces, and manufactured dramas created by the Unification, this story would be headline news.

Charles walked up to the altar and pulled out the clip of bullets in the assault rifle. "You see, Reverend Matthews, I have already had enough persecution from your lot because of my choice in lovers. God is about love, not killing a fourteen-year-old girl for your interpretation of the Bible." Charles removed every bullet from the clip and put it back empty.

He made sure to check there was not a round in the chamber, and upon finding one, removed that as well. "To your congregation, this will all seem as if it were a bad dream, that you snapped and used Halloween props to scare them. The congregation will be saved from you."

Charles leaned down and removed a tear from the girl's face, pushing some of her hair back behind her ear and giving her a kiss on the forehead. "You will be fine, my dear. Just have faith that there are those of us who truly want suffering to end for all." He straightened his vest and began to walk back out into the night.

A SWAT team stood ready at all entrances, poised to break in. He made his way back inside his car, looking out his passenger window, where the commander, a helldiver, leaned in the window. Face frozen in a contorted scrunch as he was asking a question. Charles slammed his watch shut and put it back in his vest.

". . . to move in, sir?" the commander asked.

"Yes, you are free to mobilize. Ensure the reverend is arrested alive and that nobody is harmed *before* your men dive. You know the rest of my *revised* cleanup routine." Charles rolled up his window and began to drive away. *What part of peaceful and quiet did the dignitaries not understand? How hard is it to kill a demon and slink into its shadow without witness?* He started to activate the car's automated phone process.

"Call Delilah Dumont," he said.

"Would you like to call Delilah Dumont?" the program responded.

"Yes."

"I'm sorry, I did not understand."

"Yes."

"I'm sorry, I did not understand."

"Call . . . Delilah . . . Dumont."

"That is not a registered command."

*Lovely, we can rip open a portal to hell, but you can't get voice recognition to work. We are so going to die.* He took the simpler route of dialing by hand.

"This is Delilah."

"Evening. Containment in St. Paul is under way. Did you know that your Special Forces unit was bringing helldivers in hot, ready to kill everyone?"

"Excellent news. Of course, sir. Our orders were to leave no witnesses. I assume the operation was a success?"

"No witnesses means stopping creatures from getting out *before* they get into public areas. You were going to slaughter an entire church of innocent people, you ruthless bitch! In what colossal pile-of-shit view do you think that's even remotely okay?"

"I believe," she replied in a matter-of-fact tone, "that view would be the view of a world where people such as yourself construct fortified cities to pull forth an ancient lich from the pits of purgatory. You cannot expect to have this scenario play out without broken eggs, Mr. Walsh. Besides, death allows for a deeper dive. Greater chance of ending it all."

"They are not eggs. They are humans. Living, breathing people with free thought and will. It is our job to save them. To protect them. I'm issuing a new order to you. Tell your trigger-happy special task force that from this point on, they will arrest all witnesses and relocate them to the survival shelters located around the city."

"If that is the wish of the Unification, it will be done. I will inform our second wave as well. They will be led by JJ Bollard. You will be informing the council of these new orders, then, I presume?"

"I'll take care of them. I have a meeting with them after I finish another round of personal business. Have my friend Roger Queneco meet me in my office at eleven." He hung up the phone. *This just smells wrong. The bleed was only supposed to last for three days, at best, and be located right around the ritual sites, and according to the council, placement of their location could not be helped. To make it worse, all the witnesses and apprentices in the ritual were killed. Death was bound to happen, but this . . .*

Charles pulled over on the expressway shoulder, late-night traffic beginning to die down. He rolled his pocket watch over his fingers like a coin and looked at the illuminated white Walsh Tower in the distance. 10:15 p.m. Forty-five minutes left to get real answers. He was high enough in the ranks of the Unification to know its operations and just how secretive the council was about the warlocks. Yet they gave them autonomy in one of the most critical parts of the ritual.

*Am I really ready to risk my life to learn the truth? If I die, Delilah will be the next in line to assume my position. For all its faults, the Unification means well enough. Global peace and a unified consciousness are a worthy goal. I can make the call to kill the gates, accept failure here, and hope another region will be the one to locate Lazarus. Do I?* Charles weighed the merits in silence before kicking the clutch back into gear and heading to Walsh Tower.

While the city and the area above the ground belonged in theory to the Unification, the Libraries of Dues, the ritual chambers, and other facilities below were all the personal domain of the warlock Primus Vryce. Entering uninvited was not permitted, or even an option for most. Charles opened and snapped shut his pocket watch. The reassuring ticking sound gave him focus. *I am not most people. I might lose seven years for this, but it needs to be done.*

He walked past two blooded guardsmen at the elevator and pried open the doors. It was a long way down. *Coming back up is not likely an option.* He took off his vest, wrapped it around the cable, and slid down. Any sensors or wards he triggered would be paused as his life ticked away. He opened up the doors below and stepped into a scene that looked like a painting from an epic battle.

Gabriel wielded a sickly green cavalry sabre and floated in the air, a stream of fire erupting from his hand into the face of a pit fiend. It reminded Walsh of the statue where Lucifer was cast into hell, if Gabriel the angel wore blue jeans and a hoodie. Bodies of dying demons lay strewn about, ash paused in time as they decayed and were sent back to hell.

Another sorcerer, who looked like a druid, was in the midst of slamming his staff in the ground while his animated vines ripped a fallen angel's wings off. They were all fighting to keep everyone above ground safe. Down here it seemed there was no barrier between worlds any longer.

Instead of a ceiling filled with lights, Walsh was able to see above, a sign that the area was fully immersed between worlds. A giant island floated above the city, tethered with enormous chains. Inside gashes in the earth, he could see the gray hellscape that demons were crawling from. The first circles of hell.

His path to the library chamber was clear; its massive stone door and keystone stood as imposing and impenetrable as ever. Walsh made his way through the time-stopped scene.

He knew of no deception that could be used here, nor did he intend to use any. He activated the keystone and spoke his true name, gaining entry into the hermetically sealed chambers. *Tsk. Warlocks never plan on time manipulation. You've underestimated me, Vryce. Magic can still be bent outside of time.* Instead of heading to the library, however, Walsh walked to the chambers below.

Even though the ritual was completed and etched with divine magic in every corner, it appeared mundane compared to outside. Walsh knew the room could still tell him secrets.

The first was a porcelain mask that hung on a wall, cracked down the middle. *I've already come too far to turn back.*

Walsh reopened his pocket watch with a familiar click. He still had a few more tricks up his sleeve. Since he knew the exact time the ritual took place, he could view what transpired. *Like rewinding an old VHS tape.* As he tampered with the gears, wrinkles started to appear on his face and streaks of his hair turned gray. All around him, the events of the ritual played out before him. He saw the turning point, the opening, and, most important to him, that other warlocks also betrayed the council.

"Find what you need?" said an unfamiliar voice.

Walsh spun around, his right knee giving out and causing him to fall on it. His breath was visible in the air, and his hands shivered from the cold as the temperature of the room plummeted. Frost and ice formed in fractal formations along the etchings in the ground. His heart raced as goose bumps rose along his arms, shortness of breath only adding to the panic. Sitting under the mask was a boy. He was no older than ten years of age, maybe eleven. His hair was as white as fresh snow, and he had familiar gold-and-green eyes.

"Vryce?" said Walsh. His body betrayed him, as he felt an invisible force keep him in the kneeling position. It felt as if the air itself were crushing him, and if the pressure increased, he would pop.

"Congratulations." Vryce clapped. "You are the ninth person in six centuries to see me without a host." The warlock stood and walked over with patience. Despite Vryce's boyish frame, Walsh felt miniscule in his presence.

"But how? Time is frozen."

Vryce flicked a small wooden cross on his necklace, dangling next to his ouroboros talisman. "It took me a long time to acquire this artifact to prevent your little trick. You aren't the only one with friends in low places." The child crouched in front of Walsh and held his chin with two fingers; his touch was so cold it burned. "You know, I am a firm believer in a simple truth. Do you know what that truth is, Mr. Walsh?"

Walsh shook his head.

"People are always more useful alive than dead. Wouldn't you agree?"

"If you are going to enslave me, then kill me. I'd rather die for what I believe in."

"And what is that? That mankind will be saved by the resurrection of Lazarus alone? What happened with Zeus? Odin? Thoth?" He paused. "Buddha?" Vryce moved his head to each side, inspecting him. "Age is a wonderful price to pay for knowledge. A worthy sacrifice."

"What do you want? I will not sacrifice my dignity to be your lapdog," Walsh said. His face quivered with fear, but his eyes still managed to stay focused and determined.

"If I needed another slave or gargoyle, I would not be talking to you." His eyes tried to give a reassuring look. It was like a snake telling a mouse they would be friends. "Taking your soul, stealing your blood, and turning you into a puppet would do neither of us any good. I need your willing help."

Events of the ritual replayed themselves in Walsh's mind. "You betrayed the Unification?"

"Is that what you saw? I opened the portal as requested," Vryce said, tilting his head sideways in a quizzical fashion.

"I'm . . . not sure what I saw, but it explains much. The other warlocks? You are not acting alone."

"This highlights exactly why puppets are not useful. Critical thinking skills are often lacking." Vryce rose and waved his hand. Walsh felt the weight of the air lift. He had his freedom back. "As director, you can lie to the council. You can keep the walls fueled and working."

"Why would I do that? Why should I trust you?"

Vryce nodded to Walsh and began. "If you are to trust me, I will trust you with my secret. I am taking my soul back and, in doing so, helping legend and wonder return. My vision is to allow all humans the chance to save themselves through their own awakening. The council places their faith in Lazarus alone, but they are misguided by the demon kings who whispered in their ears to open the gates. Do we really want to place the fate of the world in the hands of a creature bound in purgatory for millennia? Our ideals can be similar, Charles. You will need my power if humans are to have a chance at fighting back against ancient creatures. Join our society, buy me time with what little you have left." Vryce sat back down on the steps and folded his hands on his knees.

"I'll admit, I started with a leg up. My master rigged the game and gave me one of my shards back before this all went down." He unconsciously twirled the wooden cross. "Ten rituals. Ten warlocks with their souls shredded ten ways."

Walsh knew there was something wrong here. He could feel it in every bone he had. This creature before him should not exist.

Lichdom was not a new concept among his colleagues. After all, Lazarus was the first who had achieved such divine immortality. He was subsequently jailed for his audacity. The idea was immensely complex, even on paper. Become a warlock, having your soul shredded. Then find a way to drag fragments individually out of heaven and hell and unite them in ritual. An utter abomination of existence according to angels and demons. So much so they imprisoned Lazarus in purgatory for eternity out of fear and disgust.

The rise of a second lich, or even more, was a feat never likely to occur, but Walsh saw the puzzle fall together. *Vryce was patient and has waited for others to provide the chance.*

"So that's what you did. You—"

"I did what I was forced to do. Create a pathway from the land of the dead for Lazarus to follow home. No one said it was exclusive to him alone. If you place your faith so highly in him, then fuel this city and help the divers before it's too late. To get what I needed, I shattered the gates open farther than anywhere else. The portals here go deeper into purgatory as a result. This is the best spot for both of us. The Society of Deus will give this world a choice. I am giving *you* a choice. One for you to make of your own free will. You paid a price for knowledge. I granted it. What you tell the death lords of the Unification is up to you. You will live with whatever choice you make. I will survive regardless, even in memory. The assassins they send to snuff out my life will not change that. I have cast my lot in with every forgotten myth and legend to return wonder and awe back to this world."

Vryce made a series of circular gestures, shards of ice falling from the portal sliced through the air behind him. "Now be gone with you. I have work to do." With a thrust of Vryce's hands, Walsh was flung through the portal, his head slamming into a desk, knocking a phone and computer off it. His ears rang, and his watch was no longer ticking as the view of his office came into focus and the world moved once again.

*He let me live! Why? I still have more questions. Why give Lazarus a chance to come back? Will the Unification kill him? Is this even possible?* His hands were still shaking, both from the panic and the cold. The time on the phone blinked eleven o'clock. It was time for his phone call to the Unification.

The door to the room opened as the sly frame of Roger Queneco walked in. He looked down at Walsh. "I was wondering how long it would take before Vryce offered you the same choice he offered me." He reached down and lent a hand to help Walsh up. "I wonder what you'll say to the council. I advise caution, to a friend, of course. How would mankind survive the council's plan if nobody finds Lazarus? How, without power like Vryce's to save them?"

Walsh looked at the smirk his old friend wore. "I wish Delilah never introduced the two of us."

"Don't say that." Roger's fangs seemed to protrude farther than usual. "I just saved your life by making you seem useful to a creature that ripped open a gateway to both hell and heaven. I've your best intentions at heart. Imagine what would happen if my master decided that you were nothing more than the council's loyal puppet and an obstacle in his way?"

The phone rang. Walsh answered. "This is Director Walsh." *Time. I only need more time.* "The gates are open. May Lazarus find his path." He hung up the phone, its click reassuring, bringing him clarity. *The council would no doubt demand more information in person. I have time, though. Not much, but time enough to make my choice.*

"Charles?" Roger asked.

"Yes?"

"You need to shave." Roger smiled and spun out of the room with a slight skip to his step.

# CHAPTER 19

The thirteen lords of death sat in their chamber deep beneath the Vatican, rulers of the Unification. Twelve of them wore masks that served to represent which aspect of death they presided over. One for murders, one for unfortunate accidents, one for starvation, one for old age, and so forth. The thirteenth sat in the middle of the room, unmasked. Yet at his feet lay the grave clothes of Lazarus. Wrappings of ancient power that the thirteenth seat would have the honor of bestowing to their lord.

Every third year, the members of the thirteen would change hands within the Unification. Over three hundred occult groups signed the Treaty of Unification around the world. Some vastly more powerful than others, all of them vying for the prestige to sit on the council. It was intended as a method of ensuring that power among all within the Unification remained somewhat distributed. Dr. John C. Daneka, the current thirteenth chair, knew it was all a farce. When you pull from the same set of immortal candidates every three years, there would be no change.

Regional Director Charles Walsh had just delivered the shortest report received thus far. The final report coming in meant it was time to take an accounting.

"Very well. I have received the final report from my regional director. This concludes the first stage. Let us recap where we stand within the world," Dr. Daneka said.

Lord of Murder rose. "I am pleased to report that the ritual led by Warlock Mortiemer Ploutuns was successful, in the utmost regard, in Jerusalem." Everyone nodded in approval and held for a moment of silence. None had expected failure from Lord of Murder, who took very direct agency within his region.

Lady of Age rose and hesitated. "The ritual led by the Warlock Lucian Montague in Haiti has gone awry. It appears that Baron Samedi interfered from the land of the dead. The loa are freed from their prison, and Haiti will soon be lost to us." A moment of silence was held after her report. Dr. John C. Daneka watched Lord of Suicide roll his eyes behind his mask. The region was notoriously difficult to begin with, and Daneka chided himself inwardly in hoping that Lady of Age's wisdom would provide experience in that region.

Lord of Starvation rose before Lady of Age sat. "The ritual led by the Warlock Rasputin in Moscow was a success. No signs of influence from Baba Yaga or her lot. Events are unfolding according to the schedule." The lack of sound after his statement eerily held the room. None had expected Rasputin to play along, much less succeed. It meant the Unification had vastly underestimated his power.

Lady of Misfortune rose. "Warlock Sydney DuWinter in London was a resounding failure. The good people of MI5 intelligence had somehow discovered our activities and marshaled their forces just in the nick of time. Ah shucks, sucks don't it? So in the end, a portal was opened to some godforsaken place, and the Innocence in that area will continue to shred at an alarming rate. Let's give a big ol' round of applause to the moronic humans for muckin' with a perfectly good day." An uproar of surprise echoed through the chamber. Sydney DuWinter was a member of an occult group that drew its strength from the Golden Dawn. London had been counted among one of the Unification's prize regions. John silenced the room with a clank of his moderator hammer and dismissed Lady of Misfortune back to her throne.

Lady of Pestilence rose. "The ritual by Warlock Kiro Yamakaz in Japan did not take place under the watchful eye of the Unification. A coup by the emperor's family usurped the proceedings, to their agenda." John C. Daneka glared at each member who dared to make a sound. The fall of Japan was a calculated risk, one that could be remedied after the ritual's completion.

Lord of Suicide rose. "The youngest warlock, Peter Culmen, in Mexico City, was successful in the first act of his ritual. His silicon-based prototypes quelled an uprising by apprentices to bring forth their own Mayan gods. Peter is already assisting helldiving teams personally." Lord of Suicide gave a flourishing bow. He was the newest member to the council, and ruler over the only warlock that interwove science and magic. John felt they were growing too powerful in modern times, but his success would have to be rewarded and remembered.

Lady of Drowning rose. "The ritual led by Warlock Nefertiti in Cairo was a success. Nothing further to report." She sat back down, and all other lords bowed their heads in respect. Including John. Lady of Drowning, he suspected, was the oldest lich on the council.

Lord of the Unborn rose. "The ritual completed by Warlock Null in Antarctica was a failure to the standards of the Unification. Nothing was contacted and nothing was found." Lords and ladies looked to each other, but remained silent.

Daneka watched them shift in their seats and adjust their positions out of curiosity for more information, but none was to be
had for now.

Lady of Fate rose. "The ritual led by Warlock Verkonis in
Greenland was a failure. They have turned their backs on the
Unification and sacrificed our members to the ritual for their
own purposes." The people in the room lost control. Their largest undertaking dangling by a spider's thread over oblivion.

"Order and silence!" Dr. John C. Daneka rose from his
seat. He currently served as the death lord of those who were
killed by demons or angels. Or as the room knew him, Lord of
Heaven's Wrath. "The ritual led by Warlock Vryce in the Twin
Cities was a success." That was all he had to report. Fortunately,
his position as the thirteenth chair meant none would speak
up. Their looks, however, suggested they were filled with questions and doubts about their chances of success.

Dr. Daneka continued. "A Lilith moon has been sighted in
the sky, which confirms that the bleed will be greatest in the
northern hemisphere. Lazarus has many doors open for him.
Our plans shall not be stymied because of this interference. Let
us take this as a sign. The bleed has spread, creating even more
portals than we ever intended. Three hundred of our organizations are searching for Lazarus's prison. Will any of them
achieve the glory of his return, perhaps even unseating one of
you?

"Let us use our demons to kill the warlocks who failed.
The Seventh Age will have us as champions, to guide. In their
vulnerability, let us give them everlasting peace to end their
torment, removing their threat from the world. Their final sacrifice so that the world may be cleansed of sin and united under
one world thought." He paused. "Let us pray."

They chanted in unison, heads bowed low. Dr. John C.
Daneka stood in the middle with arms outstretched and led

them in prayer. "We saw the thrones on which were seated those of us who had been granted authority to judge. And we saw the souls of those who had been beheaded because of their testimony about Lazarus and the word of God. They had not worshiped the prophet or drank of the host's blood. They were cast into darkness to wander blind in the Land of Nod for a thousand years. Amen."

Dr. John C. Daneka loved that prayer. He spoke with every ounce of conviction he could muster forth from his dead soul. Acolytes of Lazarus had been beheaded in the past. Now, centuries later, they sat on the thrones and had taken the authority to judge humanity, to bring back their savior. *To return order to chaos.* The death lords had all eaten the hearts of the hosts and drank of their blood. They shattered their souls for power to do what must be done. They ruled over the vaults of souls. Their legions were many. The next crusades would begin soon. Lazarus and his descendants would pardon them for following in his footsteps and return from purgatory with their shattered souls. They were no longer blind. *Oh, the irony of it all.*

# CHAPTER 20

"Wake up." The voice sounded hazy to Mike.

In the shadow of the Second City's skyline, in the bowels of industrial parks once referred to as the Jungle, Morris slammed his fist, wrapped with barbed hooks around thick leather gloves, into Mike's face. It left deep gashes, yet no blood flowed. Meat hooks thrust into Mike's wrists hoisted him up on chains, yet Mike felt little pain. They were in the ungentrified no-man's-land just outside the city proper. Outdated lights dangled from high steel rafters, emitting a dying orange light. The warehouse was a giant health-code violation, yet it still shipped hot dogs to every street vendor in Chicago. Mike opened one of his eyes to look at Morris before another punch came. Even though Morris had great strength behind his frame, Mike took the blow as if it were a child hitting him.

The last thing Mike remembered was Morris looking at him and telling him to sleep after Matsen narced on him. "Really, Morris? Ya going through with this? I mean, it's not like you can torture me. I barely even feel this. It tickles," Mike said. "Frankie, talk some sense into him. I mean, this is about as effective as you putting on skin lotion."

"Oh, it's not about you, friend," Morris said. "It makes me feel better. Vampires always think they are invincible. Let's see that smirk of yours when the sun rises."

"If you want to feel better, I know a great taco stand," Mike said as Morris slammed his fist into Mike's chest, sending him rocking back on the chains like a kid on a swing. Winters grabbed Mike's shoulders to hold him like a punching bag. "Okay . . . how . . . about I mail you a fruit basket?" Mike coughed. "Everyone likes nutmeg, right?"

"I don't think you get it, friend. You created a metric shit-storm that I'll have to clean up. The world is short of punching bags that I won't break, so I might as well get some use out of you." Morris did a skip back and started winding up for another punch.

"Ahhh, fuck it." Mike wrapped his forearm around the chain. The steel beam ripped off its rusted joist as he heaved, putting his weight into a right hook that connected with a wide-eyed Morris. The punch was so hard that it created ripples on the side of Morris's head as his skull was shattered. Morris was flung like a rag doll across the warehouse, crashing into shipping barrels on the other side.

Echoes made Matsen and Winters cover their ears. They took cover from flying debris and hot dogs liberated from their packaging. Mike wound the chains on his left around his arm and ripped it free, causing shredded steel debris to rain down. Frank had taken cover inside the protective cage of a nearby forklift. "Come on, Morris! I'm just letting off some steam!" Mike shouted to the other end of the warehouse.

Mike bounced on the balls of his feet like a boxer, chains hooked into his wrists. He waited for Morris to get up. Morris bared his fangs, dropping any semblance of pretending to be human as his head restructured itself. He slowly pulled himself up. Dusting off, he picked a few bits of animal flesh off his shoulder.

Mike blinked. Morris was gone in that instant, vanished from Mike's sight. *That explains how I lost him in the alley.*

"Running already?" Mike spun the chains around, creating a zone of protection in case Morris tried to sneak up.

"Nope." Morris said from Mike's left. Mike heard a *thwump* sound. He turned and saw Morris standing at distance, arm outstretched with a small crossbow. Mike didn't feel any pain from the bolt hitting his chest, but that didn't stop him from crumpling to the ground. *Crap! Hey, why can't I move! You gotta be fucking shitting me! I can think. I can see. But I can't move. Even my eyes are stuck.* From his vantage point, he could see Morris standing over him in his dirty shoes.

"Congrats, friend. You became a vampire. You stole the heart of a big-ass demon and its strength to boot. Allow me to introduce you to your number-one weakness." Morris grabbed Mike's hair and held up his head. "Me."

"Actually, kid. It's the shaft of wood in your heart now," Patrick O'Neil said from behind Mike.

"Oh, hey there, Boss," Morris said as he dropped Mike's head, letting it thud on the concrete. "Didn't see you there."

"Showing the new kid the ropes, eh? Back in my day, this was done while walking uphill in snow, fighting off packs of the undead just to get a single drop of demon blood," O'Neil said. Mike heard a snipping sound, followed by a cigar butt bouncing off his face and landing in front of his nose. *Aw, come on, let me out! I have amusing anecdotes to say. You can't make an old-man joke like that and not let me respond.*

Mike saw more feet appearing behind Morris in the warehouse. *Women's biker boots, some nut job walking around with dirty bare feet and shredded camo pants, Doc's shoes, some combat boots paired with an axe, and some fireman's boots. Great, the village people are here. Hey, wait. Doc! Yo, Doc, let me out! Let me out!*

"What do you want done?" Morris asked.

Mike could hear everyone get closer. All he had to look at was a rusty steel chain that was rocking back and forth from the earlier fight. *So this is how you arrest a vampire. Solitary confinement is preferable. At least I can hear myself talk.* He heard himself chanting to the crowd about being sons and daughters coming from a device in someone's hands. *I'm really fucked.*

"Nice speech, kid. Knew you had it in you," O'Neil said.

"Excuse me, Boss?" Morris asked.

"Despite how good you are, Morris, there was no chance of containing the news of Golgoroth marching on the United Center. Not only did our resident hero here stop it, he probably convinced most of Chicago to start hunting down demons and killing them. The last time demons tried to invade earth, men were armed with pointy sticks." He took a drag from his cigar. A fleck of hot ash landed on Mike's eyeball. *Oh God! I can't blink! Get it off! Get it off!* Patrick O'Neil continued without noticing Mike's plight. "I'd like to see the forces of hell wander into Englewood. Shit, I'd pay for center-ice seats to see the reaction on a rage demon's face."

"But what about the Unification's plan? Our job?" Morris pleaded.

"Let's be practical. There are people far smarter than you working out all of that. Let's just handle what is thrown at us one step at a time. This is currently an invasion force of demons, slowly ripping their way into this world. Let's get our city under a semblance of control first. I have boys on the ground in the Twin Cities, figuring out what went down. They need time to cook a bit," O'Neil said.

"So what about him, then?"

"Doc, what's your prognosis?" O'Neil asked.

"Mike needs to learn his limitations. I think this could be a very insightful exercise for him. I've always been a firm believer in fringe therapy."

Even though the ash on his eyeball clouded most of his vision, Mike saw Doc's shoes tap in front of him like he was nervous.

"Maybe," Doc continued, "being undead now, he'll probably lose that near-death rush he was hooked on before. He's going to need that back to survive if I know him at all."

*Gee, thanks, Doc. That swordfish is so getting thrown in a Dumpster after this.*

"All right. Box him up. Four holes," O'Neil said.

"Wait, what?" Doc moved between Mike and Morris. "I meant test him. Teach him limits. I'm fine with a little rough-up, but you can't box him up and throw him away."

Mike's world shifted as he was rolled onto his back. He could see all of them standing over him. Four of them he didn't recognize. All looked a little too excited.

"Tough love, kid. You're a Nosferatu now, a vampire. It's slightly different for each of us, but there are a few ground rules here you gotta learn. Eating a demon heart kills the body and keeps your soul inside. You replaced your old heart with the demon's. Impale it and your body can't move. Tacos are a thing of the past now. Blood is how you stay young, whole, and moving. Usually this is where everyone in the movies says that the movies are all false." O'Neil looked up at Doc and winked. "Well, they are right. Mr. Daneka, we know what we are doing. Children only stick their hand on a hot stove once."

Mike noticed that Patrick's shirt had a few burn marks in it and ash stains. "We don't have the leisure time to bring you in slow over a decade. You're going to learn fear. A fear every Nosferatu needs. Trust me. It's for your own good."

Mike was picked up and stuffed into a barrel. *At least the ash fell off my eye.* He could feel the barrel shake when they drilled the holes. From under his arm, he could see with his left eye a beam of orange light bleed in. *You know, the undead should really make self-help pamphlets. Hand them out to new recruits. I thought they offered dental coverage. I can't believe Doc is in on this. Wait, yes I can. He's been yelling at me for years about my rooftop antics. Oh, and I gotta remember to get some damn chest armor.*

The barrel was picked up. Mike could feel the inertia from multiple hands carrying him as balance shifted. He spied out of a single hole as he was moved outside and carried up to the roof. He was placed so that he was facing Chicago's east, the skyline large enough to see some of the smaller buildings. *Ooh, a sunrise view. Come on. How bad can this be? I already know they aren't going to kill me.*

# CHAPTER 21

Lightning snapped and arched in the air, leaving behind the smell of burned flesh and ozone. *Pathetic.* The cracked porcelain mask hid Vryce's face as he raised his right hand to the sky again. A thunderstorm raged in the small Russian village. Clouds swirled, creating a vortex above him. He gestured down, summoning another lightning bolt. The flash impacting the worthless sorcerer could be seen for miles if there was anyone left alive to witness it.

Vryce had tracked down a fraction of his shattered soul in a northern province by a haunted forest near a farming village. At a helldiving site near Rasputin's ritual, a witch had recognized the fragment for what it was on a dive and sought to claim its power for herself. *I will not be denied that which belongs to me.* She put up a little fight, controlling the winds in a vain attempt to get away through flight after she ensorcelled the entire village to attack.

Vryce casually shot her in the head with his pistol before finishing her off. He snapped his fingers again, bringing down a third lightning bolt. It was always best to be certain when dealing with witches.

The twitching of her fingers in the bloodstained patch of earth was her final sign of life. Vryce moved in to claim her soul as it tried to flee her body, carrying with it a fragment of his own. He took out a small crystal, clear and made of quartz, with delicate golden rings attached to a small chain. He twisted and dialed three rings into the right position while chanting in Latin. The green soul became visible as it exited her mouth and was sucked into the crystal. Behind the mask a fanged smile gleamed with satisfaction. *Two down. Eight to go. One step closer. I just need time.*

He looked at the small wooden buildings behind him, their small populace drawn out into the streets and burned to a crisp from his initial lightning storm. There could be no surviving witnesses to his actions yet. Vryce closed his eyes and inhaled deeply as he felt a part of him return. He was becoming something more than a warlock. Soul by soul he would undo the damage that had been done six hundred years ago at the behest of the death lord Lady of Misfortune.

He took a knee next to the fallen witch, her body slowly crumbling into a pile of ash. "Of course, and you wouldn't know this, witch, but Lazarus and the lords of death guarded this secret well, even from me. Few grimoires detail that after the Room of Guf opens, my soul could be sent along the lines of the ritual. Rather than neatly entering the phylacteries, I had prepared for them," he said while picking through the burned corpse for any items of significance.

He pulled out a gnarled raven's claw that was attached to a blue cord. "Arcanists such as yourself, unfortunately, are drawn like crows to shiny objects when hunting for treasures beyond the Innocence. A fragmented soul shines brightly, and you sought to bind and steal its power for yourself. Such a waste.

If only you minded your own business. You would have been more useful alive."

*Well, that's not true. I can't actually have acolytes of the Unification running around and diving into purgatory looking for Lazarus rather than just paying lip service to the Unification. I don't want the competition. I've learned from his mistake and have no intentions of being dragged and chained in the depths of Hades because nobody can figure out what afterlife I belong to.*

Vryce worked his magic to bind the fragment into the raven's claw. His eyes remained closed as the sensation of vertigo made the world spin. Sweeter than any heart he had ever consumed, the rush of divine power flowing through him brought him to his knees. The vortex of clouds swirling above allowed lightning to dance between them. A signal to the world that divine law was being violated.

In the throes of the euphoric sensation, he felt magic of the world dance on his fingertips. A few more shards and he would be overflowing with it, finally able to rip the gates wider than initially, rather than seal them as Lazarus would.

Frozen winds swept away the pile of ash that remained of the witch. The ground near Vryce froze. Behind the porcelain mask, he gave no thought to his surroundings as he remembered his training over the years.

*It was I who discovered the Kabbalistic tree of life was the perfect road map to piece a soul back together via arcane connections.* He remembered centuries of research into the secret of lichdom via phylacteries, objects recovered from purgatory that a soul could rest within. *I can deal with the sacrifice of forever being bound to this earth, unable to walk between worlds as a cost.*

Lightning struck and rattled the ground, sending steam into the air. A second later the steam solidified back into frozen crystals, falling to the ground around him. He remembered the death lords stealing his research in the 1800s. They saw an opportunity to resurrect Lazarus with the combination of Gnostic Hermeticism and demonic knowledge. *I will not suffer the thieves buckling the will of God and ruling this earth unchallenged.*

Vryce knew that collectively, mankind was God, but individually, they were worthless, ignorant specs. *They will never organize or awaken on their own. Someone has to do it for them.* He reminded himself that vengeance was his primary motive as the raven's claw clenched tightly in his hands turned into a state of permanent frost, an icy shell of its former self. There were many tools to climb the steps to enlightenment. "I prefer a healthy dose of cold revenge after a century of the death lords' empty promises," he said as he began to stand. "Oh, Vryce, we will make you a *council member*," he mimicked while commanding the vortex to dissipate. *The Society of Deus and I played as good little leashed dogs for the past century.* "'We can return your soul anytime,' they said." He pocketed the crystallized raven's claw. With their great ritual under way, he could just collect it back on his own.

Vryce pulled out his own soul blade from the red velvet lining inside his trench coat. He sliced his finger along the curved dagger's blade and felt the world shift around him as he teleported to the next shard on his list.

# CHAPTER 22

Mike woke up to the jostling of the barrel as it was tipped on its side. The left half of his face burned with such agony that Mike wished he would just die. It was that tiny spot where the hole was drilled. Fear of that spot gripped him with terror. Even though the sun had long since set, he went unconscious from screaming in his own head hours ago. The barrel came to a halt, and he was released from his wooden sarcophagus. Several hands picked him up and set him on a table. He was blind in one eye. His face was nothing more than charred, dead flesh. It felt like his spine was still on fire.

*Sweetness.* The taste of peaches and spiced plums was forced into his throat. He then felt as if a hundred small insects crawled on his face, tiny ants picking up bits of the pain and carrying it away as his vision came back into focus. Doc leaned over him, shining a small penlight into his eyes.

"Looking for pupil dilation on an undead corpse? You don't know anything, do you?" said a girl about half his height with short red hair cut into a bob. She wore some sort of black face paint and a gray coat with the hood pulled back.

Doc gave her a piercing look. "Despite vampires being around for centuries, I've never had this chance. How many vampires have undergone experiments on their biology, type, classifications, and psychology?" He paused as he checked Mike's other eye. "Only the Nazis and my father have a clue about what exactly we are dabbling with. Most of the Unification just accepts it as corrupting your divine soul, whatever that's supposed to mean. So, let's just say it might be you who doesn't know anything."

The girl said, "I come from a long line of demon hunters and have trained my entire life for this. I know *exactly* what I'm dealing with. There are plenty of recorded studies before the Unification came into existence. Rational blokes ignore the magical and then spread that toxic science drivel, but that's not the way the world works. Angels make the sun rise, your soul can be stolen, and anything magical tastes like peaches." She gave a curt nod.

"You know gravity is a thing, right? Does God just hold your feet magically to the ground? Lucy, if you show any scientist a double-blind case study, they will believe anything," Doc said, and put his hand on the bolt in Mike's chest. "All right, buddy. I'm going to pull this out now, on the distinct promise you don't punch me. I've only tasted the blood at this point. I couldn't survive a full punch from you. Understand?" He yanked the bolt out.

Mike was gone the moment the bolt was removed, tossing back all instruments on the workshop table with the force of the wind alone. *He's gotta be close.* He willed his legs to carry him faster out of this place. He checked the bathrooms, throwing open stall doors so hard they flew off their hinges. Pictures on the wall were still in midair as he sped through the hallway, hitting the ground long after Mike was gone. *Inside clear.*

*Smoking. Entrance. Security. He's security. He's outside. The main door.*

The steel doors to the first floor of the warehouse were blasted off their hinges. Mike could see Morris with a smoke still in his mouth fixing up his scarf and talking to the barefoot camo kid. The flame from the lighter went out before Morris could even react as Mike snarled, leaned back, and kicked him with all his momentum. The kick was so strong Morris created a dent in the side of a dump truck. This time Mike was confident he had knocked Morris out. The barefoot kid was trying to light some expensive brand of hipster cigarettes and had frozen in that position as she looked at Mike.

"I'm Mike. Nice to meet you," he said, gesturing to the pack. "Mind if I bum one? I just had the worst day of my life." He felt ashamed to admit that was not a lie. *Was that really worse than living through everyone's death?* Memory of the barrel flashed before his eyes. He leaned against the wall to brace himself. It would be easier to live through the day his own son died than live through another day in a barrel. He tried to shake it off.

"Akira. Charmed. Sure thing, Boss." Akira handed over a smoke and even lit it for Mike. She was short and wiry. She reminded Mike of a gutter punk or a street rat. Her skin had been enhanced with tattoos along her neck. Bright-blue insects.

"Boss?" Mike forced himself to inhale. It was unnatural, a conscious thought. He focused on the feeling of the burn and the smoke inside him. He could feel his nerves calming from his indulgence in the decade-long habit.

"Well, I ain't too keen on being on your bad side, seeing as you just put that guy's head up his ass. Listen, pal. They ain't so good with sharing the demon hearts. You let me fight with you and don't hoard the hearts. I wanna eat one, so why not?" She shrugged. "You can be Boss." The way she twitched her head was almost like an insect.

"What is it you do for O'Neil anyway?"

"Nobody notices the homeless. So I kill people for him. Or listen. Pretty easy when nobody pays attention to you."

"All right, don't kill any of my friends and we got a deal." Mike offered his hand to shake.

"Accepted! Good thing too. I was gonna have to do it for free. Bigger Boss wanted all of us to help you out. Now I get demon hearts out of the deal instead of just blood. World is coming up, Akira!" She smiled and shook Mike's hand with both of hers.

"I'm not big on hoarding anyway. I'm a card-carrying socialist after all." Mike flashed a grin and pointed to a red fist button pinned to his green coat. "Think I went too far on Morris. I'd better go make sure he still has teeth."

Mike walked over to Morris and pulled him up. *Ah crap. It's not Morris. I got so focused on the scarf. Who the hell is this?* Mike didn't recognize him. He was, however, more than dead. Blood oozed out of his nose and his body seeped liquids like someone shot him with a shotgun. *Oh God, no . . . no.* "Hey, buddy, wake up. It's going to be okay." Mike laid the body back down and took off the cabby hat. He didn't recognize this guy at all.

"That's your dinner," said Morris. He was standing outside the dock door with a stone-faced demeanor. "Figured you would be pretty pissed when you woke up, friend. As much as I like having to repair my internal organs, I wasn't feeling it this evening."

"Dinner," Mike said. "Dinner." Mike stood up. "Dinner?" Mike's fists began to give off steam.

"Yeah, dinner. Blood, food, lunch, breakfast. Whatever you wanna call it, big guy. Don't worry about him. He was a murderer. Killed his seven-year-old daughter and his wife with over fifty stab wounds. Told him if he could survive the night, he was free to go." Morris held up his hands. "Now chill, friend. I knew you weren't going to eat just any old schmuck for your first meal. You have too much vigilante in you."

Mike looked back at him. *These guys have always lied, or spoken in half-truths.* "Prove it."

"Pull him in. Akira, go grab the newspaper." Morris flipped his cigar onto a gravel path and walked inside.

By the time Mike got inside, Akira showed him the newspaper story with the man's face plastered on the third page: "Local Man Wanted for Double Homicide." *Well, I take back feeling sorry for kicking you, douch nozzle.* Mike walked up to a column and sat down, propping his back up against it.

He felt like crying, not only from the killing, but from everything. All the days put together were beginning to catch up to him, and Morris was right. He was ravenous. Using his newly acquired strength and speed drained him, and all he craved was blood. Everyone else in the room stood there letting the awkward pause hang in the air as Mike started knocking his head against the column.

Doc Daneka was picking at his neck skin again. "Right, I think each of you should talk to me first. Even though I'd like to continue documenting this process for a case study, let's give Mike some space. He's going to need a minute to adjust."

"I'm not your research assistant," Lucy said, her voice deep and almost growling.

"Ah, but years of training burn inside of you. You'll want my father's notes to further your knowledge. That means joining us, doesn't it?" Doc said. "Come on. You first, then."

In procession they followed Doc back into the side rooms. Morris shook his head with a warning at Mike and walked out after O'Neil.

Mike was alone in the warehouse at last. He walked up to the dead murderer on the table. "I really hope you ate Mexican food today." Mike's fangs popped out instinctively as he bit in. It was only lukewarm, but it was sweet and sour at the same time. He felt his body absorb each drop he sucked out like a sponge. It replaced all fear, nervousness, and apprehension he had with raw satiation.

When the last drop was gone, Mike looked up and saw a little ghost looking at him. A small girl with knife slashes across her face. She smiled and skipped through Mike, who spun around to follow her. Three women kneeled down and gave her a hug as they started to fade from view back into the world of the dead. *Well, at least seeing the dead isn't a thing that has changed. One . . . unsettling comfort.*

# CHAPTER 23

Leaning over the drained body, Mike was lost in the reverie of his imagination. He pictured himself using his newfound powers to right all the injustices in the world while looking awesome doing it. The moment was broken when Patrick O'Neil and the rest of his merry band of misfits strolled in.

O'Neil held up a gloved finger to everyone and shook it as he walked up in front of Mike. He put both his hands in his long brown coat and started rocking back and forth on his feet while looking around the room. Mike raised an eyebrow and started rocking the same way. *I'll hand it to him. He dresses real well.* O'Neil continued letting silence fill the moment. Mike looked for answers on the faces of others. Doc, Matsen, Winters, Morris, and Akira all had expressions of equal confusion and had started looking around themselves.

The girl with a hood and face paint had brought an axe with her. She brooded in the corner. Another girl in a tight black jumpsuit stopped chewing her gum. *Damn. Of course, I'm dead and I end up in a room with a girl like that.* Even the large man in fireman's boots and pants, with the red suspenders and a Superman shirt underneath, looked sheepish. Patrick O'Neil continued swaying with his hands in his pockets. *Okay, I can't take it anymore.*

"What?" Mike said. Hands flinging out to the side, displaying new holes in his fingerless gloves from meat hooks. Patrick said nothing. He just kept rocking. "All right. I'm sorry I punched your guy and told everyone to defend their families by eating demons." Patrick only lifted a single eyebrow and pursed his lips. Mike was a terrible liar. "Okay, I'm not sorry I tried to lead a revolution against puppet masters who have kept the working class down. I draw the line there. That's all you're getting out of me. Take it or leave it."

Still nothing from Patrick. *Okay, this situation is getting close to a day in the barrel.* Just the thought of that made him shiver. "Fine, the sun hurts. Your barrel had a lesson. I get why you did it. Can we get on with saving the world now?"

"Thought you would never ask, kid," he said at last. Everyone in the room sighed with relief, and the group relaxed.

"Mike, meet your new family. They already met you at the bar earlier, but you were . . . different then. Lucy Carter is a demon hunter. Her job is obvious." O'Neil pointed to the girl with face paint and a hood in the corner. "That's Phoebe, my messenger. She can do the fastest ride from Lake Shore to Lemont. She's got her own crew of crotch-rocket fiends." As O'Neil nodded to the girl in skintight leather, she popped a giant bubble and winked at Mike. "This man in the fireman outfit is called the Captain, one of my imbedded agents at the Twin Cities while it was being readied." The large firefighter leaned in to get a better look at Mike. O'Neil continued. "You've already met my troublesome assassin, Akira. She handles things that go awry." O'Neil put a cigar in his mouth and the barefoot girl street rat lit it for him. "Welcome to the O'Neil family."

Mike stood up. "A family?"

"A family of those who gambled with death." Patrick produced two small golden pins and handed them to Mike. They looked like coins from ancient Greece. "We serve Lady of Fate. All here, including Doc and you, have been marked. You've gone farther than most."

Mike pinned the coins to his coat, underneath a frowny-face button that read: "POWs Never Have a Nice Day." Another medal from a protest.

"Kid, you've become nobility among the damned. You slew an arch demon and consumed its heart rather than making a deal. Golgoroth's heart and all his power, strength, speed, and rage are bound to you. Frank and Morris each have their own, but one thing binds all you monsters together. People who have stolen a heart are banished from sunlight forever." O'Neil walked over and gestured for Morris to pull out a chair and sit down.

"What about you? Are you . . . ?" Mike asked.

"Don't worry about me. Just know that I'm cursed to be forgotten by anyone and everyone every time an age ends. As if I was never here." He let out a small chuckle. "When this is all over, kid, you'll look back and forget I even existed. Makes for a real lonely life when everyone dies around you from old age and everyone immortal forgets about you."

"If everyone forgets about you, how do you stay employed?" Mike said. There was not a soul in the room who didn't seem interested in the answer.

"That's going to remain my secret for now." O'Neil let slip a look of remorse past his aged demeanor. Regret seemed to weigh him down and made him look older for a brief moment.

"I'll get your story someday. Not gonna forget you. You ain't gonna forget me. So, saving the world. Are demons still crawling out of the earth?"

"Yes. It's only getting worse and at a faster pace, like race-horses out of a gate. Lady of Fate chose us to operate the Second City, my city, to help the Unification conduct its ritual. They were expecting an odd occurrence here and there, some-thing money could fix or maybe some muscle in the right spot. I was expecting hell on earth."

"Where is it all coming from?" Mike asked.

"Here?" O'Neil asked, letting on that it was happening else-where. "The Twin Cities, but we are directly connected, and it looks like I was right. So I've sent Frankie up there to get field intel. We've got a guy up there figuring out a plan."

"All right. Why is this happening?"

Patrick paused at that question, his gaze focused at his feet. "A lot of us asked that question. I suppose I don't have a sat-isfactory answer, kid. The creatures that go bump in the night were tired of being confined to the night perhaps. What's done is done." He brushed some nonexistent dust from his clean pants, a nervous habit, Mike supposed.

"You brought the world to an end because you were afraid of the fucking dark? Ever hear of Netflix? Watch some damn marathons," Mike said.

O'Neil held up a single finger. "Never me. Do not ever associate my name with this plan of the Unification. I am just an old man forgotten and forced to see this through. Do you understand?"

Mike looked at him and took in his eyes. They were full of sadness and pain, old eyes that were full of loss. Mike nodded with empathy. "Okay, so *they* did this. I'm down for defend-ing this place. Are all demons like the ones we've been facing? They keep getting bigger and bigger . . ."

Lucy set her axe down and spoke. "You got lucky killing an arch demon, Golgoroth. It will take you decades of study to learn all the classifications of those past the Innocence, where all divine things reside. The ones you gotta watch out for, though, are those who look like humans. Aspect demons, lords of hell, and fallen angels."

Doc pushed up his glasses. "From what I've read, aspect demons usually go by demon of $x$. Where $x$ equals whatever aspect gives them power. Demon of war, demon of lies. The inverse is also true for their heavenly counterpart."

"Since when the hell are you religious?" Mike pointed at Doc.

"Well, I'm not religious, but it's hard to ignore the evidence. While you've been running around on rooftops and being difficult, I've been reading my father's journals on the science of how man becomes monster. Boils down to you are what you eat. Eating Sparkles might cure a case of the sniffles, an aspect demon of rage and you get . . . well . . . ragey stuff. Good info to know when deciding on what to eat." Doc stopped as Mike waved his hand.

"Already boring, don't care, have things to punch. Hey, O'Neil, people who eat a heart are stronger than those who just drink the blood, right?" Mike asked.

O'Neil smirked. "Yeah, but it's a gamble, kid. You really wanna throw those dice?"

"Well, I figure Doc's already got the important parts. You said only a few are nobility or whatever. Screw it. Let's upgrade. Akira mentioned hearts are a rare thing, held in secret or, you know . . . because they aren't on fucking earth normally. Well, now they are. You got your group of misfits. Let's go fucking hunting and get us all on the same page. Why sit around and pass up this chance? If you wanna save this place, you're putting a lot on the shoulders of . . . how many of us are there?" Mike paused to count, mouthing the numbers.

Morris looked like he wanted to object, and Lucy shouldered her axe. O'Neil held up his hand. "Save it, Morris. Kid's right. Time to restart the family business. I think it's high time the O'Neils take their place as the best helldivers again. My plan, why I chose all of you, is to put some wild cards on the table."

Mike laughed and shook his head, recalling his conversation with Frank two nights ago about all of this.

"I'm bound by an unbreakable pact to see this through to an outcome. You are under no such contract. What's going on is worldwide, but it's all connected. You'll be able to make your mark soon enough." O'Neil turned to the Captain. "Lay out how it works for us. You helped build the unholy setup."

The large fireman stepped forward with a cocky smile and snapped his suspenders. "That I did. That I did." The looks of disapproval caused him to visibly shrink. "I'm a sorcerer who was accepted by the council to help guide the ritual, but it's better if you think of me as one of the noble *Bothans* who stole the Death Star plans."

"Spit it out."

"Righto. The Twin Cities is one of the Unification's ritual sites. Think of it as a small coal furnace. The ritual being conducted is the flame inside. Souls of the dead are the coal. Since demons harvest dead souls, we bound big demons to be coal miners for us here in Chicago. The Twin Cities was built to contain the ritual, where the souls are burned as fuel. Chicago has a rich history of death and is close by, perfect for mining. It's the same basic setup at the others."

Mike raised his hand.

"Yes, Mike?"

"So what went wrong?"

"From what I guess . . . the flame inside the furnace is now a raging inferno. So the demons, bound in service, are trying to fill the demand. The ritual is requiring more souls than they have, so they are rushing out to cause more death. Since the gates are open, they are crossing out of hell to do just that."

"Okay, well, let's go put out a fire. Seems pretty damn simple to me," Mike said.

O'Neil choked on a laugh. "Don't be so quick to jump into fires. You'll get burned alive. Let Frankie get back with info on how to best douse it. You guys aren't strong enough to extinguish these flames anyway. Your first idea was right, Mike. Go out and harvest some demons. Fight together. Get stronger. I'll give you until Frankie returns for all the hunting you want. All of you can benefit from it." He stood up and started walking to the door. "With that said, don't trash my city too much." He looked back before he left. "You are my sons and daughters now. Don't die on me again."

# CHAPTER 24

Chicago had only two seasons, winter and construction. In the transition period between the two, the streets were under heavy construction, and beneath them, the tunnels were a ghost town in their own right. The plan was simple, Matsen and Winters flushed out the hellhounds with spotlights. Phoebe would herd them, and Mike and Lucy would put them down.

Phoebe and her crew of bikers on crotch rockets raced past on Lower Wacker Drive. She slowed down long enough to give a wink and flash a peace sign at Mike, who was awkwardly standing out of position. Lucy dominated their ambush operation, taking the best spot between concrete columns as thick as a car, edging him out.

The hellhounds looked like shadows running at them, backlit by the remaining rocketeers as they used their lights to send them running. Some of the hellhounds defied gravity and ran along the ceiling, iron claws scraping away flecks of concrete. The hellhounds were faster than they had anticipated, at times outrunning the motorcycles.

Mike had a look on his face like a seven-year-old who just found the puppy dog, candy, and fireworks emporium, while Lucy acted like his disapproving mother who would not let him go in. "You can stand over there," she said. Mike was sure that humor, or even smiling, was something with which the muscles in her face had little experience.

She was the first to move, slinking out from behind the column and spinning with her axe, burying it deep within the skull of the first hound. Carrying the momentum through, she ran up the wall, hurling her axe like a Frisbee at a creature running along the ceiling. She was already putting a dagger into the demon's throat before it slammed into the ground, and she continued tumbling for another.

Cornered between Lucy and the hated light, the hound snarled and snapped its fleshless jaws as it charged right at her. She dropped into a roll underneath it, sliding between its legs. Mike was ready; at least he could send this one back to hell. He vaulted into the fray with a crowbar raised above his head, knocking the hellhound over and splitting it so that its intestines splayed out on the ground. Lucy cleaned off her dagger.

"Why do I get the distinct feeling I'm the comic relief here?" Mike said, lowering his weapon and sulking back to where Lucy demanded he stand.

"If the shoe fits," Lucy said. She carved out the hearts of her kills, sealing them in a clay jar, and added them to the growing pile behind her column, which was about as tall as she was now.

"Hey, I'm holding back, you know," Mike said.

"Okay."

"This is punishment, right? Being stuck down here with you. Doc gets to go duck hunting with his shotgun. Matsen and Winters are out scouting. Me and you, She Who Not Know Talking."

"I've trained since I could walk. You?" Mike recoiled, and his mouth stayed open as he tried to work up a reply. Lucy continued. "Oh right, Mr. Lucky is going to save the day by punching things," she said. "What about the demons you can't hit? There are more than just hellhounds, genius."

"Right. Sorry," Mike said. He wanted to say more, to tell her that this wasn't him. It was just nervous chatter. *Don't make excuses, man. Just man up. Own your shit.* "Any tips?"

"Stand there and watch. These are scouts we're herding. It's only a matter of time before larger ones start appearing. Stay out of trouble. I can't let you get killed on my watch." She held her axe at the ready again and waited. Above them they could hear the sounds of the next wave.

Mike watched her work each wave, an expert at her craft of killing. On the fourth and largest wave, he saw her cast the first spell he'd ever seen. She made parts of herself turn into a charcoal-colored mist to dodge attacks. *Can't wait to see her in action once she eats a heart if she's already that scary.* That would have to wait, however. From one of the maintenance tunnels, Mike saw a flash of green light. "Hey, look! Trouble!" he shouted. Lucy was engaged in intense fighting and didn't pay him much attention.

Mike walked over to the opening, waiting for a demon to come charging out. Instead, he heard the sound of something scraping along the concrete. A pungent odor crept out of the smaller tunnel as greenish light flashed. Mike gave a concerned look back to Lucy. *Eh, it's only a little trouble. I can handle this one.* Mike heard tapping sounds, claws against concrete echoing down the small tunnel. Tap. Tap. Tap.

Mike looked inside. Gaunt and emaciated, its skin pulled so tight over its body he could see the heart pumping even in the shadows. Gray and hairless, it flickered closer and shambled on a broken leg like a stop-motion film moving closer.

With each flicker, a flash of green light came with it, adding to the effect. Mike felt its eyes level upon him. The creature reached out and tapped the wall again. Tap. Tap. Tap.

It wore a toothy grin as its stomach distended and protruded while it inhaled. *Oh no, whatever you're doing, it stops now.* Despite a sense of natural apprehension, he ran around the corner, putting his feet into the wall as he got close, copying a move he saw Lucy perform earlier. He brought his crowbar down on the eyeless creature just as locusts were beginning to swarm out of its mouth.

*Like whacking a beehive with a baseball bat.* The head came clean off, and cockroaches scattered out of the body. It twitched and shook as its stomach exploded. Mosquitoes flew forth. Some managed to get into Mike's mouth, and he could taste them, squirmy and crunchy. *Get 'em off. Get them off!* The smell was so bad he would retch if he could. Instead, he swatted everything as he began to feel the stings. He couldn't see the exit anymore. Every surface crawled and moved. In seconds the walls looked as if they were made of water, pulsing and vibrating with millions of insects.

"My how mankind has grown. I must say I like what you've done with the place," a woman said.

Mike tried to swat away beetles so that he could see, but he could only make out a figure. Someone dressed in a bowler hat with a cane and coattails stood at the far end of the tunnel. The hurricane of insects was not letting up its assault, and all Mike could do was remain standing.

"The slayer of Golgoroth brought down by mere plague demons. Well, the story will be a terrible bore if you were to perish this way. Eyes chewed out by maggots and your undead body a breeding ground for spiders."

She tapped her cane a few times on the ground, and the insects seemed to obey her command by attaching themselves to the moving walls. With them swarming up to his knees, Mike was glad he wore boots, but that still didn't stop the small ones from crawling in and stinging his feet. She was pale and had a spot of freckles running across her nose. Short red hair curled around her ears from under her hat. Not what Mike was expecting from any sort of demon.

"You asked to 'get 'em off,' and so I did. A small concession before I take that soul of yours. Oh dear, I'm sorry. I am Marcus Danbury. It is my pleasure to meet you, Mike Auburn." She bowed.

"Yeah, I don't think it works like that. Wait, fuck that. I know it doesn't work like that. You can't just listen to someone's thoughts, then do what they want and claim their soul," Mike said. The sea of crawlers was getting deeper, up to his waist now.

"An expert on demonology, are we? Men always think they know how this works. That their new tools of war will save them from our invasions. After all—" She made an insulted gasp as Mike flung his crowbar at her. It flew past her as she easily stepped out of the way. "Ahem. After all, we have centuries and centuries of sinners at our call. Banished from your ignorant gaze, yet we are never truly gone, Mike. Now you are one of us. You've eaten our hearts, killed for pleasure, and condemned a man just to feed you." She was closer to him now. He could see that her teeth were rotten and her breath smelled like a smoker who licked an ashtray. She whispered in his ear. "All your sins are laid bare to us."

*All right. Let's take a minute here. I'm up to my chest in bugs. I got a monologuing demon inches away from my face. Oh, and she can hear my thoughts. Shit.*

"Bingo." She smiled. Mike saw Akira carefully crawling through the undulating swarm. Her neon-blue hair streaks and camo helped her blend in. A brown recluse spider latched onto her cheek. She didn't flinch. "You should be proud. Your soul will fuel our needs for weeks," she said as she ran her fingers along his face.

Mike watched Akira gently move a millipede the size of her leg out of her path. *That is one big motherfucking bug.* "You know I'm a huge fan of Mexican food, right?" he asked. "I'm a child of the eighties, so the first video game I ever played was *Mega Man 3.*"

She looked confused as she cocked her head. "Yes, darling. It is a 'big motherfucking bug,' and soon the locusts will claim you."

"Marcus Danbury, you said? Why that name? You look human, but Lucy said—wait, are you a fallen angel? Is that what kind of demon you are? Neat! Tell me *all* about that."

"We all have names, child, and you *are* a demon expert. Look at you. So proud of yourself." She licked the side of his face, her tongue causing his skin to blister. "I would like to thank the Unification for breaking open the gates to the underworld."

The insects were up to his neck now, a centipede crawling into his ear. Akira slowly rose, pulling twin one-handed scythes off her belt, readying herself.

"Well, Marcus Danbury. You're welcome. It was nice to make your acquaintance."

"Was?" She spun around as the scythes closed in, cutting off her head. Akira moved with lightning precision, impaling the demon's heart and surgically extracting it from her chest.

Akira set herself to gnawing on the blackened heart like a ripe peach as insects scattered, freeing Mike from his prison. He rolled around on the floor and slammed his back into the wall as the remaining bugs scurried from beneath his clothes.

Mike was still plucking them out of hidden and uncomfortable areas when Akira spoke. She didn't look much different, only now her eyes seemed more colorful.

"It's a good thing everyone just focuses on you ignoring everyone else around them. You've that kind of presence. I think I'm going to like stalking you," Akira said. Even as a human, she still resembled insects in her body language. "Just don't mind me staring at you when you sleep." She paused. "I'm going home now. I just ate seriously the best catch I could possibly find. I really hope I can change into a giant mantis. I wonder if I can cocoon myself." She held out her scythes like claws, pretending to be one. "Thank you for your service, Boss."

Mike only managed to wave good-bye. *It's going to be a long night.* He made sure to pry his crowbar from the side of a wall. Walking out of the maintenance shaft, Mike was pleased to see that Lucy had added to her pile. *Well, just how many can there be after all?*

"Are you going to do what I said and stay put now?" She flipped her axe, waiting for Phoebe's next shipment.

"Yes, ma'am," he replied.

# CHAPTER 25

Four in the morning is a unique time of night in the city of Chicago. One could stand in the heart of downtown and scream with nobody hearing. Mike walked along vacant streets among the giant steel skyscrapers. Not a soul to be found for miles. It appeared even the demons respected the sanctum that was this holy hour in the business section of the city.

Farther north, Mike was sure people stumbling out of after-hours bars were having their early-morning stupor shaken by encounters with supernaturals. It had been a long night. Mike's green trench coat was covered in substances that no dry cleaner would be able to remove. *If any are stupid enough to remain open after a night like tonight.* Everyone else had gone back to claim their new prizes and unlock their future potential over an hour ago. Mike wanted to stay out to feel the pavement under his feet one last time before the sun rose.

One demon summoned bigger ones, and those in turn brought forth even more unique horrors. *Heh, to think only a few weeks ago I thought teen vampire fiction was the worst we were going to be plagued with as a society.* Still, the frigid night

air instilled a sense of energy into Mike. It infused him at his
core.

*The lights are magnificent. I can feel this city in my bones.
What's going to happen now?* Mike walked with heavy boots and
ran his fingers along smooth marble from an oligarch-owned
bank. *There are more demons than in past nights. By now the
news must have broadcast everything.* Mike was isolated in
combat with Lucy for most of the festivities, but the different
types that were clawing forth from the shadows meant it was
only a taste of what was yet to come.

The city, with its beauty and monolithic steel facade, still
had its gutters where the lifeblood, the working class, toiled
to erect glowing monuments to corporate greed. Underneath
them, the forgotten and homeless were left to rot in this dys-
topian paradise. *What happens if the demons that crawl forth
from the shadows cut deals with them and buy their souls for
power or money or liquor?* In a way, Mike was satisfied with this
thought. *At least the balance of power will shift. Money means
nothing to demons.*

Mike saw the bank's logo displayed in proud bold letters
high above. "I'm working for a different sort of power vacuum,
aren't I?" he pondered out loud. *People are more likely to bow
and pray to their neon god rather than wake up and realize the
truth of what happened these past days. This will all be some
upcoming movie, and the government will come in and cover
everything up.*

Mike found himself feeling cornered. He worried he might
be working for the very people he fought against for decades.

He resolved that he would stay true to himself and decided
that a bit of vandalism was in order. *It's not like the cops are
going to arrest me now. Besides, what good is super strength if
you can't indulge yourself a little?* Mike got to work shattering

marble, steel, and glass with his bare hands. The sound of his art echoed in the hollow streets with no one around to witness it.

He stood in the middle of a three-lane street and looked upon his work. "That's right! You are hollow inside! An empty shell devoid of life!" he shouted at the building. "There is nothing to you! You are nothing more than a lie; a false sense of hope you provide people! You are devoid of ethics. You do it for your own greed! Go to fucking hell and burn a thousand years in absolute suffering, you sociopathic asshole." He knew that breaking the bank would only cause more people problems and, even worse, that he was in danger of becoming the exact thing he hated. *Maybe you already are, chief. Look at yourself.*

Mike pulled a smoke out of his pocket, annoyed at the concrete dust that had mixed with some demon blood on his gloves. "Fuck this shit. I'm going home."

He wasn't sure where home was anymore, and rather than go back to his ransacked apartment, he found himself running back to the warehouse. *You know, I wonder if teleportation is possible. I'd like to never sit in traffic on the Hillside Strangler again.*

The main level of the warehouse was empty. The carnage from Mike's fight with Morris remained, beams torn, a dented truck, shattered barrels strewn about, along with the blood-stains from his first meal. Only now there was a handful of crotch rockets parked in the middle. Mike heard sounds from the sublevel. *Makes sense, away from the sun.* He trotted on down to find the entire crew crowded around a TV.

Lucy was as pale as ever, only now she was in a set of pajamas that were red silk and gold trimmed. They looked more expensive than Mike's entire wardrobe.

Akira was not kidding when she said she would try a cocoon. She was stuck to the corner of the couch with only her wide eyes blinking and a game controller in her hand, swaddled in a mix of blankets and silk threads. Her fingers were a blur as she input commands from her self-made insect home.

Doc had on fuzzy slippers with bunny ears and was in old-man flannel pajamas that smelled of pipe smoke. He was writing in a journal and, without paying attention, pressing buttons on another controller.

Mike was disappointed to see that Phoebe's choice of slumber wear was an oversized hoodie with cotton pants, mittens, and a purple hat with tassels. She lay stretched on a sofa they had brought down. Everyone else seemed to be down the hall, playing some other game.

"Where the hell did all this furniture come from? Last night this was a meat-packing warehouse. Now it's a crash pad?" Mike asked.

"Heeeey, the hero returns," said Phoebe. "Demon fight, in a furniture store, up in Old Town. Figured they weren't going to use the stuff anymore. None of us felt like going home either. Doc thinks it's safer if we all stay together in case one of us has a bad reaction."

"What the hell are they doing, then? Are they playing *Tekken*?" Mike stood on his toes to get a good look.

"Yeah, they've been going at it since they got back. I guess it's a thing now between the two of them. Akira has years of experience playing these. It's all she used to do. Now she's got some wicked-fast speed, though, so there's no point in anyone else playing her," she replied.

"So why is Doc playing her, then? Hey, Doc, you are . . ." Mike was about to say "moving like a turtle," but he realized that Doc was winning with extreme ease.

"Doc got what he always wanted, the ability to know what everyone else around him is feeling subconsciously, before they know it. He can even manipulate it. It makes for some fun matches actually. Akira has never lost this much in her entire life, but she's stuck to the couch and refuses to give up. No matter which character Doc picks, he's been trouncing her all night long." She stretched and brought a giant wool blanket over her head. "I wanted super speed. All I got was stupid prediction and some sort of *psychometry*, whatever the hell that's supposed to mean."

"It means any object you pick up, you will be able to use. Think about it. You can drive anything now," Doc said while finishing a combo.

"Buuuut I already coooould drive anything," she mewled.

Mike put his hand on his friend's shoulder. "Doc, man, fate of the world? What the hell's on the news? What's going on?"

"Right now you're expecting me to say, 'I already know what you're going to say,'" Doc said.

"Actually, no," Mike said.

"Right, because I already know what you are going to say. We've all upgraded to be proper vampires. No big fish like you, though." He finished writing with his left hand and closed his book, turning his attention to the screen. "Oh, and before you ask, I'm a psychic vampire. I feed off dreams and emotions. Yes, yours are delicious. Please stop watching bad porn, though."

"Um. 'Kay? Soooo . . . news?" Mike asked.

Lucy chimed in. "You really do not want to see the news."

"Yeah, I kinda do," Mike replied.

"I didn't know you were a big fan of pop stars getting divorced and drunks showing their tits," she said. "Wait. Never mind. That does seem like you."

"Ouch. That twists, Lucy. You left your knife in my back earlier. Now you gotta poke the wound?" Mike said. "Speaking of that. Lucy, you were a demon hunter. Now you've eaten demon hearts. How does that make you feel?" Mike fired a jab back.

"I ate a few," she replied. "And?"

"And what?"

"You're okay with that?"

"Did I turn into a demon?"

"Well . . . um, no, but—"

"Can I kill more demons now than I could before?"

"Uh . . . yes? But—"

"Do soldiers not use the best weapons at their disposal?"

"Okay. Yikes. I can't win against you," Mike said, holding up his hands while putting a smirk on his face. The room remained silent as Lucy stared at him.

"Remember that statement," she said.

Mike waited as the awkward silence hung in the air, broken at times by the sounds coming from the epic match of *Tekken* playing out in the background. "Seriously? Nothing? Just pop stars?" he finally said.

"Yeah, it's kinda fucked up, huh," came Phoebe's muffled voice from under her blanket. "You, however, are a hero and are viral all over the Internet. They keep trying to shut you down. They actually tried to cut the Internet feed, but hackers decided that wasn't going to do." She popped her blanket off and smiled at Mike. It sucked him in. "Man, they will remember you for centuries, the guy who turned Chicago into vampires and ghosts."

Mike dropped his bag. It made a clang on the concrete floor. "What?"

Doc performed a finishing move on Akira, who let out a curse that was muffled in the cocoon. "Turns out that you went viral, and rather than run when demons came, most of the people who encountered them did exactly what you said and fought back."

Mike let out a laugh. "That's fucking awesome."

Doc continued. "Some of them, after they got their own powers, started wearing armbands, organizing other people.

The armbands have green-and-black stripes from your coat, Mikey."

Lucy sighed. "A whole lot of untrained people are going to die."

Doc shrugged and looked back to Mike. "Either way, whatever the Unification wanted to hide is unhidable here. This is it, Mike. The apocalypse. A revolution is spreading. You gave it a voice. Hope you're ready for a big fight." He took a moment to size Mike up and down, his gaze leveled and serious.

"Fight?" Mike was even paler than usual, but in his eyes there was a tiny spark, a flame that was beginning to kindle.

"Phoebe picked up prediction, remember? She can guess a coin flip right fifty percent of the time. Eh, a bunch of religious prophetic claptrap I know you won't care about," Doc said.

"Shut up," Phoebe chimed in. "Short story is war is coming. Fighting and death will surround you, and you'll make a choice to join a heretic or not. Don't feel too special, though, cupcake. You aren't the second coming of Christ. I guess if this . . . all of this . . . isn't stopped, the death of dreams and the birth of nightmares will be made into flesh in seven years and darkness will rule for a thousand more while the worthy wander lost in a forest no longer ignorant of their natures."

Doc Daneka laughed. A tiny set of fangs protruded. When he smiled like a predator, Mike felt like he was being eaten by Doc's look alone.

"Then we better rise to the occasion," Mike said. "I've always wanted a revolution. We have to come up with some survival plans. I'm pretty sure world trade will come to a grinding halt soon. At least localized labor will have a place." He vaulted over the couch and plopped in between Doc and Akira. "First, though, give me that controller. I love this game, and Akira isn't the only one with speed."

As the sun, grayer than the day before, rose on the horizon in Chicago, Mike put down his third controller, broken in half by his frustration. Akira had devastated him twenty-one matches in a row. The weight of the change and the slumber that comes with the rise of the morning star claimed them. The Sons and Daughters slept.

# CHAPTER 26

Well-laid plans always have problems the moment combat starts. Mr. Bollard reminded himself of this as he stood outside the medical clinic in Minneapolis. He had been leading society containment squads for a few days now. His driver, a council-assigned butler, was there to assist him and to ensure the contingency plans were carried out according to the schedule. He would have preferred another bound demon rather than an assigned grunt from the council.

*Wheels within wheels, Bollard.*

The sounds of gunfire echoed in the night from the clinic, reminding Mr. Bollard that other activities should be holding his attention right now.

Everything had been going according to plan for some time. Glory-seeking dignitaries would move into an area primed for a dive, usually noticed by demons or ghosts bounding out of purgatory, looking for their escape. Society crews would move in to reinforce and contain the area and sometimes assist with diving in as well. It was a rather bloody affair on all sides.

His plan required sacrifice, but he was sure that his employers would understand.

*The ends do indeed justify the means.*

"Oh, I do believe we will do a fantastic job by sticking to our specialty." Mr. Bollard, secretly a rakshasa himself, knew more about the various layers of hell and its inner workings than all but the most experienced warlocks.

At each location, Mr. Bollard would enter the building alone, take on his true form, and sacrifice a handful of the building's inhabitants in a ritual to summon up another demon. Once one demon had entered the world, others in that particular area of hell would rush to that exit.

This would prevent them from spawning in random uncontrolled areas of the city. Helldiver teams would move in and launch their exploration in pursuit of Lazarus, while he spied on the paths they took through the labyrinth, looking for what he needed. He would then send in the society's Special Forces units to eliminate everyone and everything on the inside. A nice, contained, and clean operation. Each section of purgatory within the Twin Cities, block by block, was explored and mapped by this method.

*Well, each section that I am responsible for anyway.*

So far, this method had pleased Lady Dumont and allowed Mr. Bollard enough free time to engage in some personal indulgences and side business. Of course if it was discovered he was rakshasa himself, it might cause some difficulties. After all, a demon summoning forth other demons was the entire secret to his success. Something that would land him in Vryce's experimentation chambers with his heart likely consumed to grant some unworthy human magical powers.

JJ had already tried to convince Bollard that Delilah Dumont was the only human in this city with whom he should be willing to make a pact, granting her some of his blood in exchange for future services. For that to happen, however, Vryce would have to die, for the warlock would never allow Delilah to make a pact with him out of jealousy. Perhaps Vryce would get lost in hell himself or eaten alive by an arch demon. Mr. Bollard struggled with the thought. He loved and hated the idea. Stealing her from Vryce would satiate a vice of his, but his blood carried too much power. Deus was not to be trifled with, as evidenced by his current observations.

Mr. Bollard didn't expect the Special Forces units of the society to be as effective in combating the forces of hell and returning back from the pits. Dignitary helldivers were powerful, experienced, and well prepared. They would lead a squad in, and in most cases, it was only the squad that came out with information of the landscape below, lost treasures, and a few casualties.

*No wonder Delilah approves of our methods. We are perfect cover for them to eliminate competition in this race as well. A nice symbiotic relationship. Still, it's not like the society is always successful. More than a few outsiders have come back with great acclaim and mapped out significant paths. This portal, however . . . I had a good feeling about this location.*

Pulling on the leather gloves to ensure a snug fit and taking a deep breath, Mr. Bollard held it, counting for four seconds before exhaling. A plume of warm air danced in the night sky lit by the waning moon. They were ready.

"Pull up the video feed from the unit commander. I wish to see the results," Mr. Bollard said to his driver.

Mr. Bollard had chosen this medical clinic for a specific reason. Inside housed research into the uses of demon blood and children who had undergone a particular ritual from a warlock before birth. The purpose of such a ritual was to ensure their future as sorcerers. It had been done a few times throughout history with terrifying effectiveness. The warlock had sped up the process that would normally take seven generations of parents who each had a seventh son.

*Well, it's not that much of a mystery. Delilah Dumont showed him the beauty of embryo manipulation and modern-day science, allowing him to achieve those exact results.*

The truth of this medical clinic was technically above Mr. Bollard's clearance level. He was only here because the Captain uncovered it.

It was a perfect location for an expedition. The suffering, shadows, secrecy, and spellcraft surrounding the facility meant Bollard could dive deeper and longer once he removed everyone and everything out of the way. So he summoned a plague demon inside after the sacrifice of the personnel. He tipped off some divers to pave the way. He even mobilized the Special Forces unit, with little information about what they would be facing. They were expecting barghests and carrion eaters again.

Then the bastard showed up with his own crew.

Gabriel D'Angelo and his companions had not asked any questions before entering the building minutes ago. He had been freed to assist the society with their operations. He brought with him Captain Mitch Slade, leader of the first precinct and a Masonic apprentice to Master Vryce. He also brought Cael McManus, a druid sorcerer from the Unification branch in Greenland, another of his apprentices. The three of them together might as well have been the closest sorcerers to Warlock Vryce out of anyone here. In addition, a small crew of the vampiric army of the society led by Alexander Lex DuPris provided backup.

The driver had finished pulling up the video feed from Mr. Bollard's unit commander. "Bloody hell," he said, as the shaky camera offered a limited picture of what was happening inside.

"Bloody hell is right," Mr. Bollard replied. He leaned into the car window to get a better view. If he had eyebrows, they would reveal a look of surprise. "This is not according to plan."

"Which plan, sir?" the driver asked.

"Be first," JJ said, quickly taking control of the body.

The screen revealed Gabriel surrounded by a ring of red-and-blue flame. There were several other rings in the distance with soldiers inside them. Insects from the plague demon were repelled and banished back by the flames. The walls of purgatory pulsed with a sickly neon-green light, but here, a vortex led straight down.

*JJ, I thought you said he could not cast spells of high sorcery?*

"I didn't think he could," he replied, right as he looked at the driver.

"They seem to be most effective, sir. Considering only hellhounds were expected, the unit was not equipped to handle a plague demon. Judging from what we can see, perhaps even more than one. Do you think these are agents of Legion, the many demons of one name? According to our information, they should only be active within the region of the Black Sea. For them to be here, they would have to be directly summoned." He pointed with excitement. "Look! See there. On the head of the one behind the fires, the head of swine and the mark of the beast."

"You did not answer my question. Gabriel is moving objects with telekinesis, and that is an earth elemental guarding him. The others are acting according to their operational methods. Lex has transformed into the war form of dracul, Slade wields his flaming swords, and Cael is commanding summoned vines." JJ pointed and gestured to each instance as they came on camera. He radioed the commander and told him to get him a visual of Gabriel as he watched the soldiers unload round after round into the endless legion coming from the pit.

The driver interrupted. "Gabriel does not possess any of these abilities. According to Unification files, he is an unblooded witch. Born to a family who by birthright can command the blood by will. Perhaps we underestimated their lot? There is a significant amount of demon blood within that room. Or perhaps Warlock Vryce is possessing him," he said.

"Perhaps it is Master Vryce. I see no symptoms or signs of possession, though," JJ replied while peering at the screen.

*Of course. You could just be wrong about him. These are special children, though. Did we stumble onto a tool we can use later as a lure?* Mr. Bollard looked back at the clinic. Flashes of light reflected off the black windows, creating a shadow puppet show. *If Vryce has a weakness for this, we can exploit it. He'll keep all other divers away from here.* His lips curled in a smile with pointed teeth starting to grow as he gazed into the building. He reached into his coat and clicked the safety off his pistol. It had been loaded with a special ammunition blessed by papal authority.

"No! It's not him. I can confirm that Warlock Vryce is meeting as we speak with Alexandria of Ur and other dignitaries in the Libraries of Deus." The driver clicked his phone shut. "We are observing Gabriel and Legion. Look! Gabriel just sliced the head off the Unification diver himself! Sir, inform the death lords of this backstab. The society is killing off their agents."

*Shit. Delilah and the society aren't here saving Lazarus at all. I'm being used as a patsy. Or tested. How do I play this out?* As Mr. Bollard and JJ conversed with each other internally, Bollard clicked the safety on his pistol and halted his shape change.

An explosion blasted the windows out, creating a shower of blackened glass. As cold air rushed in, the flames were given strength by fresh air and blazed even hotter. Mr. Bollard could feel the waves of heat wash over him. He closed his eyes to embrace it.

"Tell me what's happening in there," JJ said with his eyes closed.

"Visual is lost, sir. Smoke has blinded everything." The Englishman tossed the tablet into the vehicle. "Would you care for a spot of brandy, sir?"

"Perhaps. What year?" he paused. "Are they dead?"

*Would that not be a tip of luck in our favor?*

"Brandy de Jerez Solera Gran Reserva, sir. I'm sure you will find it to your liking." The driver produced a flask from his suit and passed it over. "It is highly unlikely they are dead. Although judging from the popping of overheated insects, I would wager that the agents of Legion are."

"Since we have arrived here in the city, you've neglected to share that you are walking around with decades-old brandy?" Mr. Bollard opened the flask and smelled it. JJ felt pleased at the sting in his nostrils and took a swig. The sky was lit up by fleeing burning scarabs and beetles.

"One must always be prepared to carouse if you are going to remain unnoticed," he said.

The words hung in Bollard's mind longer than normal. It was interesting advice and something they could put into motion. After this scenario, they would need to engage in some carousing to cover his tracks and motives. *You got greedy, Mr. Bollard. Now it's my turn to fix your mistakes. You were too hasty trying to be first. I think we can do better.*

The doors to the clinic spewed smoke as flames ravaged the inside. First the Special Forces unit made their way out, escorting a handful of ash-covered children with rags over their faces, followed by Alexander Lex DuPris, no longer in his war form, his clothes shredded. He picked an insect from his ragged hair and ate it, looking rather satisfied with himself.

Everyone else made their way out of the building as quickly as they could: some bothered by the smoke; some strolling out as if it was air they breathed daily.

Gabriel was the last to exit. He carried an eight-year-old boy who was still in hospital robes. Gabriel wrapped the kid in his singed and blackened fleece. He even took a moment to lick his thumb and give the child a smile as he cleaned off the kid's face.

Gabriel ran back into the building and came out with a wounded doctor. JJ's heart skipped. She was the one Bollard pinned to the floor inside a summoning circle. Gabriel shouted out to Slade. "Get her to the ambulance now!" Then he ran back inside a third time. Fire had more than engulfed the building. The flames were so high they seemed to claw at the belly of low-hanging clouds. *We need to kill that doctor. She can spoil our secret.* JJ ran to offer assistance to Slade.

"Go help others. I have her," JJ said. Slade, his mutton-chops burned off on the left side of his face, nodded and ran to a soldier who was screaming as scarabs were still burrowing beneath his skin.

The doctor's eyes widened when she realized whose care she was in. Before she could scream, Mr. Bollard pinched her nose and covered her mouth with his leather gloves. "Shhhh, you don't want to live in this new world anyway. Go to heaven, dear," JJ whispered in her ear. Mr. Bollard ensured that nobody else was looking. Death by suffocation was common in fires.

Gabriel came out minutes later. He carried a small girl wrapped up in a blanket. His blue eyes had teared up from the sting of smoke, and the rubber on his gym shoes had all but melted off.

He dropped to a knee, not from exhaustion, JJ realized, but from the mental stress. A cavalry sabre was strapped to Gabriel's back, the gem in the hilt pulsing with green light.

As if Gabriel could feel Mr. Bollard staring at him, he looked over at JJ and the dead doctor. Gabriel stood and began walking with purpose in his direction. "Slade." He pointed at Bollard.

Mr. Bollard looked for his nearest escape in case things went wrong. *We can always make a run and dive into that rift. Think we can make it?*

"Yo, what up, man?" replied Slade, who shook off a leather coat as he trotted alongside Gabriel.

Gabriel looked back to the building and to the doctor. She wasn't moving. He leaned down and felt her pulse and confirmed what Mr. Bollard already knew. Slade and Gabriel gave each other a look that made Bollard's hands clammy and cold despite the flames behind them. "Slade. Take care of these kids. Get 'em home. Here." Gabriel handed over a wad of cash. "Pizza, ice cream, movies. Whatever they want. I'll check on them later. I need to handle this first. Got it?"

Mr. Bollard began to creep to the side, ensuring a clear path into the building if needed. Slade offered Gabriel a smile and a solid handshake. "Pleasure working with you. We got this. Do your thing."

The moment Slade turned around and began herding the patients, Gabriel reached out and grabbed Mr. Bollard's tie, pulling him up so only his toes touched the ground.

"You little fuck. What do you think you're doing? Pay attention to your job, you little shit. Helping a dive squad here? This area is off-limits! Everyone knows that." Gabriel shook JJ as he spoke.

"A bit rash, don't you think? Containment was needed here. Carrion eaters began to leak out first. I only took advantage of the situation, turned it into a diving mission. Besides, it leads nowhere. You saw for yourself. Just an endless vortex down. You will take your hands off me. I don't take orders from you," JJ said.

"You work as a petty squad commander in the society, underneath Delilah, who is underneath Primus Vryce. We both serve the same person." Gabriel released JJ and added an extra push to make a point.

JJ brushed himself off and regained his balance. "Yeah, the master, right." JJ wanted to add an insult.

*Gabriel has a hot temper. Don't provoke him directly. Easy to lure. Switch his focus off us onto something else*, Mr. Bollard said from within.

"You come from noble lineage, Gabriel. Have you even thought about why this site was off-limits?" JJ asked.

Gabriel's jaw was clenched so tightly veins protruded from his neck. JJ felt Gabriel's hand quivering with anger around his tie. "Because that doctor who died was the expert in treating blood addiction," he said.

"The master cherry-picks you out of a pool of dozens. Clearly, he thinks you're *special*." JJ reached behind Gabriel and tapped the hilt of the sword. "Maybe you should be investigating your selection process and question your boss on why that kid you pulled from the fire looks just like you." JJ smiled and pushed Gabriel back with a fraction of Mr. Bollard's strength.

Gabriel looked back at the kids in the distance, and it was all the distraction they needed to put steps between them. Mr. Bollard could feel the questions and waves of doubt rising in Gabriel even though Gabriel only wore a mask of rage. *Just let me have this feeling, JJ. I'll let you play with your toy later.* "Fine," JJ said to himself, even though Gabriel was standing only paces away. "Tell you what, I'll eat this error and do you a favor, Gabriel. I'll quarantine this site and let the other dignitaries know it's too dangerous. After all, they didn't return, right?" JJ laid the bait.

Gabriel looked like he wanted to go back into the burning building for a moment before shaking his head and storming off to his own car. "You're right. Lock it down. Thanks." He slammed the door so hard that the window cracked. A few of the soldiers looked at each other in awkward silence.

*This may be the best threshold for our dive yet. Can we get in long enough before the society stabs us in the back? They are clearly doing more than edging out the competition. What's our play?*

"We have time," JJ replied.

"Wrap it up, boys! That's enough containment tonight. Clean up and move out for the night," JJ said to the remaining troops as he walked back to the car, grabbing the flask from the driver.

"Time for your pleasure. Delilah will be our move and way in. Tell Heaven's Wrath that we are close," JJ said before taking a swig, letting the booze take the edge off the cold night.

# CHAPTER 27

Every warlock mastered his own personal magic. Even bound in the earth, it was a simple matter for Vryce to detach his mind from his body. No other warlock in existence was a master of possession to the degree that he was.

With that thought, his mind was floating among houses that each looked as bland and carbon copy as the next. He saw a nighttime runner trying to maintain his shape through exercise before whatever boring activity he would resume to pass his meaningless life. Vryce flowed into him, claiming the body for his own.

Ever since he had reclaimed the fifth shard of his soul, he no longer needed his iron nails. Still, Vryce wished he had some with him. Unless he nailed his shadow to the body, possession was all he was capable of. Centuries of occult knowledge and spells were still denied to him. *For now anyway.* He began his search through the London town, pausing outside each house to feel if he was close.

Vryce paused outside one house. The sound of a viola came from within. *Early morning practice?* The song "Ode to

Joy" was being played with such perfection that his hand was brought to the jogger's face to move a tear. *It's a shame that my soul resides here. This person is more useful alive than dead.* The string instrument reminded him of the only woman he had loved in the centuries before he was taught the reality of time. Now, most humans looked like pet goldfish to him. He could only watch them grow old and die so many times before such a perception set in. Music remained timeless to him.

He jogged up to the front door and waited for the song to finish before knocking. An older gentleman opened the door. Gray hair lined his temples, and he was dressed in his finest suit. The viola was still in his hand, and the moment he saw the jogger, his jaw stiffened up and his eyes showed acceptance.

"So you've come at last," he said.

Vryce had no reason to pretend. They could each feel one another on a different plane with tingles that ran down their spines. "I have. You have recovered something in your expeditions."

"I suppose I do not have much choice in the matter." The gentleman stepped back from the door and walked into his house.

Vryce stood and looked at the doorframe. "It would be polite of you to formally invite me in."

"You may come in," he said with a southern American accent. "Will you allow me the honor of a final song before you end me?"

Vryce walked into the house, a cold breeze following him. The small house was filled with historic memorabilia. A set of bills from the 1800s were framed on the walls, a suit of armor was stationed upright in the foyer as a coat hook, and a pistol from World War I sat as a centerpiece on the table. "You aren't from London," Vryce said as he looked at the framed pictures.

The gentleman was in all of them, and his age remained the same in each.

"The name is Jonas Mueller. I am a keeper of memory, just another sorcerer trying to find his place in the Unification. I paid for rights to dive here, and once I found that fragment, it spoke of its life and told me what it was. Knowing your legend, I felt it was only a matter of time before you arrived," he said.

"I see," Vryce replied. "I hope you are satisfied."

"There are many who do not tolerate the existence of your kind. Yet no one here will listen with the ritual going awry as it has." He sat down and picked up the viola once more.

"Hopefully you are not attached to what you've discovered."

"Oh, I'm going to give it to you. I request a book from your libraries. The scrolls of the Dead Sea. I will add it to my collection in exchange for what is yours. Surely the arts of scholarly exchange are something you would uphold while within my home?" He began to play.

Vryce contemplated his options as he listened to the music. It was hypnotizing and calming at the same time. It drew him in. "Very well. I will see to it you are granted access to the libraries. All of them. Rather than one set of scrolls. You will be allowed to study to your heart's content."

"Excellent. I cannot wait to attend the Libraries of Deus," Jonas said. He handed over the viola.

Vryce took the instrument and inspected it. On the inside were markings and sigils made in angel blood. He offered Jonas his hand to shake.

"Your soul sings beautifully, Mr. Vryce. You should remember that there are plenty of humans in this world worth saving." He shook Vryce's hand. He winced at the coldness that shot through him.

"It has been a pleasure. I will see you soon," Vryce said as he left the home in a hurry.

The jogger ran to the mound where Vryce was buried. Vryce contemplated his options regarding Jonas and came to the only true conclusion. *Delilah always chided me when I would let people survive. I am at a fraction of my power, either as a warlock or a lich. I can't take the chance that he will spread word of what I'm doing.*

As Vryce released the possession, the hapless jogger regained his senses. He felt the cold in his fingers from being outside, and he looked around with a panic on his face, wondering what happened. His breath was so cold that it formed ice. The mortal looked around in confusion when the hand grabbed his face.

Vryce was quick with his dagger, slicing the man's throat open. Warm life oozed from him, and the warlock drank his fill for the night. He drank not just of the blood, but of the very essence of the man. The salty, coppery taste of the blood mixed with the vibrant, sweet taste of the soul. The withered husk hit the ground, its clothes now baggy and loose.

Vryce pulled out his mask and fastened it securely. He gestured to the sky, and the clouds began to swirl overhead, lightning dancing between their energy. *Don't worry, Jonas. You'll see my libraries, just not in the way you expected.* He picked up the viola case and smiled as readied his pistol before beginning his descent into town.

Streetlights flickered and faded away as the warlock moved down the street, shadows on his heels. With each light snuffed out, he gestured and sealed the doors of the houses with his magic. *No interruptions tonight. I will not risk having this town turn against me like the last.*

The warlock came to a stop in front of Jonas's house, the moon's pale light trying desperately to stay alive through the growing storm clouds. Vryce cast a spell to open the front door and stepped into the foyer. Gunfire shattered the framed pictures on the wall as bullets ripped through the drywall. Jonas was out of sight from Vryce on the other side.

"Tsk, tsk, Jonas. Is that any way to greet your guest?"

"We made a deal, oath breaker!" Jonas said, hiding behind a tipped-over table.

"You should have left already." Vryce took a peek around the corner, a bullet ricocheted across his mask, leaving yet another crack.

"If I kill your real body, you die, remember? Go on, poke that mug of yours out again and let's see how immortal you really are. You aren't a true undead in that current state."

"How very astute. You must feel rather confident, then. If I wanted you dead, Jonas, I would have fried your house with my lightning by now. I am here to escort you alive. Look out your window at the sky." Vryce gestured around the corner with his gun at the window. He could hear a shuffle from the room.

"Jesus," Jonas whispered.

A vortex of storm clouds raged and collided with each other, building themselves up.

"He won't help you. His numbers have been on the decline, so the Unification stopped marketing him a while back. He's currently polling at thirty-two percent of the world professing Christianity." Vryce waved his pistol in a circular motion and whistled to get Jonas's attention back on him, rather than the storm outside.

"All right. Drop the pistol. Slide it over. Then come out," Jonas said.

Vryce slid the pistol over and showed a hand, then another, as he stepped out from behind the corner. He was older now, a teenager, each shard collected restoring him to his prime.

"Really? I'm commanding the weather outside, and the pistol is your first concern?"

Jonas peeked from behind the table. His true form more visible, reptilian skin and rows of fanged teeth, a hideous deformity that made him look like he'd been fed bottom-barrel blood. He held a rifle leveled at the warlock's head, hands steady, showing no signs of anxiety. "The weather is the only thing you can control right now. So yes." He looked straight at Vryce.

*Oh, you poor, ignorant fool.* Vryce looked at him with his greenish-gold eyes from behind the cracked mask. "Dance for me." As if on cue, Jonas began to move his feet and dance. Vryce gestured and manipulated him like a puppet.

"H-how?"

"That is for me to know, and you to never find out." With a wild gesture, Vryce slammed Jonas into a wall, pinning him there telekinetically. As he moved his hand upward, Jonas struggled and was heaved to the ceiling. The warlock never took his gaze off him. "If you really know me, you would have learned that I never enter a fight I haven't already won. Now let me explain to you what is going to happen. I'm going to rip out your soul, feast on your mind, and rewrite it to my own suiting. Then I'm going to ensure that you serve in my armies for a period of seven years. After that, I will give you the choice to willingly fight or be ripped apart and stitched into one of my gargoyles. Do you understand me?" There was no chance for him to respond before the warlock went to work stealing the soul.

Vryce took the time to peruse the rest of Jonas's collections, grabbing a few books to add to his libraries. He needed the time to calm down. *That had been closer than Jonas will ever know.* If that bullet had penetrated the mask, everything would have been over. He was still not strong enough to face the Unification directly. *Others will have to fight my war for me until I am ready.* A two-thousand-year-old vampire like Alexandria of Ur could easily end his existence.

Pulling the curved dagger from his coat, the warlock again sliced his thumb. The world around him spun.

# CHAPTER 28

*Need to do carousing in order to remain unnoticed.* JJ rather liked this thought, so he invited Delilah out to dinner. *Dinner might not be the correct term.* It was, after all, nearly three thirty in the morning. That time of night, near the witching hour when the universe becomes silent and angels rest.

*Rally time for us demons.*

JJ took a drink. The smoky taste of old bourbon cleared his throat. He was driven through the city to a small diner. It was quaint, with the neon sign missing a single letter. The parking lot was full of police and fire department vehicles, a place for them to relax after a night of keeping secrets. JJ left his driver in the car with instructions to wait for him and walked inside to greet the smell of fried eggs.

For a diner that had a line of people waiting to be seated, it couldn't have been more quiet. The clink of forks against ceramic plates and the sound of coffee cups being placed carefully on their saucers was all that could be heard. The faces of the customers were paler than they should be, not because they were undead, but because their world was shattering.

RICK HEINZ

They all knew it as first responders. They had seen things they could not explain or even dare to talk about.

The football game or the pop star who flashed skin were no longer relevant conversations for them, even casually. *They only have a few more days of this. Then their troubles will be washed away.* JJ walked past them, removing his leather gloves and looking for Delilah. She sat in the middle of the room at a small table. Her stick-straight blonde hair was pulled behind her. A few strands dangled in front of her face as she struggled to stay awake. A neatly stacked pyramid of coffee creamers grew taller as she added another row.

"Have I kept you waiting long?" JJ said as he pulled out his chair.

"Quite. You are four minutes and twenty-eight seconds late." She flashed a polite smile. JJ noticed the darkening under her eyes.

"Boss is keeping you up all hours again? How is work?"

"About as expected. You should have the coffee. I've had this diner, and seven others like it, import the finest South American and African coffees available. You wouldn't know it from its drab demeanor, but there's no better late-night diner in North America. They have almost single-handedly propped up the commodities market with their bulk purchases." She took a drink herself, her shoulders relaxing.

"Always prepared. I'm envious. My evening did not go as expected. Your new employee, Gabriel, might go poking around in restricted areas for secrets." JJ poured himself a cup. "Can you keep a leash on him? I don't want him showing up where I work." Mr. Bollard thought about adding brandy to it.

"Like all new employees, they always have such a zeal to them. It usually ends up with them getting killed," she said. "I have spent my evening entertaining our *friends* with the most obscure dietary habits and demands. I think some of them are of the worst kind on earth. They ignore the toll their agendas take on these men and women." She gestured out, changing the subject. "This will be another night where I pay for all of their bills, to at least give them something to go home to. They are, after all, doing a much finer job than those in Greenland."

"You have contacts with that branch?" JJ asked.

*Of course she does, you idiot.*

JJ chuckled and continued. "Have you had any contact with the other sites? I imagine none of them are faring any better." He pushed aside his menu. "Has anyone gotten close to finding Lazarus's prison? You've charged a high price for people to dive here in this city. Think any other site has a chance to beat us?"

"Don't play coy, Bollard. It doesn't suit you. The council has their specialists. What I find interesting is how they plan to put the genie back into the bottle. The McCarthy plan of media control may work, but not with what happened in Chicago. It seems the Unification's media branch dropped the ball on the viral type." She downed her coffee and poured another steaming cup. "I imagine entire branches of, well, you know, are in the process of being terminated for their estimates."

"Oh, that reminds me, speaking of terminations. I had to terminate a dignitary a few hours ago. He was inside one of the restricted areas. I cleaned the area, but I need you to cover my tracks with his cohorts. I'm not sure which dignitary he's tied to," JJ lied, hoping Gabriel and Delilah would never mention the clinic to each other.

She flipped open her tablet case and made a note. "Thank you. I'll have my people take care of that in the morning." She looked at him with her green eyes and bit her lip. "Are you actually hungry? I have until just after dawn before I'm back on."

JJ felt himself blush.

*This is tedious. Fine. Have your pleasure.*

JJ could not contain his ear-to-ear smile as he leaned in. "I did say that it should be you who ran this place, and I wager you already do by now. Let's celebrate. Your place?" He winked.

"Let's do yours. There is always business one foot away from my door, and I can't relax there anymore," she said, already standing up and grabbing her coat.

"After you," JJ said.

*Careful. She only wants to see our place.*

One of the officers in a nearby booth overhead that last exchange and raised his cup in salute. JJ pushed Mr. Bollard down deeper into his subconscious.

*Humans. Your instincts are what make you fun to play with.*

The moment they were in the car, they couldn't keep their hands off each other. Five years of stress and frustration gave way to a moment of earthly indulgence. Her lilac perfume was intoxicating, so much so that even Mr. Bollard couldn't lift a protest.

While Delilah and JJ were enraptured with each other, the driver made sure to take less traveled roads and made nary a sound or seemed to even notice. *A proper professional.* They came up the road leading into JJ's estate. He pulled himself off her and maintained deep eye contact as he held her hand, helping her out.

Cherry-red Christmas lights reflected off the untouched snow, giving the estate grounds a magical glow. Immense statues dotted the yard, each a carving of an ancient god in the old Greek pantheon, the twelve Olympians with Athena standing at the center of the round driveway. The driver handled their belongings, deftly hiding Delilah's tablet from any spying eyes and giving a hand signal to Delilah.

"Christmas lights?" Delilah asked.

"It's a neighborhood thing. What else are rich bachelors supposed to do with mountains of money, toss extravagant parties while they plan with covert societies the rebirth of the world?" He smiled and opened the large set of double doors into his palace. She only shook her head at the absurdity of the holiday and walked inside.

Despite the size and external opulence of the estate, only a small portion was ever used. Most of the manse was eternally dark and empty. JJ took Delilah's coat himself and hung it up in a nearby closet.

*Something is off.*

"It's my turn," JJ replied. He chided Bollard for forcing him to speak. Their cohabitation was based on each of them experiencing equal amounts of pleasure. Mr. Bollard thrived on doubt and envy in humans; JJ craved physical sensation. When it came to murder, they were on the same page. It was getting tiresome with so few days left.

"By all means," Delilah replied. "I'm a bit surprised that you don't have help here, or even security?" She smiled as she took off her shoes. "You do know what it is we do for a living, right?"

JJ leaned in close for a kiss. "You do know my reputation, right? Even your boss respects hospitality. After all, we are a civilized lot." He took her by the hand and led her further into the mansion by the kitchen. "I have something for you. Something rare."

The kitchen was large enough to be a condo in its own right. Intricately carved oak cabinets lined every wall. Racks of knives hung from multiple preparation counters, each with their own stainless-steel sink. There was not a single stain or object out of place.

Delilah placed her hands on a marble countertop and admired the variety of cutlery that decorated his kitchen. JJ went to one of his many fridges and started producing ingredients that would need to be cooked. Green, red, and purple vegetables, fresh from a Mediterranean deli, overflowed in his arms as he turned around. JJ began to move through the kitchen with the grace of a predatory cat as he flipped a switch to play music.

"I have always wanted to show you my craft, Delilah." He smiled.

"Delilah, who's that?" said a raspy voice from the hallway behind JJ. "Don't tell me ya brought a birdie home?" said Frank as he walked out, an open bottle of blood in his hands. "Nice to meet ya, lass," he said as he gestured with the bottle and took a swig before turning to JJ. "So the dame has to go. We got work. Pay the girl and ditch her. How many times I gotta tell ya to not bring pleasure home?"

Delilah didn't hesitate and grabbed a knife from the rack above her. Throwing it with expert skill, she landed it between the eyes of the Irishman. She ran for the door.

*Enough of your game*, Mr. Bollard growled, taking over instantly. His eyes changed to resemble a tiger's. He leaped over the counter as white fur started to grow while his muscles and bones cracked.

Delilah had almost made it to the door before Mr. Bollard, in his full form of half man, half tiger pounced through the hallway. His steel claws left marks in the floor as he dived onto Delilah. She rolled with him and used his strength and size against him, sending him into the door with a crash. "You are good, for a human," Mr. Bollard growled as he recovered on all fours while Delilah had already vanished into the darker part of the mansion.

"Usually they scream now," Bollard taunted. The lack of light didn't bother him as he pursued her into an unfurnished corridor. A shadow nearby provided Mr. Bollard with the portal he needed as he ran into it. It felt like diving into a pool of ice water.

Delilah ran to a window at the end of the hall, attempting to dive through. Mr. Bollard was following her through the shadows as if he were swimming. He waited in his icy void until her feet left the ground before he pounced.

Mr. Bollard heaved himself out of the shadow, grabbing her face with claws that enveloped her head. The momentum slammed her into the ground, and he felt her body twitch in his hand.

*I can feel her breath. She lives.*

Mr. Bollard dragged his prey while ducking under a chandelier. His feet left pools of pitch-blackness behind him.

Frank had pulled the knife out of his head and joined them. "Ya know money usually works. You don't have to kill the lass. It's not like your birdie knows me," he said.

Mr. Bollard growled back, his mouth filled with rows of pointed teeth. "This is Delilah Dumont, right hand to the warlock Vryce. Not only is she the most competent person in this city, she is also in the business of knowing exactly who everyone is." Bollard dropped her limp body. "You have just single-handedly tipped my hand with your invasion. Why are you here? Speak quickly." Bollard towered over the zombie. His steel claws reflected some of the light, creating shadows where there should be none.

"Easy there, tiger. O'Neil sent me up here to pull you out. We need your intel so we can turn this thing off. Hey, he's got the details. I'm just the messenger." He gestured to the claws. "You can put those back, tough guy. I had to break into your place with all those Deus boys around. I figured it would be best to go to ground here."

"You've fallen to a mere errand boy? You were never the sharpest tool in the shed. It is indeed best for you to go to ground here. I'm done working with rejects." Bollard yanked Frank's head from his body. The skinless face showed no emotion as the light left his eyes in the last seconds of his unlife. "Consider this a favor to your dignity."

Mr. Bollard began to shift his form to normal size as the smell of rotting flesh started to set in.

*What . . . you . . . just . . . killed him with my hand?* JJ forced himself back in control, driving Mr. Bollard down and shape-shifting to human. "Bollard, you fool. You've fucked me," JJ said.

JJ sat on the stairs and pulled out his set of leather gloves as he allowed himself a moment to think. He only had a few hours before the sun rose. "O'Neil will have to accept his son's death. I can explain that he was killed by someone else."

Delilah was another matter. She was too good at her job, but she let her guard down and left her security detail. JJ had hoped it would never come to this.

*Your kind never does. It is our path, never forget that, JJ. I refuse to allow the gates to be closed before I succeed in finding Lazarus. I want my freedom, and your boss's bitch bound me to you. My arrangement is with Lord of Heaven's Wrath. Not anyone else. If you want me gone, let me operate freely.*

"You're right. The society is betraying everyone anyway. At this point our best option is to find out what is really going on, from the person with all the answers," JJ whispered.

*The warlock will find out soon enough.*

Shadows moved along JJ's face as his eyes began to dull in color and he became more inhuman. "Removing her from the equation, we can get closer to our target, and perhaps find his vulnerability. He relies on her." JJ knew he was resolute in his next course of action.

The shadows poured into JJ, pulling him deep inside himself. He did not struggle as he surrendered to the power of Mr. Bollard. *This is the only way the world is saved.*

Mr. Bollard sent a text to his driver, requesting an emergency pickup. With Frankie dead, he would need someone else to assist him, and the Unification agent could be trusted to follow his orders. Mr. Bollard wrapped Delilah up in a bearskin blanket, taking a moment to move the hair back from her bloodied face.

*You were the only one here worth saving.*

Bollard struggled with the emotion welling up inside him. A knock on the door snapped the snarl off his face and reminded him that time was running out.

# CHAPTER 29

Mr. Bollard knew that the medical clinic from earlier was closed and under quarantine. So close to the bleed, this was the best place to hide Delilah. It was physically restricted, and he hoped the bleed would disrupt any magical means to find her as well. It would buy him the time he needed. The fires had been put out long ago, yet small wisps of smoke from the charcoal-covered walls struggled for life not unlike the skinny, bloody girl on the floor chained to a water main. He waited for her to wake up as the sun was rising. The driver waited in the shadows. As her eyes began to flutter open, Mr. Bollard opened his tool kit and removed a heretic's fork, a medieval torture instrument that consisted of bipronged forks with a leather strap. He placed it on the table before producing a set of silver nail clippers from the kit.

"My dear Delilah. Welcome back to life. I apologize for the manner and situation we find ourselves in now. No doubt you are aware that this is not according to either of our schedules," he said.

She spit out a fleck of blood on the floor and rattled her bindings to test them. "O'Neil's group. Reject assassins and second-rate helldivers. I had pegged you for a higher calling than a thug."

"Oh, I have my higher calling. Vryce is a dangerous creature, one who has been issuing orders against the new world order. There is no place for monsters such as him, or his kind. I realize now that the society has no intention of unlocking Lazarus's prison. JJ had hoped to place you upon the throne when we succeeded, but instead you will serve as the instrument I utilize to bring about this society's demise." Bollard perched in front of her. "Let us not waste time. I know you will not tell me anything willingly, but you will by the end of this session." He looked at her and studied her features while cocking his head. "First, we are going to make sure that you always see what is about to come."

Mr. Bollard kneeled, straddled her legs, and grabbed her face, letting his demonic strength hold her head still like a vice as she thrashed her legs. The nail clippers in his hand went to her eyelid. She tried to keep them shut, but that was what he expected as he snipped and peeled the loose skin. Tiny clip by tiny clip, Bollard cut away her eyelid. She refused to scream, but even with her jaw clenched shut, throated cries still came from the pain. This gave Mr. Bollard even more satisfaction than screams.

With each snip, Bollard cleaned the blood off his instrument, ensuring the pain would dull before resuming his work. The look of hatred in those beautiful green eyes was more becoming on her, even as blood ran down her right eye. He leaned in and kissed her forehead before standing up, satisfied with the work he had performed on her right eye. Her eyes darted around without control, grasping for a way out of the situation.

"Now, I suppose that the left eyelid will stay for now. You know that eyes are the gateway to the soul?" he said as he cleaned the clippers before placing them back with precision in his case.

She stammered and mumbled, gasping for air. "You will die. I will see your skin ripped from your bones and placed in front of my fireplace when this over!" She laughed as she thrashed. "You. Demon scum. You will lose."

Mr. Bollard started to hold up tools in his kit one by one. *Having fun yet, JJ? She is not looking as strong as you thought. I think the heretic's fork is most appropriate. No, maybe a simple knife?* "Perhaps, but I am a demon on the side of the light, my dear. It is typical for my kind, the rakshasa. We are allowed to choose where we stand. If one starts losing, I'll just change sides." He saw her pupils dilate as he held up pliers. "This one, then? Very well. I apologize, but we are not at the point where I can ask you questions yet. Torture is a tricky thing. If I begin asking questions early, you'll lie. If I wait too long, you'll tell me whatever I want to hear. I need to go just past that point, to the brink of death when you can only whisper and your subconscious speaks what I need." Bollard was about to resume the torture, but he paused when she giggled.

Delilah's shoulders shook as she laughed, and strands of bloodstained hair were shaken loose. She looked up at him, slammed her jaw into her chest, and screamed. Blood flowed in streams down her throat, and she smiled a bloody, toothy grin as she continued to laugh. She spat her tongue out at him as she struggled to keep her eyes from rolling back into her head. She coughed and choked as blood drained down her throat.

Mr. Bollard did not hesitate in shifting forms. He lunged and licked her throat with his cat's tongue, biting playfully and leaving rows of teeth marks along her thin neck. "Oh dear, you think you can kill yourself for freedom. You are that devoted, aren't you? You are truly worthy of the gift of blood, then. You will tell me everything. I will take you from Vryce and cause your soul to weep."

Mr. Bollard shook her to bring her back. "The *vitae*, or life, the blood of kings. You shall be forever my child. Constantly returning for more to satiate your addiction." Mr. Bollard sliced open his wrist with the steel claws and jammed it into her mouth. "Drink. Heal. Live eternally. Your soul freed from the shackles of this frail mortal frame."

At first she resisted, but the sweet nectar of demon blood, of his blood, could not be resisted for long, no matter the human. Mr. Bollard stepped back and watched the drunkenness set in, the droopy eyes, the half smile, as she began to heal the damage she had caused. He waited as the change set in. His blood was unique, regenerating the most grievous wounds.

"Well, I think now is an appropriate time to ask questions. Tell me, dear Delilah. Tell me about your master and his plans. I can keep this up all night and day," Mr. Bollard said as he picked up another tool and kneeled down. She lowered her head and gazed at him with hatred as she politely, with utmost etiquette, told him. *Everything.*

Mr. Bollard spent the day listening to her. Taking in every word, each more incriminating than the last. She even had information on the workings of other sites. North America was not playing along with the rest, it seemed. The Society of Deus would need to be dismantled and destroyed along with other warlocks. "We knew the warlocks have had their own agenda . . . but this?" he asked. "Vryce has violated the principles of divine law and sought to reclaim his soul. The others pioneer their own experiments. Every demon and angel and man on this planet should seek their demise. You are no different, Delilah."

Vryce needed to be eliminated *and* they still needed to free Lazarus. Thoughts ran through his head about how to best achieve his goal. For starters, warlocks were as cautious as skittish deer. Vryce was particularly more difficult than some of the others as the master of possession, but he did have his weaknesses. First, his real form was weak and vulnerable to attack. Second, Mr. Bollard reminded himself, and of this he was particularly pleased, was Vryce's vision. "When humans reach to the heavens, their wings melt from the purity of creation," Bollard said. In this, he found Delilah Dumont and the organization of the Society of Deus to be Vryce's weakness. In past centuries, enemies that would strike at the warlock would attempt to assault *him* directly.

*After all, for all the world is aware, Vryce could very well be a woman.*

It's surprising that immortal oligarchs on the council would plan for centuries and yet be so brazen to ignore these simple facts.

He checked his phone as the sun was setting and smiled at what he saw. The Society of Deus had been made aware of Delilah's absence and a few captains, including himself, had also gone missing. This meant that there was an opening to exploit.

Gabriel D'Angelo had been given authorization to release the rest of the army as reinforcements. The society was provoked, and they were reacting quickly, but tipping their hand. *If the army of vampires is being released, I'm going to need reinforcements. I can still get close to Vryce with her as a trump card if I can produce her captors. He is more important than my freedom. Yet I'm sure I can pull both off if I move quickly.*

"You there, come out of the shadows," Bollard said.

"Yes, sir." The Englishman almost oozed out of hiding, not making a sound.

"I need to leave the city. With Gabriel on a warpath, he'll destroy me in a second if I don't have anything to produce. Moving her at night is a risk not worth taking, so I have to rely upon you. Keep her here, in this place, for our sake. Do this, and I shall see to it you are compensated beyond your dreams," Bollard said as he cleaned himself up.

"You need not offer, sir. I know what must be done. Are you sure that this place is secure?"

"This place is dead to them now. If any do come, misdirect them away from here."

"As you wish."

Bollard left the building. He had to meet with O'Neil in person, and it would not be safe here for him anyway. Killing Frank was a mistake, but a course of action was becoming clearer to him.

The Whisper stood in the room with Delilah. He moved to release her bindings, and she shook her head against the idea. Her left eye caused him uneasiness, like she was looking into his soul.

"Thank you for not interfering. I had hoped that our training together would hold," she said.

"Of course it would. He took it further than we had expected. I do not think the primus will take kindly to the blood he gave you." The Whisper stood back and made sure to not disturb any of the scene. "What will you have me do now?"

"Get me Symon Vasyl. I need this place rigged. This isn't over yet. Let it leak through that the forces of Chicago are behind the assault. Leave Bollard out of it for now. He is mine. This, by the way, is exactly why I feel that mental conditioning is vital for our organization. Demons have too many tricks up their sleeves." She cracked her neck and wore a determined look that no longer showed any signs of fatigue.

"But you still told him the plan."

"Those on the council of the Unification have already figured it out by now. The downside of a secret society is that information moves at a snail's pace. We have our backup plan. Now go and do your work. Then resume your cover while you can. Keep Vryce out of it. He has to focus on his quest. We have to succeed on our own, understand?" She stared long enough to drive the point home.

"As you wish." The Whisper bowed and faded back into the shadows. No one would see him leave the building.

# CHAPTER 30

A low-flying fighter jet rattled the windows of the warehouse. Mike woke up under a blanket, hugging Akira's cocoon for a pillow while Doc used Mike's bunched-up trench coat as a pillow for himself. As the sun set in Chicago, the Sons and Daughters began to wake up, weary from a day where most underwent physical changes from eating the hearts of demons.

Mike felt a deep hunger in his gut, a desire to feed again. He noticed Phoebe wrapped up like a burrito under blankets and bit his lip to stop himself. *It's a burrito. With blood. That counts, right?*

Each of them stood up and cracked their bones for an evening routine. Out of habit, Akira went to make coffee. The shock wave of an explosion rattled the building and reminded them of the trouble outside. Without speaking, they all ran up to the ground floor and outside. Akira and Mike were there before the coffeepot smashed to the ground in the basement.

The fading sunset burned along the city skyline and turned Chicago into a smoldering ember. Trails of opaque smoke marched across the night sky, signaling where the battles were.

They watched as a National Guard caravan plowed through dense traffic on a nearby expressway. People had abandoned their cars and were evacuating the city in teeming masses, like a river that had overrun its dam.

The moon seemed to mock them, its half gaze a grin as it hung low on the western horizon. Mike looked back at the assembled crew and pulled out a pack of crumpled and broken smokes. *Doc put his fat head on them. That bastard.*

"Doc, you owe me a pack," Mike said. Doc handed him a menthol. It would have to do. Everyone else looked around in confusion, their mouths open just a crack. "What the fuck, eh? That's what you're all thinking." A few nods came in response. "Hey, how many of you wanted to be superheroes when you grew up?" Mike raised his hand. The Captain was the first to follow. "So let's go do that. Not much to it, really. After all, we know where the fighting is. Let's gear up." *This is going to be wicked cool.*

A moment before they were ready to roll out, motorcycles revved, echoing in the warehouse so loudly that they drowned out the sound of gunfire in the distance. Winters and Matsen's police cruiser pulled in, escorting Morris and old-man O'Neil.

A short bald man with leather gloves and a Winchester-knotted necktie stepped out of their car along with the rest. Their lips moved but no sound could be heard over the roar of the engines. Morris waved his arms like an airplane runway controller to silence them.

"I said, where the hell do you guys think you're going?" Morris yelled.

"To save the world, of course," Mike replied. "Damn, I've always wanted to say that. Did it come out right? Should I pause while an explosion rocks behind me and walk away in slow motion?"

Matsen chimed in. "Right, well, the National Guard has the city under lock-down. The riots began while you guys were asleep. People started a run on the banks to get their money out. So it's a spot of chaos out there. You have Mike's armband revolutionaries facing off against the police and National Guard. Everyone who can fight is facing demons."

The Captain held up a finger. "So they don't send in the National Guard when demons start coming out? They wait until people start looting and rioting? I'm not sure which ones we should be fighting."

"All of them," said Patrick O'Neil. "You won't have any success above ground. There is a reason the Second City is getting hit so hard. The Chicago fire, the riots, the floods, the rivers of blood from the stockyard. This city has always demanded sacrifice. She's a mistress with her own heart. Beneath this city lies a heart, an outlet for man's sin in the world to bleed through, the fuel source for the furnace in the Twin Cities."

O'Neil rocked back and forth on his feet while he continued. "It's time for your first helldive." He handed Doc a coffee-stained blueprint. "The Deep-Tunnel Project runs close to it, but you'll have to follow this map. Just know that you can't actually kill the heart of the city. It's in your best interest to not let this demon that's bound there talk to you either. But I'm sure you'll find a way to seal it off."

The bald man with the fancy tie flashed O'Neil a glare but remained silent.

"Let me guess, Unification oversight?" Mike said as he pointed at the bald man.

"No, this is JJ. I sent Frank to retrieve him," replied O'Neil.

"Oh, sweet. Frank's back. Where is he? He knows this city better than anyone. We could use him," Mike said.

Morris chimed in. "Frankie's dead, Mike. He didn't make it back."

Mike revved his engine and almost broke his handlebar from yanking too hard. He had nothing to say as he drove past them, almost running over JJ. *See you soon, buddy.* Morris tried to stop them by shouting and reaching out as they drove past. O'Neil called him back to his side.

The bike hit the interstate at full speed with the rest of the Sons and Daughters behind him. Mike may have been faster on foot, but it made him hungry rapidly, and only Akira could match him. They got behind a National Guard caravan full of recruits praying. One of them looked back at their new followers and pointed. He gestured to the others in the transport, and soon they were all cheering and had a look of hope in their eyes.

Mike looked back at his crew and smiled. He screamed at them, "Remember who you are fighting for! It's your families and friends! Armbands are your friend!" Mike gestured to his arm as he took off his bandanna and tied it there. His showboating almost cost Phoebe a bike as he lost balance, but he recovered seconds before a wipeout. Mike peered back to see his crew put their faces in their hands, he thought for a moment that Lucy was blushing in embarrassment. *These soldiers are just people caught up in their games, faced with hell. Just like me.*

Phoebe rode up next to Mike, her helmet solid black with a visor that hid her face, but she gestured with her fingers to follow. More than once as they sped through the city, she had to stop and wait for everyone else. Signs of the riots and fighting were everywhere: broken windows, cars tipped over, and trash spilled down every street. Some places were still ablaze, with no fire crews available to respond. No longer afraid of the light, a small handful of imps picked apart a victim of the violence.

At first, they would stop and scare them away, but as they drove farther south, it became so frequent that they just had to keep riding. By the time they reached the entry into the Deep-Tunnel Project, everyone in their crew either kept their visors down or had a look of determination on their face.

The entry they had chosen was near the water-pumping station of a neighborhood called Cicero, a place that was underfunded and under construction. It hadn't been part of any gentrification projects for a long time. Fires created an orange landscape from the residential areas, a true devil's night.

The Sons and Daughters paused long enough for Doc to memorize the map. Mike ripped off the barricade preventing entry, tossing it aside like a crumpled piece of paper.

The tunnel was massive, large enough to fit a fire truck through. As they rode in, their bikes' headlights shined hypnotically on the walls. Mike could taste the dampness in the air, water that had been still for so long, it festered with mold. They pulled up to a maintenance steel door with a rusted handle like the wheel that opens a submarine hatch.

"This is it," Doc said. "This door should be sealed off and welded shut. We should be under the heart of downtown right now. Behind here it's all tunnels, slagged iron, catacombs, and the ruins that Chicago was built upon."

"And most likely a crap ton of demons. Do you think any of them have been here longer than the past few days?" Mike asked.

"Yes. The Second City has always been very close to the dead. Hauntings, the Catholics, riots. I bet my life that O'Neil himself got his start down here," said Lucy.

"Well, I'm going to go on official record and state that the entire Unification plan is stupid," Mike said. "Next time they want to open a gate to hell, don't pick a fucking populated city." Mike started to pry the door open. It made a scream of resistance as steel buckled under his strength before giving way. A flood of rats washed over their legs as the rodents ran for their lives. *It's always a bad sign when the vermin run. Looks like we aren't the pinnacle of evolution after all.*

The Captain said something in Latin as they entered the tunnel. His hands lit with a sick green-and-black flame. Akira's eyes took on a red glow as she began to crawl on the ceiling. Lucy produced an iron lantern that illuminated the area in front of her with a soft, warm glow. Phoebe removed her helmet, tied a blindfold around her eyes, and kept one hand on the wall. Even Doc seemed to smile and move through the darkness like he belonged there, every one of his senses heightened. Mike had to stop, pull off his backpack, and fumble with a nearly dead flashlight.

"Wait, wait. I'm the only one who didn't get cool night-vision powers?" Mike said. "That's bullshit."

Akira chuckled from above. "We'll let you know when a door needs to be moved."

Phoebe said out of the blue, "What's going to happen, guys, is that we are going to have to fight through a lot of hellhounds. We will face Tindalos himself, the demon of loyalty. Bound here for we know what. He wants to be set free. If we agree, this will be easy."

"Uh, well, that makes things easy. What happens if we don't?" Mike asked.

"No idea. We say yes. I had a vision about it."

"Well, that takes out the suspense. What if I don't want to say yes?" Mike said.

She paused and let the deep booms from above, the trickle of running water, and the pulsing sound in the distance set in. "I didn't say it was you," she replied.

# CHAPTER 31

The construction of the pathways dated back further than 1906, first built for telephones by the Chicago Tunnel Company and later by private enterprise. Saloon owners once used them for smuggling during prohibition. Metal rails crumbled underfoot as they walked through. Curved concrete walls and criss-crossed conduits and cables overhead made Mike's head spin with vertigo.

The tunnels here were barely taller than his head, and Akira insisted on cramming herself above him. They were, to the best of their ability, attempting to remain quiet as they got close to the sound of gnashing. Arrhythmic gnawing and crunching began quietly at first, only heard between the tiny scuffles of their footsteps. *It's like someone is taking a grapefruit and constantly bashing it against a wall.* Mike could feel the granite in the walls and taste dust from the past century hanging in the air. The sound became louder with every tunnel junction they crept through, inspiring them to move slower.

More than once his fingers brushed against bloody wet spots on the wall. Fingers found farther in, ripped off at the knuckles and still stuck in the wall, confirmed the blood was human. In the light of Phoebe's lantern, Mike saw Doc give a thumbs-up as they entered a junction with vaulted ceilings. Tunnel entrances littered every wall as far as they could see in the dim light.

They were on the third floor of tunnel junctions. Looking over the edge reminded Mike of a beehive cut in half, catacombs and pockets of subway and freight tunnels hidden in every nook. On the floor at the very center of the junction lay a pile of concrete rubble with mounds of ash in neat stacks. A stone cross with Gaelic carvings jutted out from the rubble of the makeshift grave, defiant in protest from the rest of the decay around it.

Shadows below them slinked along the exteriors, darting in and out of the tunnels. Mike saw something different, however. He saw a gaping hole where there should be a floor, swallowing up debris that fell into it, down into a whirlpool. He saw hands clawing up the side, followed by faces. Gray faces with no real features, just heads twisted in pain as they kept slipping along the edge, trying to get out but never finding purchase.

Deeper in the hole, a grayish-green glow emanated like lights underwater. *Oh shit. The actual land of the dead. Is that hell?* His crew started making moves to crawl down and get closer. He followed, climbing between protrusions to make his way down. The closer he moved to the pit, the colder he felt on the inside, like diving into a pool of ice water. *Well, that does it. I've officially climbed into hell.* Even though fragments of the real world remained, like the tunnels, everything took on a duller, ashen appearance. Above him, distances seemed to stretch, creating a sense of vertigo.

Mike felt a dull pressure on his hand when he touched the rail. He looked up to see a black reptilelike claw pinning his hand to the wall. Then he saw a hellhound's head appear from the tunnel. It was larger than the ones they herded before. Its drool landed on Mike as it tilted its head to look at him with a glowing eye. The saliva burned so bad that Mike could not help but scream in pain. It reminded him of the barrel. It was boring through him, eating away at his shoulder. He let go of the ledge.

A second and third head came out and bit down on Mike. He quickly looked for which of the three hellhounds he would hit first. His eyes followed their leathery skin along their necks down to a single set of shoulders. *Four feet . . . three heads.* As realization set in, he felt the teeth slice into his arm and heard the crunch of bone as it clamped down. It ate away his flesh, peeling back his skin and curling it, while frying it at the same time. *This is motherfucking Cerberus! Get off me!*

Mike saw his friends as he was flung around in the air. They were airborne as well, jumping off the ledges and down to the pit to avoid hellhounds that were coming out of the tunnels. Some were the small bony hounds with their detached spines. Others were large with three heads.

Ghosts cowered in the tunnels on the first floor. The tunnels were brimming with the dead, trapped between the hurling abyss of hell and hellhounds above them. *What the fuck? I thought I had it bad.* He was out of time. The third head came around and latched on to Mike's leg, ripping the flesh off his thigh and splaying him out between the middle head.

An arm and a leg locked in the jaws of a demon hound pulling them apart was not how Mike imagined dying. Cerberus was wasting no time. The mouth of its middle head drew back in a vicious snarl as it lunged forward to claim its prey. *I'm not going to be dog food.* The demon matched his strength as he struggled to free his arm and leg. Crunching, pulling, and trying to twist every way possible, he found he had no leverage. *Oh shit!* The canine ripped into his midsection, the crack of half his ribs being ripped off as his torso gave way echoed through the junction.

The Sons and Daughters were faring no better than Mike, taken by surprise, they had to leave their ledges and dive to the floor, only to find it was a sandpit of ash, slowing down any movement to a winter's crawl.

Only Akira and Lucy seemed to be doing well, Akira running along the walls as an insect slicing the heads off the hounds when she could, Lucy turning to a gray mist and reforming before burying her axe into hound after hound.

When Cerberus bit into Mike, it dived to the floor and shook its head like a dog with a bone. Mike's left hand started to glow bright red as fangs protruded from his face. Wild eyes of frenzy, a mouse in a snake's mouth, fighting for its life, he slammed his fist into the face of Cerberus so hard that ash from the floor was swept into the air. His hand became a blur striking again and again. Each strike caused the creature to growl and wince, until finally the hellhound's fangs shattered. The three heads let go at once and started tending to the middle head, its jaw bludgeoned in.

Mike fell, his leg in scraps and half his body hanging open. Rage was all he could feel. *I will not die here.* Snarling back at the hound with his fangs, he used his good leg to vault himself back up at its throat.

The Sons and Daughters didn't hesitate as they regained their footing from the initial onslaught. Each of them shifted targets to Cerberus. The Captain's flames mixed around Lucy's axe as she and Akira moved toward the animal. Phoebe and Doc took aim with their guns at its eyes. Their bullets struck at the same time, ripping the beast apart as it had done to Mike.

They drank its blood. The taste of peaches and spiced honey was addictive. Soon they found themselves ignoring the room around them as they drank together, wounds healing themselves. The other hellhounds crouched low and backed away as the alpha was killed, unsure of the new hierarchy.

It was the sound of slow clapping that caused them to cease their ecstasy. Mike looked to the sound, his ribs slowly rebuilding. A man stepped out of the inky shadows, covered in fur from head to toe. As he came into the light of Lucy's lantern, he revealed himself as a hellhound that was half man, walking upright on two massive hound legs with an elongated jaw and teeth at all angles. His deep, growling voice echoed throughout the chamber.

"Well done. Well done," he said. "If only entirely reckless. I could have killed you while you were enthralled. Do you know why demon blood heals you so quickly? It is not a gift of life. It is used so you can be tormented eternally."

"Oh, great. We got a talker," said Mike. "Yeah, okay, Tindalos. Go back to your pit. None of us are taking your deal." Mike's vision of the dead lands was clearer than it had ever been, with something he never noticed before. Standing now, on the other side, he could see a pathway back into the living world. Near an empty tunnel stood four familiar ghosts from his life, showing him the way. Nobody else on his team even glanced in that tunnel's direction. *They can't see that? Oh, wait, mega-arch-super demon. Nobody else cares about my ghosts.*

"O'Neil needs to send better ambassadors next time. It's a pity you're not interested in an alliance. After his betrayals, at least one of us still does our job." Tindalos began to sink back into the abyss behind him.

"Wait!" said Lucy. "Don't listen to him. We need your help to close the rift. What is it you're looking for? Why are you here?"

He stepped forward and moved more into her light, revealing his eyes, which looked like a night sky with stars in them rather than pupils as he moved his jaw a few feet away from her. In Lucy's light, it almost appeared as if barbed chains were thrust into his back and trailed off like puppet strings into the abyss. They didn't match his motif, however, red and gnarled with hooks. Small curled flames decorated them.

"So one will listen?" Tindalos seemed hopeful. "I am the demon of loyalty. You've been killing my children for days now. Your Unification put me into service," he said. "I serve them as you do now. My hounds dragging souls, not to hell or heaven where they belong, but to some soulless heathen's kingdom in the north."

Tindalos wrapped a paw around a red chain and slid it forth into Lucy's light. A gnarled iron lock dangled, holding five chains together. "The key, is what I wish. This place—" He spat on the ground. "It's one nexus point where your lords of death eliminate their competition. Ssssooomething has weakened the barrier, and now my hounds are visible. I've heard tales on their lips of what it is." He leaned back into the shadows, chains scraping on the ground. His eyes shined like a starry night sky. "A new prophet cometh."

"Yeah, as Lucy said, there isn't much of a choice. We are here to close a rift, buddy. I assume that's through eating your heart," Mike said.

"Dibs!" Akira shouted as she peeked around Mike's coat.

"Yes, that would be wise for you, slayer of Golgoroth. You've already slain an arch demon of war. Saving the Second City from him. Killing a demon prince, *the* demon of loyalty's heart would make a fantastic addition to your collection. Imagine what you could do." He lifted the wrought-iron chains. "Here I am all chained up as well. Unable to defend myself."

Lucy slapped the broadside of her axe into Mike's chest. "Shut up. You can't kill him. Angels make the wind blow, the trees grow, the tides flow. They make the world turn." Lucy placed herself between Mike and Tindalos. "Demons deal with human-made things. Lust, apathy, loyalty, love, hatred, and even hope. They twist and test our virtues. If you kill him, loyalty will cease to exist. Imagine a world where the concept of loyalty is but a memory . . ."

"Oh, that's just rich coming from the self-proclaimed demon huntress herself." Mike laughed. "Listen. We make our own fates. We need to stop hounds from fucking *eating* people!"

"It was you who said that my death was the answer." Tindalos crept around the edge of Lucy's lantern. "O'Neil sent you here to make a choice. Set the stage for you to act. Let the Unification use this city as part of their ritual. The *choice* to bury *her* here was theirs." He tapped the iron cross that jutted out of the concrete three times.

Tindalos snarled. "This was placed here by Lord of Heaven's Wrath decades ago. It's the body of a girl who was never born in this world. She-who-shudders-with-the-lidless-eye is her name. She's quite dead, or rather, never born to begin with. Her eyes stolen by the fallen king, Balor. A remnant that the Unification needed to eliminate, and inside her grave is what I need," he said. "Freedom so close, yet untouchable by my kind."

"To what end?" Doc asked.

"*She* is the only thing that knows King Balor's true name. I've been chained here in servitude to keep her dreams of that name contained. Forcing souls through her as a conduit to fuel their ritual. She is the link that ties these cities together. Upon completion, she will die. Which will erase an old legend from history when Lazarus closes the gates. Killing one to pave way for another. How else does one pull off something so grand if not over the graves of enemies?" Tindalos began to shift into a hellhound made of shadow.

His voice continued to echo in the room around them. "Set me free, and I stop feeding the neverborn. Her dreams will spread back into the world, paving the way for the Balor's return. My hounds leave, and the Second City is free of my demons. Kill me, and my hounds will scatter indeed. Loyalty would become a forgotten trait among your kind. Either way, this ritual will wither and die in nights to come. Make your choice." His teeth dripped acidic saliva, and his eyes glowed white as he began to stress the chains.

"If we do nothing?" Mike held out his hands to calm the beast, not ready for a fight yet.

"You are just monsters who roam this earth, wrapped in the chains of your keepers. My hounds will continue to drag this city to be used as kindling in a great spell," he snapped. Out of the shadows behind the hound, smaller hounds began to creep out.

"Eh, isn't this the pot calling the kettle black?" Mike remarked.

"You'll break your loyalty to one side or another. Even if you are unaware which side you are truly on yet." Tindalos chuckled deeply. The chains behind him were lifted by the smaller hounds, allowing Tindalos to move closer.

Doc held up his finger while bouncing on the balls of his feet. "Uh . . . sir? Excuse us for one minute, please." Everyone moved into a huddle as Doc frantically tried to organize them. "Okay. I say we do nothing. We just set up containment points. We just stay here and keep killing hounds. Stopping any more fuel going to the Twin Cities."

The Captain swatted Doc on the head. "No, you moron. We fucking kill it. We need to seal the rift. What demon in their right mind wants to die? Of *course* he wants us to do nothing or set it free. Besides, his loyalty thing is a crock. Humans are already selfish lots who act in self-preservation."

"Nightmares ain't so bad, I reckon," Akira said while picking her teeth. "Look, so what if some king of nightmares comes back. We already got 'em. If he's a problem, won't Lazarus just smite him anyway? Besides, sounds like a fairy tale. I always liked those."

The scraping of chains across the floor caused the group to look up as Tindalos yanked on his bindings. Behind him, another pack of hellhounds crawled out of the shadows.

"Down, boy. We're workin' here. Tell me what happens when you seal this portal thingy to purgatory," Mike said.

Tindalos smiled as best a giant hound could. "I take my hounds and go back to my real purpose. Hellhounds leave your city. The dead stored here will wander until properly judged or guided. It is not my purpose, so I don't care. I'm willing to bet your city will have to get used to turning up the thermostat for dear old dead grandma with the way things are going, however."

"What kind of fucked-up deal is this?" Mike asked, he picked up a small rock and threw it at the ground. *Damned if we do. Damned if we don't. Damned if we eat him.*

"Fine," said Lucy. "I'll get it." Before anyone could respond, she had already turned into a mist, her lantern disappearing with her, and she flowed into the gravestone.

Tindalos let out a deep howl. "Freedom!" He paced back and forth, looking down.

Below, Mike could see her flying among the souls. *It's good she can fly. I would be stuck on the wall.* "Tindalos, I'm the one who's going to make the deal, so if it goes south with the Unification, it falls on me. I'm not letting anyone else die around me because of it. Understood? Leave their names out of everything."

"The slayer of Golgoroth is willing to bear the consequences of her choice? It shows how loyal you really are to your friends. I will make sure that history never forgets you, Auburn. I'll sell your tale that you dived in, freed Tindalos, and betrayed the Unification." The hound's eyes glowed green for a second. "If you want this in your name, then you open the lock."

Lucy returned quickly. Mike could see her already flowing back up from the rivers just a minute after she left. She rematerialized back into solid form among them and jingled a set of keys with a pink rabbit's foot on them. "Before you ask, the lantern shows what's hidden. It's how I hunt demons. Turns out it also works on keys lost in the first layer of hell."

"Toss me the keys, Lucy. It will be better for everyone if your name isn't attached to this deed," Mike said.

She hesitated and looked back at Mike. Phoebe gave her a nod of approval. "You're going to save me, a demon hunter, from making a deal with one?" Lucy said, her eyes widened.

Mike only nodded. She gave a genuine smile as she threw the keys to Mike. He approached Tindalos with measured steps and placed his hand on the lock. *Yeah, who am I kidding. Lucy has the right call. This is what she meant by 'you can't kill every demon.' Who cares if O'Neil sat on the fence? He let us determine fate.* With a twist of a key, sparks flew out of the lock.

Chains all around the junction lit on fire and fell to the ground. Ashes rose in the air. Howls could be heard from every tunnel, almost drowning out a slow chuckle from Tindalos.

"The creature with the tattered green trench coat, the Auburn, will be remembered by history as the leader of the Sons and Daughters," Tindalos said. "Now leave before my hounds seek glory at feasting on the heart of the slayer of Golgoroth."

"What about our deal?" asked Doc.

"I am the demon of loyalty. I've tested your bonds, and our deal stands. Yet you remain as sinners and betrayers, fit for my hounds to take with us." Ink was already swirling around him as the shadows in the room danced at his command. The gateway below them was beginning to close.

Hounds leaped around them. Grabbing Phoebe's hand, Mike ran for the exit, his ghosts frantically gesturing to hurry. Looking back, he saw his friends right on their heels. All but one. The Captain was deeper into purgatory as hounds dragged him away. The light in his eyes was already gone.

"Thank you for freedom. Now, little creatures . . . run," Tindalos whispered over the howls.

# CHAPTER 32

The city looked grayer by the time they got above ground and back on their bikes, no one saying a word. Buildings looked more aged than usual, marred by stains and burn marks. As they drove past some of them on the south side, Mike would catch glimpses in the windows of ghosts flickering in and out of reality. He looked at each one, hoping to see the Captain or perhaps Frank standing there. Mike pulled over and stopped his bike. When Akira slowed down to join him, Mike rushed to her and swiped her smokes from her pocket.

"Hey! What the hell?"

"Deal. I'm bumming one. Take it out on Doc. He's the cause of this," Mike said, lighting one up, leaning against a pole.

Getting off the back of Akira's bike, Doc put his hand on her shoulder and said to Mike, "Let it go."

"Fuck that. I'm not letting shit go. You crumpled my last pack of smokes."

"Mike, about the Cap—"

*"Don't even mention it."* Mike pointed at Doc. "It was your bright idea to look into this whole thing. Now look, another

person I've met is dead. Besides, people die and we barely knew him."

Phoebe tried to chime in. "Kill the tough-guy act. We all know—"

"I said don't mention it. I'm getting pretty damn used to seeing the dead walk around all the time and all these fucking ghosts lying about. City looks kinda cool covered in ash all the time. The Captain had iron balls that clanked when he walked. He was a flame-wielding, sorcerer-supreme badass."

"Hey," Lucy said. "About that. Mike, how did you know which tunnel to take?"

"The obvious one? I mean, the same ghosts that are always around me guided us out of there."

"Mike. What ghosts?" she pressed. "What city of ash?"

"You know, the land of the dead? Shedding your innocence and all that jazz. It's the reason we see the world differently, because we drank the blood."

"That's not how it works. You see vampires and demons that are walking around you clear as day. Sure. But you only see ghosts and the lands of purgatory if you actually step across. The city, or anywhere, only looks dead from the other side. The barrier between worlds may be weakened, but it's not shattered. We're trying to stop that shattering," Lucy replied.

"I'm done," he said, flicking his smoke. "I said don't mention it. You guys all got night-vision powers. It looks like I got special ghost vision." He picked his bike up and began to jet off. *So what if I could see them before.*

They made their way back to the warehouse. The long night had calmed most of the city's violence, and the bitter cold deprived even the heartiest of the will to fight. Looting, however, still seemed fashionable. The steel roll-up doors of the warehouse rattled open as they got close. Morris had opened the doors for them. The grim look on his face and his blood-stained shirt told Mike that their night was not over yet.

They pulled into the warehouse and cut their bikes. Soldiers from the National Guard were strung up on meat hooks, with their blood draining into bowls beneath them. O'Neil and JJ were having casual conversation near some tables and chairs. Morris went back to work on the bodies.

"What the hell is this?" Mike shouted, hopping off his bike and stepping up to Morris.

"Wait. Wait. Wait." Morris had his hands out. "They were already dead. We didn't do this. They were killed by a plague demon near here. I saved the rest of them. They ran, though."

"So you are just going to eat the dead, then?" Mike asked.

"Uh, yeah, actually. I'm a vampire. That's what I do. Be real, friend. Where else are you going to get blood?"

"Ugh, can't we find serial killers or something?" Mike asked.

"Do not get all righteous on us. You are a predator now. Act like one," Morris said as he leveled a meat hook at Mike.

Mike couldn't help but feel the draw to drink. He was still hungry even after he feasted on that demon. Human blood just seemed more enticing. He grabbed a bowl. *Fuck it. I'm not really that noble after all. Everyone dies someday. I might as well make a meal out of it. Besides, their souls leave their body and walk around. Sometimes they haunt me. I could deal with a few soldiers hanging around. Never know when that could help.* He walked over to O'Neil and JJ. Everyone else was busy cleaning themselves off and getting ready to unwind.

"It's done," Mike said. "Power is turned off. World's saved. Woo-hoo." He plopped down and used a spoon to eat his new nightly soup.

"You came back." O'Neil smiled. "With more of your crew than Morris would have expected. I knew you had it in you."

O'Neil snipped off the end of a cigar. "I'll let JJ fill you in on what comes next."

Mike looked up at him and raised an eyebrow. Slowly bringing the spoon to his lips and slurping slightly as he stared.

"Primus Vryce, warlock of the Society of Deus, is responsible for the damage so far. He betrayed the Unification and opened the Innocence further than it should have been. He's been part of a conspiracy to create an army of undead soldiers for conquest and to fight back against Lazarus, all so he can become a lich himself," Mr. Bollard said as he folded his hands in front of him.

"You did just speak English there? Is this a comic book? He's the arch villain, right? Doc! Are you sure I'm not nuts!" Mike shouted down the warehouse.

"Nooope," came a distant reply from Doc.

"Well, so Mr. Bad Guy has an army of vampires and wants to rule the world. How is that any different from Mr. Good Guy Lazarus? All I see is a bunch of vampires and a conspiracy to rule the world," Mike said, slurping more blood.

JJ and O'Neil looked at each other for a minute, debating how to best respond. Finally O'Neil spoke. "I said I'm bound to see this through to the end. You are under no such obligations. Let the rest of the crews up there know what he's up to and set them upon Vryce. The ritual at the Twin Cities will wither and die on its own. We can just hope that some other location finds Lazarus so he can fix everything and make the world forget this ever happened." O'Neil sat down.

JJ slammed his hands on the table, causing Mike to spill blood all over his coat. It was almost not green anymore. "It's not just that. He has an army. If he achieves becoming a lich, he won't need fuel from here. If we are banking on Lazarus sealing the gates, then you should bet another can rip them open. This could be the end of earth itself. We can't just sit here and hide.

We have to do our jobs, kill him, and free Lazarus. Sure, the others might get lucky and wander through the long way, but we can skip right to the cave with my information. We are the ones in a position to strike."

O'Neil raised an eyebrow when JJ mentioned the location. O'Neil let his trademark awkward silence hang in the air as he thought.

"So while you guys sit on your asses waiting, what happens to everyone in Minneapolis while this rift is open, eh? Just like here, I imagine? Yeah, screw that jazz. I'm with baldy here. We go up there and do what we must. Besides, they killed Frank. I haven't forgotten about that. Hey, what's the name of the guy who killed him?" Mike asked.

"Gabriel D'Angelo, the right hand of Vryce. His soldier of death," JJ replied.

O'Neil and JJ looked at each other in another long silence. Mike waved his arms, trying to get their attention at first, but settled with tossing his boots up on the table with a loud thump. O'Neil gave JJ the final nod as he lit the cigar, the light from the flame kissing his aged face. "Fate. Mr. Bollard. May the fickle bitch smile on us before she smacks us back down."

"I'm going to get my shit," Mike said as he stood up from the table. It was getting near dawn, and he knew they would be leaving at nightfall. Still, sleep wasn't on the table for him. Mike walked over to one of the Captain's fireman coats and grabbed it off the hook. He spent the rest of the day cleaning his protest trench coat and sewing it back together. He added a single new patch underneath the two coins from earlier. "Minneapolis Fire Department Engine 1."

# CHAPTER 33

*'Make enemies,' he said.* The thought hung in Gabriel's head as he looked down at Roger Queneco. "While the cat's away, the mice will play. Is that it?" Gabriel asked as they were escorted through downtown Minneapolis on foot. His personal security detail stopped people that would bump into him. One of the Twin Cities most despicable traits was that everyone was so consumed with themselves they never watched where they walked. Sometimes stopping in the middle of the sidewalk to look at their phone. Gabriel elbowed a human with frost-tipped hair out of his way.

The homeless were a different story. He hated them. One homeless man was being particularly persistent tonight. He asked Gabriel twice if he had a smoke. They were so persistent in chasing Gabriel down, always asking for a smoke. *You can't get a job if you reek.* Gabriel outright shoved one away hard enough to cause Roger to pause.

"Easy there, Hercules. You never know who works for who," he said.

"No. If the trash wants something free, they have to work for it." Gabriel fumed.

"You woke up on the wrong side of the bed. Listen, I know this is impromptu, but you have to start sorting through our allies and enemies. Delilah's gone missing, so tonight's meeting with the dignitaries falls on me. I have to track what has been uncovered with their dives." Roger picked up his pace to match Gabriel's.

Gabriel pushed himself through a line outside a street taco vendor. *People call them a fad, but these damn trucks are popping up more and more every night. Ugh, Mexican food.* "Yeah, so why bring me? You need to take notes on me because I'm the apprentice?"

"A quick study you are! Yup, yup! It's not far up ahead. You got the book I sent you?"

"I made it my own."

Gabriel stopped without taking his eyes off the binder to avoid a taxicab. He opened his binder to review his notes. On the side he had titled it "Book of Expendables." The red light from street signs reflected off the plastic pages. The book contained information on all the groups hunting within the city from different Unification branches, like the priests of Xipe Totec or the Vodun from Montegue. It listed where they had been, and it included sales pitches for them. A marketing guide for the apocalypse. Gabriel was to convince them to donate their findings to the Library of Deus, in exchange for better diving grounds within restricted areas.

"The Society of Deus boasts one of the world's largest collections of arcane texts and original artifacts relating to magic, so naturally, sorcerers, would-be warlocks, and vampires interested in picking up a spell or two were drawn here." Gabriel looked back and smirked as Roger looked annoyed with his public candor.

"Peter Culmen in Mexico City has at his disposal some of the world's most advanced and yet unreleased technology. It's technology the world is not ready to handle, like cloning, mind transfer, and android tech. Shifters and constructs are drawn there. Few vampires, though. Rasputin had the largest amount of imprisoned demons taken from near all the world's religions, everything from djinn to Japanese *oni*. Ghosts, revenants, and vampires flock to him. See, I got this, right?" Gabriel said.

"Chap, we are in fucking public. Watch your tongue," Roger hissed.

Gabriel put on a defiant smirk and walked backward. "As payment for their services, each warlock was granted permission by the council to charge a service or fee for the rights and privileges to helldive within their walls. Having different requirements draws different crowds."

"Yes, yes, you moron," Roger said as he had to jog to keep up with Gabriel's long strides.

"What are you so worried about? If we win, all these people will know magic is real and start using it. Who gives a fuck?" Gabriel laughed. "So naturally the gaping hole in the Unification's armor is the loyalty of its ranks. They were all drawn together from millennia of secret societies."

"I'm starting to rethink my choices tonight," Roger replied with a dry tone and a sharp look.

"Once the Unification Council had achieved enough influence throughout the world, smaller societies would sign on or forcibly be crushed and brought into the fold. In the past century, the Unification started to eliminate many alternative cults that stood against them. The council had a goal in mind, and no one could stand in their way once they had control over the world's finances." Gabriel laughed louder as they neared Walsh Tower.

"All right, go ahead. Spoil the fun. Continue on. Just spill it all. No worries," Roger said.

"Haven't you noticed yet?" Gabriel stopped and leaned down. "You going to cry yet? Nobody gives a shit! Nobody is listening. They are ignorant masses."

To prove his point further, Gabriel walked up to a couple as he turned the page. *This page is about my family. One of the forced acquisitions.* "Forced into service were Italian merchants and fortune-tellers who manipulated fate and chance to their favor. They had the economic might to stand alone for ages. Their pure-blooded sorcerer lineage gave them an edge against the demon-blooded swine that the Unification would send as enforcers." He read out loud. They looked down and hurried past, slipping through piles of fresh snow to get away.

"Okay. You've made your point."

"Have I?" Gabriel chuckled. "I'm the best at what I do. I don't need to read books. Shit's fucking easy."

"No, you've made the point that you'll be the perfect ass-hole to continue pissing everyone off."

"And that's exactly why we are here tonight. Me pissing off all the Unification divers helps you be a straight—"

The ground shook beneath them. For ten eternal seconds, the buildings of the Twin Cities rocked and creaked with the world around them. Roger dropped to the ground, placing his hands above his head as Gabriel struggled to keep his balance. The city panicked, wide-eyed people gripping the nearest person or object as the sounds of a quake echoed through their bones. A rush of ozone swirled through the streets between buildings that gave protest to the ground moving beneath them. Looking to the horizon surrounding the Twin Cities, Gabriel saw a shimmering aura vibrantly flare up along its edge, its colors rapidly changing between shades of deep red and vibrant blue before settling on a soft, dying green light.

Then it ended.

The aura of the quake faded away as quickly as it had appeared.

"Roger?" Gabriel asked as people recovered, pouring into the streets from buildings to survey the damage. Sounds of the shock wave were replaced with horns of cars involved in accidents and distant sirens. "Roger!" he shouted again. Yanking the little vampire off the sidewalk as he gripped a magazine rack for his dear unlife.

"Okay. Okay." Roger stood up and dusted himself off. "I have a clue of what that was. Let's calm down."

"Sure thing." Gabriel chuckled as a fire hydrant started spewing cold water into a crowd.

"Vryce isn't here."

"Nope," said Gabriel. "Off collecting."

"Walsh is busy."

"Yup, oversight."

"Delilah's not here," Roger said.

"Nope. MIA."

"That makes me in charge here," said Roger.

"Yup, looks like it."

"Our source to power the ritual just got shut off."

Gabriel hummed, watching the first case of looting he'd seen in the Twin Cities.

"We've got a week of soul energy at best," Roger said.

"Yup. We're screwed."

"Always a plan B, chap. Always a plan B. However, that means, you, my good friend, need to do a really, *really* good job at selling to all these dignitaries. You're the lowest apprentice, and I need to run."

"I'm not sure this is what I'm cut out—"

Roger opened the glass door into the building. "Beauty before age, friend. You'll do wonderful! Just barter library time for demon hearts. It's a buyer's market, I hear." He held the door for Gabriel to enter first. "Oh, and start taking notes on who is who. You'll probably have to kill most of them later. Don't want any mix-ups now, do we?" he said with a grin.

Gabriel walked into the meeting room. High above the city, he was thrown to the wolves. Unprepared and socially inept for the intense pace of negotiations, he was shredded. Weeks of time alone with the Emerald Tablet were purchased for marbles. Entry into the sacred Libraries of Deus was traded to helldivers that had mapped out only tiny portions of the underworld. The who's who of names thrown around him in dizzying fashion trashed any preparation he had. Everyone inside knew the obvious: Deus was on a clock.

# CHAPTER 34

Entering the ritual site in Greenland was a shock, even to Vryce. He quickly dived to the ground to dodge debris from a forty-millimeter grenade round. His ears rang as he struggled to regain his bearings, a luxury he was not afforded before another struck nearby. A shard of silver shrapnel lanced through his leg. His real leg. One he could not repair. Even behind his mask, now with eight of his shards near him, he could do nothing but clench his teeth and hiss through the pain.

Wolves, larger than the Humvee firing from its Mk 19 grenade-launching machine gun, ran past him. Their translucent blue fur glowed brightly, matching the night sky, a rainbow of colors illuminated along the aurora. Through the pain, Vryce recognized the mythical beasts. Geri and Freki, some of the legends in Odin's pantheon. He smiled even though he was in pain. *Magic is returning.* He surveyed his wound from his ill-fated teleportation and was not pleased with the results.

The Unification had mobilized their own troops for containment, armed with weaponry built to handle the supernatural creatures. Clad in deep greens with mesh hoods, they had the appearance of monsters themselves, wielding customized ammunition. The result was that his leg was useless for the foreseeable future. The wolves, spiritual creatures of legend, had less to worry about from physical weaponry. They tore through the soldiers as machine-gun fire riddled through them.

Despite the appearance of the wolves, it looked like the battle was not going well for his loosely connected ally in Greenland. Verkonis was one of the few warlocks who assisted in altering the ritual for his own means. The city of Nuuk was his location for the ritual, and from the looks of it, the small population had mostly been evacuated already. The backdrop of the Sermitsiaq mountains were illuminated with the sparks of battle waging. Winged warriors and mythological beasts battled Unification helldivers, vampires, and Special Forces units as they fought to usurp control of the warlock's inner sanctum. A foretelling of what Vryce would face if his society could not keep Walsh and the council distracted.

He spied a small squad heading down a road in his direction, three, maybe four reinforcement vehicles, creature types Vryce could not make out at this distance. He reasoned they could be anything from sorcerers to regular humans. Either way, they were the enemy, and there was zero possibility of him hiding in time. Focusing his will, he commanded the clouds to form a raging storm and steeled himself, waiting for the right moment to call forth death from above.

All four vehicles rounded the mountain pass, and Vryce snapped his fingers. Nothing happened. *That is most unfortunate.* He snapped again, only to watch his storm clouds dissipate as quickly as they had appeared. *How rude. Countermagic. Isn't this exactly why I recruited Gabriel?* "Oh, what an inopportune moment to be really here," he said, lying his head back on the mound of dirt.

"There is no room in this world to be soft," said a deep voice.

Vryce craned his neck back and saw Warlock Verkonis standing meters up the hill beyond him. A bear of a man, more strong man than body builder, dressed in brown-and-gray finery. His long beard and hair were braided neatly, tied together with trinkets of power. His most defining feature, however, was his fake left eye, a crystal that housed within it every color found within aurora borealis. "Command of the elements is not my only trick," Vryce hissed.

"No, but it is not your specialty. You are relying on the classic spells. Why is the master of possession here in person? That would be like me, the master of spirits, walking around without my ethereal guardians," he boomed. Behind him, his spiritual companions, Norse legends and ghosts, spread around them, creating a shield wall.

"Possession was the plan. You seem to have evacuated all your humans, however. Speaking of soldiers?" Vryce pointed to the caravan. The soldiers rolled past, giving a salute to Verkonis.

"Not all humans deny magic. My town has decided to join the fight. They are helping me resist a full onslaught from the council, so we fight to protect them as well. Here, this is yours. You should know better than to assume you would have to steal it. Have some honor." He threw a small rune stone with Vryce's fragment bound inside onto his chest. "Still trying to become an unholy abomination, I see."

"And I see you are still trying to be the spitting image of Odin." Vryce placed the rune stone in a pocket.

"We each have our means, and the gulf between us is eternally wide. Yet we are both friend to myth and legend. The cost for this fragment of yours is safe haven and access for any of my people, at any time, whenever they need it, with the utmost hospitality."

"Very well," said Vryce.

"I want your word upon your true name."

Vryce sighed. He knew relying on allies and favors was never free, but this was worth any cost. He paid it gladly.

Satisfied, Verkonis loomed over him. "You should return home. They will be assaulting your walls soon enough. You must keep your portal open until the twenty-first. I hear they've already shut down your neverborn in Chicago. Do you have a plan?"

Vryce picked up his personal soul blade and sat up fully. "I have my people working on that. Lineages are a powerful source of energy. Do you have a plan for yours?"

"I have my spirits working on it. The will of humans is a powerful source of energy. Remember, Vryce, if you gamble with the lives of others and lose, you must pay thrice."

Vryce grimaced as he sliced his hand again, teleporting into his sanctum deep beneath the Twin Cities. *That little trick is why so much is possible. How I can collect my fragments before time runs out. I am so close.*

His leg still tattered, he moved a cane to his side for some mobility and placed the porcelain mask on the wall with the viola case underneath it. With a steady hand, he fixed the raven's claw to the hilt of his soul blade. Satisfaction was beginning to creep up within him, almost making him gloat to himself. *Oh. Not yet. There are still many players left in this game. There will always be players.* He sheathed the blade and hobbled out of his sanctum, pulling two iron nails from a table full of other ritual components before emerging into his grandiose underground living quarters. Dozens of familiars and small homunculi worked at cleaning the arcane tomes that would be added to the library above them later.

It was decorated with personal belongings he had acquired over the years. A banner from the carnival he served with during the dust bowl in the 1930s. A Freemason's Grand Master robe. A wicker man from the Salem days. The smell of vanilla incense and dusty fabric mixed in the air. It was a museum of his life, items to remind him of who he was and who he could become again. Outside this room Sven would be waiting for his master's possession. Two iron nails later and a spell to alter appearance and the warlock could enter his city without fear of death. *Well, unless one of the homunculi gets the bright idea to stick a dagger in my eye.*

The tenth fragment was his coup de grace, recovered by someone on the council after they stole his research. Removed for so long, it was hidden from his senses. It's why bait was needed. The deepest portal into purgatory lay just below the Library of Deus. All he needed to do was locate a descendant of Lazarus that would inevitably come calling. *After all, lineages can carry powerful magic through them.*

# CHAPTER 35

The convoy of vans raced along the expressway. Mr. Bollard was an aggressive driver when he needed to be, and despite the snowy weather conditions, he made sure every car moved out of his way. Mike sat in the passenger seat, pointlessly trying to make the window fog up with the thick wet snow on the outside. Mike knew they had enough of an arsenal in the three vans behind them to ensure they would go to prison for a very long time. The engine made a loud clanking noise and sputtered out every time Bollard floored the accelerator.

"You're gonna stall us out," Mike said. *Man, O'Neil needs to hire better drivers for his personal militia.* They were coming up on the Twin Cities any moment now. Through the snow, Mike could not see anything on the horizon. *Like driving in a snow globe.*

The car ride had been near torture for Mike. Bollard was a dick who wanted silence and slapped Mike's hand every time he reached for the radio. *Meditate on the mission, my ass.* Mike decided to tempt his fate for the thirteenth time and used his speed to attack the volume bar with zeal only to have Bollard swat it like a cat playing with a mouse. *Son of a bitch. Should've brought some headphones.*

"All right. Fine. You want to focus on the mission. Tell me again what the hell this plan is," Mike said, banging his head on the window in frustration.

Mike could almost feel Bollard roll his eyes before he responded. He revved the van up close to a poor sedan, almost running it off the road. "For the seventh time, in your language, there is a bad guy who did a bad thing and we are going to stop him," Bollard said at last.

"Yeah, let's go over details. You have this guy Vryce. What's he doing that's bad compared to you guys specifically? You Unification guys want to bring back Lazarus from the dead, so you ripped holes into hell to do so. This guy Vryce was one of your guys who was tasked with doing that job. He did it. What's the problem?"

"He is violating divine law. Not that you would understand. It is above you anyway."

"Try me, genius. You know, maybe your personal problem comes from the fact that you guys need to take a few management classes and focus on branding."

Bollard gave Mike a sideways look and smiled. "Very well. God, the big man, the big bang, the creation of the universe, made the heavens and the hells. They govern the earth, and each performs specific tasks. The sun rises because angels move it. The wind blows because there are angels who make it so. Demons were created with their purpose as well. They deal with and test human-made concepts. Without them, the world would be a static picture, never changing. Do you understand this concept?"

"You know that things like gravity, evolution, and friggin' dinosaurs existed, right?" Mike replied. "Yeah, I know what you're going to say, they are both right and true, divine will accounted for all of it and that the religions are all wrong. We've covered that."

"God himself rested when he was done, and the universe was created. He did this by creating humanity. He made them *in his own image* is the phrase, but what this means is he died, and humanity was born to live within his creation. Demons and angels are doing their part behind a veil that separated their world. We call this the *Innocence*. Since humanity is divine, they still have the ability to add to creation through their dreams. Look to history for examples, but even other *gods* were made at times." He flashed the van's lights on another slower-moving vehicle and sent the message to move. "You follow?"

Mike grabbed the handlebar above the passenger window to brace himself. *Good thing for oh-shit handles.* "Yeah, we are God, and we messed things up pretty damn well. Why didn't everyone wish for a better life and hold hands and sing 'Kumbaya' to create a utopia?"

"Irrelevant. Some men are weaker than others. You are no longer part of that equation either. Once a human drinks or eats of the forbidden fruit, they choose to kill that tiny part of themselves that was once divine in exchange for power." Bollard swerved the van and almost slid off the road. His lips pressed thin as he focused, the only sound in the cabin was the thumping of windshield wipers.

Bollard continued when they were back on the road. "That material power can serve to bend the masses to someone's will, thus grant said person, by proxy, the ability to control the world. Egyptians were the first to put this into practice, and look what they did with it? It is summed up by the choice that humanity makes with its own fate. This is humanity's world, after all. If they choose to follow a monster, that is upon them."

"So back to the bad guy?"

"Right. Throughout history, humanity has always needed a prophet every millennium to guide them, or they would ravage themselves to the breaking point. Everyone knows Jesus and Muhammad, but there was also Isis, Thor, Buddha . . . the list goes on. Ones with the backing and support of the Unification tend to stick around. You don't hear much about Mithras or Ukko. They've effectively been stomped out. The Unification is going to return Lazarus to serve as a new prophet to reset the wheel and start the next age. Vryce and others like himself have figured out the game. Watching the world turn for a few centuries does change your outlook."

"A few? This isn't rocket science. More like a fairy tale," Mike said, checking behind them to make sure the rest of the crew was still there.

Bollard ignored the comment. "Warlocks have found a way to take the blood, hearts, and souls of demons and angels, claim their power and work magic that remains among the most guarded secrets in the world. The magic of manipulating the barrier between the worlds and souls themselves. Then, on top of this, Vryce wants to steal back his soul, his divine spark. That is a violation of divine law. Even worse, since warlocks are aware of how to use that spark more than any, reality itself can almost be bent to their very will in certain areas, provided they know the correct names and words of creation." His gloves creaked on the steering wheel as if he tried to strangle it. "A necessary evil, we only allow those warlocks chosen by the Unification to exist."

"That sounds pretty hopeful, actually. So there is a way back for all of us?" Mike asked, pausing for a moment before slapping his head. "Wait a minute! You guys are fucking idiots. Talk about classic inequality. Let's just erase anyone else who doesn't want to play ball?"

Mr. Bollard snarled at him and raised his hand to threaten Mike. "Fool. Becoming a lich breaks the very foundation of creation. It opens cracks for things-that-should-not-be to enter. It turns angel, demon, and man against you alike. It binds you to this plane of existence, unable to pass through the gates of heaven or hell for eternity. You would wander this land, cursed and immortal, unless you are physically dragged and imprisoned elsewhere."

"Yeah, but with awesome powers." Mike held up his hands. "Whoa. I get it, tough guy. Don't worry. You're all a bunch of monsters who are tired of being second fiddle to the Kardashians. Stings, don't it? Closing the rift here does immediate good. I'm down." Mike watched as they raced past a car that spun out. "This has been done before, hasn't it? I mean, there are already"—Mike switched to his best impression of Tindalos—"things that were never born."

"Yes, it has. More than we would like to admit. We have a chance to stop this one. It is a long process. Vryce must reclaim fragments of his soul before seven days. If we kill him before then, it stops."

"You know we are up here to seal that rift, right? Let's not lose sight of the mission at hand, Mr. Bollard."

"We've already killed the main source of energy for that. Vryce will do whatever it takes to keep the rift open for a day or two. This is why the Unification used two cities. In case we needed to end a ritual early. But you've given me a bolder and better idea. We are also going to dive into purgatory as well. Like it or not, Lazarus can seal all of the rifts. This is the best place to do both at once."

"So why not just drop a bomb on him if it's that big of a deal, or shoot him with a sniper rifle," Mike mused.

"Because he never comes out in his real body. You're dealing with a warlock who has survived in the shadows for centuries, studying the occult for his entire existence for this chance. Shredding the Innocence is something that can only be done on a certain date, by certain people, in coordination, around the world. The Unification had no other choice but to use him, and him them."

"Bullshit. What a load of motherfucking bullshit." Mike leaned his seat back and put his boots on the dashboard. "You assholes had a choice. A choice to *not* do any of this. But just like every other group of self-entitled pricks, you want to rule the world. Only it came back and bit you in the ass, and now it's up to us to try to save a part of it. You know what I could have been doing today? Eating some terrible Chinese food and crying in a bowl of ramen over the *Iron Giant* movie."

Mike let the silence resume between them. He really didn't feel like talking anymore. The orange lights of street lamps fluttered past, and he watched the thick, heavy snow fall. He didn't give a crap about what Bollard had said. He knew he was alive deep down inside. Now he just had the ability to make a difference.

As they were getting closer to the cities, Mike began to squint his eyes and shot up out of his seat as he rolled down his window for a better look.

A massive wall built from green pulsing bricks at least fourteen stories tall loomed ahead of them. Mike knew he was seeing the world for what it really was, not what everyone else saw. To him, the snow appeared as falling ash now. His ashen world. Atop the wall, chains as thick as cars hung leading up to a floating island that hovered above the city, right over the top of a tall white building with a *W* stamped on top of it. As they rode through a tunnel in the wall, Mike gauged its thickness. He could swear that he heard the sounds of distant screams as they traveled underneath.

"Oh, you can see that?" Bollard said. "No wonder O'Neil wanted you recruited. You already had one foot in the door. That's rather interesting. Welcome to the Society of Deus, personal domain of Vryce."

Mike still had his head out the window in awe when he replied. "So how do we kill this guy?" He brought himself back in.

"That will be covered when we are safe at the hotel. Everyone needs to know that, and I hate repeating myself."

# CHAPTER 36

They pulled up to a shady motel outside downtown St. Paul that advertised free cable TV. Bollard had rented the entire place, given the staff a weekend off, and passed out room keys to everyone.

Mike had just enough time to fight with a vending machine for some gum and a pack of smokes before they all were to meet in JJ's room. The lot of them crammed into a room that smelled of sex. Cases of assault rifles were stacked on the single bed. Winters and Matsen had been stealing gear from the Chicago PD for a while. The look on Winters's face suggested he was pleased with his collection, but Mike suspected he'd kept the best for himself. Once they had gotten cozy in whatever corner on the stained rug they all chose for themselves, Bollard began to unfold the plan.

"We have only three days to complete our objective. You have allies here within the city who will serve as reinforcements. The Unification has their own array of agents who have been working within the walls. They have so far been waging a covert war to identify key personnel within the Society of

Deus." Bollard pulled his own tablet out, flashing a devilish grin as he caressed it.

Shaking the feeling off, he continued, "The Society of Deus has been building an army of vampires from the rejected, eliminated, or criminals of the Unification. They were sent here to be reconditioned so they could be useful. The Society of Deus commands roughly three hundred undead warriors."

Matsen chimed in. "Sir, there are only twenty of us."

"That won't be a problem. They may have high numbers, but most of them are so brainwashed that they cannot act without their commander. It's a master-slave arrangement. Our objective is not to fight them head-on, but to eliminate their key personnel. Within the society there is a position known as the ridari. Each ridari commands a small squad of undead, and each of the undead in turn commands a small squad of blooded soldiers. I am one of the ridari myself. I hope that my cover is still intact, as it will allow me access to their communication networks."

"I should've brought more sniper rifles," said Winters. "Any chance we can just get them all in one location and then blow them up?"

"That would be ideal. There are, of course, complications. Vryce has a few apprentices, sorcerers of high potential that serve him. The first and most dangerous among them is Gabriel D'Angelo. He is new, a wild card. He has been given the strength of many from his master, but he is an easily goaded and provoked hothead. This is his weakness. He is a deadly instrument of war, though I would not rate him as highly intelligent or savvy." JJ held up a photo of Gabriel. His fleece turtleneck sweater and blue jeans did not appear to be that of a mass murderer.

"Okay, so we send in Lucy to talk to him for an hour. I'm sure he'll be raging at the end of that." Mike flashed a wink at Lucy, who answered with a murderous smile.

"The next group of threats is Captain Mitch Slade, a fire sorcerer and also the leader of the Twin Cities Masonic police force. He will be armed and most likely traveling with Gabriel and a squad of blooded Special Forces soldiers." A swipe on the tablet revealed a stocky individual with muttonchops and aviator shades.

Phoebe dived over the mattress and swiped Mike's pack of gum. A quick wrestling match ensued for the fate of the Juicy Fruit. Phoebe emerged the victor.

Bollard waited for the tablet to be passed around the room and moved on to the last apprentice worth noting. "Cael McManus, a druid, controller of plants and wildlife. He is a solitary figure, usually restricted to the society's libraries." The picture of Cael dressed in dirty robes with a gnarled wooden cane did not impress anyone.

Bollard gave them a predatory smile. "The rest of Vryce's apprentices are sorcerers that haven't finished their training. He will put them in harm's way. After the ridari are eliminated, if Vryce wishes to command his armies, he will have to do so himself. In his real form. There is no way he could command that many creatures and still maintain possession."

"So, Phoebe, any visions on how this is going down?" Doc asked as he pulled at his neck skin.

A pop of bubble gum broke the silence. "Yeah, this will be down to the wire. Some doctor's office is a risk, a better place is near a pyramid with a lot of books. You'll have to be invited in. One way gives you a better shot of killing Vryce, the other a better chance of finding Lazarus. As long as Vryce is killed and Lazarus is freed, there will always be a chance. Siding with one side over the other is also a choice," she said, chewing on the hard-won gum. "I know, it's all pretty vague, but hey. Prophecy."

"I think we need to flank them. Sir, you mentioned we had allies in this? Are these the same allies that worked with Frank? If he was killed, how do we know that they are still in play? Or even trustworthy?" Matsen asked.

Bollard kept his cool demeanor. "They are the same ambassadors that Frank was dealing with under the table. Their work of smuggling out artifacts and copying texts has been under way for a while. It's how we got Daneka Jr. some of his dad's journals. Since they are Unification loyalists, I'll keep you and them separate so nobody gets hit with friendly fire. It is unwise to place all our assets in one basket. It is only at the final moments that they will strike. Chicago is our fallback point. Once the society falls, Chicago will serve as the hub of operations."

"So when do we begin the party?" Mike asked. He had folded a paper airplane out of a steno pad after writing, "They are using us as cannon fodder. Be ready." *I was gonna send it to Phoebe, but no, thief of gum, Doc gets secret classroom notes.* He let it fly in Doc's direction.

"We'll rest for now and begin tomorrow night," Bollard said.

Doc unfolded the paper airplane and read the note as they left the room. Doc gave Mike a nod, and they headed out into the night. Mike lit up a smoke and took in the skyline, still in awe of the massive walls surrounding the city. The island was still there above them. It billowed black clouds of smoke into the sky. The Twin Cities was far calmer than Chicago. *If I'm going to fight here, I need to walk the streets. Feel this city's pulse.* Mike hopped over the second-floor railing and wandered off into the night to explore this new battleground.

# CHAPTER 37

The crew was still filing from his room when Bollard reached out and grabbed Phoebe by her shoulder. She spun around and glared at him as she moved a purple streak of her hair behind her ear.

"Hands off, chief," she said.

"I need you to stay here. You are in charge of that entire biker crew. We need to go over the mission planning," Mr. Bollard responded. He took his hand off her and moved with catlike precision between her and the door, shutting it.

Phoebe plopped down onto JJ's bed and made sure that her boots, still wet with snow, made a nice puddle as she curled up her legs and began to rock back and forth. "All right, plan away. What's the scheme?" She took off her leather jacket.

Mr. Bollard's hand grew larger and full of white fur as he shifted and moved in to swipe at her. Phoebe moved to dodge the blow, the talons slicing her hair as she ducked and rolled off the bed, throwing the sheets up between them for a quick distraction. "Wait," she said after she had distance between them. "I already know how this plays out."

"Do you, my dear? Then you understand why this is needed." Mr. Bollard shifted back into human form, cracking his neck and fixing his cuff links.

"Yeah, pretty simple. You can't let them have their resident psychic. All your plans would be spoiled if I was sitting around. So you eliminate me, take me out of the picture before I walk out of the room." She pointed at him. "Except you aren't going to kill me. You can't. So you were going to slam my head into that desk until I blacked out."

"Really? I admit even I had not thought that far. Particularly the killing-you part." He grinned and stepped forward with caution, making sure he was cornering his prey.

"Yep. That's what happens. So here's what's going to happen now. You are going to open your tool kit over there. You have a syringe and a vial. I'm going to inject myself and knock myself out for the next day or so. Then you're going to have us all imprisoned. I won't say anything, because the end result is good for both of us. We'll both get what we want." She motioned to her bare arms and slapped her wrists as she spoke. She was still on the balls of her feet, though, ready to sprint if something went wrong.

"I wish all future prisoners were as interesting and able to recognize the inevitable as you." Mr. Bollard opened his tool kit and produced the required instruments.

"No, you don't. You are a shit-for-brains demon who gets off on Machiavellian manipulation, thinking you can con your way into freedom. Nothing gets you hard like watching people fail as you claim their success. But you've killed the wrong person, and pissed off someone very determined. So you need me alive for your plan to get close. I don't fear you, alone, in this room." Phoebe caught the vial and began to work, handling the syringe like an expert junkie.

Mr. Bollard grinned with pointed rows of teeth, his eyes gleaming red. "You are far too dangerous to let run around. You lied to Mike when he asked you if there were visions. Left out information. Why?"

"Have you seen him? It's on us to save him, not the other way around. It's all or nothing with him, and he's better off as a wild card. Not knowing what's in store for him. Hope is a fragile thing. If he knew the truth, it would break him." She winced as she injected. "See you on the other side." Her eyes rolled back into her head, and she collapsed.

Bollard picked her up and placed her on the bed. Moving her hair away from her face, he felt JJ remark at just how beautiful she was. The plans were coming into place. Soon, he would be the one who captured the Unification's forces that were responsible for turning off the fuel and "killing Delilah." Right in time for Primus Vryce to have his grand ceremony in his libraries. With Delilah out of the picture, he could position himself close enough to Vryce to strike. Afterward, the Unification would have all the tools in place to control this city and its rift.

JJ forced a thought to the surface for Mr. Bollard. *You really think Vryce is going to show up when he is at his most vulnerable? No wonder demons are nothing more than hearts to be eaten by warlocks.*

"Silence. He will be there. Once he's dead, we finish our goal and then circle back to Delilah at our leisure."

*Use her new addiction to blood and force her to repurpose this city for our agenda.*

"I told you this was the only way," Bollard snarled.

*This is how the world is saved.*

"From itself." Bollard pulled out his phone and a coin with the laws of thermodynamics printed on it and began rotating the coin in his fingers.

"Yes, this is Ridari Bollard. I'm alive. I need a daytime assault crew. I have the location of the group that kidnapped Delilah and myself." Mr. Bollard frowned as he looked into the mirror. A rogue white hair had sprung up on his head. He plucked it out with a twinge of pain.

*Leave no trace. This is my body after all.*

"Deal." Mr. Bollard smiled to himself.

# CHAPTER 38

Mike kept his hands in his pockets as he walked around downtown St. Paul. Unlike the Second City, St. Paul did not accept the sacred hour of 3:00 a.m. as one of peace. People bustled about among the Gothic architecture of the city as if it were daytime. Shadows were cast at odd angles, adding an element of depth to the city. It was a place that hid many secrets in its walls. He did not like this city. It felt *wrong* to him. The young man out jogging at this hour; the couple walking down the street, holding hands, smiling; and the salaryman flagging a cab with his briefcase after a late night were all out of place. Mike stood out like a vegan in a barbecue house. His trench coat was dirtier, but also filled with more of his own flavor. His boots told a story. Everyone else seemed plastic, and Mike realized what was bothering him.

*None of them are going to die as it stands.* Not in a car accident, not of a gunshot, not of disease, not of a piano falling from a building. Nobody out at this hour had any chance of dying, even of old age. Maybe that's why they didn't panic like the people did in the Second City. They kept their heads down and did their jobs and trusted in the government. *Heh. As immortal as these guys might be, they don't seem to have much of a life either.*

A girl's scream broke the night air, followed by the bellow of a shotgun. Nobody reacted. They just kept about their night. *Oh, hell no.* Mike broke into a sprint. He heard the sound from behind the cathedral and climbed on a parapet to get a better view.

A dozen or so men and women, naked, with black leathery wings stood handcuffed in a line below. Black tears rolled down their faces, making them look like a sad Goth parade. A soldier in full riot gear grabbed the next in line and threw it against the wall.

Its form changed from man to woman back to man again, each more pleasing to the eye than the last as it begged. Without hesitation a firing squad unloaded into it. Mike could see the glint of silver rounds burning its flesh as it was ripped to shreds. As the creature fell to its knees, it was already turning to ash. In a blur, the captain of the soldiers rushed in and ripped out a heart with his wicked set of long, reddish claws.

"Men, who captured this succubus? Was it you, Thomas?" the captain said.

"Aye, Ridari Westin," said the soldier as he saluted.

"Claim your prize, then, and load the next. We rendezvous with D'Angelo in twenty minutes. Our break only lasts so long. Pick up the pace, scum." He threw the heart over to the soldier, who began to devour it with zeal as he stepped to the side and another one took his place on the firing squad.

*This isn't a fight. It's a damn execution. Never thought I would feel bad for the demons, but damn. Frankie did say not all demons were bad. Well, we are supposed to take out the ridari. I might as well cross one off the list.* Mike jumped from his perch, almost reaching as high as the top of the bell tower before falling down to his target. The soldier leveled his gun at the next succubus in line, his finger on the trigger and a greedy smile in his eyes.

The soldier didn't have time to scream before he was crushed when Mike landed on him. A quick right jab buried the head of the next soldier into the brick wall. Mike stayed close to the ground and ran to the third soldier, bringing his foot up to kick him, crushing his ribs and sending him flying out of the alley, where he crashed like a broken doll into a car.

The remaining four men and Westin were still recovering from the initial impact. Mike didn't hesitate before grabbing a shotgun from one of them and using it as a baseball bat on another, burying him into the wall.

"Time to redecorate, boys," Mike said as he cracked his knuckles and pulled out a cue ball in a sock from his pocket. He began spinning it.

"Interesting," said Westin. "Get him." The remaining three and Westin closed in. Westin was a blur of speed himself as he tried to claw and rip at Mike.

Mike spun the cue ball around and whipped it into the first soldier's face. The weapon ripped out his jaw. Westin's claws found purchase in Mike's side and were beginning to rend his guts out.

"Really? That tickles," Mike joked.

Mike brought his knee up and elbow down to dislodge Westin with bone-crunching force. Westin fell to the ground with a look of terror on his face. Raising his boot to curb-stomp him into oblivion, Mike brought it down with full force only to crumple the concrete below. Westin used his speed to retreat to the end of the alley.

A shotgun blast from a soldier behind him brought Mike to his knee in panic. A wooden bolt jutted out of his chest, just below his heart. *He missed! Oh my, that's luck.* Mike brushed himself off and looked back at the soldier. "Ouch, man, what the hell! I like this coat. Who said you could use a gun?" The soldier's eyes went wide before Mike buried his head into the wall next to the succubus. Mike grabbed the foot of the body and threw it back at Westin, who was turning into mist already. "Ah, shit. He got away." He turned to the succubus. "Did you know he could turn to mist?"

"Yes," the creature said, changing shape to a pretty female with large eyes and short green hair. "Thank you," she said.

"Uh, you can talk. Great. That makes it harder. Also, I'm dead. I don't think seduction is going to work," Mike said.

"You are a vampire. Seduction is your thing, and it works just fine. Besides, I'm not trying. Are you going to kill us or let us go? We aren't here to enslave the world or whatever you guys think. We just want out of the pit. Wouldn't you run from hell if you got the chance?" she said.

"Point taken. All right. I don't have the time for this any-way. Tell you what. Leave this place. Go west. I bet Sin City is a perfect place for you guys. I can't believe I'm saving demons from humans. What the hell is going on?" Mike gestured out of the alley. "Get out of here before I change my mind."

"We'll remember this, honey. The hounds already spread rumors of you. You've earned a favor from us. You vampires never know when you need one returned. Our master, Dorian, will remember you, the one in the green coat." She pilfered a set of keys from a fallen soldier before they made their way out into the night. "Your name?" she looked back before she left.

"Auburn," he said. *Well, I'm just going to keep this between me and this wall. What the hell is in these guns?* Mike reached down, took out a shell, and examined it. It was custom-made and filled with silver. The shell had a strange occult marking on it, almost like a rune. *Great. Magic bullets. Well, I've caused enough noise. I need to get back. I think I'm going to enjoy beating these guys up.*

The crummy motel was silent by the time Mike returned. Everyone was already asleep or bedding down before dawn. Mike let himself into his room on the first floor and closed the door. He flipped over the "No Smoking" sign on his nightstand and lit one up as he inspected the drapes. He didn't like the security they offered against the sun and decided that he was going to sleep in the bathtub. He moved a few pillows and all the bedsheets to the yellow-stained tub and shut the door. *Maybe this is why the legends always sleep in coffins. Better than motel bathrooms.*

Mike, nestled in his bathtub, was jostled awake at the sound of a grenade. He was tired. Moving sluggishly, he crawled out of the bathtub like he had the worst hangover. A single small ray of sunlight leaking through the bathroom door scorched his hand. Flesh burned off in an instant, and Mike let out a howl as his bone was revealed. *No, not again. Not the sun.* His mind raced in panic, anything to avoid the terror of the barrel again.

He heard the door to the motel room slamming open, the chain snapping off its weak screws with a loud ping followed by the sounds of another object bouncing. The door to the bathroom rattled after another explosion. Soldiers filed in after. "Clear the drapes! Flip the bed. Let's bring the sun, boys." A series of shotgun blasts littered the room.

It would take them seconds before this door was kicked down and he was sent to his burning demise. *Think, man. Think. You're fucking trapped in a bathroom and you led them here. You let Westin get away. Wait. Daytime. They are humans or just blooded like Matsen. If they come in here, I can still kill them.*

Mike sluggishly pulled himself into a fight stance in the bathtub. He put his hands against the slimy tile behind him, shaking from fear as he lifted his boot out and placed it on the floor. It didn't burn. *Good.* Still he had seconds to come up with a solution. *Maybe they are just as scared.*

"You come in here and I'll rip your heads off, assholes," Mike said. "I've got a toilet I can rip out and smash three of you with. Nobody wants to die by getting hit with a shitter."

The response was not what Mike had hoped for as the gunfire started. Flecks of plaster and drywall filled the air as bullets ripped through Mike's body. Diving into the bathtub for cover as the barrage continued, he curled up in a fetal position. The specks of sunlight just above had pinned him inside a porcelain prison.

"Our orders are to capture you alive. You are pinned down on all sides, and we know exactly how to get that room full of the sun," shouted a voice after the gunfire stopped. The sounds of them reloading did not set Mike at ease. Nor did the thought of being paralyzed again and at their complete mercy.

*Ahhh, bloody hell. Might as well go out with some glory and try to escape.* He grabbed the end of the bathtub from inside, knocking moldy tile aside as he heaved. Rolling with the bathtub, he yanked it out of the wall. Water showered the room. Burying his head and hands in the tub for cover, Mike pushed out like a football player moving a defensive lineman. He threw the tub with the force of a moving car through the wall toward the gunmen behind it. Before the sunlight blasted him, Mike shouldered a sidewall into the next apartment. It gave way like papier-mâché.

"Ooooh yeah!" Mike shouted, remembering the Kool-Aid man as he dived into the next room. SWAT soldiers were already zipping up a body bag in there. The light was not as profuse as it was in Mike's room. *Why is my room so special?*

*Light is light. It should be everywhere. Are they using mirrors? Fucking hacks! That's a great idea! We should steal that tactic.*

He pounded a soldier's head off and then elbowed another one in the skull, knocking him out. He grabbed the body bag and ran through the wall into the next room. *Ha! They fucked up. They should have taken out the guy with super strength first.*

He continued to slam through the motel, bullets ripping through his legs and gut, with little effect. A bolt was sticking out of his back by the time he reached the end of the motel. The goons were far enough behind that he had some more time to look at the situation. The parking lot was crawling with them. They were loading body bags into armored carriers. *Of course it has to be a sunny day, one of those annoying ones without a cloud in the sky.* Mike would have to worry about his team members later. *If I die now, there will be nobody to save them later.* Inside he knew it was because he was terrified of the sunlight. Even if he wanted to step out, he could not.

He was trapped in the farthest motel room, and soldiers were starting to close in. He couldn't run or hide. The weight of exhaustion from the day pulled on him. Even with all this action, he wanted nothing more than to crawl back into bed.

It was the cage of the motel that was the problem; if he could make it into the city, hell, the sewers, Mike was sure he would be fine. *Sewers.* Mike yanked a tattered mattress with dirty sheets off the bed, hoisting it over his head like a makeshift umbrella. He screamed as he kicked the door to the outside off its hinges. Trying his best to carry whichever friend was in the bag and balancing a dirty mattress on his back, Mike scurried outside. *Ooooh, I'm so dead. This is how it happens. You know, death by sunburn.*

He stumbled for a moment when a bullet ripped through his knee. The shift in balance exposed his left wrist to the burning sun, and he collapsed. The sewer lid was paces away still,

and the world felt as if it were on fire. He crawled with desperation, trying to get closer, when he heard the car coming at him.
The SUV was barreling down on his location, and Mike was
running out of strength. He jammed his arm into the asphalt
and braced himself for impact.

The taste of blood and metal filled Mike's mouth as the
vehicle crumpled into him. Skin began to melt off his face as
glass and metal shrapnel shattered around him. The SUV tumbled and flew over him. Mike grabbed on. Momentum carried
them closer to his destination. Tumbling with the crash, he
buried his fingers into the sewer lid.

His wrists were liquefied, in flames from the sun as he
ripped off the lid. Mike thrust the body bag down the hole
and dived in after, banging his head on the far side with a loud
clang. He tumbled down into the water below and snapped
his leg on impact. He wished he were really dead. The pain
from the sun was intense. He tried to pull the body bag, but his
hands were only bone by now, except the parts hidden by the
gloves. *Blood. I need blood.*

Mike clumsily opened the body bag, hoping it was Phoebe
or one of her girls. Instead, he found Akira, who had an arrow
sticking out of her chest. *Fuck. Well, hopefully you can save me
now.* A flash grenade exploding in the water nearby deafened
Mike and blurred his vision.

With his limbs all but useless, Mike did everything he could
to get the bolt dislodged, eventually resorting to biting on it to
pull it out. It tasted different than wood, like it was covered
in blood and ash. Akira opened her eyes wide. She took one
look at Mike, who was beginning to pass out when the first set
of boots landed in the small stream. Akira sliced the soldier's
neck with a claw, so fast it was like a wound simply appeared
on his neck. *I knew she was fast . . . buuuut.* The thought was
lost as Mike faded.

"Mike, take my hand. Do not move. Whatever happens. Do not move." Akira grabbed his bloody hand. Mike winced in pain. "Do not move." Pulling themselves as far to the side as possible, she thrust Mike and herself under the chilling water that filled the storm drain.

More soldiers filed down and checked their dying member, administering what first aid they could. Teams went each way through the sewer, passing them by inches. Boots landed so close to Mike's ear that he could hear the squeak of leather and feel ripples of water when they walked past him. Yet they never noticed him or Akira, because neither needed to breathe. The fear never left. The weight of the daytime activity was unbearable. Every nerve in his body was still on fire. Yet he could not move through the entire day. He had to trust Akira.

# CHAPTER 39

The three apprentices walked along the torch-lit corridors beneath the Twin Cities. The walls were made of rough, porous stone and smelled of damp mold. Gabriel thought Vryce could use some air fresheners and a few maids.

The torches and stone slab served a purpose. Within these walls, the gargoyles they created blended in, serving as the deadliest last line of defense. Stone creatures made from blooded humans and magic intertwined to make the perfect guardians, even if their creativity was rather limited.

Deep below the city, in Primus Vryce's personal sanctum, many magical experiments were conducted. Gabriel understood next to nothing about them. Cael, the druid limping by Gabriel's side, was down here more frequently as the highest ritual master. Slade preferred combat operations and population control, so he tended to avoid the underground unless he was summoned.

Each brick of this entire place had more magical wards inside than even the Unification's headquarters in the Vatican. Every stone in the facade had been dipped in demon blood.

Arcane glyphs would serve to ward against demons, angels, and unwanted trespassers.

He ran his finger along the hilt of his cavalry sabre, reminding himself that the knowledge he had came from the deceased Visago, residing in the blade. Having the magic of ten apprentices was intoxicating, but Gabriel wished he could cut down some of the dignitaries that had been around for a thousand years.

It was six at night. Gabriel had spent most of the day in bed, planning instead of getting his beauty sleep. Tonight they were to start crossing names off a list.

The master wanted to see them after his return. Despite the need for the special rock that made up these walls, Gabriel decided that you could still provide camouflage and spice the place up some. He resolved that he would be installing a throw rug, picture, or perhaps even a nice suit of armor and a coatrack the moment he had free time.

He paused outside the door to the lab and looked at his two companions. Cael seemed bored, his hair wild and unkempt. Parts of his beard were singed and tangled from his nightly ritual routine. Slade had his hands in his leather jacket and an unlit smoke dangling from his lips. Gabriel wrinkled his nose at the smell of brandy wafting from him.

"The three of us don't exactly look like we're going to be meeting our master," Gabriel said. He kneeled to tie his shoe.

"Meh," was all Cael said as he shrugged. He plucked something from his beard and ate it with a crunch.

"Last I checked, only the army of vamps had a dress code. Vryce only cares about results. Besides, I don't see you in robes that look like drapes either." Slade gestured to Gabriel's jeans.

"Robes get in the way actually. I prefer functional clothes." He reached for the knocker on the door and gave it three raps. "We have a lot to do tonight. Let's get started."

The door opened on its own, scraping the ground with a grating sound. Primus Vryce was inside, shirtless, with tattoos running along his arms and back. Strands of blood-red silk were woven through his fingers as he operated on a translucent green body in the corner of the room.

A massive eight-foot-tall creature made from solid obsidian stood over him, holding a golden bowl that Vryce would dip the strings into before resuming the stitching of the jade body. In the middle of the room, another being that looked as if it were made of pure shadow lurched and waited with an anticipatory edge, like a father waiting for the birth of his child.

Also present on a slab on the far side of the room was a monster larger than the lithe jade body that Vryce worked on. Made of a shiny black metal that gleamed in the torchlight, it had spines and spikes protruding from it at odd angles, as if it was meant to inspire terror.

"You're late," Vryce said as he continued his work.

"Apologies. Dignitaries have been diving nonstop ever since we were placed on reserve energy. Putting the final notes on what they found took time," Gabriel said. While true, he had also drifted asleep. He elected to leave that part out. "Are you finished with all your bindings?" The door closed behind them as they walked into the room.

"Apparently, the Unification discovered our true goals and took action without going through Walsh first. We need more time. I'll finish my bindings later when I'm fully ready." He finished the last stitch and ripped the thread off, throwing the remains in the golden bowl. The obsidian assistant set about cleaning up the rest of the components.

"What happened with the Unification? Does it affect our mission tonight?" Gabriel asked.

"After they got what they needed from Delilah and put us on a clock, they mobilized a strike force from Chicago. Ridari

Bollard escaped and allowed a daytime assault on their make-shift base of operations," Vryce replied.

"Fancy." Slade chimed in. "So we won, right? That was easier than I thought."

Vryce smiled. "In a manner, yes. I present to you the for-mer officers Winters and Matsen of the Unification. I'm going to call him Onyx." He gestured over to the shiny black creature. "And she is Jade. Their souls have been bound into these new gargoyles, which will help us. An old pastime of mine, the cre-ation of such things. This is why I say that people are always more useful alive than dead. The rest of the group is currently undergoing the brainwashing required for integration into the army. We will turn our enemy against our enemy." Vryce bowed slightly with a sense of triumph about him.

"How do we know these things are loyal?" Gabriel asked.

"They will obey your commands. My magic binds them, so be careful of the way you phrase your orders. It takes time, perhaps decades, for them to understand intention."

"Commands we give them, sir?" Slade asked.

"With only nights left, expect a full-scale assault. I'm giving each of you one of these gargoyles. I will take Obsidian. He has been with me the longest and was my first creation," he said. The assistant holding the bowl nodded in acknowledgment.

With a snap of Vryce's finger, the form made of shadow slithered into the middle of the room. "Cael, you will take Epsilon. He is a shadow walker and thus suits you best."

Cael bowed low, holding his gaze to the floor. "My master, I thank you. I will ensure that your vision, the return of magic and wonder to the world, will be defended." Cael slammed his cane to the floor and gestured for Epsilon to take his side.

Vryce poured a swirling green-and-red vial of liquid into each of the two dormant bodies. They seized for a moment before waking, rock and earth given life with human sentience.

"Slade, you will take Jade. I've given her the ability of speed at the expense of strength, but since you have enough guns, a scout will help," Vryce said as he lifted his creation's head up.

Slade knelt as if he were a knight in front of a king. "Boss, with your gift, I will ensure that your enemies are destroyed. Who wouldn't want a hot jade statue standing by their side? Roger is going to be jealous." He smiled and lit his cigarette. A small ring of fire appeared in his hand, and he walked over to Jade and placed it around her finger.

Vryce continued. "Lastly, Gabriel, you will take Onyx. You still need a shield to guard you. Onyx is the most durable of the set. As the youngest of us, Onyx's assistance will help you against creatures that have been around for centuries."

"I do not approve of the methods you use to bind them. I would rather have somebody who will fight for the cause willingly than a walking risk that might crush my head in," Gabriel said.

The room remained silent for a moment as Vryce looked upon his apprentice. Slade and Cael seemed to distance themselves as much as possible without being obvious. A wry grin slowly crept along Vryce's face, revealing fangs. "Very well. If you must be insolent, order him to stand in a broom closet. Finish the task before dawn if you are so brazen to do it alone."

Cael stepped forward, breaking the tension. He placed his cane under Epsilon's chin. "Follow me." The shadowy figure moved like a panther behind the druid.

"Fair enough," Gabriel said. He snapped his fingers to capture the attention of Onyx. The eyes looked stoic, like they were aware, yet not of who he once was. "Let's go." He gestured back to the door. Onyx simply stood there and looked at Gabriel as he walked away.

"Go where?" A grating, deep voice came out.

"To kill people. I don't know. Let's go," Gabriel replied.

"Kill people. Okay." Onyx crouched and started moving over to Slade, who raised an eyebrow and took steps back.

"Stop," Gabriel said. "You are a flaming idiot, aren't you? Stand behind me and follow me until I point at someone for you to kill. Seven steps behind me. Understand?" He snapped his fingers and rolled his eyes with frustration. *This guy is going in a broom closet for sure.*

"Yes." Onyx followed exactly as he was told, his large frame casting a shadow over Gabriel once he took his position. "I desire free will," he said. Even Vryce stopped what he was doing and looked back. Obsidian dropped the bowl, dashed over to Onyx, and looked up into his eyes.

"I want him, Vryce. This one is mine," Obsidian said.

"It is rare that they maintain knowledge of their condition." Vryce pondered, his lips curled in a smile like a fascinated scientist. "Officer Winters must have been the strong, silent type. I will give him to you, Obsidian, after Gabriel is done with him. It will be a good lesson in leadership for Gabriel, a test for Onyx, and a lesson in patience for you."

"Let's go, sweet cakes. Follow me," Slade said as he tapped Jade's shoulder. "So, off to the murder fest, are we now? All geared up and ready to end the world?"

Vryce cleaned off his hands with a rag. "Yes, let's." He smiled and admired his handiwork. "There is one more thing. Some of them escaped. One of them has eaten the heart of an arch demon known as Golgoroth. The one with the green-and-black trench coat. He would make a perfect addition to our forces. Bring him in alive. We have Bollard to thank for tipping the tide of war in our favor. I wish for him to see dawn."

# CHAPTER 40

Slade, Cael, and Gabriel had just left the sanctum, walking through the geofront back to the elevators. It had been quiet for days since they managed to cleanse the area of both angels and demons that poked their ugly heads through the tear in the Innocence.

Gabriel pulled out his Book of Expendables, filled with more notes after his terrible negotiations. He wasn't sure what bothered him more, the fact that Vryce hadn't spoken of it or the haunting thought that he was really just going to be discarded because of it. He wasn't going to be caught unprepared this time.

"The Society of Deus is a vital stronghold we have to protect," he said to Onyx, looking up and shaking his head at the large creature who couldn't care less. "Do you follow?" Gabriel said.

"I am following," said Onyx as he walked exactly seven steps behind Gabriel.

Gabriel spun around and held out his hand. "Okay, stop following. Just stand there and listen."

"Okay," Onyx replied.

Gabriel bent the end of his pen in frustration. "You want free will, and I want someone who knows why they are fighting. So pay attention."

"Listen for how long?" Onyx asked.

Gabriel put his hand on his forehead and let out a deep sigh. Slade leaned on a nearby wall and let out a cackle. Cael only shook his head.

"Until I am done!" Gabriel said. "Cancer, aging, disease. All of these things can be cured with magic. We don't want to turn the world back to the dark ages, just bring back the power that humans had when there were fewer of them around." Gabriel paused as he flipped through his binder to look something up.

"Are you done?" Onyx asked.

"What part of *listen* do you not understand?"

"I understand *listen*. I do not know when you will be done."

"Were you this annoying in life?"

"A friend taught me."

"I'm going to knock his teeth out. What friend?"

"I don't remember."

"Fine, I will wave my left hand above my head when I'm done. Don't speak until then."

Gabriel shifted his stance to ensure he had his attention. "Roger assigned me to go through the list of all sixty-three actively diving dignitaries." Gabriel flipped to his own handwritten section of the binder. "Comparing them to Roger and Delilah's notes, I've narrowed the list down to thirty-four members who will not attend the library opening tonight. We know that they will instead make a dive of their own. Their goal, we assume, are three dive sights that we've declared restricted, because each will bring them close to Lazarus. We've named them Mather's Church, Succubus Alley, and the Clinic. We need to kill them before they get to the underworld, where pursuit is impossible."

"What about the others?" asked Slade. "Aren't we getting rid of everybody?"

"I'm not sure. Roger has something planned for that. He asked me to make enemies of everyone days ago. I'm sure me murdering over half of them will go a long way with that. I don't know his end game. How much do you two trust him?" Gabriel said.

"Implicitly," said Cael. "Social maneuvers are his specialty, and if it wasn't for your birthright, he would be standing where you are now."

"That doesn't mean it benefits me," Gabriel said. He raised his left hand above his head and waved.

"None of this helps," said Onyx.

"Quiet, you. Now are you going to do the same and stop these guys from trying to rule the world?"

"Not by choice. The master commands I follow you."

Gabriel turned to Slade and Cael. The six of them stood in a hallway near the bottom of a very long elevator leading into Walsh Tower. "Do yours give you this kind of problem?"

"You will learn how to command a creation. It's less verbal than you think," said Cael. With a flick of his wrist, Epsilon took a knee at his side.

Gabriel ripped out a sheet of paper and handed it to Onyx. "Our first target is Vertovi. All three of us will be needed there as Vertovi is Alexandria of Ur's prize helldiver. He's got his own squad with him, and if Alexandria is lethal, so are they."

Gabriel handed envelopes to both Slade and Cael that contained their targets' known powers and pictures. "The element of surprise will be key," Gabriel said.

"Why don't we just put them all in one room and blow them all up?" Slade asked.

Cael looked at him and rolled his eyes. "The old way is more fun. Their heads must be ripped off, stakes plunged through their hearts, and they must be buried in coffins of rosewood. Then they must be thrown into a stream of running water until sunrise."

Gabriel scoffed. "That's a bit overkill, don't you think?"

"If you are going to do something, do it right," Cael replied.

"Faaaair enough." Gabriel continued, "Let's make a coffin maker happy right before Christmas. Vertovi and crew will be in St. Paul getting ready in a three-story building across from the church. We'll ambush them there."

"We'll let you run the show here, Boss. It's cute watching the low-man plan," Slade said.

"Cute," Onyx added, a slight smirk etched into his stone face.

# CHAPTER 41

Their destination was nestled between square brick office buildings, built for function. Yet in St. Paul, it was these buildings that looked out of place with the backdrop of the cathedral across a large street. Flame-orange lights lit up the cathedral from varying heights, while wooden planks for some sort of track were placed on scaffolding that stretched and winded through the streets. The construction for the Crashed Ice Festival had been abandoned due to recent events, and instead of being filled with citizens cheering a sport where Minnesotans fly on illuminated sheets of ice at breakneck speeds, it sat isolated and alone. Joy was just as absent from the air as heat. The smell of ozone had vanished days ago, and now the green aura that surrounded the city was barely visible.

Zipping up his fleece to protect him from the biting wind, Gabriel wondered if anyone really had a plan about the death of their ritual and an alternative fuel source. They walked through scaffolding up to the freight elevator. His breath steamed in front of his face while he rubbed his hands together. All five of his companions, breathless, just stopped and stared at him.

"What? It's cold out?"

Slade activated the elevator. "You know eating a demon heart makes you undead and a lot more resilient. You're already banished from the sun anyway, so you might as well."

Gabriel pulled out his cavalry sabre and sliced his thumb along the blade, activating its power. The eye of Mammon glimmered with a dying green light that pulsed slowly as the elevator descended. Cael and Slade both readied their wooden staves embossed with glyphs. Slade's was smaller, the size of a baseball bat, while Cael's gnarled and twisted staff extended full-length.

The elevator opened. The three of them looked at each other before Slade broke out laughing. "So much for looking cool before getting on. Remember this pose for when we get off." They all agreed and boarded the elevator.

The freight doors lifted up with a rattle on the top level of the empty loft. The floor was filled with planks of wood for the track being constructed outside. The light from the cathedral parapets shone like beacons through the windows, creating oddly long shadows on the floor. Iron lanterns, silver crosses, and other diving equipment lay piled along columns.

Vertovi, in a slick black suit and diamond cuff links worth more than Gabriel's house, looked up from a backpack full of gear. Vertovi smiled when he saw the six of them getting off the elevator and filling the hallway, with weapons brandished.

"Evening, gentlemen. My escorts for purgatory, are you?" he said. His dashing good looks had the ability to disarm most people.

"You could say that," Cael responded and slammed his staff into the marble floor. An arc of lightning zigged across the floor in odd angles. Vertovi spun with the experience of a dancer and ran past the windows, his shoes so polished they reflected the arcing electricity on the floor. He ran past them before the electricity detonated where he was seconds before.

"Thanks for holding the elevator." Vertovi thrust his hands out to his sides to begin the spell. The windows bent and distorted, causing the cathedral outside to appear warped. Columns of metal and glass screeched as they began to buckle. The elevator doors shattered and crumpled. Then, as the spell neared completion, everything else behind him, including Gabriel's own allies, was thrown into the middle of the hall.

Vertovi was the first to recover. His unnatural speed gave him enough time to remove his cuff links and roll up his sleeves. "You've been shanking us inside purgatory for weeks, one by one, by—" He became an unintelligible blur as Slade received a kick in the face, Gabriel's feet were pulled out from under him, and Cael was pulled to the ground by his hair.

Gabriel spun when he lost his footing. It felt as if a thousand impacts bruised and broke his body before his face bounced off the cold concrete floor. The iron taste of his own blood streamed from his mouth. The ground shook twice as Cael and Slade were both slammed down. With one eye half-open, Gabriel could see Vertovi's shoe crush Cael's skull, spraying thick green blood everywhere. Vines quickly sprouted from the wound, writhing around, collecting what blood they could.

Slade winked at Gabriel, and then pushed himself up without a scratch on him. After dusting off his leather jacket, he flipped off Vertovi. "Oh, we are done with the one by one. It's time for the big show. That's all you had in you? And you bit me? Really now." Slade's small staff ignited into flame, and he whipped it in front of him. A long tendril of fire snapped in the air. Slade made the living fire dance ever longer, whipping around him on all sides and snapping the air at each end.

Vertovi laughed and moved to the ceiling, dodging and weaving between the whip of flame, rushing into Slade's personal space. Gabriel saw each blow land on Slade, cracking columns or the planks of wood nearby instead in an impressive display of transference spellcraft.

Gabriel used his pain as a source of focus, summoning forth a ring of white fire around all of them. He could feel the angel blood dancing in his fingertips as he raised the white fire to the ceiling, paint curling off the walls from the heat alone. A sense of euphoria washed over him as the pain flowed out of him. *Should've killed me first.*

Vertovi was trapped between the red fire stroke from Slade and the walls of white fire from Gabriel when the bodies of the three apprentices began to levitate. Cael's head looked like an array of vines, spilling and lashing out in every direction.

With nowhere to run, bound between them all, Vertovi's knees were blown out from another arc of lightning. Before Cael could impale him with his staff, Vertovi flipped a hand-held trigger.

The explosion came without delay, blasting out the floor beneath them. Intense heat followed by a suction of cold air from outside and an infusion of oxygen caused the flames to spread between planks of wood and along the scaffolding outside.

The three apprentices hovering in the air looked beneath them with indifference. Vertovi crawled to safety. His companions were all waiting below, a maroon-red light oozed through the room from a doorway to Hades nearby, where barghests reinforced them. Somewhere in this city, a demon was supporting them.

"Well, if they are going to group up for us," Gabriel said.

"Makes our job easier," Cael said.

"Jade, kill them," Slade commanded.

Gabriel was grateful for their newfound reinforcements. The three of them had planned to ambush Vertovi and friends separately. Together, they posed an actual threat. As they descended, he took in their ambush spot. Anything that could be used as cover was moved aside and set up as a barricade. All of them were prepared for the fight. Some stood with spells at the ready. A seven-foot-tall shadow beast loomed by the door, and the last diver had two hand cannons leveled at the three of them.

Gabriel noticed their eyes widen. On closer look, the barricades weren't set up as barricades at all. They cleared the floor to make room for more explosive charges to blow the next floor out. *They are going to bust in through the bleed a different way.* He wanted to test the limits of those who would stand in their path. *This useless trash needs to be taken out.*

The gargoyles rearranged the stage set for battle by blasting through their makeshift barricades with ease. Gabriel set to work countering the spells of the sorcerers. *Cheap, pathetic, blooded fools.* Slade controlled the flames to cut off any escape. Cael threw his staff into the middle of them, growing vines that lashed out to grapple anyone.

Gabriel felt himself get lost in the battle, exchanging partners to parry attacks with magic interwoven between the rock fists of their new pets. Light and shadows cast at disjointed angles as the air grew so thick with a bloody mist that Gabriel could taste it. Telekinetic attacks ripped columns out of their steel foundations. Flames swirled around them and melted the flesh off those who came close.

His ears rang as thunderous shotgun blasts ripped chunks out of the gargoyles and spells of ice and petrification found their mark between lapses of Gabriel's countermagic as the Unification creatures fought without the same coordination. As they rallied, Gabriel felt the torment of immense pain when bullets riddled through his gut. That was instantly followed by an intoxicating euphoria as he summoned white fire. He was getting drunk off the pain, craving *more* so he could release it. Reckless and wild, Gabriel let himself go.

Until the pain came, with no euphoria after. He backed up into a broken column and grabbed his stomach, feeling so much warmth flowing over his hand that he was afraid to look down. White dots began to flood his vision, and his head was ringing.

His heart thumped in his head as his vision dulled. *Tha-dump.*

Gabriel saw Slade grievously wounded from the shadow beast, a hundred swords lashing through his torso.

*Tha-dump.*

Lashes of flaming whips entangled a diver as Slade used the last of his leverage and strength to pull them both into a nearby inferno. The vampire let out his final screams of unlife when the fire consumed him. Gabriel saw no sign of Slade emerge from the inferno as ash clouded his vision.

*Tha-dump.*

Cael transformed himself into a large moving tree and slammed another victim into the ground, splattering his skull, only to find himself blasted apart by machine-gun fire.

*Tha ... dump.*

Gabriel's vision faded as he collapsed. The clattering of metal next to his face from the soul blade drowned out the other sounds. His last sight was the pulsing eye of Mammon.

# CHAPTER 42

*"Why do you deny what you are?"* A delicate voice welled up within Gabriel.

"We've got him! He's down! Get 'em outta here. Now!" Vertovi screamed.

Gabriel saw the bright, warming lights of St. Paul Cathedral through his blurry vision. He was moving, being carried by something. A creature. He could tell because of the claws burrowing into him. The night air offered a brief moment of relief before the impact of being thrown into the back of an SUV. One of the helldivers, the shadow beast, threw him in. Above him, he could still hear the sounds of fighting in the building next to Succubus Alley. *Are we losing?* As he tasted his own blood, slightly salty and copperish, his eyes rolled back into his head and the vehicle rolled away.

*The instructions say . . . head around the city counterclock-wise at five miles above the speed limit. Stay on Hennepin and shadow I-94.*

Gabriel's eyes shot wide open. A sharp pain sat just behind his eyes, like needles covered in hot spices were being thrust into his skull. A thought . . . not his own . . . invaded his mind. He jostled mildly in the back of the SUV, thankful at least, for modern suspension and a carpeted interior. The bindings tying his hands and legs were a new, unwelcome addition. He had been unconscious for a while now, it seemed. His abdomen and chest hurt with each breath, and a ripped-open first aid kit lay near his head. *I've been shot. A few times. That won't do.* He barred his teeth through the migraine as another thought crawled in. A small sliver of light leaking through the trunk was enough to overwhelm him.

*They should've known the price of evil. Can't believe it's going to go down this way. Bollard is pulling a sick move.*

"You need to turn left up here. The Clinic is that way," a deeper voice said. Gabriel thought it sounded like one of Vertovi's men.

"How many of us do you think are going to make it? This is the big dive, right?" a female voice said. Her next thought jammed its way into Gabriel's head. *I'm going with twenty. The plague demon scared the rookies shitless.*

"Thirty. Vertovi and the other three are taking out the war-lock's apprentices. They'll dive in back there. She said that all restricted areas are a good bet. Bollard's banking on the Clinic, and he'll kill Vryce himself."

"Can you really trust her info?" she said. *Delilah is a ruth-less predator. I've seen her follow through before.*

"Yeah, she spilled the whole bowl. Even the warlock's real plan. Haven't you seen the way she looks at Bollard?" *I bet those two have been shacking up for years.*

"Strength in numbers, I suppose, regardless. They said tonight was the final night for diving anyway. Gates gonna close here after tonight, just before the deadline as well." *I'd follow Delilah now that I think about it. She's effective.* "So why him?" *Why alive?*

"Sacrifice. Guess that was the plan for him all along. Besides, he's a fucking asshole. I'll feel a lot better after I pin him to a wall with knives in all his organs one at a time. I mean, unless you would rather kill one of us to pry the Innocence open an extra hour or so. I'd rather have an escape plan." *Aaaannnd this should be it.*

Gabriel listened to some minor conversation as they slowed down over the remaining blocks. *None of the apprentices in the soul blade were capable of telepathy.* He grasped around the best he could for the soul blade and felt the chill of losing something critically important. *The heart? That angel's heart is the source, then?* As the vehicle came to a stop, thoughts came racing in from every direction. He needed it to stop. He needed to breathe. He needed to focus. *Make the world small. Focus on what's in front of you. The microcosm.* The taillight went from overwhelming, to just a taillight. The invasions faded into the background, along with their troubles, as he concentrated on the pain in his chest.

"She's inside, yeah?"

"Yeah, Bollard says she isn't leaving there till this is over. Get the asshole."

Multiple doors were opened and shut. Gabriel could hear their thoughts, and let one or two in if he focused.

*Cute.*

The SUV crumpled in from the top, as if a wrecking ball landed on the roof. The world went dark to Gabriel as his head knocked sharply on bent metal.

*Have faith. The world grows. You grow. Know thyself.* The voice was eerily familiar. Graceful and feminine, yet mewling and weak as it pulsed in the back of Gabriel's mind.

He recalled the image of the angel, her ribs flayed open and the pulsing heart in his hand slowly being raised to his lips. Suddenly, a vile taste in his mouth brought his vision back as his heart was jump-started by Onyx's stony hand slamming Gabriel in the chest. Everything was overloaded. His vision was filled with white light around the edges. His body burned and revolted against itself. Blood flowed from the bandages around his stomach like a shattered bottle of wine. Nothing compared to the taste in his mouth. A sick, rotten taste and smell of sewage made him vomit. Onyx held the head of a hellhound, pouring the blood over Gabriel.

"S-t-op," he stuttered in between heaving. The taste was still in his mouth. He could not get rid of it. *I have to get . . . this . . . out.*

Onyx only looked at him with a deadpan reaction and dropped the hellhound's severed head.

His arms flailed for the soul blade in Onyx's other hand. The rush of power helped deaden the pain as he mentally sorted through the spells contained within. *Healing. Need to drink demon blood first.*

*It is better to die,* the voice chided. He crawled to the hellhound's severed head and began licking its blood off the street. With each lap of the tongue, he felt violated. *Why is this denied to me? I do not want to die.* He forced himself to swallow, a thousand daggers going down his throat. He quickly cast the spell before the heaving began again, turning the poison within him to lifesaving. He clutched the blade close to his chest. The sounds of the soldiers firing guns brought him back to earth.

"You have eaten an angel," said Onyx.

"Yes." Gabriel coughed.

"Then you cannot feed upon the blood of others for strength."

"I guess not."

"That is weak."

"Fuck you. I still got the spell off."

"Because of that sword."

"Who cares?" Gabriel said as he lifted himself back up. *Warlocks are made from eating the hearts of both, their souls shredded in the process. If even just a taste of demon blood felt like that.*

*It is better to die.* The voice rang inside.

Gabriel looked at the carnage outside from Onyx's landing on the SUV and formed his plan while hiding behind both Onyx and the shattered car. The helldivers had all gathered at the Clinic, the remaining assistants anyway, with no sign of Vertovi or the other vampires. *I count thirty. Guess we know who won that bet. Only blooded sorcerers at best. People of my birthright are useless unless facing another Unification sorcerer, right?* "Onyx?" he asked.

"That is my given name."

"Crush them."

# CHAPTER 43

The medical clinic had been quarantined, surrounded by road barricades and police tape. The shattered windows were replaced with plywood, and when Gabriel looked closer, iron nails held dead herbs in nooks and corners. The Lilith moon cut through the spotted cloud cover and gave ample light that reflected along the light snowfall. The smell of burned wood still hung in the air.

Gabriel pushed one of the barricades out of the way and walked up to the building, leaving Onyx to chase after those who fled after the tide quickly turned against them. Without anyone around for a block, Gabriel was free of the thoughts of others, and his headache started to subside.

Until he made his way up to the broken doors of the burned building.

*It's Gabriel. Delilah said to stop anyone but Bollard coming in. Yet I must follow his orders. An interesting conundrum.*

Gabriel felt the thought flow into him from behind the doors. The shadows were thick inside, yet he was sure that thought belonged to one of the inhuman soldiers under his command. It felt cold and reminded him of Alexander Lex DuPris.

"Yes, you do need to follow my orders. Now step into the light, soldier," Gabriel said.

Gabriel was completely surprised when Ridari Bollard's driver stepped out of the shadows. *I saw him earlier at the Clinic.* Even with the debris on the ground, he made not a single sound as he stepped out through the large hole in the door. He gave a slight bow and then resumed his attention stance. "What can I do for you, sir?" he said, displaying not the slightest surprise that he had been sighted.

"What is going on here? Why are you here? Lex is out right now battling who knows what that crawled out of some pit. You are supposed to be with him," Gabriel said as he readied his blade for trouble.

"There was a disturbance here that I was sent to investigate. It turned out to be minor, and I've already handled the situation," he said.

*I'm waiting to see what comes of Delilah's plan.*

Gabriel smiled. *I could get used to this.* "Really? And Lex or Bollard ordered you to investigate this *disturbance*?" Gabriel held up his fingers and made quotation marks around the last word he spoke.

"Yes, sir," he replied. *Not exactly. I suppose I could say that it's true. Delilah runs them all.*

"Well, I have a new order for you, soldier. You are to report back to Walsh Tower. Enough of this deception. Fall back in line underneath Alexander DuPris," Gabriel said as he gazed inside.

"Very well, sir." There was no further thought as he went back to the car. Gabriel traded places with him and stepped inside the building. *In hindsight, a fight like that would be a cinch now that I've gotten better. Heh. Demons beware. Gabriel is here.* The Clinic still smelled of burned wood and the chemicals that had been used to put out the flames. The cleanup crew had moved around much of the debris, stacking it up in very odd angles around the place.

Gabriel thought it looked as if some worker had a passion for either abstract art or strange fêng shui. He knew Delilah was in here somewhere, and if anybody knew the answers about this place, it was her.

Gabriel stepped over debris and searched room after room for Delilah. He called her name a few times with no response. After clearing out and searching the upper floors with methodical scrutiny, he headed into the basement. It was clear that much of the furniture had been arranged to the side and stacked up around columns. Someone even took the time to nail shoddy wooden boards into the ceiling for makeshift supports.

Finally, he spotted Delilah, her clothes covered in blood, handcuffed and chained to a steel beam in a corner. She stared at him with a sense of authority that made him want to apologize. It took Gabriel a second to regain his composure.

"Ms. Dumont. What is this . . . predicament you find yourself in?" Gabriel asked. She looked dangerous, and he maintained his distance.

"It is none of your concern. You have a mission to complete. I advise you to get back to your work for the master," she said. *Of all the people to come here, it of course had to be the most dangerous one.*

"I'm willing to bet, that our *master* will find what I've heard about you and your recent actions more than a curiosity. It looks like you've been bartering for your freedom. But—" Gabriel curled his lips in a grin. "We'll get to that. Since you are indisposed, I'm going to take this opportunity to ask you some questions. Pull up a chair. We might be here for a while."

"We will not. Leave and resume your work. I have everything here under control," she said as she wiggled a bit and rattled some of the chains to sit more upright. *Here comes the interrogation again. Children with power. Just what the world needs.*

"What is so special about this place and the children that were here?"

"That is above your clearance level," she said.

Gabriel was surprised that there was no follow-up thought. No flashes or images or anything to betray what she was really thinking. "Really? That's it? Just above my clearance level? Then why do I feel a kinship with this place? As if I've been here before. I grew up in Italy. I'd never set foot in this state until I was summoned."

She didn't even dignify him with a response. She just stared at him as if he were beneath her. *I've read your dossier.* That was the only thought in her head.

"I thought we were both on the same team. You can't even give me the slightest hint? I mean, you not saying anything is enough to help me draw some conclusions. So what? Was I born here?" Gabriel asked. He clenched his fists, and his jaw tightened.

"Believe what you will and draw as many conclusions as you like. This facility, much like the entire city, is the property of someone else. I am not at liberty to discuss those secrets unless ordered to, and I do not take orders from you. I can, however, give them to you. Follow my command to leave this place and resume your mission, or I will inform Primus Vryce of your treason," she said. *That will go over well. Master Vryce, one of your descendants needs to be brought to heel and executed. He coddles them too much. Children like this need to be given a stern awakening into this world.*

"Aha," Gabriel said. He cracked his knuckles and twisted his neck, the popping noise echoing in the basement. "Treason? Would you like to tell me exactly why you've been working with Bollard and the rest of the people he sent here? Maybe I'm not the one who should be reported to Grandpa as treasonous." He bit his lip in frustration. It was her fault that events were playing out against them, and he was growing impatient.

If Delilah were ever to play poker, she would be a world champion. Not even the slightest display, not even a twitch on that poker face. *Mind reader. Of course. Hello, Gabriel. Nice trick of yours. I won't fall for it again. Mr. Bollard is not who he says he is; he is working for O'Neil and a demon king himself. His objective is to get close to Vryce and eliminate him. He captured, tortured, and imprisoned me here. When he returns, the Whisper will kill him. Now go about your mission.* She tilted her head to the side an inch and waited to see if Gabriel responded.

"So you were interrogated, yes? And yes, it is a nice trick. I'm still getting the hang of it. What did you reveal to him?" Gabriel said.

"Everything," she said aloud. "I have no chance to resist the powers of a rakshasa such as him." Her thoughts matched the words coming out of her mouth. Now that she was aware of Gabriel's secret power, he doubted she would ever let slip a stray thought again.

Gabriel drew his blade and leveled it at her. "Everything. And *I'm* the one you accuse of treason!" He kicked over a file cabinet. "We have been under assault, and they closed the Chicago portal. You let them know exactly where to dive! I'm sure they've gotten into those places by now! Even worse, you never bothered to fucking tell us. So we've diverted a lot of resources to look for you, soldiers that could've been used to prevent the assault on the headquarters! Instead, JJ Bollard is on his way right now to receive acclaim from Vryce himself for capturing the forces that took you in. No, instead you have plans within plans and clearance levels while you sit in the ba—"

"I am aware of my plans, soldier. Now you take your orders and do as I have commanded. It is not your place to question, you impudent tool. You have a mission to salt the earth with the blood of the society's enemies. Go forth and spread your flames at those who would do the society harm. Let them know our wrath," she commanded.

Gabriel's face was a tint of red after the dressing down. "Oh, I will burn our enemies. Including you! Useless pile of trash." Gabriel snapped his fingers and set her ablaze before she could respond.

She slid out of her chains quicker than he would have guessed possible, activating a trigger switch she was hiding in her palm. Her flesh was bubbling from the flames, and Gabriel could see that she was dying before the entire room began to crumble around him.

Small explosives detonated under the stacks of furniture at each column. Out of the makeshift ceiling, silver spears and daggers fired like shrapnel. Gabriel ran for his life. If he had been any closer to Delilah, he would have been impaled and trapped under a mountain of weapons.

He made it to the stairs just as the rest of the basement ceiling collapsed, crushing everything underneath it. "Her plan was to take them both out," he said to himself. *Well, maybe she was more determined than I gave her credit for. Still, she needed to die for her manipulations.*

Gabriel picked himself up and brushed the concrete dust off his jeans. By now, he needed a brand-new pair, as no dry cleaner, even a magical one, would be able to help his wardrobe. It was beginning to set in that he was related to Vryce, but it made sense. *Not sure why all the secrecy. Was it really so hard just to admit that? He better not go all "I am your father" on me, though. I can't handle that without laughing.*

Gabriel took a moment to let the night's events set in. Right now he and the Whisper were the only people who knew of JJ Bollard's treachery, and he intended to finish what Delilah did not. *If I kill him instead of her . . .* He needed to revise his plan, however, to account for Bollard being aware of the entire operation. He will strike at Vryce right when the ritual here ceases to be. At least, that's where Gabriel would strike if he were Bollard.

Delilah had not anticipated Gabriel snapping and trying to kill her. *No. I saw that in him the moment he walked in the room. He's become bloodthirsty, getting drunk off that blade.* She shook the thought out of her head and focused on her real mission. She sat underground in a makeshift escape hatch and looked at the fallen room. *That trap was meant for Bollard. It would not kill Gabriel.*

She picked at her left arm, small bubbles of flesh had already begun to blister, and she could see white flecks of bone in her hand. The smell was the worst part, the sick taste of burned hair and skin flooded her senses. Symon had done a fantastic job with the trapping, but he should have collapsed the stairwell as well.

She heard a cry of pain coming from upstairs. She smiled as Gabriel swore about a "motherfucking bear trap." While it was nonlethal to Gabriel, she had no doubt that the silver teeth on that trap would cause severe injury, if not finish the job, on Bollard. *Never mind. Well done, Symon.*

All the planning thrown out the window because of a child's temper tantrum. Now Delilah would have to carry on the rest of the operation with wounds, deal with the fact she had recently been blooded, and stay out of Bollard's way. He needed to think that she was dead for years to come now. *Gabriel is so damn shortsighted. Our plans go beyond this month.*

Delilah still had backup plans, but her first step was to crawl her way out of this pit and make her way back to the prison. One of the vampires needed to be released and set after Patrick O'Neil in Chicago. The Unification would not rest as long as they had their local spymaster.

As she crawled in the cramped tunnel, her face hurt from a burned smile. She had hoped to use the nerve gas as a treat to celebrate Bollard's death. Still, it would make her feel better. *It's like a little Christmas present to myself. Sometimes you have to appreciate the little things in life.*

The cold air in the back of the Clinic felt like the best medicine in the world to her. She closed her eyes and felt the steam rise off her as she tried her best to shake the pain away. It worked to some extent.

She made her way through the snow and pulled out a small package that Symon had left there per her instructions. It contained her tablet, a change of clothes, and a set of car keys. At least she would make it back to the prison and library before Vryce's bastard son. *Luckily for me, if everything works, I won't have to see him again.* Checking the schedule, she realized that the meeting of all the dignitaries in the library was minutes away. If her luck held, Gabriel would be tied up by Symon's trap for longer than needed and she could do her work.

- ~~Kill JJ Bollard.~~ <-Move to later date.
- Get a fresh cup of coffee.
- Open Christmas present early.

# CHAPTER 44

Mr. Bollard removed his leather glove as he stood before the hermetically sealed gates that granted entry into the great Library of Deus. Despite all his planning, his stomach was still an icy pit of nervousness. All he had to do was place his hand on the keystone and speak his true name.

Bollard wasn't particularly keen on entering the library. For one, the black keystone felt warm to the touch. It would dispel any shape-shifting and return him to his natural form. Second, he was nervous about speaking his true name. The revelation of his true name was a secret any demon king guarded with his life. Any sorcerer, no matter how petty, armed with that information could summon and bind him.

Yet it was only within these walls that Primus Vryce would reveal himself in his true form, for if he did not offer the dignitaries this courtesy, he would breach centuries-old etiquette. Among the damned, overt use of power in areas of sanctuary could be taken as a mortal insult. Even Vryce had avoided public gatherings for decades, sending Delilah or Roger in his stead. He could delay no longer. He needed this for their society to have any relevance. If Mr. Bollard was to have an opportunity to strike him, it would be here in front of the great ambassadors of the Unification. Killing Vryce would send the message that all those who betray the Unification would meet their demise, no matter how protected they believed themselves.

Mr. Bollard hoped nobody was listening inside the keystone room when he revealed his true name, despite the simple fact everyone believed Primus Vryce when he said that no one, including himself, was listening and that there were no ways around the keystone chamber. Bollard assumed that Vryce was vastly more cunning than he let on and that he had found a way to have his cake and eat it too. It was still the only way in, however.

With trepidation, Mr. Bollard caressed the keystone. His hand was the first to change as the claws and striped white fur grew. His tendons made cracking sounds like snapping whips as his body transformed into his full demonic tiger form. "King Ghatotkacha of the Rakshasha, son of Bhima, father to Anajaparvan, and slain by Karna."

He felt the magic of the chamber take hold as his hair stood on end and goose bumps covered his entire body. The massive stone doors grated on the slab beneath them as they gave way. Before anyone on the other side could see him in his real form, he tried to shift back into the human form of JJ.

Panic started to set in when his body refused to shift back. The doors were open enough that a sliver of light creaked through. He refocused his willpower to force the change, yet still nothing happened. Frantic, he ran to the edge of the chamber. *Think! Think! What is this? Why can't I shift back? Nobody said anything about this. Why hasn't anybody mentioned this! I have sent countless people through this chamber. None of them encountered any problems after the magic set in. What did I overlook?*

He heard the voice of the announcer, Sven Mereti, on the other side of the doors. "Ladies and gentlemen of the Unification, our next guest has arrived! I present to you Ridari Bollard from Turkey. Mr. Bollard and his vast financial efforts have provided this city with much of its funding and defense programs. In addition, he has donated original works of Hindu mythology and the broken helmet of Karna, the great Hindu warrior who slew the demon king."

Panicked, Bollard was still hiding out of sight, but he had mere seconds to come up with a plan. *All will be lost if I reveal myself here. You are a millennia-old trickster. Come up with something. Hurry. Illusion?* He took a quick breath and tried to calm himself, but his hands were still shaking. He uttered an incantation of illusion. If it worked, everyone in the room would believe him to be what they expected to see.

If there was any doubt, however, they would see him as they wanted to see him, whatever they imagined. It was a trick to scare villagers, child's play, a cantrip almost. *Hopefully this lowly spell was beneath the notice of an arcane warlock.* Bollard did not place much faith in such a cantrip. However, he was out of time as the doors swept open.

The library was grander than he had imagined, which said something for a creature as old as he. He had walked among the great libraries of Alexandria and been within the temple of King Solomon himself. Ornately carved wood stood three stories tall, every bookshelf, chair, and table was made with amazing craftsmanship. *No, not made. There are no cut marks. These were grown by druidic magic.* Chandeliers the size of small cars hung from wrought-iron chains affixed to the air itself, suspended by magic inside a vaulted ceiling.

The ceiling itself was almost translucent, displaying the night sky above it. Guests had a clear view into the cosmology of the heavens, a look at the stars as they actually were, not as men believed.

Bollard smelled the mixed scents of oak, lavender, and even someone's vanilla pipe tobacco. On three of the walls, massive hearths with warm fires provided a sense of calm in the room. *I have to hand it to the warlock. For all his insolence and violation of divine law, he knows how to build a proper library. I think I will preserve this establishment.*

Bollard was so in awe of the wonder of the library that he forgot for a brief moment that there were people in the room, and all eyes were on him. Sweat beaded around his neck, and he prayed to himself that his cantrip had worked.

"Taken aback by the wonder of the library? This isn't your first time in here, is it, chap?" said Roger Queneco, the court chancellor who had been leading much of the negotiations regarding the library.

"I do believe it is, sir. Ridari Bollard has been out on field assignment, and as this is the grand opening of the library, he has yet to be given a tour," said Sven Mereti.

Queneco offered Bollard his hand. Bollard refused the handshake. The cantrip was only good for vision. Anybody who touched him would feel the truth. "Ah, yes, it is indeed. While I have donated, I had to wait like everyone else," he said, letting out a sigh of relief as everyone in the room seemed to go back to their business.

"Well, this is fortunate for you, then. I have a room full of people who are just dying, or undying, to meet you. Talk of the town, you are. Fantastic work bringing in those betrayers to the cause. I tell ya, some people just don't understand what it means to be a member of the Unification," he said as he gestured with his fist like he was giving a pep talk.

"Betrayers? But they were members of the Unification."

"Nay, they were a rogue group that had been calling themselves the Sons and Daughters. Luckily, you were among the ones who were taken. Jolly good luck that you were among their captured, wouldn't you say? Your escape paved the way for our success." Roger leaned in closer than Bollard would have liked, looking him right in the eye.

"Yes, fortunate." Bollard pulled back. *Are these the lies that the society has been feeding the dignitaries?* "Should we get on with introductions, then? Is Primus Vryce here already?"

"Yes, indeed he is. He is standing over there by the Dead Sea Scrolls, talking to Alexandria about the finer points of the church's decision to exclude them from formal doctrine. A divine creature if I do say so myself, and I do. A beauty such as hers does everyone good to see. She's quite the looker for a two-thousand-year-old vampire." Roger reached out his hand to place on Bollard's shoulder as he led him out of the room.

When Bollard jerked backward, Roger gave him a disapproving look. "Don't like to be touched, eh? Still got a bit of the nerves from the unspeakable torture they put you through. I understand. PTSD is a terrible thing. I know just the person to introduce you to first," he said.

"Uh-huh. Yes," Mr. Bollard mumbled.

*This little man has an unnerving ability to disarm you.* JJ spoke from Bollard's subconscious. *Oh, how cute is it that the demon pretends to be the courtier.*

Roger kept rambling. It was no wonder that Vryce had him as his personal herald. Mr. Bollard kept his attention on Alexandria and Vryce while Roger introduced him to some doctor.

Vryce was not himself. Mr. Bollard had gambled his entire plan to strike at the real body of Vryce here. Instead, Vryce mocked his well-laid plans by possessing some twenty-year-old body with dyed white hair. To add to the insult, Alexandria seemed to be in on the game. She placed a diamond necklace around Vryce's neck and toyed with his hair. He could almost feel them snickering at him as they looked in his direction.

"And that was Dr. Bowling. He'll just talk your ear off, and yet all he donated were original medical journals from the London grave-robbing era. Next, I want you to meet Baron von Adawulf, or as we simply call him, the Baron. He is a vampire of impeccable taste from Vancouver. I think you will find something in common with him, if nothing else because of your love of fashion." Queneco went on and on.

Sven Mereti continued to announce dignitaries as they arrived, listing their accomplishments and donations while Queneco took Bollard around the room at a dizzying pace. A beer baron named Alice Macgregor. A master surgeon of pediatrics Jacob Accardo. Ozinga, a hideous vampire from some sewer in Michigan. Arriana Mortgana, a demoness. The list continued as Bollard was spun from introduction to introduction.

In every other scenario, he would have his wits about him and carry on the fine art of socializing, but something about Queneco was disarming him. It didn't help matters that he had just revealed his true name and his gambit was falling apart. *Arriana was not supposed to be here. She is supposed to be with the others diving at the Clinic. Does she think to kill Vryce herself?*

Instead, he was being paraded around and toyed with, introduced to a shape-shifting coyote who was a pediatric surgeon. Everyone he spoke with brought up some parable of his heroic defeat of the terrorists and wanted a further invitation to discuss some text or some book or some spell.

Jacob Accardo was the worst of them. Not only did he continue with them from group to group, but he kept writing things in a small steno pad and asking questions for some archive report he was making. He wanted details on the full capture and a full interview after the main event tonight. His tiny round glasses and nosy attitude would interject into every further introduction to which Bollard was paraded.

The fact he remained in a half-coyote, half-man form as he walked around bothered Bollard even more. Coyotes were trickster spirits, laughing at everyone's folly when they had the upper hand.

In all the confusion, Mr. Bollard's head was spinning.

*Oh, I can see it from here. You are indeed being made into a joke.*

Mr. Bollard realized he was being turned into a war hero, a prize of the society. They weren't going to kill him. They were going to stuff him, hang his head on the wall, and give him so much prestige that he would be unable to break rank. No room to take a piss if he wanted. Fame was his worst enemy, and he walked right into it. *If they spread my true name around, I'll be answering summons for eternity.* He needed to leave.

He excused himself from an introduction to someone called Trouble Jones from New Orleans and made straight for the exit. He could no longer tolerate this room or the presence of Queneco, that disarming little shit of a man. Sven Mereti saw him heading to the door and clapped his hands.

"Ladies and gentlemen, dracs and leeches, and all of you fine sparkling creatures of the night. I do believe it is time for the main event, an opening speech from our primus, the founder of this library. After his speech, we will all commence reading the sacred texts on display. The special event of the evening will be a reading from the first edition of the *Arcannum Arcannimusim*," Sven said.

Bollard stopped in his tracks. He knew he was trapped in this room now. Leaving at this moment would be even worse than an outright assault. He turned and watched the thirty-some creatures assemble as Vryce put down a glass of wine on an oaken table and took to the center of the room. Despite his otherwise fine clothing, iron nails were still bolted into his bare feet.

# CHAPTER 45

Bollard watched as Vryce stalked through the room, waiting until he had everyone's attention before he spoke.

"As above, and so below. The magi of the world know this simple statement to be truth. It is through the will of mankind that the heavens are shaped. It is from the power granted unto them from the heavens that they shape it." He paused as he held one hand high and the other low, the spitting image of the magi from any tarot deck. "We have worked for centuries to ensure that this simple truth remains as such. Hidden in the shadows, we creatures don't have that power, because our divine right was stripped from us the moment we tasted the blood." He lashed out his lower hand and tipped over his wineglass. Blood flowed out and hovered in the air, suspended by magic.

"Yet with this power we have"—Vryce pointed at the blood—"influenced the minds of weak-willed men for count-less centuries, shaping the world as we saw fit. Humanity is nothing more than a collection of sheep to be herded by shep-herds whose eyes are open." Vryce brought both hands to his side and fanned out his fingers before snapping them shut.

Books from shelves on the third floor fanned out and opened themselves up, forming a new ceiling. "Welcome to the new age. Welcome to the age of enlightenment. I know each of us can feel it within our bones. The dawn of the Seventh Age is but a night away." Vryce closed his hands and lowered his head in a moment of silence.

*You should leave now.* Mr. Bollard heard JJ's voice in his head. *We may have our differences, but I don't want to end up as a personal pet of this warlock any more than you do.* Mr. Bollard held his head low in concert with the rest of the room but looked for an escape. Roger Queneco twirled his handlebar mustache and flashed him a grin and a wink when they made eye contact. Mr. Bollard felt like a caged animal.

Vryce broke the silence as he summoned his glass, refilled with blood, back to his hand and continued. "To commemorate this occasion, I have assembled within these halls the combined works of the centuries from occultists, prophets, and scholars." He gestured to the dignitaries. "You will each be given sanctuary from the sunlight over the next day within these halls should you so desire. Humanity will need your direction in the coming years. To prevent mistakes of history from repeating, I offer you the greatest gift of all. Knowledge." He paused and raised his wineglass as polite applause rang throughout the room.

When the applause died down, he pointed his finger back to the ceiling of books. "However, one among you is a traitor to this cause. It seeks to interfere with our success to satiate its own desire." Vryce slowly took in the room, pausing to look into the eyes of each person there. Bollard felt as if his knees would buckle underneath him. Queneco even gave him a snubbing look. "Arriana Mortgana," Vryce said. "Did you not receive a special invitation from my dear friend Roger due to your impeccable donations of books about demonology?"

All eyes in the room snapped to the thin woman in a black dress that had decorative lace curling around her neck. She became so pale that she made other vampires jealous as blood drained from her face. "Yes, Primus," she said with a curtsey.

"And you thought it would be wise to swap some of the books recovered in Hades with a copy, to be smuggled out by your companions tonight? Knowledge gained here is free for the taking provided the physical copy does not leave these halls. You are free to memorize anything you learn in these books and from these artifacts, but their removal is forbidden. Anyone who violates this rule must die." He gave her one final look before he nodded. "*Ignis vitae*," he intoned.

Arriana collapsed to the ground as her very blood boiled. Flames exploded out of her in crimson jets. In mere seconds, there was nothing but a pile of ash and bone. The gallery of viewers stood silent before offering Vryce another round of polite applause. Bollard let his eyes roll back into his head, his cover had somehow been maintained through all of it. He was going to be okay after all.

"Her companions are already being rounded up. Even our dear Alexandria had to let go of her own Vertovi this evening for his involvement. We must all sacrifice for our goals. In light of this, I've decided to offer a bit of entertainment for the rest of you. We are all scholars in our own right, so let's begin with a bit of theological debate," Vryce said.

The warlock moved to the middle of the room, setting his bloody bare feet in the ash of Arianna. "I have a question for each of you. Depending on your theological stance, you will file into two groups. Based on my judgment, the victors will be granted the first viewing of the *Arcannum*."

Mr. Bollard watched Vryce pace back and forth, leaving footprints of ash. It reminded him of a lion circling his prey. "Fear not," Vryce said. "There is no wrong answer. Among scholars, everything is subject to debate and testing. You understand, yes?" The room was his captive audience.

Bollard was familiar with this. After the murder of Arianna, the remaining people were just glad to be alive and would play along with whatever game he set forth. They were all his now.

When Vryce spoke next, his voice seemed to echo from every shadow in the room. "In the coming nights, do you believe that humanity should be shepherded and protected? Do you believe they are too weak to survive the return of demons into the world, to have the veil lifted from them? Should we continue to shelter them from the shadows? There is much merit to this idea. When humanity is threatened, they feed on their own panic and risk their own destruction. Greater threats are always clawing at the minds of men, and without a proper shepherd, wolves will descend on the flock and spoil the herd."

Mr. Bollard knew he was speaking of Lazarus as the shepherd. *Once Lazarus returns, he could bring humanity back to its innocent state as their savior.* JJ agreed with Mr. Bollard internally.

The warlock stopped pacing and let the thought sink in, the smoking remains of Arriana now scattered. "Or do you believe that we should thrust humanity into a new age and have faith that they will find the strength they need to survive despite the fact that billions will die? This idea also has merit. For the greatest works of humanity have always been borne from the greatest tragedy. Each is a gamble. Each has merit."

Mr. Bollard let out a scoff that caused the boring Dr. Bowling to distance himself a few paces away.

Vryce resumed his former position. "Will those who begin the night with the viewpoint of the latter please take a position to the right of the room, and the former to the left. After an evening of debate, we will take a census again." He gestured to each side of the room. The hearths in the fireplaces flared and each took on different colors, lighter yellow and white flames for those who chose to shepherd humanity and darker green and blue for the others.

Bollard watched as the diplomats looked at each other. Some knew where they were going already. Most of the guests Bollard had been introduced to chose the latter option, to present humanity to magic. It was no surprise to Bollard, though, that the beautiful Alexandria chose to shelter them.

"Oh, my dear Vryce, I'll play your little game. It's amusing to see how you've grown up so much since you were a little boy. Regardless of which side you choose, though, surely you know I am going in first. My descendant, Roger, wouldn't have it any other way." She gave a wink to Vryce and took a stance among those wishing to shepherd humanity. It seemed to lend courage to others in the room as well.

One by one, they filed into position like good little followers. Bollard took his stance on the side of those who would shelter mankind. He had seen humanity at its most vile, and during its greatest triumph, and he knew that they could not survive without shepherds.

*There is hope for your redemption yet, Mr. Bollard. The side Alexandria is on is the safest bet politically.*

Mr. Bollard realized one diplomat had not yet chosen.

The Baron stood in the middle of the room. He raised one eyebrow and looked to those on his left. Then he nodded at those on the right. Everyone seemed to wait for him to make a choice before he stepped forward and gave a very long and deep bow to Vryce. "Primus Vryce, I see where this is going. A vampire of my age is used to such things. It has been a pleasure to visit your library and see your society during this ritual. I hope you find my contribution of notes taken during the signing of the Treaty of Unification as something of historical significance to your collection." He held his bow and waited for a response.

"I have, my friend. You may rise. What troubles you so?" Vryce said, a look of genuine concern on a predator's face.

"Since I cannot play this game, and thus disqualify myself from membership in your organization, I request that we remain allies. You are personally welcome to my estate should you ever wish to discuss this topic further in the coming days. As to not spoil the activity, I request that I be allowed to leave and return to my home. I think I shall like to watch the moonset from my own back porch." He rose from his bow.

Whispers crept through the remaining dignitaries, most of them wondering why they had not thought to do what he did.

Vryce applauded. He jaunted to the Baron and firmly shook his hand. "It is a pleasure and an honor to have creatures like you in the world. I look forward to my future visits. Please, the exit is actually over there behind those shelves. I'll see to it that your bags are ready," Vryce said as he took the Baron's spot in the center of the room and waited for the old vampire to exit.

Not a word was said. Bollard could not help but feel that the smartest man just left the flock to a wolf who was staring at his dinner. The dignitaries would not fight now. Their will had been crushed. Alexandria playing along, only cementing the feeling.

The green-and-blue flames grew in strength, and Vryce's voice echoed in the library. "You who have chosen to thrust humanity into a world of magic, I admire your courage. You have the first viewing. I will stay here and entertain debate with the others. When the last of the first group returns, it shall be the shepherds' turn." Vryce gestured to a side chamber, and the group filed out.

Alexandria walked up to Vryce and gave him a demeaning kiss on the forehead before she sauntered off with the others.

Aside from her, no one remaining had the nerve. That, or they actually believed him. Bollard searched for any exit that he could run to.

He suddenly understood Vryce's game. He was going to keep everyone distracted and locked in a night of debate while his apprentices finished his work. Bollard had sent everyone else to launch themselves at restricted locations, yet he needed to kill Vryce and take the best gateway himself, which was near the library. All before the twenty-first. *Vryce is stalling us.*

Ambassadors began to debate with each other. Bollard ruled out each possible entrance and exit, including the one the Baron had used earlier. All of them were sealed. *Perhaps we should have swapped roles with the other crew diving at the Clinic.*

"The rest of you can die," Vryce said suddenly. The body he was possessing collapsed on the ground. The fires in the three fireplaces all went out, and Bollard felt the effects of nerve gas dispersing.

First came the constriction of pupils and tightness in the chest as the dignitaries began to panic. All of them tried to escape, using a variety of talents at their disposal. Bollard knew it was already too late for them in this hermetically sealed chamber and braced himself for the coming pain. This particular method of death would not be permanent for him, but it was certainly unpleasant.

The others in the room were not so fortunate. Blisters filled their eyes, and they twitched with myoclonic jerks. Bollard vomited on himself as his nervous system gave way. The souls of the people in the room left their hosts, spiraling upward. Bollard watched them go, and then saw Vryce as he truly was.

He stood on the books that had formed the ceiling before his speech and stared down at them like they were pathetic. He wore a long black coat with a red lining and held a soul blade in one hand with a viola case in the other. Even though he was wearing a gas mask, Bollard could feel his toothy grin. It was no doubt filled with vampire fangs and the tongue of a snake. Mr. Bollard counted nine objects of power upon him, with one phylactery missing. *Likely empty.*

The warlock threw the remaining souls into the green flames of the chamber hearth. With each ambassador added to the fire, the great ritual was granted another hour of life, just enough time to keep the Twin Cities active, limping along in the final nights. More importantly, there was no one left to kill the warlock before he finished. As Bollard's eyes blistered over and his vision was lost, he tasted defeat.

Vryce whispered in Bollard's ear. "I think not, Ghatotkacha. Demons are always more useful alive than dead. Only silver will kill your kind. Your fate is for another to decide. A favor I will repay gladly. Yet my last soul fragment is what binds you two together. So I'm taking that back. You'll survive. JJ will not."

Warmness flashed over his flesh, replaced by the cold feeling of snow beneath him. Then he felt himself plunge into ice water.

"We can't have Lazarus's descendant so close to the gates, now can we?" Vryce said.

Vryce sent Bollard back to the city with a spell, right into the river dividing the Twin Cities. Pain in Bollard's eyes and lungs gave way to severe aching in his muscles as his body regenerated. He pawed his way in every direction to find purchase. He was driven by a desire to survive and a fear of the pit, of being sent back to the abyss.

Fear subsided after a while, and his vision returned. He lay gasping for air on his back, his body twisting and pulling at itself as he shed JJ's mortal coil. The warlock had freed him, the soul fragment that had bound him and JJ together, the first one ever pulled back, was Vryce's all along. Bollard had gotten exactly what he wanted, yet it was empty and tasted of defeat. All he could do was scream into a night where no one would hear him under the ghostly walls of the city. His hollow cries joined the wails of a thousand souls imprisoned by the soul stealer.

# CHAPTER 46

Mike had spent the past days and nights in uncomfortable positions, finally crammed in between some rusted pipes. Akira had managed to keep them hidden before stuffing them into a more secure spot. He vaguely remembered her feeding him blood in his fugue state. From time to time, she would relocate them away from a patrol still hunting during the day, and by nightfall his wounds had healed with enough blood. For the most part. The soldiers had used special ammunition that slowed recovery. His face still felt sunburned, but the sharp tingling pain in his arms and chest was fading.

Mike felt Akira start poking him in the forehead to rouse him as the sun fell. He cracked an eye open to see her staring at him.

"Just five more minutes," Mike said. "And stop poking me. I've been awake for a while now." Mike attempted to dislodge himself from between the pipes. *I don't even feel like poking my head out of these sewers. Everyone around me is dying, just more ghosts to haunt me.*

"We don't have much longer if we are going to kill Vryce," Akira said. She pounced back into the tunnel, splashing up some rainwater before leaning against a wall.

"We won't be killing Vryce, man. The whole job is a bust. They fucking routed us during the daytime. I probably led them back when I killed those troops on my nightly walk." Mike took off his coat and shook it out. He inspected his wounds.

"Oh. Okay, then. So, to California?" Akira said.

Mike checked one of his fangs as he let the silence hang for a while. He was not sure what he would do. Heading west did not seem like a bad idea. *Go underground? Start a new life? Nah, who am I kidding? It's not going to work out that way.* "You know, this is where you are supposed to provide some sort of pep talk in a moment of doubt, right?"

"Pep talks are your thing. I kill people. If we're done here, then we're done. If you want to be an idiot and wallow in self-pity because you think everyone getting caught is your fault, I'm not going to stand in your way," Akira said.

Mike patted around in his pockets. He pulled out a pack of waterlogged and useless smokes. Disgusted with their smell of feces and moldy water, he threw them down. "Well, we smell like shit, there are only two of us, we have an entire city to search, and we've lost our inside man and the entire team. We are pretty much fucked." Mike walked down the tunnel, splashing as he went.

"Wait, where you going? Are we outta here?" Akira picked up the pace following behind Mike. "Like, California is a long-ass walk. We should steal a car."

"We aren't going to California. There is no way I could walk away from this as long as I'm still"—he beat his chest with his fist and smiled—"sort of alive."

"So how the hell are we going to kill this guy or his generals?"

"We aren't. You want a pep talk? The old mission is scrapped, at least the song everyone wanted us to dance to. It was kind of bullshit anyway. We were being set up as cannon fodder by Bollard and O'Neil. Which I suppose is fair considering we're all the new recruits anyway. Well, at least I am. So here is how I look at it." Mike was quiet for a bit as he looked for a way out.

Spotting a ladder twenty yards down the tunnel, Mike gestured to Akira to follow and climbed up into the city. Large skyways weaved between buildings like a spider web. The Twin Cities were known for their skyways like Chicago was known for the "L." Mike pulled himself out and smiled at a runner who tried to ignore him. He reached in and helped Akira out before kicking the sewer lid back in place. With his strength, it was like kicking a pebble. *I'm getting better at this. Good.*

"The way I see it, Akira, all of these creatures and forces are trying to preserve this city regardless of their goal, just like in Chicago. When I saw their crews killing demons in an alley, I learned these guys are way better at it than we were. They have better toys, and their citizens aren't going to die from either demons or cancer from what I see." He paused, taking in the sights of the city. "We need to disrupt the setting. I saw them loading our friends into cop cars. Chances are they just arrested them for interrogation. So let's start a motherfucking riot and set this city ablaze. That should stretch their troops thin and allow us to get close and see if we can't rescue anybody who was captured."

"Light the city on fire and cause chaos? Could work. If nothing else, it will draw them to us rather than making us hunt them down. Where should we start?"

"First, we get some smokes, food, and bikes. Then we will start on the outside and work our way in." Mike pointed up to the white skyscraper of Walsh Tower. The massive floating island still hovered above the building, connected to ghostly iron chains that led to the green walls surrounding the city. Brighter now than when they had arrived. *Did they refuel those?* He noticed pulses of energy flowing up the building to the island, then along the chains. "Heh, it's going to be the incredible climbing bad guy syndrome," Mike said.

"Yeah, what's it with that? Why don't they just have a nice apartment on some main street near a café? Why always the top floor of the tallest building? Oh, wait, compensation. All right. Food, smokes, and bikes. See, Mikey, told you pep talks were your thing." Akira smiled and stalked down the street. Mike shook his head. He felt better with her at his side.

It took them about an hour to find something to feed on. Streets were either abandoned or flooded with people creating their stockpiles of supplies. To most, what was happening was unbelievable, and they ignored what they could by bunking down, hoping that it was worse for someone else. Still, in times like this, people committed a lot of crimes against others. Mike and Akira were fortunate enough to do at least one good deed by locating muggers to feast on. Smokes were an easy acquisition, but bikes were not in their forecast. They had to settle for stealing a delivery van parked while the driver was away. As they drove, Mike assured Akira the poor fellow had car insurance. They agreed that insurance companies would have to update their policies to include vampire-related damages.

They drove around for a while before Mike found a run-down area of town. Akira kept asking "Are we there yet?" Mike told her they were looking for the city's poor. He was not expecting it to take so long. Over the years, the Unification had spent a significant amount of money on the gentrification of this city. The neighborhood might as well have been considered a middle-class area in other parts of the country. Mike parked the van on the side of the busiest road and got out, lighting up a smoke and taking in the night air as he waited.

"So what's the plan? Why we waiting?" Akira asked.

"Need fire," Mike replied.

"You have a lighter, man."

"Not that kind. Just wait. They will come through soon enough."

"The magic cigarette trick?" Akira asked.

"The kind where you step outside of a restaurant for a smoke and by the time you come back, your food is on the table? Works for anything, actually." Mike flicked his smoke and ground it out with his boot as the sound of sirens echoed from down the street.

"Be ready. Our fire has arrived," Mike said. He stepped into the middle of the street as the police SUV came around the corner. It was speeding on its way to some crisis. Mike assumed it was going to where the demons were, and that was exactly what he was looking for.

The vehicle tried to swerve and get out of his way, but Mike used his supernatural speed to dash in front of it. As the driver slammed on the brakes, Mike raised his fists high and brought them down on its front. The siren died in a sickly wail as the front of the SUV crumpled and imploded from the impact. Mike pushed it down so far that the axle snapped and the right tire spun off into another parked car. Sparks showered the road from its belly as it ground to a halt, pushing Mike back ten paces.

The two officers inside the vehicle wasted no time. The officer on the passenger side rushed out of the vehicle with great speed and leveled a shotgun at Mike. As the driver kicked open his crumpled door, it became clear they had been given the gift of demon blood.

Despite the vehicle's armor, Mike had managed to crush it like an aluminum can. Akira appeared out of thin air using her oversized mantis pincers to slice off the hands of the officer with the shotgun. Before he could realize the pain, Akira had already removed his head. The officers may have been blooded, but they were still human and could be killed.

Mike grabbed the driver and raised him overhead, slamming him into the ground and jamming a knee into his chest. While the cop gasped for air, Mike leaned down and snarled at him, baring his fangs. "Talk and you'll live. Got it, chief?" Mike ripped off the cop's pistol holster and threw it to the side. Then he ripped the badge from his body armor. "You aren't an officer to protect and serve. You're a soldier in a war. Let's not lie to each other." Mike did not care that there was a small crowd of people poking their heads out of stores. They would probably call the police, which is exactly what he wanted.

"Bite me," the man coughed.

Mike shrugged. "Okay." He latched on to his shoulder, biting as deep as he could. His blood tasted sweet and full of life, more vibrant than the meal he had earlier. It took dedication for him to pull away and wipe the blood off his mouth. He wanted to keep drinking from this person, yet it still felt off to him. *Like Chinese and Mexican food had a love child.*

"Now, unless you want to be eaten, tell me where you were headed. Where are the demons? We are here to help you, even if you don't realize it." He lifted the officer off the ground and pushed him into the broken car. "Ever imagine what it would be like to be eaten by a lion?"

"Jesus, man! For Christ's sake, we are just doing our job! There are reports of activity in that housing complex right up the street, on Elm. I didn't know you were one of us," he said with wide eyes darting around frantically.

"What did you do with the criminals you took earlier this morning at the motel in St. Paul?" Mike asked as he picked him up and spun his body before landing it on the hood. Mike wanted to keep him disoriented.

He spit up blood after the impact knocked loose a tooth. "Same as we do with everyone who is a freak like you. We deliver them to the boss, Captain Slade. Seriously, man. Just let me go. I don't know jack shit about any of this. I only got the blood a few nights ago, and the mission briefings right after that."

"Oh, I'm letting you go. Tell Captain Slade that I'm bringing a horde of demons to Walsh Tower later tonight. Your operation is busted, and I'm going to show the people of this city what you guys are really up to. Now get the fuck out of here before I name you dessert." Mike shoved the cop away, and he ran off through a small crowd of people who were recording and watching.

Akira followed Mike as they took off in a light jog to Elm Street. "Hey, try not to be so lethal, man," Mike said.

"I don't have any choice. I either kill them or I do nothing," Akira said. Something in the sound of her voice told Mike she wasn't being mean about it. It was as if something in her demanded those absolutes. "I don't really have a middle ground." She shrugged.

"Well, then wait for my signal to do something. Unless I'm dying. Then kill everyone. Let me be the target. Let them come at me. They will ignore a skinny lass like yourself," Mike said. "This crowd is probably lost. They won't follow us or start a riot with us. Still, we need the demon. Maybe the next crowd will be better."

# CHAPTER 47

Roger Queneco stormed into the Library of Deus after receiving the newest field report at sunset. The sorcerers and vampires that remained were those who had chosen to side with the Society of Deus. They spent the night and entire day drinking their fill of demon blood and poring through the knowledge Primus Vryce offered them.

"May I have your attention, please?" Queneco asked, rubbing his hands together in a scheming manner. "On this day of celebration, the final night of this age, we have been gifted with another round of entertainment. Will everyone please accompany me up to the twenty-fifth-floor ballroom? It appears that Auburn, slayer of Golgoroth, is about to launch the final assault on our city."

The request was met with indifference, as nobody wanted to leave the books. Roger made three clicking noises with his tongue and utilized his own power of the blood. Everyone would feel a compulsion to take a contrary action to what they were currently doing. They placed their books down and paid attention to the herald. Roger knew he needed to get these people out of the library and put on a showcase of the society's strength at the same time. Any faux pas made through a compulsion or two would be overlooked by his master.

"Why, thank you. You are all too kind. Too kind. We have captured one of Auburn's friends, the child of John C. Daneka. We are about to watch a momentous undertaking. Now, if all you cattle will please follow me," Queneco said with a bow and a flashy grin.

Outside a redbrick apartment complex on Elm Street, three older ladies waited among parked cars, smoking long Virginia Slims. They wore oversized fur coats that complemented their sandy gray hair along with grimaces that seemed to scold and criticize everyone. Judging by the carnage on display in front of the small building, Mike and Akira had found the location. Windows were shattered inward, and large cloven footprints had melted the concrete leading up to the unit. Mike jumped out of the van and ran up to the ladies.

"Are you guys okay?" he asked.

They recoiled from him and looked to each other before one answered. "Who are you?" Mike imagined the grating sound of her voice was enough to make children run in the opposite direction.

He didn't know how to respond at first. "Uh, the guy who is here to help. Can't you see the commotion across the street?"

"Oh, there is no burglary. The lord has sent Beelzebub to drag the Bell family screaming and kicking to hell, where they belong. Bunch of pissant lady men. They are always out at night causing trouble," one said. The second nodded in affirmation.

"Oh, our prayers have been answered at last. Ever since their Rottweiler attacked my poor little dog," the third began.

Mike wasn't going to sit around and let crazy old judging ladies distract him all night.

"I told you, Betsy. God has a plan. Ever since the Antichrist was elected president, it was only a matter of time," the first said as they watched Mike and Akira trot away. They shuffled across the street, closer to the building.

Mike cracked his knuckles and entered the front door. Sounds of snorting and heavy breathing filled the air. The tracks left behind small bits of fire leading up to the second floor. *Very kind of the demon to leave a trail of hot coals.*

Body parts along the floor and blood streaks on the wall meant the Bell family was not doing so well. Mike followed the tracks to the bedroom. The rest of the family splattered the room in a collected mutilation.

A demon, the spitting image of a classical devil painting from the 1950s, was sitting on the bed panting and getting its rocks off on a torn torso. It was shiny red with a goat's bottom, massive curled horns, and cloven hooves. Mike had hoped for a plague demon or a hellhound or even another succubus.

Instead, it was some new, almost cartoonish kind, just the sort of thing he thought the ladies outside would have imagined a demon looked like. Mike buried his face in his hands.

"Listen, pal. This is how it's going to go. I'm going to knock you unconscious, then parade you around town, showing everyone what you are. I'm not going to kill you, because you would just disappear, leaving no evidence. You follow?" Mike said as he cracked his knuckles.

The Krampus demon spun its head around and stuck out its elongated tongue. It was met with the iron piston of a vampire's right hook. Mike had to pull his punch to make sure he didn't kill the comical thing and cringed when its head bounced off a nightstand before hitting a radiator. A cat pounced and starting clawing its face. Mike shook his head, grabbed it by the hoof, and carried it outside.

The three ladies looked at him with such hatred and vitriol that he wasn't sure which demon he should be parading out.

"All right, Akira, light the building on fire and pull the alarm. Let's flood this parking lot," Mike said. "Wait . . . scratch that. Pull the fire alarm . . . *then* torch the building."

"It's getting pretty easy to take these things out, isn't it? I mean, who knew that bullets and modern weapons and even baseball bats worked just fine. Why was anyone ever afraid of them?" Akira said.

Mike shrugged. "The big ones we haven't heard of yet are probably tougher. But I think we would put up a pretty solid fight. We have some pretty big guns. I mean, we aren't sitting around loading trebuchets these days." Mike gestured with his thumb over to the building. "Fire?"

"Right, right," Akira said as she jogged off.

The fire alarm started its annoying high-pitched squeal that would alert all connected buildings for evacuation. Small explosions that sounded like someone was putting Christmas ornaments in microwaves came from one of the buildings. Mike spied Akira through a window, running from one microwave to the next with an armful of silverware and Jack Daniel's.

Mike leaned back and smoked as the parking lot filled with grumpy people who had been disturbed from their nightly television. Never mind the fact that there was a demon sitting under Mike's right foot. They seemed to neither notice nor care. *Why should they? They didn't know or hear when their neighbors were ripped limb from limb.*

"You can't stop what's coming," one of the old ladies spat at him. "The rapture is at hand."

Mike just rolled his eyes. "Lady, I don't have the time to put up with your drivel. How holy is it to wish harm on a neighbor?"

The second chimed in. "That is God's will! We had nothing to do with that."

"Oh yeah, how many prayers have you said wishing *judgment* upon that family?"

"That is just proof that God exists and our prayers have been answered. You'll see!" The third pointed her bony finger at Mike.

Akira returned stealthily and appeared at Mike's side, lighting up a smoke of her own. She took one look at the old ladies and raised an eyebrow at Mike. He just shook his head.

Together they watched the growing crowd that now included spectators from across the street. The heat from the fires washed over them, fighting back the snapping cold air.

The longer the groups watched, the closer they moved together, asking each other questions. After another building caught, the fire had become self-sustaining. The people worried. Their calls to emergency services had been placed on hold or weren't being answered at all. The longer the fire burned, the closer they came to panic.

This process of searching and waiting for help caused a slow awakening from their slumber. It had taken them far longer than Mike expected. In past protests, the anger would spark much faster. *Still, fire cleanses all, including willful ignorance.*

A short girl who was still in her work uniform from Delilah's favorite coffeehouse finally noticed the unconscious demon under the boot of one undead guy in a green coat and his shorter companion. Akira was looking into the driver's side mirror on their van, practicing shifting her face to look like other people around her. The crowd started to focus on them rather than the burning homes. Mike flicked his cigarette to the side, lifting the demon by its neck while hopping on top of their stolen van.

"So you finally woke up to the world around you!" Mike shouted. "Welcome, people of the Twin Cities, to the reality of your lives. The police, the firemen, the government are not coming for you. They will ignore you tonight because of this!" Mike thrust out the demon.

The crowd fell silent as Mike began his speech. "They are trying to end the world as you know it by harvesting these creatures for their own *greedy*, sycophant needs. They fight a secret war, but you still pay the price. To them, you are nothing more than people who will serve them. Your needs are not significant or important beyond your abilities to wash their feet." Mike smiled as he saw the old ladies standing in the back with their mouths open.

He continued. "The American dream is a lie, and they fucked it up. Hell, the whole damn world we *all* live in has been a lie. And *they* fucked it up." Mike hopped off the van and moved among the crowd, showing them his fangs and the demon before resuming his post near the van.

"They fucked up because they got greedy like fat pigs at a trough. They summoned more of these things than they could contain in this world. Area Fifty-One. Roswell. Raiders of the Ark. These are legends that have truth to them. They have managed to lure the populace of the world into a state of ignorance where such things are fantasy." Mike leaned back on one foot and kicked the van, sending it flying over the crowd and rolling into a burning building. An explosion added more weight to his words.

The crowd listened with a mixture of fear and awe. "These monsters are now ready to come into the world and claim it as their own. Your elected officials are in on the game, along with every other bastard who had enough to buy their ticket to immortality. But there is hope!" Mike punched through the demon's chest and ripped out its heart. In a plume of sulfur, the comical demon became a pile of dust, leaving only his blackened heart in Mike's hand.

"These were the rarest things on earth, the secret to the power of the world. We have one night to claim this power for ourselves, because on December 21 at dawn, their objective is complete, and it won't matter anymore. It won't matter how hard you've worked or what you've done or how good you were to your fellow man. You will be washing the feet of Charles Walsh and the rest of the royals that have been harvesting this power." Mike raised the demon's heart up above his head.

"That's right, everyone. Charles Walsh, the one who built your low-cost housing, the darling of this city, and the richest son of a bitch here. He has an entire building dedicated to giving out these hearts to his elite friends. Walsh Tower is where they are summoning forth these creatures in hordes. That is why there are no cops or firemen to come help you and your homes." Mike ripped the heart into a bunch of smaller pieces and passed a handful of them to Akira.

The girl in the coffeehouse uniform looked around and spoke up. "So what are we supposed to do? If it's filled with Bram Stoker wannabes like you, we can't do anything."

"You can save yourselves. I'm going to give you the choice to protest. I'm going to let those of you who wish to voice your names together in unison as the Sons and Daughters of the Twin Cities. This is the heart of the demon that burned down your homes. I offer you a sense of retribution and rebirth. That choice is yours. Do you let Walsh and his cronies run you down? Do you let them deny you the chance to protect your family? Or do you march, let your voices be heard, and show them strength in numbers?" Mike shouted.

The coffee-shop worker stepped forward in front of the crowd. "Why should we believe you? You guys are clearly monsters yourselves. How do we know you aren't lying?" she asked.

The crowd behind her seemed furious and ready to riot, but this little dance needed to be carefully orchestrated or Mike could lose them all.

"You're right. I'm a vampire now. I was just like you only a few weeks ago. I did this same kind of thing in Chicago. I'm kinda famous for it now. Granted they keep trying to cut my video down, but it keeps popping up all over. Pull out your phone and search for Sons and Daughters." Mike held out his hand.

A few people pulled out their phones and began to look him up. A moment later the first person hobbled up with a focused look. "I saw these creatures in Iraq years ago! I was discharged when no one believed me!" he shouted. He grabbed a piece of heart and ate it. He was the kind of person who looked like he had nothing to lose, filled with scars and injury. *The power of the Internet and viral journalism.* Only moments after he ate the first piece of heart, the veteran's war wounds healed.

"It shouldn't surprise any of you that the theater of war was a place where soldiers would see things like this. You've heard conspiracy theories your entire lives. Now is your chance to blow one wide open."

With each passing minute, Mike listened to the sounds of video clips playing on phones, often preluded by a movie announcer or followed by a "Coming soon to a theater near you." He chuckled at the idea of Unification-paid movie producers spinning his battle as an action flick.

"Hey, do you think we get to be extras?" an attendee asked her friend.

"No way. This shit's real. That's him!"

"This is just viral marketing. Don't you follow See Phoebe Ride on Twitter?"

"Whatever. This sounds fun."

Others in the crowd drew their own conclusions. Some exclaimed that there was clearly something going on in this city. They shared stories about clips they had seen of small strange dogs or insects swarming in other cities. The effect was the same. More people started to come up to Mike and Akira to accept parts of the demon heart.

"Ladies and gentlemen, welcome to the Sons and Daughters. Let's start fanning the fires of rebellion. There are more demons out there for you to see with your own eyes before we march on Walsh Tower. Follow me, and I will show you how to change your world," Mike said.

Even Akira was looking up at him and clapping. Mike leaned in to Akira and whispered, "Don't tell them I gave almost the exact same speech on Wall Street, including how they were vampires. Little did I know then how right I was."

"Oh, how did that work out for you guys, then?" Akira asked as they walked.

"Not good. We didn't have demon hearts, and the police closed down our camps even though their pensions were being sold out from underneath them. Only the future looks kindly on protests. In the present, people hate protesters because the protests disrupt whatever creature comforts they currently have," Mike said.

"Hey, did you hear about that Twitter account?" Akira asked. "I'm totally going to follow that," she said with a devilish grin.

The crowd took a few minutes to marvel at how much better they felt, some of them began to display small hints of powers. *We're coming, Doc. Just needed to get more friends.* They began their march, heading to a busy street now that they had finally gotten the "fire" Mike wanted to start. He had completed the first step of his plan. All he had to do was let the crowd get rolling into a full-blown riot, then get close enough to Walsh Tower to bust in while Vryce's forces dealt with his own citizens. A riot full of blooded, near-immortal citizens. *I think I've got my stride back.*

# CHAPTER 48

The ballroom boasted large windows to give a stunning view of the city on all sides. Each of the corners housed smaller televisions broadcasting news stories from around the world and local events within the city.

Stories of chaos and riots in all cities were the norm as the talking heads tried to downplay events. Walsh shifted all the channels to a local feed displaying Auburn giving a speech outside a burning building. Throughout the ballroom, servants poured sweet demon blood in crystal goblets held by members of the society as they toasted to each other. Tiny clinking noises echoed in the room as they listened to the speech.

"Not too shabby," said Roger as he took a swig. "He's a bit off the mark that we are hoarding it, though."

Walsh grabbed a glass himself and took a stance next to him. "And about me as well, and no, Roger, I'm not going to cry about it. I'm saving the most people possible, regardless of their beliefs or what side they are on. Our crews are still out there fighting to keep people out of it. Plus, it's not over yet anyway."

"Well, that guy has the crowd eating out of the palm of his hand. Reminds me of the Occupy movement. Do you think this is dangerous?" Roger asked.

"Nah, the first time they find a real demon, I bet half that crowd goes running. Pretty words only carry you so far." Walsh chuckled at that thought.

"Pot calling the kettle black," said Roger.

"Quiet, you. There is nothing we can do but watch." Walsh fidgeted with his pocket watch.

With each block they marched, they attracted more attention. People of the city would trickle in and join their riot as it fed upon itself. Every human in the world could tell deep down that something was wrong. No matter how much the Unification tried to cover it up, there were always leaks of information. Uprisings, market crashes, and cries of the End Times were just the start.

Bad things happened when families in other cities had been killed by mysterious animal attacks or when someone saw something they could not comprehend and called their relatives. It had been stewing for too long, and all they needed was a spark to light their fire for protest. People often ignore what they think to be impossible, so demons coming forth in this world were easy to ignore. People see tragedy happen elsewhere, and if it doesn't affect their local life, they move along. Unlike Chicago, where Mike brought it into the spotlight, the Twin Cities had few open encounters. The society had hunted down creatures far more effectively. Mike was damn sure it wasn't out of a desire to keep things hidden, however.

Mike ran at the front of the riots, carrying a parking meter, smashing it into the head of a vampire hiding in a police uniform. The riot had made it seven blocks. He lifted the head of the creature and showed the fangs to the rioters. "See! This isn't a horror movie or Bigfoot!"

The crowd cheered.

Akira led part of the crowd into a nearby police station while Mike led people outside in the time-honored tradition of flipping cars. *All legends are borne from human imagination.* "There is a truth that you know deep within yourself. There is more to this world than a ball of dust that travels around the sun. Believe in something greater than yourselves." Mike heard a priest chant as the riot descended upon a demon that was flushed out nearby.

Mike supposed that was the entire plan of the Unification. As a group, with the power of collectivism, humankind achieved great things. He was glad to see the rioters taking the message to heart. Even if he hated the Unification's means.

In the ballroom above the city, the sorcerers continued to comment about the riots. They laughed at the crowd below. Walsh and Roger gave each other a more concerned look.

"You should send out some other forces. Looks like they're picking up more steam than you expected. With each demon they kill, they grow stronger," Roger said.

"Even worse, some divers made it through in Succubus Alley. Slade and Cael did make it back, however. When Vryce recharged the ritual, we thought everyone had been dealt with. Instead, the society has more challengers," Walsh said. "I was okay, stepping to the side and buying you time. The Unification wasn't perfect, and it was already happening elsewhere, but I will do everything I can to stop the bloodbath that is about to ensue when the society strikes back against this many."

"We are returning magic to the world by tearing open the Innocence that far. Of course you are going to see the proliferation of demons. Calm your tits and call some men. A show of force should break 'em."

"Don't dismiss the severity of these riots. Arrogance doesn't suit you. I'll make some calls and ready more troops. Slade!" Walsh said, setting down his goblet.

Mr. Bollard stalked behind the growing riot from the shadows. He watched Auburn from a distance with a hungry grin, feeding on the energy. "We've underestimated his strength, JJ," he said to himself. No response came from within. Mr. Bollard would not be long for this world without a companion to possess. He needed another soul to mask his presence before an angel, demon lord, or simple sorcerer sensed him. The last thing he needed was for someone to rip out his heart and consume it for lunch.

Stopped in an alleyway, Mr. Bollard finished the incantation to summon a series of rage demons. Creatures with one leg and one arm in this world and the other half trapped in hell. The souls of these creatures were damned to imprisonment for the crimes of wrath. Bollard would set them loose among the rioters. He hoped they would be consumed quickly and their power transferred to the crowd.

He knew that the Sons and Daughters would never take him back after his betrayal. Feeding the riot with demons bought him time to process what happened, and to get used to JJ's absence. They had known each other's every single secret and desire. O'Neil had been the one to recommend JJ to the Unification as a helldiver years ago. Yet Mr. Bollard worked for older, more ancient forces, the death lords themselves. How old was O'Neil? For some reason, ever since the riots with Mike started, Bollard had a harder time remembering details about him.

Shaking his head as he felt the heat from a Molotov cocktail exploding outside the alley, he pushed the thought out of his mind. He had time. JJ had been an exceptional host. Together, they had plans within plans. Yet he was still a human. Not a rakshasa. JJ was just an identity he wore like a suit. Their joint ownership of the same body made more sense to him now. *Perhaps if I steal another one of Vryce's fragments, I can find a new human to possess. He is the master of possession after all. It's why it worked the first time, I wager.*

Yet now, standing in the shadows of the riots, lurking in the background, he felt . . . insignificant. The humans ripped his demons limb from limb and feasted on them for strength, all to fight other humans that challenged the very nature of the world. In their war, demons were but an insect under the boots of conviction. It wasn't his defeat by Vryce, or his ill-gotten freedom, or the fires of the crowd that got him. It was the diminutive feeling of being irrelevant.

*Humans are so alien to me now. Look at them go.* He finished opening one last portal. *I want . . .* He struggled to find the right word as he sunk into a nearby shadow. *Purpose.*

Mike dashed in front of a hail of gunfire, taking the bullets from soldiers that were meant for the rioters. To Mike they were just as important as those anywhere else in the world. "If it takes everything I have to convince you of the truth, I'll give it. The Unification stacks the deck! They make you believe you have more to lose by fighting for yourselves than being passive."

Akira darted forward with her super speed and collected the guns from the militarized police force. She blew them a kiss as they turned tail to run to the next fallback point.

As Mike looked upon his flock, he saw them squeezing an imp, healing a man who had been shot by draining the blood out into him. Mike walked over and lifted the man off the ground, patting him on the back. "They keep people like you bloated with creature comforts. So when you see an injustice, fighting against the system would cost you everything." The man lifted up his shirt and watched the bullet wound close. "Now they no longer have that power," Mike added.

Block by block and neighborhood by neighborhood, they lit fires, they rioted, and more people trickled in. They came in swaths as they found rogue demons running for their lives. They were hungry from the blood and hearts of the demons. This much was certain.

Mike led from the front line, making every effort to protect them from any larger threats. Kicking a sewer lid into midair, he threw it like a Frisbee, shattering the skull of a cloven-hoofed demon. Ripping another parking meter out of the ground, Mike played baseball with the body of a hellhound. Behind him, he heard the chants. "Auburn! Auburn!" The more outlandish stunt he pulled off, the more cheers he received. It was intoxicating. He felt alive.

After taking the heart out of a plague demon with a crowbar, Mike helped one of the first rioters off the ground, the girl who worked at the coffee shop. "Hey, you okay?"

She nodded and picked a scarab trying to burrow in her arm. Blood flowed from the wound like water, and her hands trembled.

Mike ripped off a portion of his shirt and started wrapping her wound. "Listen, when your dream is at stake, even your own life, you rise to fight. You are doing a great job. You see how we fight back? They've been oppressing us forever. Keeping us in the dark. Together, we can get through this alive. Even if not . . . we set the stage for those who come next."

The impromptu bandage had turned red by the time he was done talking. She saluted him and ran off, back into the riot. Mike hoped he was able to get the crowd enough strength to fight back against the evil that resided within these walls. Even more, he wished it would spread to the rest of the world in time.

Akira tapped Mike on the shoulder. "Hey, Boss, what's up with those guys in the back?"

A few people near the back were looking to the horizon. He saw the fresh bloodstains on their chins, and some were still eating a demon's heart. He followed their gaze to the Lilith moon; its violet hue made their surroundings seem surreal. *They are starting to see the magic hidden in the world.*

"They are becoming awakened, Akira. You are watching regular people have their illusions torn down around them," Mike said.

"You must be super charming, then," she said.

"I do what I can." He smiled.

# CHAPTER 49

Roger Queneco twirled his mustache in frustration. His own anxiety was beginning to spread to the celebration room as well. The monitors showed the riots fanning out to other parts of the city and slowly marching in. Thousands of people were making their way to them with violence in their hearts.

"Their numbers are growing," said a silken voice as a feminine hand was placed on his shoulder. Roger turned and saw the divine face of Alexandria by his side.

"They are. That one has a way with words," Roger said, pointing to Auburn. "What camp did he come from? I've never heard of a player such as him."

"My child, he has been given the heart of an arch demon by someone I've almost forgotten. O'Neil, I think his name is. A player who comes and goes throughout the ages, arranging such things. Always stepping back into the shadows near the end."

"It's not like you to forget a rival, Alexandria. Are you faring well this evening?" Even Roger had already forgotten the name she mentioned. Inwardly, he cursed himself for forgetting. The name danced just beyond his memory, like a song he forgot the name of. Instead, he just kept coming up with Auburn.

"Auburn will need to be handled by more than your foot soldiers. Did you mention he had companions that were captured? What do we know of them?"

"Always looking out for me, you are." Roger twirled his mustache. "I think I have a better angle," he said as he grabbed another glass of blood and began telling Alexandria of the captives.

After a batch of little one-legged demons ran into the riot, Mike almost lost control of the protests. People who killed and ate their hearts quickly became the most violent protesters in the bunch. They began to invade homes, yanking others out into the streets and forcing them to see as well.

Akira elbowed him. "The blood reacts strangely in people. Sometimes it makes them killers. Not everyone is as noble as you." Mike wasn't sure if she was talking about the rioters or herself.

The forces of authority did not remain silent during the growing rampage. Exhausted police officers who had been working around the clock showed up to stop the riots. A sergeant among them, hair peppered with age, leveled a shotgun at a civilian trying to run past the blockade. A one-legged, one-armed demon, its skin black and oily, lashed out and ran its hand through the runner's chest. Shots rang out as the police fired into the crowd. The sergeant opened fire on the demon. He fired one blast after another as he inched closer, his face twisted in rage. Demon blood painted the building facade nearby as the sergeant kept firing round after round into its lifeless body.

Another shot went off into the crowd. The sergeant called for his men to stand down. One by one, guns were trained on demons instead. They were scared by what they had seen over the past month but didn't have an easy way to lash out. As the initial blockade was overrun, the wave of first responders began to march with them, joining in their riot. After another blockade, even the police began to chant, feast, and fight, swept in the fervor of the night, now fueled by the blood of demons.

As they moved closer to Walsh Tower, a large group of soldiers showed up. They were the blooded forces of the society, with their vampiric powers, shape-shifting, and sorcery. Actual battles broke out in the streets.

Like pouring gasoline on the fire, the first SWAT officer hurled a fireball into a group of protesters that were ripping a hellhound limb from limb for its blood. The attack reinforced everything Mike had been preaching the entire way. The salt-and-pepper-haired sergeant screamed. "See! They are hoarding power! I knew it!" The message spread as a news crew from KMSP caught it on camera.

One of the rioters, endowed with a bit of strength, cut a horned demon apart with a chainsaw in front of a camera. Like a pack of wolves, they descended upon the demon, claiming what parts they could before it turned into ash. The journalist's hands were shaking as she gave her report. Mike swept in and grabbed her before the rioters turned to her.

"Look, lady, stay back a bit. I'm all for the press, but we are at war here," he said.

She quickly regained her composure. "Who are you? Are you the leader of these riots?"

Auburn cleaned some blood off his face and straightened his bandanna. He showed the camera his armband with the symbol of the Sons and Daughters. "Yeah, I'm Auburn. I want those who are hiding in their ivory towers to know that we are coming for them. Walsh and his people are the ones who have been holding satanic sex parties to bring about the end of the world," Mike said.

Akira jostled up on-screen beside Mike and flashed a smile. She held out two fingers in a peace sign and winked. Her camo pants and black tank top were far cleaner than Mike's clothes. "Lady, these people are your neighbors. They are just fighting against the End Times, End Times orchestrated by people hiding within Walsh Tower. When the police state is as corrupt as it is here, ya gotta expect some violence."

"Do you have any evidence that would implicate Walsh as the one responsible?" she asked as rioters hurled Molotov cocktails in the background.

Mike moved closer and pointed at the police down the street. "Zoom in on the one in the back." As if on cue, the SWAT officer took a swig of a black vial before hurling a ball of green fire back to the protesters. His unit patch identified him as a member of Captain Slade's unit. "Stick with us, lady. You'll get your story and your evidence. Just stay safe, okay?" Mike placed his hand on her shoulder to reassure her as she nodded.

Akira slapped Mike on the shoulder. "These people have been kept ignorant for so long. Once you lit that fire under their asses, it couldn't be put out," she said.

"Yeah," he replied. "Hoping for that. This has already turned into a war." Mike looked to the distance and saw Walsh Tower, closer than it had been before. He was becoming increasingly concerned about what to do with the ashen world he saw around it. *Tackle that problem when it comes.*

# CHAPTER 50

Sharp pains along the corners of Delilah's mouth reminded her not to smile. After watching the effects of the nerve gas attack she had arranged, the pain was worth it. For far too long she had advised her master to eliminate his rivals in the swiftest fashion rather than toy with them as he preferred. *At least when it matters most, he listens to me. Not that he had much say in the matter.* Delilah had more than a few tricks up her sleeve to direct the society when she needed to.

It was difficult to coordinate a schedule as precise as the one they had just performed when you had to anticipate the movements of others. All her master's souls had to be returned to him before sunrise. A feat even he could not achieve alone. Delilah had anticipated that it would be Bollard who would return to claim his kill. Still, she had hoped she would be able to capture or kill him. *Unless Vryce decided to monologue and allow Bollard to escape, I fulfilled my service to him. He should have all his fragments now.*

She had enough time to tend to her wounds in a medical lab beneath the city near the prison that stored the rest of the society's army. A cream paste mixed with herbs and a spell offered relief to her burns. The nurse on hand wrapped her arms and torso in bandages up to her chin. Any more and Delilah thought she would look like a mummy.

*We just have to make it through this night,* she assured herself. Riots had started in the city earlier tonight, and they were already beginning to coalesce around headquarters. Even though she had Symon and the Whisper with her, they alone would not be enough for absolute victory. *Or any victory at all. Luckily, I have an army.*

She slapped the nurse's hand away before she could be injected with a painkiller. "No, I have earned this. It is giving me focus. I still have work to do. I can't be of dimmed wits," she said. Getting off the table, she put on a fresh suit that a servant had retrieved for her, unconcerned with the people in the room as she changed. "Come. Let us finish what we started. Time to release the hounds, as they say." Delilah did not look back as she power walked out of the room, forcing Symon to stop toying with beakers. The Whisper was more prompt and already on her heels.

As Delilah stormed through the facility, her fingers danced on her tablet, entering all security codes and setting in motion the release of the entire army. By the time they made it to the cylindrical chamber that stored the remaining soldiers, blood had already begun to flow into the sleeping soldiers. She paused when she noticed a handful of the cells on the bottom level had new people inside them. They paced around in their cells like caged lions, an eclectic bunch.

"Who are they?" she asked.

"I believe that they are . . . What's the word? Fresh recruits," Symon said in his French accent.

"My lady, those are the soldiers from Chicago captured while you were otherwise occupied with your work. Thirteen soldiers of the Unification, already blooded, and fully changed. Awaiting your conditioning," the Whisper said.

"Thirteen? I count twelve. Who authorized them stored here?" she said.

Without hesitating, she pulled up a security footage feed. Indeed, it showed thirteen people originally locked in glass chambers. Then hours later, according to the tape, one of them turned into a black-and-gray mist and walked through the wall itself. The mist had tried to free everyone else but failed before it decided to leave. No doubt it was time to go and get assistance. "Never mind. I see who made the authorization." *Stop toying with your prey.* "It appears we have another assassin in our mix. I fear that the Unification will never stop trying to kill our master."

"They say that the crown is a heavy burden. Do you think Master is . . . ehhh . . . up to the task?" Symon asked.

"When their resources include a demon huntress from Chicago who can walk through walls, even magically reinforced walls"—Delilah looked inside the cells—"it's better to not take any risks." Methodical gears shifted in her head.

Daneka stood up, his leg twitching from a restless knee. "Impressive facility. In need of a psychologist perhaps?" He smiled. "I would love to work here with all of these fascinating experiments you are conducting." The slight bit of a fang jutted out from beneath his grin. From the look on his face, Delilah knew that he knew he would not be in captivity very long. His stance and posture was that of a prisoner who knew someone was coming to release him.

Delilah took a step back and observed each of them. Of the twelve prisoners, most of them paced liked caged lions, brimming with anticipation for their release and ready to fight. Some of the girls in biker clothes fidgeted. She watched them closely long enough to see the occasional hint of doubt. Two of the twelve, the toothy-grinned psychologist and a girl in biker armor, had little care in the world. Delilah entered a keystroke into her tablet. The glass on all the prisons turned opaque, and white noise was activated to prevent them from gaining contact with the outside world. "I know one of them. The mortal child of Lazarus's right hand, Lord of Heaven's Wrath, Dr. John C. Daneka."

She paced to the center of the room, where the four remaining vampires were entombed. "We can make this work for us. I have an idea," she said.

The large cylinder rose from the ground as Delilah released Rafiq from his chamber. Her prime assassin was trained for only one task, to give his life for the elimination of a single target. He would answer only to her, regardless of what other pressures or magical spells were placed upon him.

Rafiq was built and trained to kill other creatures who could control minds. Like every vampire older than a hundred years, Rafiq was shorter than most. He looked Delilah right in the eyes after he bowed from being released. He was silent as Symon handed him two red-handled, curved daggers.

"You will go to Chicago. You are to eliminate the creature known as . . ." She paused as the name escaped her for a moment. She referenced her tablet and continued. "Patrick O'Neil."

Rafiq began a swift jog out of the room. He would not need any more orders than that to achieve his goal. Besides Alexander Lex DuPris, he was her finest work.

"Whisper?" she asked.

"Yes, my dear."

"Get me a line to Queneco up in the ballroom. Make sure he is away from Alexandria, if possible. Where are Gabriel and Alexander DuPris?"

"Gabriel is still en route to Walsh Tower at this time. He's been occupied by the riots. Alexander DuPris is in the ballroom," he replied as he picked up a landline phone and made arrangements for a secure line.

"Choices. It always comes down to choices," she said as she walked over to pick up the phone.

A crystal goblet shattered on the marble floor within the ballroom, breaking the silence. Mike Auburn just got one of the society's soldiers to cast a spell on live television. Sorcerers within the society looked at each other with trepidation. The society wanted magic to be returned, but Roger could feel the tension rising in the room. One by one, all eyes in the room began to look to him for guidance.

"Worry not, friends. Our best moments have yet to come. I told you there would be entertainment tonight. What kind of host would I be if the show was always our victory?" Roger said as he clapped his hands.

Walsh maneuvered himself closer to Roger and leaned in with a whisper. "Where is Vryce? He should be here for this."

Smiling to the crowd, Roger replied through his teeth. "He is busy. Now is not the time to question him."

"I don't think a group of betrayers to the Unification are interested in anything less than perfect success. Vryce's continual absence is becoming a problem," he said.

Alexandria leaned in. "He's still afraid I'm going to kill him when he shows himself." She paused and put her manicured hand on her chest. "Oh, sorry for eavesdropping. I'm enjoying this game. I haven't seen anything like it for a millennium."

Roger shooed the crowd and turned to his companions. "Our primus has a lot of . . . interesting allies. It is prudent for him to remain mysterious. Otherwise, even you might find him boorish, my lady."

"Well, why don't you entertain me further yourself, Roger? You were talking of the captives from earlier. Bring them here. I wish to dine on them." She laughed. "I mean with them."

Alexander DuPris, clad in his long military coat filled with society medals, marched up to Roger, flanked by Vryce's two apprentices Cael and Mitch Slade. "Peasant. You have been summoned."

The crowd heard DuPris applaud a display of power on live television. The group seemed to relax when the general of the army approved. He looked at them. "Enjoy the fruits of our king's work. We are all monsters, yet you choose to cower, pretending to be humans rather than claiming the night for yourselves. This is why you are useless—"

"Now, now, clearly you have had a long night battling demons," Roger said as he grabbed DuPris by the elbow and escorted him off to the side of the room. "What is it?" he whispered.

"Delilah wishes to speak with you." DuPris handed him a phone.

Roger took the phone out into the hallway, away from prying ears. Alexander DuPris positioned himself close enough to keep his eye on the room and listen at the same time, however. "My dear Delilah! What can I do for you on this fine evening?"

His smile faded as he listened. DuPris watched Roger nervously bite on a fingernail while pacing around.

"That's a very big gamble. You have no way of knowing such things will happen . . ." Roger said. "Yes, I agree it has merit. It's a nice backup plan. But you are betting on two wild cards . . .

Don't worry about my ability to convince them. Worry about what he'll say . . . I'm sure he'll cry over it, but that's not the point. You can't mind control something like that. It's gotta be their choice . . . You know I'm on board with it. If your intuition is right, it's golden. If it's wrong—but you have to do me a favor. You owe me . . . I'll do my part. I need you to release the captives up here. Trust me, it will add to the impact. Alexandria is starting to get bored . . . That choice is above you. Her strength alone is a deterrent. You scratch my back; I scratch yours. Now finish your end of the plan, and we'll see what the wild cards do." Roger hung up the phone and stared down the hallway for a moment.

DuPris intercepted him before he could return to the ballroom. "What are the orders?"

Color was starting to flush back into Roger's cheeks, and he twirled his mustache. A forked snake tongue danced out of his mouth for a quick second. "You are going to be deployed very soon. This night is going to be either very boring, or magnificent. I can barely contain the excitement to see what choices people make."

Roger walked into the room with the grace of a circus ringleader. "Some of you may wish for a more active view of the entertainment. You have been authorized to go down to the courtyard for front-row seats!" he said with a flashy bow.

Alexander watched the reactions of the dignitaries in the room. He assumed they all knew this was a poor attempt to get them out on the front lines. "March forth. The battle comes to us. It is time to meet it head-on."

Hours after the first flames, the riots reached Walsh Tower. The city was glowing from the fires in the background. Mike had built an army in a single night, and all he had to do was turn the people against their masters and give them the tools they needed.

Along the way, he found the tools he needed. He found a crate to stand on, his own personal soapbox, and a bullhorn. In the courtyard of Walsh Tower, with its massive lights shining up, illuminating the carved columns of marble, the rioters flooded into the courtyard, faltering only at the final glass doors.

With every word he shouted, the crowd's anger grew fueled and focused. With every moment he had to speak, to chant, to rally, the protesters were one step closer to giving their lives if needed. They were ready to rip Charles Walsh apart and storm the building.

Those inside the tower had come out as well, strange-looking people in robes. One had a full, wild beard and walked with the aid of a staff. They lined up in front of the doors and watched and listened. Not a single person who walked out of the building seemed even the slightest bit moved by Mike's speech. At times, they clinked glasses of black ichor and chuckled among themselves.

Akira faded into the crowd at their arrival; throughout the night she had been practicing looking like other people and decided now would be a good time to disappear to the side and wait.

At first Mike thought one of the protesters was walking up to him. He was a six-foot-tall skinny man with blond hair, covered in dried blood from a night of rioting, his right leg wrapped up with bandages like it had been mangled in a car accident. He looked familiar to Mike, like he had seen his face before.

Mike noticed a second too late the cavalry sabre strapped to his back and realized it was Gabriel D'Angelo. Gabriel kicked out the soapbox from under Mike. He reached up and grabbed Mike by his coat collars and held him in the air. His face twisted with anger.

"What the fuck do you think you're doing, you little shit!" Gabriel shouted.

"Doing what you bastards should have been doing, saving this city instead of killing it. Now let me go," Mike said. He pulled back and head-butted Gabriel in the face, breaking Gabriel's nose. Mike reserved some of his strength for now and let Gabriel reel backward. *He doesn't know who I am or what I can do. Play it cool. Hold back until you have his measure, man.*

Gabriel held his face with one hand, and with the other, he gestured for the forces of the society to stay back. "Don't engage. These are our citizens and people. I won't stand by and let you slaughter them. I'll handle this guy."

Alexander DuPris and Cael looked at each other and shrugged. A handful of armored soldiers took up defensive positions outside. Inside the building, massive statues of stone inched closer to the entrance and resumed their vigilance. The gargoyles were waiting for their command to move.

Mike began to shuffle his feet like a boxer. "How noble, tough guy. How's it feel to know that all that stands between your monsters and demons and a city full of innocent people is you. A tool, serving a demonic overlord hell-bent on destroying the world for his own personal greed. You sure you aren't on the wrong side of this fight?" Mike darted in and led with a restrained right hook. Gabriel blocked with his left. With that opening, Mike rammed his elbow into Gabriel's chest, adding a bit more strength, cracking a rib, and sending him flying back into the crowd.

The protesters descended on Gabriel, kicking and tearing at him with glee, as he was an easy target. Mike lost sight of him among the chaos of the crowd that swallowed him for a moment.

At least a dozen people were thrown in the air from a massive shock wave emanating from Gabriel, his spell of force freeing him. He skipped up with his sword in his hand and cracked his neck before gesturing to Mike.

# CHAPTER 51

One hundred forty faces watched Delilah from behind the walls of glass. She entered her authorization code, and the walls slid down into the floor. Her prisoners—now her army—stepped forward as one. It was the last time any of them would have to be imprisoned. "Gentlemen and ladies of Amo-a-Deus, the army of the damned. The dawn of the new age is upon us. Your orders are as follows. All command of Gabriel D'Angelo has been revoked among your ranks. The only person who out-ranks me is the primus of the Society of Deus. Is this clear?"

The soldiers saluted. Each of them was equal to a small Special Forces unit. With supernatural strength, speed, and a plethora of other tricks at their disposal, Delilah also made sure they were aptly equipped for war.

"The final night is upon us. At dawn the ritual is complete. The legions of heaven and hell will descend upon this planet to claim it for their own. We will show them the will of man. This is the day that humanity will be pushed back into darkness, back into legend. Any who do not submit, you will slaughter to a pulp, water the ground with their blood, and drink your fill.

This is the day that monsters will come out of the shadows to lay claim to territory. You will defile them and eat their hearts to grow your own power and claim dominion for the society." Delilah smiled as she took their measure.

"You each know your assigned section of the districts surrounding the city. Arm and awaken your citizens, slaughter those who refuse. Now go forth, you damned armies of the night. Bring our own version of hell to this world and usher it into the final dawn of a new age." Delilah saluted her vampiric soldiers. Their eyes glowed red with hunger. They armed themselves with weapons from caches and marched in unison out of their prison.

"Do you want us to go with them, my lady?" Symon asked.

"No. You and the Whisper will be leaving with me after you escort some prisoners to the ballroom," she said as she watched the soldiers leave.

"Leaving, my dear? Are we not staying in the Twin Cities?" the Whisper asked in earnest. A look of confusion was impossible for a creature with no facial features.

"Oh no." Delilah smiled. "I have other plans for our future, which I need time to set in motion. Meet me in front of the eastern walls past the third gate at dawn. Say your farewells to Lex. He will remain here. The primus will need his power more than we will. At this point, the Unification Proclamation, and all agents that swear fealty to them or any other organization are to be executed on sight. These walls will only house the members of the society from this point on," she said.

"As you wish. I shall pack a bag and remember to bring wine and a tool kit." Symon bowed with a flourish. The Whisper gave a slight nod, and the two of them left after the final soldiers had filed out of the room.

"I will meet you later. I need some time with them first." Delilah nodded to the captives.

Delilah waited until she was alone. She slowly shut down each of the cells to conserve the facility's power and because it bought her time to think. When she got to the cells of the new prisoners, she read their entry logs before swiping her tablet, which allowed her to view the people inside again.

Delilah spoke in a calm voice. "I am no fool. I can see that you do not intend to be within these walls long, and I have seen enough bravado to tell the difference between true knowledge and a cocky attitude. One of you is a fortune-teller or a psychic. If I kill you, chances are, a necromancer will revive you elsewhere. If I recruit you, it will not last. Cutting a bargain with you is futile. I will, however, not make your release any easier and ensure that you remain off my master's chessboard as long as possible."

Delilah made a few keystrokes and turned her tablet to them. "I've turned off all new oxygen going to your cells. I will cut you off from the outside world and entomb you here. I'm not sure which of you needs air to survive. Either way, all record of your imprisonment is erased from any log. Enjoy your solitude and reflect upon your crimes." The glass faded to an opaque white again. The last thing Delilah saw was varying degrees of doubt take hold. Some even rushed the glass. All except the girl in the biker armor. *That's the fortune-teller.*

Delilah walked in front of that singular cell and turned it clear again. The girl inside lay on her cot, gave her a cool look, and went back to staring at the ceiling. "Thought I was to be imprisoned in eternal darkness, stricken from all records," she said.

"Tell me your name," Delilah responded.

"Phoebe. And before you ask, you want answers to a few prophecies. I've accepted fate as what it is and let horrible things happen to people I like all for this chance to stick a fork in the road of an even worse future. Let's have a girl chat, and when we are done, you are going to do something for me." She sat up and rapped the oxygen vent with her knuckles.

Delilah made a keystroke to begin the flow of oxygen again and listened with intent to every riddle-like word that Phoebe spoke to her. Her eyes were white as she spoke, with no irises, a rare and powerful gift. Delilah memorized every word. Much of it an enigma, but clear enough to change with immediate action. Some of the predictions were rapidly becoming unavoidable. When Phoebe was done, she asked Delilah for a single favor.

Delilah released the Sons and Daughters from their prisons and nodded to Phoebe. "I'll honor your request." She brushed the dust off Daneka's jacket. "I will arrange to escort you to the society's gathering."

"Me?" he said. "I'm not leaving."

"All of you are going," Delilah said. "Now leave."

Delilah waited until they boarded the elevator. She broke into a sprint, running as fast as her wounds would allow, to the ritual chamber. She was uncertain if she would make it in time, but she had to try before Gabriel brought Mike down here. It was unlike her to let enemies go, but the only way to have a chance at victory, even if it took centuries, was to put them back in play for now. *I'm starting to sound like Vryce already.*

# CHAPTER 52

A column of fire erupted under Mike's feet. The heat singed off his eyebrows. He used his vampiric speed and ran for his life to a nearby fountain to douse the flames. They hurt more than regular fire. *Right, this guy is the deadliest of them. Maybe I should stop pulling my punches,* Mike thought as the ice-cold water offered him little relief.

Before Mike could leave the fountain, the water itself came to life, forming fists attached to streams that hammered into him, slamming his body against the concrete base. *Ow! Son of a bitch! Okay, relax, man. Morris is worse than this guy. You don't need to breathe.* He tried to focus as water hit like iron pistons, ramming into his back. He yanked in his legs and kicked like a mule at the fountain wall, sending bricks like missiles in Gabriel's direction.

The bricks were stopped in midair by some sort of telekinesis, but it also stopped the water from animating. Mike did not wait for another opening. He used his speed to close the gap and grabbed Gabriel by the back of his head, throwing him at a column in front of the building.

One of the statues came to life. A hulking winged creature of solid black flew up and caught Gabriel. The force of the throw sent them both crashing into the column, but Gabriel took none of the impact. *Huh. The fucking giant stone statues can fly. Great.*

Mike cleared the courtyard in the blink of an eye, maintaining the momentum of his assault. He was about to smash the statue's skull when the creature made eye contact with him.

Sad stone-gray eyes drooped and looked ready for the release of death. They had the same shape of worry that Winters displayed when he arrested Mike for the first time. That single look stopped Mike from throwing his punch.

Gabriel finished a spell and repelled Mike away with a force that sent him tumbling back into the courtyard. Mike regained his balance, eventually skidding to a stop on his feet.

"Yes, that's your friend Winters. We call him Onyx now. You are here to save them? Maybe if you were not so ignorant of your cause, you would see that *you* are on the wrong side of this fight," Gabriel said as he hurled a streak of fire in Mike's direction.

Mike used his speed to sidestep the fire this time. The flames shot into the crowd behind him, and Mike noticed how Gabriel got pissed that he hit someone else. The protesters backed off after one of their own screamed in agony as he burned. *Jesus, I can't dodge his fire here. I'll kill the people I'm trying to protect.* Mike gave Gabriel a taunting sign. "Over here, buddy. Keep your focus on me. I'll fucking kill you for what you did to my friend. I've always wanted to see if I can punch someone through a ceiling."

"You sure you wanna do that, tough guy? You can't dodge my spells now. The difference between you and me is I'm willing to kill for my cause." Gabriel sliced his finger along the sword's edge and summoned up two elementals of living rock from the ground. He sent them lumbering over to Mike. "I already know who you are and what you are after. It's plain as day. You have no chance here. What is one man and a mob of peasants going to do against our armies? You lead your flock to slaughter, Auburn."

"Don't patronize me." Mike smashed the two elementals with the ease of a child squishing a Play-Doh creation. "You are not going to kill these people any more than I am. You have a terrible poker face. You are just as pinned in this as I am. Bollard told me all about how to goad you." Mike ripped out his own chunk of earth and sent it flying to Gabriel, only to have Onyx dive in front of it again and take the blow himself. "You know I would beat you if it was just you and me. I'm too fast for your spells. I should have just crushed your skull with my head butt," Mike said.

Gabriel laughed. He was about to say something before Mike closed the distance and smashed Onyx, sending the creature shattering through the glass walls on the first floor of the tower. "Sorry, man" was all Mike said before picking Onyx up and smashing him headfirst through the marble floor. Onyx stopped moving, and Mike took only a second, hoping he would live. *Well, he is made of stone now.*

Mike's body stopped moving. An invisible force yanked him back into the courtyard and slammed him into the ground. The impact was so hard it even caused blood to bubble up in the vampire's mouth.

"Over here, buddy. Keep your focus on me," Gabriel said. "Now stand still so I can tell you why you are barking up the wrong tree. Imbeciles. What's wrong with you people? Just *pay* attention."

"You don't know me at all if you think I'm going to stand still. Let's dance."

Mike used strength and speed to close the gap and find openings for left hooks, right hooks, elbows, and knees. Gabriel was on the defensive, using every spell at his disposal to summon objects to block blows. He placed walls of flames to shape the battlefield and give him space. He threw telekinetic attacks to keep Mike at bay or try to deaden the impact of fists that could crush cars. Neither had room for words as the courtyard exploded in fury while both forces of the society and crowds of angry rioters watched in awe.

The doors lining the lobby inside Walsh Tower exploded in a cascade of crystal glass as Gabriel and Mike thrashed through them. Gabriel could not get a word in despite his best efforts. It took everything he had to keep the relentless vampire at bay, and he was losing ground with every second. Even with all the sorcery at Gabriel's disposal, Mike could throw a brick at him with enough force to punch a hole through the side of a Sherman tank. Throwing fireballs seemed like throwing water balloons in comparison.

He knew Mike's thoughts. That was the saving grace that was keeping Gabriel alive. Telegraphed attacks allowed Gabriel to erect defenses, summoning earth golems to pop out of the ground and take a punch or conjuring a telekinetic blast to push Mike away.

The courtyard was filled with walls of fire, melting snow on rooftops across the street with their heat. When Gabriel had a brief second to go on the offensive, he tried to isolate a section of the battlefield to cut down Mike's mobility. Once Mike could no longer dodge, he would rain down fire from the sky and end this battle.

Gabriel was not sure of his ability to finish it in time. He already had a mangled leg and a few broken ribs. Each time he felt he had a second to breathe, Mike was already on top of him. At one point, Mike even pulled off his boot and threw it at Gabriel to stop a spell. *Years of training to counter magical spells, and all you need is a boot to the head. Genius. That's what I get for trying to levitate.*

Gabriel summoned a water golem from the smashed fountain and commanded it to attack Mike before throwing himself onto shards of broken glass to duck a reception desk that Mike hurled back at him. A security monitor fell off the desk as it flew over his head and landed with a cracking noise on the arch of his nose. "Ow! Fucker!" he exclaimed as he pulled his bloody hand away from his face. His vision was blurry from the impact, and he hesitated too long.

He felt Mike's hand grab him by the throat before they were both drenched in the water from the dismantled golem behind Mike.

"Got you, you son of a bitch," Mike said as he raised his fist. Mike stood still for a single second.

"JJ sold you to us!" he shouted. His didn't blink as he looked Mike right in the eyes. Gabriel's voice quivered, and his hands were clenched into fists so tight that his knuckles turned white. It was all Gabriel had been trying to say for the entire battle that had destroyed the whole lobby and courtyard.

When the explosion hit, Gabriel checked to make sure he was still alive and that it was not Mike's fist coming down. Relieved, he noticed Mike's attention had turned outside as well, and Gabriel's gaze followed. His soldiers had opened fire on the crowd of rioters, and new reinforcements were running out of the elevator.

One of them was on his knees after firing a rocket into the crowd. He was reloading. The rioters lunged at the soldiers that had already been standing outside. Among the flames, Gabriel saw Alexander Lex DuPris change into his hideous dracul war form and scream as he charged into battle.

"Get the fuck off me, Mike, if you want them to live." Gabriel didn't ask as he forced Mike off. Mike seemed stunned, either from Gabriel's words or the slaughter that was about to take place. Gabriel didn't care. He cast a spell to grab Lex with his mind. He yanked Lex across the broken glass into the lobby proper. "I told you to stand the fuck down. You are disobeying a direct order," Gabriel snarled as he put his foot on Lex's throat.

Gabriel felt a thought come into his mind from Mike.

*If I can beat the shit out of Gabriel, I should be able to make mincemeat out of these soldiers . . . I count . . . twenty? Thirty?*

"And don't you think about running out there yet either. You've beaten me, fine. Good for fucking you. If you would have just shut up and stopped trying to hit me, I would have told you sooner." Gabriel pointed at Mike. He knew being between two vampires was a risk.

*Phoebe did mention being invited in. By some pyramid?* Gabriel heard. "I'll get to that in a sec—"

"I don't serve you any longer," Lex said as he shifted back into his ragged human form and rolled out from under Gabriel's foot before standing up and looking him in the eye. Lex's golden wolf eyes glimmered in the dim light. "The command of the army has been transferred to the primus. The Unification is sending in real forces soon, and we have been given authority to recruit who we wish and slay anyone who is against us. Looks like you took too long with your little fight." Lex looked over to Mike. "I've been ordered to kill all of you. Nothing personal. I have enjoyed watching a vampire of your kind battle the golden child." He gestured to Gabriel. "Was a treat to watch. You, Auburn, might have risen to even greater heights in nights to come. You're someone who earned what he has rather than this shithead who was born with his daddy's silver spoon in his mouth." Lex's hands started to crack as the fingers formed into three massive claws.

"Oh no. It's not personal," Mike said. "From the looks of it, you're a vampire, and you don't have much longer until the sun rises. Think you can kill me and then finish your mission on time? Or do you wanna end up a failure like this guy?" Mike gestured to Gabriel.

"Will all of you stop pointing at me? Bastards." Gabriel dusted himself off. "You aren't killing him, DuPris. He's my prisoner for reeducation. When he's done, at least he'll know who he works for, unlike you." Before Mike could protest, Gabriel added. "Unless you don't want to see your friends again? Think you can beat it out of me before the sun rises and still make it to a safe spot?" He raised an eyebrow.

"Well, aren't we all a cheeky, self-repeating bunch," Mike replied. "Go enjoy killing your own people there, Lex. It looks like I'm slated for *reeducation*." Despite Mike's flippant demeanor, he looked ready to pounce on either of them if they made a move he didn't like. Lex walked away from them backward as his skin began to darken and stretch along his bones before he resumed his war form and ran into the courtyard.

"Are you really going to let him go kill all those people?" Gabriel asked.

"No, and neither are you. But this crowd is going to disperse in a flash now that we stopped fighting. Without leaders, chaos will take hold. Both sides will turn their attention to the demons. There is only one way to stop this. I assume the primus is Vryce? He's the one we have to stop," Mike said.

"Let's make this clear. You aren't going to stop him, or us. You are on the wrong side. I respect your conviction. We are both fighting to break a cycle of control. I just don't think you know that yet. It's the only reason I'm going to take you to your friends. But it's not for free either. You are going to do something for me as well. I can't help the stone guys. They are lost. I'm after JJ Bollard, and so are you. From the thoughts in your head, you had suspicions you were being used as cannon fodder. Don't accept that bullshit. You owe the Unification nothing. Unless you want the world enslaved under a depraved god who will rule with an iron fist, that is." Gabriel limped toward an elevator. "You coming?"

Gabriel looked back at Mike, who stared out the shattered windows. At first, the rioters fought well thanks to their newfound strength. Later, they broke and ran as more monsters flooded out of Walsh Tower to take the fight into the streets. Many were gunned down as creatures began their pursuit. Gabriel watched Mike's smile fade and listened to his thoughts. *The only way to save the people is to close the portal. I'm so close.* "I suppose I've made my point that you guys have been hoarding power and using it to rule over them." *They have their tools to fight this now. If I fight with them, I'll never see this end. Fuck, man. Nobody should be sacrificed like this.* "It's its own animal now, that will spread like wildfire." *No, it's not sacrifice. They made the choice to fight. We all do this. Together. As one.* "Might as well come with and finish this." Mike jogged over and got into the elevator. "Penthouse level, right?" Mike smiled.

"Nope. Basement." Gabriel pulled out the blood-red coin and slid it into the elevator slot, activating the descent to the geofront below.

"I am going to stop him, you know. I'm not going to let Vryce flood the world with demons and destroy it," Mike said to break the silence as they descended in the elevator.

"Destroy the world? Well, maybe, but that depends on what people do with their new gifts. Yeah, people like us will thrive in the world after dawn. But so can everyone who wants to. If they die, it's their own fault."

"Like I am supposed to believe that? You fuckers are the reason Chicago has been overrun with demons. What the hell is that?" Mike asked as he saw the buildings and strange plants below ground.

Gabriel smirked. "Believe what you want. We make the impossible real here. Now before I go and make my dad very unhappy by telling him he has to release your friends, let's finish our deal. I need you and your people to do something for me. After all, as *he* says, people are more useful alive than dead."

Mike did not take his eyes off the geofront. Gabriel could hear his thoughts, and from the sound of them, Mike could see things that even Gabriel could not. "What do you want?"

Gabriel coughed up blood and leaned on the wall. The cold glass felt good on his skin, giving him a bit of relief, and he sighed for a moment, letting the thought of what he wanted bounce around in his head for a bit. "I want something that you will probably come to enjoy doing. There is no way that you are the first wave, or the second, or even the thirtieth battle we will have with the Unification. They sacrificed you and your friends to die here just to scout and see what we had. I want you and your friends to leave here and, when you are set up and ready again, to swear that you will resume the fight against the Unification."

The elevator came to a stop at its destination, and Mike was the first to step off. He looked around and even touched some of the plants that grew nearby, strange fauna with red vines and amber flowers with nectar that looked like crimson syrup dripping from them. "Take me to my friends first. I can't sign them up for something they won't agree with."

Gabriel leaned on the elevator doors. "Oh, we won't be seeing your friends first. There is only one creature here who can truly set them free."

"Then I'm not making any deals," Mike said.

Gabriel struggled to move along the dirt path as the pain of the night's fights was starting to catch up to him. "I think I need to find a healing salve and fix myself. You broke more than ribs."

"The world doesn't have to change, you know. This can all still be stopped," Mike said. Without even listening to Mike's thoughts, Gabriel knew he was looking into another world, either heaven or hell. "Let me cut the subtext and spell it out-right. Why work with me?"

"Look at what you've done. You're basically the poster boy for our end game. Regular guy, now aware of magic. The world's eyes are on us, and you're good at spreading fires. You'll send a message one way or another." Gabriel gestured. "This way." He started down a smaller path that led away from the ritual chambers and libraries. *Even if it could be stopped. Would you really want it to, Mike?* Gabriel kept that thought to himself.

# CHAPTER 53

In the ballroom the beautiful crystalline voice of Molly LeMuse rang throughout. Her form and body matched the voice with luscious red lips and hair held together by diamonds and sapphires in a dress just as opulent. Her songs were filled with beautiful sadness and caused even the coldest vampire to give heed to lost mortality. A powerful moment for the society members returning from the battle below.

The smells of spiced meat cooked over low fires drifted through the party as servers brought racks of food to the still-living members of the society. Kevin Yukito was a smarmy-looking man with a thin red tie and tiny gold spectacles who discussed various diets that people were fed to produce certain tastes in their blood. He was a veritable blood sommelier for the undead that looked at humans as if they were cattle.

It was enough to make Daneka sick to his stomach in short order. It did not bother him that he was underdressed for the soiree, where everyone who was involved wore their best. What bothered him most was that his fame was not his work, but his father's name. When he saw his best friend fighting for their lives on the monitors, footage being rewound and played again, Daneka felt his knees buckle.

"Easy there, darling," said Alexandria. "I'm sure the leader of your cute little Sons and Daughters will be up here soon enough."

Like scavenging hyenas, the room descended upon the rest of his friends, pulling them into private conversations. Doc could feel the energy in the room, a ravenous hunger mixed with terror. From the creature standing in front of him, he felt a sense of pride.

"Like father and mother, you awoke in the most unique way, didn't you, Joseph? You feed on emotions," she said.

"How do you know that?" he replied.

"I was the one who gave your father his heart, and his father before him. And so forth. We creatures, those who can command demon blood, born as the seventh son, are the descendants of Lilith. The first wife of Adam. Of course, we adopt any into our ranks who are able to claim the heart of a divine as their own, as Lilith did herself. In a way, I am your true mother." She paused and ran a finger from her cheek down her slender neck. "Or a very old great-grandmother."

"So what is that supposed to mean? Lady, I'm not the kind to develop an Oedipus complex. So you can chill with the seduction." Doc reached out and grabbed a glass of water from a nearby tray. "You, however, have a list of issues that need help. I assume you do not have health insurance."

Her eyes were cold as she spoke. "Lazarus was the brother to Mary Magdalene. In Gnostic texts, ones hidden by our kind, she was the lover of Jesus. They spawned heretical lineage, indomitable souls, protected in secret by monastic orders. I convinced the chief priests to murder him in secret a second time, hoping that his first resurrection was a singular trick."

She lifted a chalice of blood, drank deeply, and looked away. "Unfortunately, it turns out we need him and his wretched bloodline. Your father and I need him—"

"My father was never the religious type," Daneka said.

"—to marry our lineages together, a union of bloodlines that were never meant to be, who will bear the children of the neverborn. Your father will wrap grave clothes around Lazarus at dawn, securing his mortal coil in this world yet again. So I assure you, he is religious now."

"So why are you telling me this?" Doc drank from his water.

"Because I think"—she leaned in closer and ran a sharp nail along Doc's face—"that you, a descendant of Magdalene, you would make a fine prospect for one of my children."

Doc's eyes looked around quickly. Sweat formed in the palm of his hands. "Me? A descendant? Marriage?"

She placed her arm around him and ran her nail along his throat. "Prophets told me of your lineage. The mark of Magdalene is the ability to see the dead, unlike the Lilim, born of the seventh son, with the power to command demons." She leaned in and whispered, "The children our lineages will bear will shape the future for all eternity."

"Uh-huh." Doc forced himself to swallow. He wished he were still in the prison cell below as her nail began to draw blood.

"Don't worry. Lazarus shall grant his blessing as payment for freedom." She began to press harder.

"But I can't see the dead," Doc said before it was too late.

"What?" she said. Her grip was crushing his shoulder. It seemed everyone else in the room was oblivious to their conversation.

"This is why the scientific method is better than prophecy. Do you know how prophecy can be applied to largely anything?" Doc said. His hands were trembling. "You've got me

all wrong. I'm just a vampire who feeds on and controls emotions." *Even my own. Checkmate.*

Doc's hands stopped trembling. He calmly placed his
glass of water back on a server's tray and adjusted his glasses.
Alexandria looked as if she had the wind knocked out of her.
"I'll pass on your message if I ever see my father again. Thank
you for your voracious appetite and narcissistic desire to brag
about your motives. It was the most delicious meal I've had to
date. You should really see someone about that."

As Alexandria quickly regained her composure and
retreated to the side of the room, Doc made his way into the
nearest crowd as fast as he could, introducing himself as the
son of John C. Daneka to get their attention. *Mike, buddy, just
stay down there. You do not wanna be up here.*

# CHAPTER 54

Delilah bit her lip as she opened the door to the ritual chamber. It was the only way into Vryce's private quarters that lay beyond. She crept down the spiral stairs to the floor below. Despite a bandage getting caught on a jagged part of the wall, she made it down onto the chamber floor without making a sound.

The carved inlay of the tree of life built into the floor had taken on a sanguine color over the past month, and the ceiling had certainly grown darker. From the edges of the wall, a darkness oozed its way into the center of the ceiling, corrupting the otherwise beautiful artwork that had been there. Delilah assured herself that it was a side effect of the ritual and not the more unfortunate scenario that her master was manifesting himself right behind her.

Despite her otherwise unwavering loyalty to Vryce, it was a loyalty less to the individual and more to his vision. Phoebe's prophecy told her he would bring about the downfall of his own vision if he were left to continue unchecked. His downfall would not come about through some sense of greed, or by his short temper, but rather by what was coming to end him.

The council of Unification lords were going to ensure that all warlocks died one way or another, either now or in the future. Delilah was not the sorcerous type and left the world of the occult to her master, but she knew that he was engaging in the process of reclaiming his souls. She also knew that as an insurance policy, he was binding them to important objects in some sort of arcane manner.

When Vryce would eventually be killed, he would reside within the objects until they were gathered onto a suitable host. *Or something like that.* She slinked along the wall to the doors that lined the back of the ritual chamber. No longer were there giant stone forms guarding the doors. She produced a key to unlock the doors to his sanctum and exhaled with relief as they opened without any alarms going off.

She entered the warlock's personal chambers, knowing the ever-burning candles would provide all the light she needed. It was rather cozy for a chamber deep beneath the earth, filled with opulent rugs, drapes, and candelabras. *Add in a few women, and he's got his own personal harem.* Personal memorabilia littered the chamber as if he had been diagnosed with clinical hoarding.

There were enough wealth and historical objects in the room to make sure that anybody who found the treasure trove would never have to work a day in his life again. She wasn't interested in the objects having only sentimental value, like the wagon wheel of a carnival he traveled with in the 1920s. She sought items of power, like the set of iron nails that he was set to the stake with in the 1700s. *The nails will probably end up as one of the phylacteries.*

Hair rose on the back of her neck as she poked her way through the shelves. Someone was watching her. She spun around quickly and was greeted by an empty room. Delicately placing a crystal necklace back on the shelf, she tiptoed into the middle of the room, keeping a direct line of sight to the exit. The shadows danced in the flicker of candlelight, but nobody was in sight. Waiting motionless, she listened for any sound and was rewarded with a creak of a floorboard in an adjoining room. Step by step, she made her way into a room with more arcane objects and wooden floors. Seeing no one, she let out a sigh and relaxed her shoulders. Despite the long shadows in the room, only a child could find a hiding spot there. If anything was within, it was one of Vryce's homunculi. *But this room is bound to have what I need, his phylacteries. Now which objects will he bind?*

Delilah started picking through memorabilia with delicate precision, looking for the item she desired most. If Vryce was successful in his ritual, the one to bind the pieces of his soul, then the linked items should be artifacts that were connected to him. It was only when he would die that they would become more sinister. All his power would be divided and added to the artifacts, granting whoever wielded them all the power of the lich without the drawbacks. She knew well enough that his soul would survive within the objects, exerting some control over the bearers. *Yet there were even limits to how far the master of possession can stretch himself at a single time.*

Depending on who found them, everything the Society of Deus worked for could be undone. She resolved herself to steal the most important one, the mask.

*After the death of Vryce, when the armies of dead march, the one with Vryce's porcelain mask will shatter the walls of the society and pave the way to bring ruin to its foundation.*

She shook her head in dismay as she surveyed the room, unable to locate her query. *How can I change the future if I can't steal what I'm here for? Asking him for it will do no good. He's as stubborn as they come. If Gabriel gets the mask, everything will be lost.*

"What are you doing in here?" Vryce's voice pierced the room. Between objects, the shadows stitched themselves together as a breeze chilled the room. Vryce stepped out of the corner and threw his viola case on the floor. He was already reaching for a dagger before a look of realization crossed his face. It did not stop him from holding the short soul blade to her throat as he snarled. "You've changed. Whom do you work for now? Whatever was done to you has triggered my alarm."

Delilah held her composure, slapped away the dagger, and gave him a piercing look that liquefied bravado. "You were the one to take the gamble with my life in regards to Bollard. Did you think that I would survive unscathed? The fact that his blood instead of yours was used to change me is the price you pay for your pathetic game." She tilted her head as she sized him up. He was a man in the prime of his life again, his flesh restored with power.

Any aspect of physical attractiveness, however, was cast aside by an intangible creepiness that seeped out of him, giving her goose bumps. He was wearing most of his trinkets tied to his waist, including the mask she was after. "I'm going to assume by the obvious fact that just standing next to you feels like my skin wants to crawl that you have completed your ritual," Delilah said.

"I reclaimed that which is mine. All that is left is the binding. The phylacteries have all been chosen and set. Now I need to prepare this vessel to channel their power. I do not intend to have what I've reclaimed taken away or banished into the underworld." He began taking off objects from underneath his red-lined coat and placing them on a shelf in the room. "Regardless of the blood that runs through your veins, you will always be my daughter and my right hand in affairs. No one can take that away from you."

"Sentiment does not suit you. I am a tool that you use and nothing more. Without me, you would have had to spend another forty years learning civil engineering, psychology, and accounting software. I am here because I need to speak with you. Knowing that you were near completion, it is obvious that this is where you would hide." Delilah started picking up objects, dusting them off, and placing them back on shelves.

"Hide?" he responded.

"Yes, hide. Call it what you will, but if I wanted to kill you right now before the binding, everything you've worked for will be lost. As such, until you are safe, you will cower down here until you are done, or your hand is forced above."

"Careful. You still work for me. Your tongue will be the death of you."

"Please, if you were going to kill me for chiding you on your ignorant behavior, you would have done that years ago. Just because you hide and cower down here does not mean it is wrong. After all, you cannot let Alexandria get anywhere near you until you are done. Of course, if you listened to me, you would have killed her years ago, rather than let her dance around and control you."

"That is because you understand little of the life-span of someone who has lived centuries. Killing anyone who steps in your way or could be a threat makes unlife extremely boring. Not to mention, I will have Alexandria under control once I finish my ritual. Without her . . . What's the phrase you used in the past? Ah. Nuclear deterrent." He paused, took the mask off his belt, and ran a finger along the crack before hanging it on the wall. "Without her, I would not have had success in attracting as many other vampires to this city. It would have only been sorcerers. Like it or not, some creatures are tired of hiding, despite the fact you dislike them for being more powerful."

"It's not power. It's that you let her get away with anything she wants, along with your newfound toy, Gabriel. You surround yourself with brats while giving them unlimited power. Therefore, you can do so without me here. I have fulfilled my end of the work in this city. Your ritual is near complete, the portal is opened, and the control of the army has been transferred to you." In the process of dusting objects, Delilah snuck the set of nails into her pocket, peering out of the corner of her eye to make sure he was distracted.

"Taking your leave for your pet project of creating the archive, then? I prize all knowledge as something worth preserving, so of course I will sponsor you heading out to catalog and map the changing landscape over the years."

"So you are choosing Gabriel over me to remain here, then?"

"Jealousy doesn't suit you. You were pleased when you brought him to me. Why the sudden change in demeanor? He has as much a role in this as you do. Sure, he will never have Roger's tongue or your knack for organization. Neither of you, however, can fight the way he does. The only way for him to learn is to give him so much power that he will either break under its weight or learn how to wield it correctly."

"It's not jealousy. It's outright questioning of your intelligence. You dance with the Unification. You dance with Alexandria. You dance with giving children weapons of unimaginable power. You dance with the forces of heaven and hell. And during all of this, you seek to make yourself a lich, the very thing that they all hunt. I do not see this ending well for you. Which is why, for the sake of our mutual vision, you are going to listen to me now, more than you ever have."

He shot her a glare during her speech, and his fingers twitched as he placed the ouroboros and the inverted rosary on the shelf. "Well, I did not expect you to so thoroughly dress me down before we were to part ways. We make every situation a victory and always hedge our bets. That includes you heading off to form the archive. In time, perhaps a hundred years, perhaps two hundred years or longer, this landscape will be changed and ruled openly by demon kings, vampires, sorcerers, and many other creatures, including the Society of Deus, which I will rule here. Your task is to grow in power while charting and mapping these new territories, and in time sabotage them for our ends."

"Yes, our ends. Not Gabriel's. Not Alexandria's. Not the Unification's. You may not like what I do, or how I say it, but you trust me with your innermost secrets. Now, in order to pull this finale off, you are going to do the unthinkable and give me your sorcery." She crossed her arms in front of her and stared directly at him.

"Demanding, aren't we. Let's make one thing clear." Vryce snapped his fingers, and Delilah felt herself lose control of her body. As he twirled his fingers, she spun around like a ballerina. "Each warlock has their forte. Do not forget that possession and soul stealing is mine. Your bravado is admirable, but even if I were to perish by your hand, it would be to serve my own ends. You are a young creature. You are less useful to me now as my conspirator than as simply my great-great-great-granddaughter. You have been soiled. You were the most effective human being I had ever met. Now, you are on a path to become nothing more than another monster, learning the misery of existence with power at your fingertips, and nothing but dust at the end." He held his hand flat to the ground, and Delilah stopped spinning to face him.

Her look told him she wanted to kill him. He tilted his head sideways and continued talking. "The children that survive will be the ones to carry forth the vision. You are just a tool of the divine now, trapped in a prison of addiction until you claim the heart of the rakshasa." He took two fingers and held her by the chin. "Welcome to my pain for the past six hundred years. If in this next thousand you manage to learn how to follow in my footsteps and reclaim what Bollard took from you, then you can be my daughter again. Until then, you are my employee." With a gesture, he let her go, and she collapsed like a broken doll on the ground.

She picked herself up and grabbed his wrist before he turned around. She pulled back and backhanded him with every ounce of her strength. It was strong enough that the knuckles on the back of her hand split. Despite his physical prime, Delilah had a sense of nobility now and the courage to hit him.

Delilah gestured to the belongings in the room. "Let's not forget that without my assistance, you would still be wallowing in that pain. Without the plan we came up with, you would be ruling over a pile of ash in fifty years. Now, if you are going to give your son a soul blade, I'm going to need a few things of my own to get started. I'm taking Symon, the Whisper, and a few other handpicked soldiers of Amo-a-Deus with me. I'm also taking your porcelain mask and inverted rosary."

She let it sink in for a second, and when he raised an eyebrow, she continued. "Don't look so surprised. It's not like it will cost you. They are empty shells, and unless you intend on dying in the near future, it will provide me with a link to you. Just teleport directly to them if you ever feel the need to wear them. I, however, need the rosary to stop those who walk through time, and the mask to stop any mind reader. You should need neither crutch anymore." Delilah hoped her gambit would work. Being forceful and determined with him often got her what she wanted. It could also get her killed. He was like a giant predatory cat at times, toying with his food.

Vryce wiped his face with the back of his hand and slowly licked the blood off. A smirk crept along the edges of his face before he broke into a full-hearted laugh, which could mean that she was either dead or he was giving her what she wanted. "Oh, my dear Delilah. I do so hope you follow in my footsteps."

He flicked his fingers, and the mask and rosary flew in her direction. "Now leave and set about your task. I have no further use for you in the Twin Cities. I need only to cast the final spell."

He turned his back on her and began to disrobe in preparation for his own ritual. Green ethereal serpents slithered out of his body as he released the souls he had gained. His shadow took on movement of its own and started picking up the shards of souls that moved around the room. Delilah did not understand what came next, even though it was described in his work, the *Arcannum Arcannimusim*. It was too arcane for her to fathom. She knew enough to know that it involved the mind, body, and souls coming to terms with their new existence. *Warlock magic, always overly complicated.*

Delilah grabbed the objects as they slid along the ground and scrambled to the exit. She kept her voice calm as she opened the door. "There is one more favor. There will be someone tonight you will meet. Mike Auburn. I think you will enjoy him as much as you do Gabriel. Kill him before dawn. The alternative is Lazarus returning in both power and name."

Delilah slammed the door shut and grasped her chest. Somehow, he was too preoccupied to notice. She managed to get what she needed from under him. Now she had to get as far away as possible before he *did* manage to notice the nails were gone.

She ran to a hidden tunnel that would lead her above ground, far away from any chance encounters she wanted to avoid. When the three items began to pulse with a green light, she knew his binding spell was beginning. *He will know I stole the nails, yet he hasn't stopped me. Is he letting me take them?*

She slid on the rosary and the mask as she made her way out of the city to meet Symon and the Whisper. They would keep her identity secret and shield her from people scrying upon her. With the mask on, her sight of the world was markedly different.

For starters, she could see the magic lines flowing through the ground itself and could actually see the giant walls surrounding the city. She could trace lines of power mirroring the chains above, heading below. *As above, so below.*

Among the soldiers that were still fighting rioters, or ridari who were carving out demon hearts to hand to their soldiers, she was almost invisible as she slid past them through the sectioned gates. While she wore the mask, everyone gave her a wide berth, assuming it was the master. Despite the ease of movement, she could not help the feeling that there was a whisper gnawing at the back of her mind. Like her own shadow trying to speak to her, its voice formless and silent, yet if you listened just right, you could hear an unintelligible murmur. *So this is what it is like to wield some of his artifacts. Or rather, my artifacts.*

She strolled through the west gate to find Symon and the Whisper standing next to a few jeeps that were packed to the brim. "Oy, don't you look lovely, Delilah," Symon said.

"Don't call me that anymore," the mask wearer said. Its voice already changing to sound both male and female at the same time, formless and silent, yet audible if you listened just right.

"Uh, right . . . So what do you want to be called then, miss?" Symon said as he looked around and fidgeted with some car keys.

The figure got into the back of the jeep and waited. "You may call me the Praenomen from now on." *Yes, I rather like the sound of that. The first one named. After all, we were his first daughter. The first rejected. The first accepted. We are eating and devoured at the same time. The alpha and the omega.*

"Sure thing, Boss. To Denver it is. We can make it a few miles before sunrise," Symon said as he started up and rolled off.

Choices. It always comes down to choices.

Vryce sat alone in his sanctum, naked as he ran a spool of blood-dipped iron through his feet, ensuring that with each stitch, he grabbed a part of his shadow. It would be more difficult the further along he went, for he would eventually have to stitch his entire body to the shadow. Meanwhile, the shadow of himself wove and stitched threads of shadow of its own back into Vryce's physical form.

It was only at the completion of the final stitch on the crown of the head that he would be able to divide the power of the warlock and his divine soul equally among himself and each of his phylacteries upon this vessel's death, rather than tumbling or being imprisoned in purgatory like his predecessor.

"I always enjoyed you, Delilah. Every one of our conversations went exactly as today's went. Even the way you demand things by being as forceful as possible one time and as gentle as a mouse another is charming. You are my very quintessence and the logical side of me I had forsaken long ago for this insanity I crave now. I shall acquiesce to your instinct. Tomorrow we shall both stand bare in the world, watching the black sun rise while we devour its rays. You were always my first to be welcomed. And you are the first of my children to leave," he said to nobody in particular, his voice barely audible and almost formless as he jammed thick iron wire through bone in his ritual of self-mutilation.

# CHAPTER 55

Mike followed Gabriel into the cavern. Neither of them had much to say to each other as Mike waited for Gabriel to heal himself. *Time is a-wastin.' Who the hell gets caught by a bear trap anyway?*

Some of the spiked vines in the gardens had gnarled and desiccated demons wrapped in them. It appeared as if the vines were draining them dry. On more than one occasion, Mike jumped back when a demon's eye opened in a jolt. *Motherfuckers are still alive. Jesus H. Christ, what the fuck is this place? It's like someone took acid and read a Dr. Seuss book while standing on their head.*

Even so, it was nothing compared to the building that was just off center of the cavern. Built from glass and stone, the pyramid hummed with magical energy as it towered over deformed trees. Mike could see a river flowing beneath it, so green it looked like the Chicago River on St. Patrick's Day, while above it there was a shimmering golden tree filled with sparrows that would flutter and fly throughout the cavern. Both locations seemed very distant, as if he were seeing them through a mirror tunnel. Yet at the same time, Mike felt he could just reach out his hand and catch a sparrow or dip his hand in the river if he got close enough. *Aha! Jackpot.*

Mike lit up a smoke and took in the sights as they wandered empty paths. "All right, fluffy, stop wasting time and get me to the big shot or to my friends," Mike said as he ground his boot on a bulbous plant, causing it to pop like a whitehead.

"That's strange. There should be more people down here. The plants have changed all the paths as well. Yesterday I knew this place like the back of my hand," Gabriel replied as he shook his head. "I'm a stranger in my own home."

"Still might be if you ask me. Have you seen what these plants eat for breakfast?" Mike said.

"How about you cut us a direct path to the pyramid there?" Gabriel asked.

"Through the demon-eating plant things that keep blocking our way there? I think your boss is trying to tell you he doesn't want any Girl Scout cookies."

"No, it's not that. Well, maybe. We took the main entrance, the one the others take. There has got to be another door around here." Gabriel squinted and looked off in the distance.

Mike saw a ghost walk across the pathway behind Gabriel, moving into a thick part of the plants. A pale-green hand stuck back out and gestured for Mike to follow. He did.

"Where you going?" Gabriel asked.

He entered the thicket, an absurd forest of oversized plants. Every few paces, he would spot an arm or a glimpse of a ghost just out of the corner of his eye. Gabriel followed closely. As long as Mike moved along the correct path, winding and chaotic as it was, the forest let them through. They continued for moments in silence. Always looping back around to face the building in the middle.

As the forest broke, Mike halted in his tracks, throwing his arm out to stop Gabriel from stepping forward. Within the shadow of the pyramid, Mike saw it. An indescribably deep hole into purgatory itself. Claw marks from demons that escaped scarred the pulsing translucent walls within, but there was no sign of any nearby. *Is this the portal Phoebe was talking about? I was invited in here, wasn't I?*

"Hey," Gabriel said. "You came for your friends, ones that are still with us. I don't know what you can see, but don't think about helldiving here. Besides, you don't even know the right spell to get in there anyway." He nodded up to the pyramid. "Door is up here. Let's go."

Taking a final drag of his smoke, Mike walked to the edge of the abyss before flicking his stub behind him. "I am here for my friends. They got me in the door. I'm just one guy who has had one foot in the afterlife for a long time." Facing Gabriel, he gave a two-finger salute. "Who said you need a spell to enter the afterlife?"

Mike fell backward.

The world above him stretched and looked farther and farther away. He fell through layers of purgatory. Mountains of vertical catacombs constructed in an ever-expanding universe spread out before him. His entry point, a brilliant warm light the size of a horizon moon, grew smaller, and other entry points became visible, if less bright. This continued until there was an illusory night sky above him. The stars were gateways from Mike's world into purgatory. The planets were the ritual locations. It felt peaceful, like Mike could spend eons staring at them. Then he hit a walkway, crashing through it as he fell farther. Then another. His luck had run out. Then another.

The eighth catwalk was the one to not break. Peeling himself off the ground, a rush of vertigo finally caught up to him. Even though Mike did not move, the ground snapped back, closer and closer, and the distance he had fallen rubber-banded back. The catwalks and the catacombs rushed past in the other direction before settling down. *All right. That was kind of fun.* He patted himself down and took stock of his location. He was deep, far deeper than he was with Tindalos. The catwalks of varying levels all had streams of dead souls that flowed through in a crisscrossing fashion in all directions. Some of them had ghosts that seemed more real, more solid. Occasionally a demon crossed another. His bridge was no different. Some ghosts of people he had known gestured for him to follow.

Without his guides, he might have wandered forever, or easily walked into demons. With them, a ten-minute jog led him around all obstacles or potential enemies. Mike didn't need to question why or how. He just knew. He was marked. Always part of the afterlife. Always with one foot in the door. Regardless of how the dead, the damned, and the demons tried to get out, he was always racing to the edge to dive in.

The entry to Lazarus's prison was completely ordinary and mundane. At least, as normal as possible within the pits of purgatory. It was simply one of many catacombs along this particular catwalk, on this particular level. The only thing that stood out to Mike was that this one had a small, rusty padlock that looked about a thousand years old. A few mounds of ash lay nearby, but other than these small oddities, it was no more special than the millions of other souls that lay resting and waiting.

The padlock crumbled into rusty dust in his hand, and Mike heaved the gate open. He lowered his head as he stepped within the door. It felt cramped. Down here, there were no smells, odors, or sounds. The revelation hit him like a brick.

*Gabriel just saw a shadow and mentioned needing a spell. He didn't seem concerned at all about me getting close. Every one of the crew stayed huddled by each other and couldn't see far out on our dive below Chicago. Except Lucy with her special lantern. The Unification has opened all kinds of portals to create light for diving in. Because nobody can fucking find this tomb. There is nothing in purgatory. No senses at all. But I can see just fine. Wow, that thought of eternal darkness for everyone is pretty scary.*

Mike walked into the tomb. It looked like he imagined it would. A small, cramped room filled with decorative carvings within the walls. On a stone slab lay a small body. Mike guessed it was perhaps four feet tall at best. Walking up for a closer look, he could tell it didn't glow like the rest of the place. It was like him, physically there, in a body rather than being ghostly. A collar bound around his neck chained him to the slab. Its mummified, tiny naked body just lay there in front of Mike. *That . . . that's it? This is the thing that is supposed to solve the world's problems? I don't even think it could see over a countertop.*

Its hand feebly touched Mike's wrist, the first real sensation he had since being down here. Mike jumped back like a spider just crawled along his hand. Lazarus used no words, but his thoughts and feelings were as clear to Mike as if they were his own. Lazarus wanted freedom. Not freedom from this tomb, freedom from existence. He wanted his torment to end. In a single touch, he begged Mike in a thousand languages to end him.

*Is this really what the Unification wanted? To kill him? Or were they planning on dragging him out of here in his undead state and shackling him to their schemes?* He made up his mind. Reaching out and grabbing the hand, Mike poured his emotions out, thinking of everything that had happened and trying to explain what was happening in the world. It begged for release. Mike acquiesced. It took far more strength than Mike thought it would, but with a grinding effort, he twisted and finally snapped off the head of Lazarus. In an instant, the body turned to ash. *What a total letdown. Well, he's free. Free from everyone. Now how the fuck do I get out of here?*

He stepped out and looked up at the false sky, easily finding the rift where he entered. It was the largest and closest, a ball of light that seemed ever expanding. Ever growing. An explosion of orange-and-red light blinded him. There was no sound to accompany it nor any physical sensation or wind, just a jubilation of light. Mike squinted his eyes and fell to his knees at what he saw.

Replacing the vision of the catacombs was a wildfire of light that spread and tore at the ceiling of the cavern all the way down below him. Flames seemed to wash over him in waves even though they held no heat. In the flames, Mike saw his ghosts, everyone he knew recoiling as they were consumed and turned to ash and sucked to the center of the cavern in a vacuum.

He dived for the smallest figure, but when his arms wrapped around the little ghost, it too was blown apart by the explosion that only affected the spirit world. In the second that it happened, it was gone. Gone too was the vision of the river and the illuminated tree above the building. His ashen world appeared to be a desolate landscape, devoid of its previous wonder and inhabitants.

It was silent.

There was no trace of anything out of place, other than being beneath the ground in a world where plants fed on angels. The charred landscape he saw only extended to the cavern walls but made him feel infinitely empty inside, which made it all the easier for him to close his heart off and deaden his emotions. Something just nuked the spirit world. A single moment after he freed Lazarus.

A man approached him. Shadows danced and flitted around his feet in patterns, as if he had more than one. With each step, plants near him withered and died as they were frosted over.

Mike noticed the man's red-lined black coat, his white hair short and combed back. With each step, he moved seven steps closer in a flicker. As he got closer, Mike saw his mismatched eyes, one red and one white. Sparks of electricity danced between his fingertips. Arcane tattoos crawled and moved across his skin.

When he was finally in front of Mike, he placed a pocket watch into a vest and took a deep bow. To Mike, it was like he was looking at a puppet, an animated doll that had several ghosts stitched together inside it. When he rose from his bow, the pendant of the ouroboros, filled with gold and gems, stood in contrast to the rest of his outfit.

"Wonderful night for a stroll, do you not think, Mr. Auburn?" His mouth stretched open, revealing fangs and a hollow emptiness where the green light of souls swirled in the black. Mike had been to hell and back. He'd seen a lot of shit. But for some reason, this freaked him out the most.

"What the fuck are you?" Mike replied.

"Tsk, tsk. Don't be rude. It's a pleasure to meet you. I know all about you. Your thoughts and doubts have filled my cavern. Your legend precedes you. I am, as Alexander DuPris called me, the lich king. I am Warlock Vryce, primus of the society, historian, and so much more. You are the first outsider I have met in the new world. Shall we go above ground and watch the festivities of the eternal night? Our city will be boasting a fantastic fireworks show, and the great vampire singer Molly LeMuse should be giving a private performance for all the members of the society as we speak," he said with a charming look.

"No fucking way. Nope. Nada. I'm here for my friends' freedom. Not to frolic and dine with elites. That ain't my scene, buddy. Turns out the Unification pinned their hopes on the wrong dead guy as well. So why not just step aside so we can go after the person who screwed us."

Gabriel joined them. "Good choice, Mike. I knew you wouldn't side with them. Or us for that matter, but at least not them."

"It is a holiday, my apprentice. This day, there shall be no violence. It is sacred. The time of man is at an end. And yet, it is just beginning," Vryce said.

"I hope your enemies feel the same way. You should stay down here until this blows over. Up there, you are exposed." Gabriel looked worried as he came to his master's side. Mike could tell Gabriel was more afraid of him than he was worried about Vryce.

"I am exposed. That is why you are here with me. I will not cower in fear and hide as the Innocence is shredded and mankind is awakened into its truest state of divinity. I will not miss the day the barrier between the lands of the dead, heaven, and hell are all thinned and magic returns to this world. Destiny awaits each of us. Now, let us not delay. There is much dancing, feasting, and music awaiting us."

Vryce raised his left hand, and six of the shadows below him mirrored the gesture, like a knife cutting through clear gelatin. He tore at space itself until on the other side, a portal opened into a ballroom party already under way. He looked back and smiled as Mike saw his friends dancing on the other side. *Guess I can only keep going forward.*

# CHAPTER 56

Roger Queneco was at their side the moment they stepped into the room. He took Mike by the arm in a formal fashion, locking their elbows. "I present to all of you, Auburn. The slayer of Golgoroth. The man who bloodied Chicago. I told you all to prepare for a roller-coaster night. Who among you had the foresight to bet that he would be standing in here tonight? Eh? Eh?" Roger pointed awkwardly to a room that was brought to a standstill.

Eyes were not on Mike. They were on Vryce, who strode over to the windows. While Vryce looked outside, Mike got a good look at the news on the monitors.

From what Mike was able to glean, it was about midnight. Some sort of eclipse had caused the sun to turn black in other parts of the world. Scientists were baffled, as no satellite footage picked up any object large enough to cause such an eclipse. Yet as the sun rose over the horizon, it was inexplicably blackened as if it were an eclipse. The talking heads rattled on about the Mayan calendar and its end being significant, while climate change experts pointed to a sudden change in the atmosphere.

These explanations all fell to the wayside as panicked news reports urged people to remain calm and stay indoors while footage of the dead rising and demons pouring from the earth filled the screens. On some televisions, Mike noticed that ghosts from purgatory moved in the background in areas where the blackened sun rose. With every new city or news report that aired after the black sun rose in their area, the gathered members cheered and raised their glasses of blood or wine in celebration.

It was New Year's Eve for monsters.

"Master Vryce?" asked Roger. "Might I steal your guest for some introductions?"

Vryce seemed oblivious at first, then nodded his head. Roger jerked on Mike's elbow, but it felt to Mike like it was a three-year-old child trying to pull him around. *Awww, it's cute. He thinks he's strong and important.* "Dude, I can walk on my own. Hi. I'm Mike."

Queneco ignored him, gleefully introducing him to clique after clique. Mike thought he saw a wispy ghost in the background poking her head through a wall. He focused his gaze on where he thought she was. She winked at him and was gone. *Like trying to catch mist.*

In one cabal, vampire soldiers drank blood in the company of Kevin Yukito.

"I call this batch organic humans," Kevin boasted. "Humans who were fed a strict vegan diet their entire lives. Certified organic grass-fed humans. Delicious, yes?"

One of the vampires stared at Mike with unblinking eyes and tilted her head like a mantis. "We follow your lead," she said, looking right at Mike, "on how to best produce blood, Kevin."

The other members of their group had been swept up and carted around just as Mike had. Doc was thrust into a conversation about how the psychology of a person would affect them in the change after consuming a heart. "After all, some people are born with such determination to break any influence," Doc said as Mike walked past. "Not everyone can control their emotions and not talk too much." Doc raised his glass. Mike knew he was feasting on information from those around him.

Phoebe had been cornered by Alexandria and looked like a teenager who was bored. Alexandria was asking sly questions about the future in between polite conversation, and from the looks of it, she was getting what she wanted. "Don't worry, love. The dead will walk again," Phoebe said while squirming as Alexandria tried to seduce her. "Don't you read the book of Revelations? I told you the dead will walk again. But that's not why we came here." Mike saw Phoebe point over to Vryce, who still stared out the window. Mike realized that to Alexandria, it appeared as if Phoebe was simply pointing out the window to the sky.

"Enjoy it while it lasts, hero," Gabriel said with a smirk as he popped a piece of meat into his mouth. Mike noticed that while he was looked upon with great regard, Gabriel was alone. Everyone in the room looked at Gabriel like he was the village asshole. "Guess we have a choice to be a pawn or not, after all. It will be dawn here soon," he said as he knelt down to retie his shoes. He had a look of determination on his face as he stayed close to Vryce. Gabriel looked extremely out of place in this room. Everyone in the society was dressed up, wearing lavish gowns and suits with dashes of arcane sigils or ancient jewelry. In contrast, Gabriel wore a T-shirt, ripped-up and bloody jeans, stained shoes, and messy hair.

*Fuck. If he wasn't terrible in another life, we could have been friends.* Mike looked down at his own battle-torn attire and fidgeted with a union button pinned to his green trench coat. The World War I coat was still holding up after everything it had been through thus far. *They don't make 'em like they used to.*

Every time Mike was about to get close to one of his own, Queneco grabbed his arm and clicked his tongue. Mike found himself standing in front of another group of soldiers being quizzed on how he had awakened Chicago. They were voraciously thrilled to see him stand by their side on this glorious day.

It took Mike every ounce of will to summon the strength to break free from Queneco's influence. The night was being lost. If there was any chance to stop this, he had to act soon. *Remember everyone who died, man. Remember why you are here. Stop listening to everyone. Give a shit again. This isn't you! It's a trick!*

Pushing himself away from Queneco felt like leaving a cozy warm bed on a winter morning. Mike knew the moment he stepped away and felt the despair and emptiness of his lonely heart that pain was his strength. *I was a fool to hide it. I need the cries of the forgotten.*

Queneco tried his best to rope Mike back in by mentioning Molly's music, but Mike was already ignoring him. "You bastards killed my friend Frankie, turned some of my team into stone monsters, and are no better than the ones you are trying to stop," Mike said before planting his shoulder into the little man's chest, knocking him into a table and causing goblets of blood to spill on the floor.

Without looking down, Mike had pushed him away with a flick of his strength. He used his speed to close the distance to Vryce and Gabriel.

The room went quiet. Gabriel drew his sword when Mike appeared next to them. Vryce continued to gaze at his domain below.

"Tell me, Mr. Auburn. Look below and tell me what you see," Vryce said.

"There's no point, asshat. You have the power to shred these portals open, that means you have to have some way to reverse it," Mike said.

"Perhaps I do. But insults will not help you. Look below and tell me what you see." He gestured with his pale hand to the city below.

Mike looked around the room, and indeed, all eyes were on them. Realization set in that the sycophants had ignored the happenings of the city after the riots ended. Now even he was curious about the people's current status. He placed his hand on the cold glass and looked out, expecting to see fires, chaos, soldiers shooting civilians, and mass looting.

But he saw a different sight. Riots and fires did not light the night sky. Instead, a peaceful light snow fluttered down onto military trucks where people formed lines around the block.

Mike saw them handing out weapons to civilians along with clay jars. He saw calm, order, and unity as vampires openly handed to the people the very power that Mike started the riots with as they fell into line.

Sometime in the night, the society had taken his rioters and turned them into more soldiers. Instead of continuing to kill each other, the society troops joined ranks with the rioters and fought against demons, teaching them how to best take them down. They also gave the rioters blood, power, and the means to defend themselves against what was coming, from their own stashes. It started as a clash between two forces, but in the span of a full day and night, the society soldiers had used their strength to appease the riots. *You gotta be kidding me. He actually listened to what his city was demanding? When does that ever happen?* His mouth was hanging open in shock when Gabriel put his sword away.

"You and I are not so different, Mr. Auburn," Vryce said. "We both want humanity to succeed in the face of adversity. The room behind us contains power. That is true. These are creatures who have mastered their changed states. But they are weapons that will be used to save those below. Those people below are being given a choice, to become something more than what they were, or face oblivion. We are not hoarding our power as you championed. Today is a holiday, and the world is changing. If it could be stopped, would you really want it to be so?" he asked.

Emotions swelled in Mike as he looked out the window. It felt as if the battle had just begun and the trenches of war had been dug within the hearts and minds of the people. Listening to Vryce felt like making a deal with the devil himself, a false promise. *Even if he declares this day sacred, we could never work together.* Secret societies like this were what he had spent an entire lifetime trying to fight and expose, and to just let it go felt like a betrayal he could not tolerate.

At the edges of his vision, Mike felt a familiar sight return to him as he peered into the edges of the underworld. Phoebe was still cornered, but he saw her smile at him.

Vryce looked to the room behind him. Mike knew he saw Phoebe's smile. Mike noticed an emotion on the creature's face. It looked like resignation. "Mr. Auburn, Gabriel—"

"You know what? Fuck all of you. I'm not your endorsement. You want a message to carry on. Here is one. Gods can fucking die." Mike's fists clenched to the point that bones in his hand cracked and began to burn with agony and rage.

The rest of his friends leaped from their various positions and began fighting everyone in their way on a warpath to the warlock.

Lucy manifested from behind a wall nearby, with her twin axes already brandished, her ghostlike form rapidly becoming solid. From her proximity, she had to have been stalking her prey this entire time. Akira dropped the ruse to turn into her giant mantis form, the skin of a soldier sloughing off her like a cocoon at the feet of Kevin Yukito, while colorful wings expanded so she could take flight and close the distance.

Doc inhaled deeply with his pointed fangs exposed. Those standing around him grabbed the sides of their heads and fell to the ground. Even Queneco was disabled by the psychic attack as he consumed the very thoughts in their heads.

Phoebe was the least fortunate, as Alexandria had grabbed her by the throat and ran out of the room with the prophet as soon as her pupils dilated.

Mike met the eyes of the lich. "Impressive" was all Vryce said when he began to raise his hand to cast a spell at the oncoming attackers.

His ashen world returned into full focus, barren and soulless. *The dead will walk again.* Mike was an unclean coil filled with rage, hands burning red from heat. *Nobody gets what they want today. This isn't going to stop.*

Gabriel winked at him.

At this distance, there was nothing the lich could do when Mike took his head clean off his shoulders with a left hook. The impact shattered the lich's jaw into an array of fragments that scattered across the room as blackened blood exploded onto the window like a shotgun blast. Mike saw the twisted and blackened shadows implode inward on themselves before scattering like the splinters of Vryce's face.

His perception of time slowed to a crawl. He felt every tick of a second after his fist had landed.

Gabriel drew his blade, looking at Mike. He summoned pillars of flame to cut the room in half, dividing the Sons and Daughters from the majority of the creatures in the room. "You had a choice," he said with his face twisting in anger.

From the hallway, Phoebe shouted one word. *"Run!"* Lucy was in midair with her axes. She hit the ground in a tumble and hurled both her weapons into the window, shattering it. The sound of glass exploding caused the rest of the room to take action.

Mike ducked the fireball that hurled out of Gabriel's hand and moved to end the fight they had started earlier. An uppercut that landed squarely into the sorcerer's ribs gave a satisfying crunch.

Akira used her pincers to grab Doc and flew out the window before any spell from Cael landed on them. Lucy jumped out the window and turned into smoke. It seemed too late for Phoebe. Alexandria had impaled her fangs into Phoebe's throat and was drinking her fill. Phoebe's crew ran for any escape they could find.

With Gabriel gasping for air, Mike saw his chance. He could stay and fight, putting an end to Gabriel now, or leap out the way Lucy had made. *We aren't so different. I only choose differently. You don't fit in with these monsters, Gabriel. Join us when you wake up.* His duct-taped boot crushed Gabriel's sword hand, and he kicked his blade across the room just in case.

He pivoted to jump into the frozen morning air. He paused for a moment to mourn Phoebe. As if she knew his eyes were upon her, Alexandria returned the gaze through the flames and grinned sadistically at Mike. Despite how fast Mike was, she appeared to teleport in comparison as she dropped Phoebe to the ground at Mike's feet and vanished just as suddenly. He didn't care as he grabbed Phoebe while she gasped in labored breaths. *You're still kickin'. Don't die now.*

Mike vaulted through the closest window and out into the night air. He plummeted to the ground, his coat flapping like a broken parachute. *This is going to hurt.* Mike rolled onto his back and held Phoebe close, hoping she would survive the impact as seconds flew by.

Unlike in his mortal days, there was no surge of adrenaline, no more gut-wrenching feeling of falling or losing his balance. No heartbeat to flood his ears as he flushed with fear. Just the sound of wind racing past.

The impact came not from the ground, but from Onyx smashing into their side in midair. Mike opened his eyes and looked into those of Officer Winters. The gargoyle was able to land them with the grace of a forklift that had tiny wings as they crashed into the concrete below near the rest of the Sons and Daughters. Matsen, or Jade as she had become, landed more gracefully. She looked more confused than anything, like she had just woken up from a bad dream. A sense of relief washed over all of them as they realized they had done it.

"Well, aren't we just a bunch of fucking superheroes? Look at us saving each other in the nick of time," Mike said with a giant smile on his face as he slapped Onyx on the back.

Lucy was the only one who did not share in the immediate celebration. "We need to run. Now."

The Sons and Daughters sped off. Mike followed at the rear. He noticed that everyone's hair started to rise from static electricity. The peaceful snowfall had stopped. Looking up, he saw storm clouds swirling in a vortex. He slowed to a jog, then a trot. He stopped and looked back up at Walsh Tower.

Gabriel was gasping for life and coughing up blood as he crawled to the tattered remains of Vryce. The room was in a sense of shock, and with the pain from Auburn's punch, he could not prevent the thoughts of everyone from flooding into him.

*The betrayer let the assassins in.*

*Gabriel just killed Vryce. This was planned. Did you see his gargoyle save one?*

*I've inherited the world. Nothing can stop me now.*

*I told you to make enemies of everyone. Now we can be friends.* The last thought was clearly Roger Queneco. The pain was overwhelming in both his mind and his body as he reached with shaking hands for the ouroboros pendant that hung around Vryce's crumbling body in front of him.

"Ladies and gentlemen," Roger said. "The Unification has killed our primus on this sacred day."

Gabriel felt life fading from him as his hand clasped the pendant. In an instant, all pain and thoughts of the world faded away into silence. And power. "No. I am the primus now," he said as he levitated off the ground, his voice echoing from the shadows.

Gabriel did not need to read the thoughts to know that an entire room of sorcerers and vampires were about to descend upon him and kill him. *Blooded sycophants who have no interest in the true salvation of humanity.* The thought was feminine and male at the same time. It was his, yet others' as well. He braced himself for their assault when he heard a sound from Roger.

Roger clicked his snakelike tongue while twirling his handlebar mustache, with a look of satisfaction on his face. Instead of assaulting him, the room took a knee, thanks to the subtle magic of Roger. "My lord. Vengeance must be served to prove your power," Roger said as he took a knee.

The flash of lightning came out of the night sky and hit Mike, bringing him to his knees and flinging the remaining Sons and

Daughters farther away. Embers of fire singed Mike's hair as he rammed his knuckles into the ground to stand back up and look with defiance at the top of Walsh Tower.

Gabriel D'Angelo floated in the air, one hand raised high above him holding a black cavalry sabre, its green gem shining in the night sky. With his other hand, he grasped Vryce's pendant. A sadistic look crossed his face as his voice echoed out into the night, loud enough for everyone to hear him. "Slaves, bow to your master. You were created to serve me."

Onyx and Jade tried to fight but found themselves giving in and taking flight to protect their master. Mike looked at the rest of the Sons and Daughters; they seemed ready to fight. Phoebe held her hand to Doc's face to get his attention and shook her head. Mike knew what it meant as they took steps away. *I'm okay with going now.* Mike took off his coat and threw it to them before an array of lightning snapped out of the sky. Mike's body burned white as lightning strike after lightning strike rained down from the sky.

Daneka ran with Phoebe curled up in his arms. They cringed with each impact of a bolt. Mike would stand after each one until his body was burned to a crisp, and even still, he remained on at least one knee with his fists implanted into the ground until his ash flew in the wind.

"Indomitable. Indomitable." A voice rang out from Gabriel above the city. Doc gazed up at Gabriel with his heightened vision and looked the creature in the eyes, one white and the other sky blue, and nodded in acknowledgment. *Indomitable. Alexandria mentioned that.* Gabriel flew back inside the building, Winters and Matsen followed, completely subservient to their new master.

"Let's go," Doc said. The rest of them nodded in silent agreement. Akira held Mike's coat close to her chest as they ran away.

# CHAPTER 57

It took hours for them to return to the Second City. The Sons and Daughters saw the black sun give off grayish-white light. It looked and felt like a cloudy day, only without the clouds. As a unit, they hurried through the city, their home, a city being born again as the dead ushered in new life, with a healthy dose of shock. Still, after over a week of fighting demons, those within the Second City were ready for anything.

Lucy ordered the crew around. Even Morris jumped at her command regarding diving supplies, lifting gear up to the skyscraper under construction. Miles above the circuitry of oblivion below. The concrete void. They loaded lanterns, food for weeks, blood, weapons, holy water, and axes. Twenty-four hours. She had twenty-four hours to take action.

Charcoal lines were drawn under her eyes, an incantation uttered, a spell to grant sight. A hood to shield her face, less the demons and dead notice her. She dipped her fingers in the blood of demons to grant the sensation of touch, vital when wandering lost.

Her grandfather stood nearby, smoking a cigar. He was there to make amends and tie up loose ends. Putting his arm around her, he walked her over to the edge, out along the steel I beam. She put on Auburn's coat. He flicked two copper coins off the edge. Lucy turned to face the Sons and Daughters.

"We'll be seeing you. Good luck in Texas." She tumbled into Hades before it was too late.

Lord of Heaven's Wrath knelt in the ceremonial chamber, decorated with crimson-and-silver-trimmed banners. Running his fingers through the grave clothes of Lazarus, he admired the beauty of them. Fourteen hours had passed since the dawn of the twenty-first. Yet there was no sign of his return. Lord of Heaven's Wrath wept.

All that remained were the signs that prophecy had come to pass, and the black sun had risen. Many neverborn and forgotten gods buried at the ten locations had been consumed by the ritual. Four survived, and within his region was one of them. The Unification had brought the heavens one step closer. One less divide separated all minds. So he prayed.

Within the Unification, some fractured and broke ranks, showing who lacked the vision to do what was necessary. It illuminated to him those who cared not for the torment that is purgatory, and within his region was one of them. Yet the dead, damned, and demons that flooded into his ranks swelled his armies and legions of dead because of their weakness. The same was true among the loyal death lords. The Unification had brought all within purgatory to the world again, allowing them to see, hear, feel, smell again. So he mourned.

"What is Lazarus if not but a name?" he asked. "If not but a concept that the Unification can rally behind to complete their work?" Lord of Heaven's Wrath had many debts to pay. The children of Lilith demanded a union among their descendants. They had been working centuries together for this task. In exchange for immortality and the thirteenth chair, Dr. John C. Daneka promised them the blessing of Lazarus over that union. So he poured the gasoline over himself. For Lazarus was burned by the demons.

If the dead walked again among the living, a prophecy of Lazarus's return, yet there was no Lazarus, then perhaps he needed form, someone to take his name, someone to control the Unification. So he wrapped the grave clothes around himself.

The Unification had committed a great atrocity for the greater good. Yet someone must suffer. One must take responsibility. So he lit the match.

Lazarus was reborn. In name only.

The Second City was not a place familiar to Rafiq. Still, he knew he would find his target inside the Drake Hotel. He slid between shadows as he moved unseen past a gathering of damned souls.

Ever since the morning, the dead were everywhere in the city, going about their ghostly lives as if they were trapped in the last moments of life, only beginning to realize they had an effect on the world again. Everything appeared older than it was, more decayed and blackened than before. Parts of the Drake Hotel looked like they had been built before the great Chicago fire.

He made his way to a bar that O'Neil's agents used as a base of operations and climbed a column where he could spy on its inhabitants from safety. His skin changed color like a chameleon to match his surroundings. From his perch, he looked in the room and saw the deformed and rotting vampires giving each other a toast. The bartender was an old man, still human, judging by the blinking of the eyes and the movement of the chest that still took in air. From every bit of info he gathered since being released, this was his mark.

A vampire wearing a cabby hat and a checkered scarf put out a cigar on the bar even though there was an ashtray right next to him. He reached down and gave a salute to the bartender and pulled out a sign with a small chain on it. Rafiq overheard their farewells and commiserations as he watched the cabby-hat man go to the door and hang a sign that read "Closed."

One by one the denizens of the establishment finished their drinks of blackened ichor, turned their glasses upside down, and set them on the bar before giving a nod and a final word to the bartender.

None of them would rise and complete this tradition until the one before them had left the building. Rafiq waited, ready to pounce if that bartender took a single step to the door. At last Morris poured himself a shot of the black ichor and completed the ceremony himself, pulling the scarf around his face as he exited and locked the door. With only the bartender remaining, Rafiq crawled along the ceiling from column to column above his target.

The bartender stared at the TV as a final news report was finished before it cut to an emergency broadcast message that would repeat itself. He pulled out a coffee-stained map labeled "Deep-Tunnel Project" and began to study strange arcane markings on it.

Without a noise Rafiq fell from his perch, his daggers at the ready. The only sound was the decapitated head of the bartender thumping against the wood bar and falling to the floor. A sensation of completion washed over Rafiq.

He had killed his target. Satisfied with his work, he pulled the white towel from the counter and cleaned off his blades. He had gotten lost in his own cleaning ritual when the door from the kitchen opened. A janitor moved into the room. They took each other in as the janitor looked at the scene, back to Rafiq, then back to the scene.

"Who are you?" Rafiq asked, unsure why he bothered asking.

"I'm nobody." The janitor shrugged. "Just an old man forgotten in time. Who was that?" he said as he gestured to the dead bartender. He placed his hands in his pockets and began rocking back and forth while looking around the room.

Rafiq wanted to answer, but somehow he wasn't sure himself. He just knew that was the one Delilah had sent him to eliminate. So he answered the best he could. "I think they called him . . ." Rafiq knew that this was the right answer. There was no need for a name; the person was simply a spec in history. Forgotten already.

"No matter, then. I suppose I'll just get a mop and clean it up. Would not be the first time this hotel has had a famous person killed in it. You might want to take your map with you, though."

"Yes, you do that. I am done here. Have a good day, sir," Rafiq said, rolling up the map. He felt that rather than sneaking out, he would simply use the door this time. He took one last look before he walked out into the changing Second City. *That man was a dangerous legend? I'm pretty sure the world is going to forget him pretty quick. Maybe it's the map that's really important. It leads to some grave under the city.*

Gabriel placed the ouroboros pendant on a shelf full of remaining phylacteries in the sanctum chamber, pain returning to his broken body. He fell to the floor and crawled to a wall. He propped himself up to catch his breath, breath which frosted in the air and tasted like iron from all the dried blood.

Shadows moved along the floor, and Gabriel was released from Vryce's control. Being possessed did not suit him.

"After our conversation in here earlier, how does it feel to claim the position of primus?" Vryce's voice sounded torn, more fragmented, than when he was alive.

Suppressing the fear took a second of conscious choice. No matter how hard he tried, however, reading his father's thoughts was beyond him. It sounded like glass being etched with an iron nail when he tried.

Gabriel coughed up blood and tried to follow the shadows as they flitted about. "Anyone could have done that. What if it was anyone else? You should have told me you intended to die like that."

"Power is a choice. If you hesitated, then you did not deserve it."

"So that's it? Now I'm trapped leading a society of monsters?"

"Are you not one yourself? You will either rise to the occasion or you will die. Either way, word will spread quickly of my death. I am free."

"But without a body, you'll just sit in this room. I refuse to be a possessed pawn."

"I expected nothing less. You already saved my children. One of them will suffice. You will rule in my stead. I have a hundred years of research to undertake." A small dagger slid across the room to Gabriel. Vryce's soul blade. "Both blades of Deus are yours now, but I would not rely heavily upon them for long. We may have use of them outside these walls, and you are not my only child who needs assistance."

"I've always had a question about these," Gabriel said as he began to lose consciousness. "If you need these forged by an apprentice and a master, and neither Slade nor Cael have one, who was your first apprentice that made this with you?"

The room was silent.

"I was the apprentice. Yet I forgot my master's name in 1920."

As Gabriel's eyes closed, he saw a girl from the medical clinic step out of the room filled with rugs. She picked up a viola case and left with shadows trailing behind her.

# AUTHOR'S NOTE

We've come to the part of the book where I, Rick, also known as Richard Heinz or CrankyBolt depending on what bowels of the Internet you stalk, get to speak in my own voice rather than the characters.' I like to imagine who you are or where you've been reading this book. Surely, it's in the loft of a cathedral with epic storms crashing outside while you listen to metal music. Or perhaps it's curled up under a blanket like a burrito for a few days while you avoid contact with the outside world. I wrote this book on a computer set in the corner of the room while drinking coffee by the truckload late at night. I loved every minute of it. Hopefully you did as well.

Regardless of your reading style or how this book came into your hands, I want to extend my thanks to you and offer a bit of social media fun. If you feel so inclined, hit me up on Twitter @CrankyBolt and share with me your thoughts, the music you listened to, and what you are looking forward to in the sequel.

# ACKNOWLEDGMENTS

My acknowledgments for this book start with the giant flaming ball of life that hangs in the sky while we hurtle around it. The sun. My aversion to this heat source is what started my drive to tell stories and play games with friends from a very young age. It inspired many other people to do the same, and together, over the years, some of us in the Chicagoland area banded together to create a universe in our imaginations.

I want to thank every one of you who played in, brought art and inspiration for, and continue to expand the setting. From the dedicated players all the way to the ones who would poke their heads in to witness our madness. Thank you. If you had never sat through my countless hours of storytelling, I never would have had the dedication to write a book like this.

The one creature who does not get an acknowledgment is the spider. Screw spiders and the alien ship they crashed in before starting an invasive conquest of our planet.

# ABOUT THE AUTHOR

Richard Heinz's inspiration for *The Seventh Age: Dawn* traces back to his history as an electrician and especially to his love of crawling through the hidden underbelly of a city to uncover its secret wonders—not to mention countless caffeine-driven hours spent playing *Diablo*. *The Seventh Age: Dawn* is Rick's first book, as well as book one in the sprawling urban fantasy epic the Seventh Age series.

You can follow Rick on Twitter @CrankyBolt or go to www.Seventh-Age.com to uncover more about the world of the Seventh Age.

# LIST OF PATRONS

This book was made possible in part by the following grand patrons who preordered the book on inkshares.com. Thank you.

Adam Candee
Adam Zoelick
Ashley Witter
Bob Heinz
Brandice O'Donnel
   & M. K. Watts
Brian Cable
Carl Durnavich
Cheryl Nabors
Chris Knuth
Chris Piecha
Crystal O'Donnell
Don Pecina
Dustin Majewski
Eric Schulke
Erica Irene

Fransz J. Murphy Holtrop
Gabriel De Angelo
James Mosingo
Jason D. O'Brien
Jason "Synthas" Peercy
Jaysin Schoebe
Jerud Colbert
Jessica Van Camp
Jesus Gonzalez-Feliu
J.F. Dubeau
Jim Heinz
John Cunningham
John M. Christy
Joseph Asphahani
Justin Solarski
Karen Hess

Keith Kuchaes
Kevin Caroll
Lisa Hall
Louis Mazza
Manny Popoca
Mary Mapp
Mary Melchiori
Matt Harrison
Michael A. Falco
Michelle Heinz
Mike Zavislak
Moose Oudoka
Pat McCandrews
Paul E. Reynolds III

Peter Hartman
Phyllis Wiencek
Raghav Mangrola
Saulius Bertulis
Sheri Corcoran Jay
Timothy R Harrison
TJ Roberts
Tony Durnavich
TPK Gaming
Tyler Reid
Vince Frank
Hans Shinn
Zachary Tyler Linville

# INKSHARES

Inkshares is a crowdfunded book publisher. We democratize publishing by having readers select the books we publish—we edit, design, print, distribute, and market any book that meets a preorder threshold.

Interested in making a book idea come to life? Visit inkshares.com to find new book projects or start your own.